BEYOND REACH

Graham Hurley

An Orion paperback

First published in Great Britain in 2010
by Orion
This paperback edition published in 2011
by Orion Books Ltd,
Orion House, 5 Upper St Martin's Lane,
London WC2H 9EA

An Hachette UK Company

3 5 7 9 10 8 6 4

Copyright © Graham Hurley 2010

The right of Graham Hurley to be identified as the author
of this work has been asserted by him in accordance with
the Copyright, Designs and Patents Act 1988.

All rights reserved. No part of this publication may be
reproduced, stored in a retrieval system, or transmitted,
in any form or by any means, electronic, mechanical,
photocopying, recording or otherwise, without the prior
permission of the copyright owner.

All the characters in this book are fictitious,
and any resemblance to actual persons, living
or dead, is purely coincidental.

A CIP catalogue record for this book
is available from the British Library.

ISBN 978-1-4091-0234-2

Typeset by Deltatype Ltd, Birkenhead, Merseyside

Printed and bound in Great Britain by Clays Ltd, St Ives plc

The Orion Publishing Group's policy is to use papers
that are natural, renewable and recyclable products and
made from wood grown in sustainable forests. The logging
and manufacturing processes are expected to conform
to the environmental regulations of the country of origin.

www.orionbooks.co.uk

To Nick Waugh
with love

Acknowledgements

My thanks to the following for their time and patience: Dave Anderson, John Ashworth, Gary Cable, Scott Chilton, Martin Chudley, Deborah Cook, Roly Dumont, Diana Franklin, Mark Hall, Alan Hunter, Liz Harkin, Andy Harrington, Simon Hodgekin, Richard John, Dean Juster, Martin Law, Tina Lowe, Terry Lowe, Bruce Marr, Teresa Norton, Paul O'Brien, Rosie Rae, Matthias Reiss, Tony Tipping, Danielle Stoakes, Wayne Tommans-Parker, Doug Utting, Alyson West.

Simon Spanton, my editor, loyally supported Paul Winter's trek into the fictional unknown while my wife, Lin, kept him from his worst excesses. Winter owes them both.

Love that is not madness is not love.

Pedro Calderón de la Barca

Prologue

More than twenty years later they were still with her, shards of memory, broken by terror and by time.

She'd been partying that night, an end-of-year celebration. She'd had a lot to drink earlier in the evening, toasting her mates and the sunset with bottles of cheap red on the beach beside the pier. She remembered lying on her back, her eyes closed, enjoying the warmth of the pebbles through the thinness of her T-shirt. A first in Social Studies was more than she'd really deserved. As ever, she'd been lucky.

After the beach came a disjointed series of parties, moving from address to address, following the trail of pissheads and celebrants. On a balcony overlooking the harbour mouth, she'd fended off a drunken lecturer from the Art College. Later, in a basement bedsit on the seafront, she'd buried herself in a corner with a guy she'd been fond of in the first year. The relationship had come to nothing but they were still friends and that was nice. Later still, with a girlfriend called Beth, she'd ended up at the Student Union dancing to Bob Marley and Wham. Beth had pulled a 2:1 in French and German, and was already looking at a couple of job offers. 'Wake Me Up Before You Go Go' seemed a pretty good way of kissing goodbye to three mad years at the Poly.

Getting back to her own place was a mystery. By now, she was drunk enough to insist on walking home alone. It was less than a mile, for Christ's sake. Her balance might be dodgy but her feet knew the way. She was a homing pigeon. She was a strong girl. She'd scored a First. She'd be just fine.

Key in the door. Don't bother with the hall light. Try and follow the worn strip of carpet. Bounce softly from wall to wall. Finally make it to the last door on the right, the door before the steps down into the shared kitchen, the door to the room with the big window. The window opened onto the tiny square of garden. On hot nights she always lowered the sash, pulled back the curtain, let the air in. Habit, like innocence, dies hard.

Chapter one

The post-mortem started later than planned. Steph Callan was a uniformed sergeant on the Road Death Investigation Team. After the delights of last night, using a torch to help retrieve lumps of flesh scattered across the B2177, she now found herself looking at the tiled emptiness of the post-mortem room at Winchester's Royal Hampshire County Hospital.

One of the technicians emerged from the cubbyhole they used as a kitchen. Instead of his usual scrubs he was wearing jeans and a blue Pompey top. Steph could smell toast. The post-mortem was clearly hours away.

'Where's Jenny?' Jenny Cutler was the on-call pathologist.

'Sick. We're expecting a bloke called Dodman. He's just rung. Shit traffic getting out of Bristol.' The technician stifled a yawn. 'You want coffee or tea?'

Steph had never heard of Dodman. She settled for coffee, producing her mobile, glad of the chance to make a call or two of her own. P/C Walters was still in bed.

'Skipper?' he grunted.

'Hit-and-run in Portsmouth, Sean. Southwick Hill Road. Happened last night. Bloke called Munday. No witnesses at this stage. That's all we know.'

'And this bloke's dead?'

'Very.'

The first officer on the scene had described the injuries as 'horrible'. Steph had arrived after the body had been taken away but six years on the Roads Policing Unit told her that traffic cops were no friends of overstatement. Another guy, the driver of the Crash Incident Tender, had been blunter. 'Roadkill,' he'd muttered.

Now, on the phone, Steph told Walters to organise a couple

of P/Cs for door-to-door enquiries. A web of residential streets lay to the south of the B2177 and there was a chance that someone might have heard or seen something. Examination of the road surface had revealed nothing as helpful as tyre marks but vehicle debris had been recovered and bagged. Munday's clothing would be submitted for forensic examination and the post-mortem, once it got under way, might also tease out the beginnings of some kind of narrative. Walters grunted and said he was on the case. Steph brought the conversation to an end.

From the kitchen came the roar of a football crowd. One of the technicians had installed a portable TV. Steph pocketed her mobile and stepped across. There was interference on the picture but she recognised the brimming terraces of the new Wembley Stadium. These were news pictures. Less than twenty-four hours ago, a single goal had won the FA Cup for Pompey.

The technician in the blue top turned to find Steph at the door. He'd been up at the final and hadn't slept since.

'Magic, eh? Who'd have thought?'

Steph was still gazing at the screen.

'So where's Dodman?' she said.

The pathologist arrived an hour and a half later, a tall lanky figure in his mid-thirties. Steph talked him through last night's sequence of events.

'The body was called in by a passing motorist,' she said. 'His wife's still in shock.'

Dodman was tucking the bottom of his scrubs into the tops of his wellies.

'You've seen the body?'

'Not yet.'

He glanced at his watch. 'Better get on, then.'

The technicians retrieved the corpse from one of the big fridges. Munday's body was still bagged from the scene of the accident. Steph followed the trolley into the chill of the post-mortem room.

The body was transferred onto the slab and one of the technicians scissored through the attached ID tag before unzipping the bag. Two years on the Road Death team had armoured Steph against moments like these but what lay inside amongst the puddle of bodily fluids belonged in an abattoir. The guy on the crash tender had been right. Roadkill.

The technicians tugged the bag free. Munday's body was still clothed but the paramedics at the scene must have removed one leg of the soiled jeans. Steph could see the roughness of the cut, way up near the crotch, and the whiteness of the flesh below the knee, peeled neatly back from the bone beneath. The exposed calf muscles glistened under the lights, a plump shiny redness veined with purple that reminded Steph of prime beef. Tenderloin, maybe. Or rump.

The Scenes of Crime photographer was circling the body, taking shot after shot as Dodman dictated notes into the overhead microphone. Flaying injuries to the lower right leg. Oblique fracture of the tibia. Lacerations to the upper right thigh. Abrasions and bruises on both arms.

Steph was staring at what remained of Munday. One or more wheels must have run this man over. Not just his right leg, stripping the flesh from the bone, but his chest and his head as well. His face was no more than a smear – a suggestion of a nose, a glimpse of yellowing teeth where his mouth should have been – and the head itself had been flattened.

Dodman's murmured commentary faltered, then picked up again. Crushed cranial vault. Visible extrusions of brain tissue through multiple scalp lacerations. Steph tried to keep up, tried to focus on the fat grey threads of jelly that laced what remained of this man's head. Memories, she told herself. Intelligence. The very stuff of what we are, of what we do. Billions of nerve cells that should have warned him to take care when crossing the road. She closed her eyes and took a tiny step backwards, secretly glad that something like this could still shock her.

Three hours later, the post-mortem complete, she looked up from her notes. The technician had discovered that the photographer was also a Pompey fan. Better still, he lived in Portsmouth and was happy to offer a lift back to the city. The technician, who'd been planning on taking the train, peeled off his bloodied gloves and washed his hands. A mate had told him the team would be parading the Cup for the benefit of the fans. Open-top bus. Civic reception. Then a monster crowd on Southsea Common. Harry Redknapp, he said, was a fucking genius.

Steph got to her feet. The Investigator from Scenes of Crime was deep in conversation with the pathologist. Dodman was confirming the exact configuration of the wedge-shaped fracture in the tibia. The base of the wedge was at the front of the bone, which meant that Munday had been facing the vehicle when it knocked him over. A near-identical fracture in the other leg – same configuration, same height – offered another clue. In all probability, he'd simply stood there, not moving.

'Do we think he was pissed?' Steph asked.

She didn't know Dodman. A blood sample would be sent for laboratory analysis. In the absence of lawyer-proof results, some pathologists refused to speculate.

'Of course he was pissed.' Dodman gestured vaguely back towards the post-mortem room. 'You could smell it from here.'

Whenever he ate out on Sundays Winter always went for the roast. Normally it would be one of a handful of Pompey pubs. Today it was Sur-la-Mer, a Southsea bistro with a reputation for good food and an interesting clientele. Marie's choice.

She sat across from him at the table near the window. Blonde, leggy, beautifully dressed, she'd survived nearly twenty years of marriage to Bazza Mackenzie and still turned heads wherever she went. Winter had always been fascinated by the relationship, but since he'd become part of Mackenzie's entourage, he'd found himself getting closer and closer to this wife of his. He liked her strength of mind, her cultured little ways, and he was flattered by the confidences she occasionally shared. He also knew that she valued his advice. Bazza, all too often, was a firework, bursting with brilliant ideas but easily bored. Up like a rocket, thought Winter. Down like a stick.

'Where is he?' Winter wanted to know.

'Out there somewhere.' Marie nodded at the army of Pompey fans swamping the street outside, making their way to the nearby Common. 'He tried to get the team to the hotel for a big reception but the club said no. He'd never admit it but that definitely pissed Baz off. Sometimes it's like he invented the bloody club.'

Winter laughed. The Royal Trafalgar was the jewel in Bazza's crown, a handsome meticulously refurbished seafront hotel with views across the Solent towards the Isle of Wight. In the absence of a team reception, Baz would doubtless be renaming one of the function rooms in honour of Pompey's sainted manager. The Harry Redknapp Suite. By Invitation Only.

'Did you see the game?'

'I was out riding with Ezzie. Did you?'

'Yeah. Crap.' Ezzie was Marie's daughter.

'So why did you bother?'

'I've no idea.' Winter picked at his bread roll. 'Maybe it comes with the territory.'

'Bazza or the city?'

'Both. Tell you the truth, I've never seen the difference.'

It was true. Bazza Mackenzie had always been indivisible from the city of his birth, and as a working detective Winter had quickly recognised just how tight the tribal bonds of loyalty could be. The guys Mackenzie used to fight alongside during the glory days of the 6.57, exporting football violence to terraces across the country, were – a generation later – exactly the same faces he relied on to turn fat bundles of cocaine money into a prospering business empire. Now part of that empire, Winter could only admire the strength of the glue that stuck these guys together. The police, he knew, could never match it. Not then. Not now.

'You think he's on the Common? With his rattle and his scarf?' Winter said.

'Of course he is. He had a ring round this morning. They took a chopper to Wembley yesterday. God knows how much it cost.'

Winter had seen the quote on Bazza's desk only last week. Skywise Helicopter Charters. £2,875, plus endless sundries. At the time he'd dismissed it as some kind of fantasy. Now he knew different.

'It's a game, my love. Pompey got lucky. Most pub sides would beat Cardiff.'

Winter reached for the menu, keen to change the subject. The lunch, like the venue, had been Marie's idea. Before they got down to business, he had something of his own to get off his chest.

'That email of mine ...' he began.

'Which one?'

'About the Trust. I've made contact with the bloke now, scoped him out. Everyone I've talked to says he's the business. Lateral thinker, big reputation where it matters, plus he can't wait to get away from London. The way I read it, he wouldn't be after a fortune either. Just in case you were wondering.'

Marie had the grace to smile. As Chair of the Tide Turn Trust, she'd worried constantly about money, yet another reason why Winter was desperate to surrender what little authority he really had. Back last summer, when the Trust was a gleam in Bazza's eye, the title of Chief Executive had sounded promising. Months later, a great deal wiser about the realities of coping with problem youth, Winter wanted out.

'To be fair, Marie, it was never my bag. You know that. There are some things I do well and some things I don't. Playing Mr Nice to a bunch of twat kids isn't one of them.'

'Mr Nice isn't what we had in mind.'

'Mr Nasty, then. Whatever. The fact is you need special gifts. You need experience. You need patience. And you need to be on top of all the bullshit that goes with it. You know how many forms you have to fill in to stand any kind of chance of raising grant money? Hundreds. Thousands. These guys want every last piece of you. You know anything about CRB checks? Prolific offender protocols? Youth Offending Teams? List 99? The Independent Safeguarding Authority? The Bichard Vetting Scheme? Public liability insurance? I thought I'd left all this bollocks in the CID office. Turns out I was wrong.'

The smile on Marie's face was fading but Winter wasn't about to stop.

'Something else ...' he said. 'Tell Baz I've sussed him. I know what he's up to. And to be frank, my love, it's not my job to help.'

'Help how?'

'Help him get his knighthood ... or whatever else he fucking wants. The guy's creaming it. The business is making you a fortune. And this is *legit* money. So why on earth do you need the Tide Turn Trust?'

'Because Baz wants people to take him seriously.'

'Exactly. The knighthood. The gong. But not me, eh? Not through my bloody efforts.' Winter folded the menu and sat back, turning his body away from the table, staring out at the street. He seldom lost his temper, but he knew Marie would carry every word of this conversation back to Bazza, and Bazza had to know that Winter meant it.

'He wants to go into politics, Paul.' She said it softly, as if it was a family secret. 'The Trust's all part of that.'

Winter didn't move. The street outside was a river of blue shirts.

'He wants to do *what*?'

'Go into politics. Get himself elected. Sort this city out. He told me the other night.'

'He was pissed.'

'That's what I thought.'

'He meant it?'

'I'm afraid so.'

'Really?' Winter finally abandoned the street. Marie's smile had gone.

'It gets worse.' She leaned forward. 'I think Ezzie's having an affair.'

D/I Joe Faraday stepped into the chilly gloom of the Bargemaster's House. After the overnight flight from Montreal, he'd paid a surprise visit to his son, still living in Chiswick. J-J, it turned out, had acquired company in the shape of a Russian actress called Sonya, and the three of them shared an awkward breakfast before Faraday cut his losses and hit the road again. The flight, the breakfast, and then the drive back down to Pompey had wiped him out.

He bent to the doormat and quickly sorted through the pile of post. Apart from a Mahler CD from Amazon and the May edition of *Bird Watching*, he was looking at nothing but bills, free newspapers, credit card offers and pleas for cash from sundry charities. Ten days away, he thought, and I come back to this.

He dumped his bag in the lounge and gazed at the stairs. Gabrielle had left the week before Christmas, flying to Montreal to take up the offer of a visiting fellowship at McGill University. The offer had come out of the blue, the kind of bombshell that he'd always dreaded. At first she'd dismissed it. She loved the Bargemaster's House. She adored living with her grumpy *flic*.

She was looking forward to throwing herself into the research for a new book. It was all, in a word, *parfait*.

Too perfect. Watching her face at the breakfast table that morning, the way her eyes kept returning to the letter, Faraday knew that this new life of theirs, the relationship they'd so carefully built, was doomed. As an anthropologist, her publications were beginning to attract serious attention. It was only a matter of time before someone came knocking at the door, seeding that curiosity, that hunger for the unknown, which was the essence of this woman who'd come to occupy the very middle of his life.

And so it had proved. As autumn slipped slowly into winter, Gabrielle spent longer and longer on the Internet, exploring the implications of saying yes. The fellowship was only for a year. Montreal was an interesting city. Canada was a mere six hours away. They could take it in turns to make the trip over. The twelve months would be gone in a flash. All of these things were true, but deep down Faraday knew that their affair, their life together, was probably over.

Confirmation came on the day she left. Gabrielle always travelled light. Years of fieldwork in remote corners of the world had taught her how to survive on the contents of a sizeable rucksack yet it gutted Faraday to realise just how little of herself she'd deposited in the Bargemaster's House. Carrying her two bags out to the car for the trip to the airport, he'd somehow assumed he'd return that evening to find lots of her stuff, her books, a handful of clothes, her *smell*, still strewn round the bedroom. Yet there'd been nothing, not a single item to remember her by. Standing in the darkness, listening to the carol singers up the road, it was as if their time together had never happened.

He remembered that moment now, a feeling of despair, of abandonment, even of betrayal. It had taken him weeks to come to terms with it and if he was honest with himself he knew it had never really gone. There were ways of burying it – work, for instance – but even a series of challenging homicides, one still unsolved, was no substitute for the anticipation of another evening together, of meals round the kitchen table, of conversation spiked with laughter and bottles of Côtes-du-Rhône, of the countless ways she untangled the knots inside him and left his soul at peace. Without her, without what she'd brought to this solitary life of his, he was nothing.

Now, he stooped for his bags and climbed the stairs. The PC was on the table by the window. He fired it up, gazing out at the brightness of the afternoon. Breaths of wind feathered the blue spaces of the harbour and he reached automatically for his binos at a distant flicker of movement. A raft of brent geese. A pair of cormorants. Closer, only yards from the foreshore, a lone turnstone.

He turned back to the PC, pulling the curtain against the glare of the sunshine, scrolling quickly through ten days of emails. For once he didn't pause for birding news from an e-chum on Portland Bill. Neither had he any interest in a message flagged 'Urgent' from his bank. All he wanted, needed, was word from Gabrielle. He'd left her barely twelve hours ago, a goodbye hug in the departure hall at Montreal-Trudeau. It was less than an hour back to her third-floor apartment in St Michel. She'd have had the rest of the evening to compose the email of his dreams: how much these last ten days had mattered, how nothing had changed between them, how much – already – she missed him.

Nothing. *Rien.*

He sat back, staring at the screen, knowing in his heart that it had to be this way. The essence of Gabrielle, that quickness of spirit that had captured him, was what had taken her to Montreal in the first place. She was a bird of passage. Her life was a series of roosts. Lucky the man who got to share even one of them.

He reached for the keyboard and began to compose a message of his own but the phrases felt leaden. *Easy flight. J-J shacked up with some Russian actress. All well at home.* Was this the way he really felt? He deleted everything and started again, the truth this time. *I miss you. You should be here. We had a brilliant life, didn't we? What did I ever do to drive you away?* He stopped, knowing he'd never send it, knowing he was talking to himself.

The fact was he'd never driven her away. She'd gone because another door had suddenly opened and she couldn't resist finding out what lay on the other side. That was her nature. That was what had turned her into one of life's nomads. Already, the head of her faculty had hinted at a permanent academic post, most likely a lectureship. Soon, there'd be someone else in her bed. Both men, inevitably, would be disappointed. Because Gabrielle, a slave to her own curiosity, would inevitably move on.

Dommage, thought Faraday.

Chapter two

Bazza Mackenzie was a rare visitor to Winter's top-floor Gunwharf apartment. Still in his dressing gown, Winter looked hard at the stocky figure of his employer in the video screen above the entryphone. Jeans, Pompey away top and an obvious hangover. The image told its own story.

'It's eight in the morning, Baz. You should be sleeping it off.'

'Tosser. Just let me in.'

Under Mackenzie's direction, Winter brewed coffee. No milk, three sugars and the promise of a tot of something stronger to brighten his mood.

'They won, Baz. In case you'd forgotten.'

'Very funny. Why weren't you there? I'd have found you a spare seat.'

'It was a sell-out.'

'I meant the chopper. We could have squeezed up. Room for a fat bastard like you. No problem.' He frowned. 'You been sniffing round Mist again?'

Winter had finally laid hands on the remains of a bottle of Bacardi. As Bazza knew only too well, it was Misty Gallagher's favourite tipple. Some mornings she preferred it to tea.

'Wouldn't dream of it, Baz. Fat old bastard like me.'

'Good. I expect you to fucking behave yourself. You got that?'

Winter carried the coffee into the lounge. With his boss in one of these moods, it was barely worth bothering with a conversation. Not unless you had something really pressing on your mind.

'Listen, Baz. If you've come round about the Trust—'

'The what?'

'Marie's had a word, yeah? Last night? First thing this morning? About Tide Turn? Fact is, Baz, I've had enough. You're paying me to make money not work fucking miracles. If you really want a social worker you'd better find some other monkey. As it happens, I think I've found one. Bloke called Scott. Can't wait to get you an invite to the Palace.'

'I'm not with you, mush.'

'This isn't about Tide Turn?'

'No.'

'What, then?'

'Ezzie.'

Winter hesitated. Yesterday's lunch at the restaurant had lasted long into the afternoon. Marie had poured her heart out about her daughter's marriage, chiefly because she hadn't a clue what to do. The last thing she'd extracted from Winter, out on the pavement beside her new Porsche, was a promise not to say a word to Bazza. Now this.

'What's up?' Winter knew it was time to be cautious.

Bazza threw him a look, then got to his feet and went to the big picture window and the view across the harbour towards the Gosport shore. There was anger in his face when he finally glanced round, and something else that Winter couldn't quite place. A family thing. Maybe disappointment.

'None of this gets back to Marie, right?'

'Sure.'

'If it does, I'll break your legs. *Comprende?*'

'No problem.'

'Right, mush. So this is what we know.'

'We?'

'Me and Stuart.'

Stuart Norcliffe was Esme's husband, a City banker who'd spent the last couple of years running a hugely profitable hedge fund. Winter had only met him on a handful of occasions but had sussed what turned Esme on. The guy oozed power and money. On top of that, if you had a taste for sheer bulk, he was a bit of a looker.

'So what happened?'

Mackenzie returned to the sofa and ran a hand over his face. He'd let himself go a bit over the winter but recently he'd returned to the gym and was back on his toes.

'Listen, mush ...' He kept his voice low as if the neighbours might hear. 'Stu gives me a bell last week. That's a hard thing for a bloke like him to do, believe me. Why? Because he thinks his missus, my fucking daughter, is having it off with some wanker at that noncey spa hotel she goes to.'

'Based on what evidence?'

'You're talking like a copper.'

'Old habits, Baz. Just tell me.'

Esme, it turned out, had spent most of last year complaining about the chore of driving twenty miles to the gym and pool she used. The facilities were attached to a four-star hotel on the edge of the New Forest. The pool, she said, was too small and some of the guys in the gym, mainly visiting businessmen, were distinctly chavvy. What she didn't need in her precious spare time was some spotty sales rep asking whether she was up for a spot of hand relief in the sauna.

'So why didn't she jack the place in?'

'Good fucking question. That's exactly what Stu wondered.'

'And?'

'She met someone.'

'Like who?'

'Like the guy she's shagging.'

Stu, said Bazza, hadn't sussed it to begin with. Looking back it was obvious, but at the time, working twenty hours a day, Stu was just glad that Esme had stopped moaning. For whatever reason, she was driving over there two or three times a week without a word of complaint, and if that floated her boat then so much the better. Then, last week, a mate of Stu's had given him a ring. This was a guy Stu occasionally played squash with. He'd been over at the hotel for a business lunch and afterwards he'd wandered down to the gym to check out the facilities. The place had been empty apart from two figures in the corner.

'Adjacent running machines, mush. Thump, thump, thump. Really pushing it. Then she gets off, silly cow, legs totally shot, and he's all over her. Kissy kissy. Towelling her face. Squeezing her arse. Fetching a drink from the machine. The works. Stu's mate couldn't believe it. One of the reasons he phoned up was to check about the divorce. They hadn't played squash for a while. Maybe he'd missed something.'

'Did Esme see him?'

'He says not. The way he tells it she only had eyes for lover boy.'

'And Stu? He's tried to check this guy out?'

'No. That's the whole point, mush. That's why he came to me. He says he doesn't trust himself. He says he'd kill the bloke. And what good would that do?'

Winter nodded. He knew exactly what was coming next but there was a move of his own he needed to make.

'About the Trust, Baz.'

'Fuck the Trust.'

'My thoughts entirely ... but listen, we need to get one or two things straight.'

'Yeah, like my daughter's bloody love life.'

'Of course, Baz. Not a problem. Leave it to me. But we're talking unfinished business here.'

'Too fucking right. You see him off, mush. You find out who he is, you take him to one side, and you tell him from me that I'll rip his bollocks off if he ever goes near my little girl again. Have you got that, mush? Only it might get very messy if you start fannying around.'

'Since when have I ever done that? Listen, Baz. This is the deal. There's a guy you need to meet. His name's Scott Taylor. He's a phone call away. He's a hotshot social worker, the real McCoy, exactly what Tide Turn needs. The moment he takes it off me is the moment I sort out our little problem.'

Mackenzie studied Winter for a long moment. He looked, if anything, amused. At length he reached for his coffee, gulped a couple of mouthfuls, followed it with the Bacardi, and wiped his mouth. Then he settled back against the leather sofa.

'You know something, mush?' He patted Winter's arm. 'You were *born* fucking evil.'

Faraday had been at his desk barely ten minutes before DCI Gail Parsons appeared at his open door. Since the recent reorganisation, she'd become the top detective on the Portsmouth-based Major Crime Team. Martin Barrie had departed to headquarters, leaving Parsons his office, his conference table and the lingering whiff of the roll-ups he used to smoke beside the ever-open window.

Parsons eyed the litter of unopened mail on Faraday's desk.

Faraday, less than halfway through his list of waiting emails, wondered if she might start this conversation with a kindly enquiry about his trip to Montreal.

'We need to talk about *Melody*, Joe. Have you got a moment?'

He followed her along the corridor. She was a small, forceful woman with an aggressive dress sense and a huge chest. She was rumoured to be extremely close to the Head of CID, Geoff Willard, and given the depth of her undisguised ambition Faraday was inclined to believe it.

Since Barrie's departure, his office had been transformed. On Mondays Parsons arrived with armfuls of fresh flowers and there was a small gallery of family photos carefully propped on the windowsill behind her desk. In the absence of a husband or a partner, two of them featured a black Labrador called Nelson.

Parsons waved Faraday into the chair in front of the desk. Whatever the occasion, she had the unhappy knack of making visitors feel they were under oath.

'Remind me, Joe. Where exactly are we with *Melody*?'

Faraday had spent the last minute or so trying to visualise the file. Operation *Melody* had been running for nearly nine months. A teenager, Tim Morrissey, had been stabbed to death on Guy Fawkes night. The murder had taken place in a remote corner of the city's King George V recreation ground, traditionally the site of the city's biggest bonfire. Thousands of people had come for the fireworks yet months of painstaking investigation had failed to turn up a single witness. *Melody*'s intelligence cell had built up an in-depth picture of the dead boy and Faraday's squad had few doubts about the name of the killer. All they needed was evidence.

'We're nowhere, boss. The file's still open.'

'But we have a prime suspect. Am I right?'

'Yes.'

'And his name again?'

'Kyle Munday.'

'That's what I thought. Have you seen this?'

She angled her PC screen towards Faraday. He had to get closer to read the details. Every morning, details of overnight developments force-wide were available for anyone to check. It was called The State.

'Here. Second entry from the bottom.'

Faraday followed Parsons' finger. The news that Kyle Munday had died in a hit-and-run brought a smile to his face. Parsons hadn't finished.

'Frankly, Joe, *Melody*'s been a bit of a disappointment. You don't need me to tell you that. Half the city were up there for the fireworks and that gave a lot of people a stake in what happened. It wasn't our finest hour, by any means. As our friends on the *News* pointed out.'

It was true. For a week at least the press had been brutal. KNIFE SLAYING MUM TALKS OF HER PAIN. COMMUNITY GROUPS DEMAND ACTION. NO ARRESTS IN PROSPECT.

'There may be some crossover here, Joe. The Road Death lot obviously have ownership but maybe that should change. If we could establish some kind of linkage with *Melody*, we might be able to bring last night's little episode into Major Crime. I could certainly talk to Mr Willard.'

Faraday nodded. Parsons, like most bosses, was constantly pushing to expand her empire. In the case of *Melody*, she'd call it closure. A more exact term might be a raiding expedition. Someone else's turf. Someone else's trophies.

'You want me to ...' He didn't need to end the sentence.

'I do, Joe. There's a woman called Steph Callan. She's a sergeant on RDIT. She's got the lead on Munday.'

The Road Death Investigation Team worked from offices in Eastleigh. Faraday had come across them on more than one occasion and had been impressed.

Parsons glanced up at the clock on the wall, her eyes gleaming. 'I've asked Callan to drive over,' she said. 'She should be here by ten.'

Steph Callan was early. Faraday glanced up from the last of his emails to find her out in the corridor, checking the name on his door. She looked to be in her early thirties, no more. Uniformed, she wore a sergeant's stripes. Tucked under one arm was a large manila envelope. Steady eyes. Nice mouth.

'D/I Faraday?' Flat London accent.

Faraday invited her in, tramped down the corridor to fetch a couple of coffees, returned to find her inspecting his modest gallery of bird photographs. The envelope was now propped against his PC.

'Did you take these?' She was looking at a family of coots.

'Yes.'

'And this one?' She tapped a column of gannets plunging into the sea.

'My son's. That's an old shot. He got lucky with the focus.'

'It's bloody good. Clever boy.'

'That's what he thinks. What's that?' Faraday had noticed the envelope.

'Part of the PM file. I understand you've had dealings with our Mr Munday.'

Faraday emptied the contents of the envelope onto his desk. These were post-mortem shots. The one on top offered a close-up of a head, three-quarter profile, the flattened face a blancmange of blood and gristle. Faraday felt a rising wave of nausea. Even Kyle Munday didn't deserve this.

'Quick, at least,' he heard himself say.

'Yeah ... for sure.'

She sat down. So far, she said, they'd drawn a blank with witnesses. There was no CCTV at the scene, no tyre marks on the road. Munday's clothing had been submitted for forensic examination, and the stolen-vehicle examiner attached to the Scenes of Crime team at Cosham was already working on debris recovered from the road.

'Like what?'

'Bits of an indicator unit and more stuff we think might have come from one of the headlights.'

Faraday nodded, sliding the post-mortem photos back into the envelope. A single tiny flake of paint or a splinter of glass could identify the make of a vehicle, even its year of manufacture.

'What about the post-mortem?' Faraday asked.

'Interesting. Have you ever come across a pathologist called Dodman?'

Faraday shook his head. He'd never heard of him.

'He's a locum. We'll have to wait for his report, obviously, but he was prepared to take a punt on what might have happened.'

Callan described the injuries to Munday's lower leg and the

provisional conclusion that he must have been facing the vehicle head on when it hit him.

Faraday nodded. According to *Melody*'s intelligence profile, Munday had a talent for confrontation, pushing even casual encounters to the point when something was bound to kick off. He enjoyed frightening people, loved hurting them. Tim Morrissey, in all probability, had been only one of his victims – though the rest, mercifully, were still alive.

'The guy was a monster,' Faraday said quietly, eyeing the envelope. 'How did you ID him?'

'The blokes on the scene found a breach-of-the-peace summons in his jeans pocket. There was a driving licence too. Matching the face was a bit of a problem but it was the same name.'

'Next of kin?'

'It turns out he lives with his mum.' She named a road in Paulsgrove, a sizeable council estate on the slopes of Portsdown Hill. 'I sent a FLO round. Half past three in the morning. You know how these things go with the death message but she wasn't best pleased.' FLO meant Family Liaison Officer.

'She's a smackhead,' Faraday told her. 'And she deals too. She hates us.'

'That's what the FLO said. She's driving the woman over to Winchester this morning for the ID. Apparently the house stank. There's a dog there too. Shit everywhere.'

'That was Munday's. It's a pit bull. He used to let it off the leash to savage other dogs. Just for the laugh.'

Faraday was staring out of the window, trying to imagine what had happened. Southwick Hill Road took traffic from the top of Portsdown Hill to the edges of Cosham, one of the city's mainland suburbs. The road was steep, maybe a mile in length.

'Whereabouts are we talking, exactly?' He turned back to Callan.

'About a third of the way up. Past the hospital.'

'Which side of the road?'

'The upside. The south side.'

Faraday got to his feet and checked the map of the city on the wall beside his desk. The road was at its steepest at the bottom. The big Queen Alexandra hospital on the left-hand side occupied the first quarter of a mile, maybe more. Beyond there was nothing but bare hillside, falling away to the estate below. The vehicle would have been moving up the hill, gathering speed all the time, but giving Munday plenty of time to see it. So why was he standing in the middle of the road? Letting himself get run over?

'He was probably pissed,' Callan said. 'According to Dodman.'

'Yeah. But maybe it's more personal too.'

'I'm not with you.'

'Maybe he knew this car, whatever it was. Recognised it. Gave it the finger.' He shrugged. 'Whatever.'

'Sure. And maybe he didn't. We just can't tell.'

Something in her tone of voice told Faraday to slow down. She was staking her claim, protecting her turf. Our job, she was saying. Our shout.

'You said there were no tyre marks on the road surface?'

'Nothing. We checked again in daylight on Sunday morning.'

'Isn't that unusual?'

'Very.'

'So the vehicle made no attempt to stop? Is that what we're saying?'

'It made no attempt to stop quickly. Not quite the same thing.'

'But ran him over?'

'Obviously.'

'And didn't hang around afterwards?'

'No.'

'How long before the body was spotted?'

'We can't know for sure. But it's a mainish road, so we're talking minutes at the most.'

'Time?'

'The treble nine was logged at 01.23.'

'Could have been longer, then? That time of night?' Faraday had returned to the map. 'This treble nine. Who made it?'

'The driver who spotted the body. He was with his wife. They live in Wickham. They were en route home after dinner with friends.'

'Going up the hill, then?'

'Yep. Just like the other guy.'

Faraday nodded. Had this couple been coming down the hill they might have passed the sus target vehicle, might have remembered a detail or two.

'Down here we've got plenty of CCTV.' Faraday tapped the tangle of main roads south of Cosham. 'That time of night you're not looking at lots of traffic. If our guy came up from the city, odds are he's been clocked.' Faraday glanced round at Callan. 'How are you for bodies?'

She returned his gaze, unsmiling. There was a steeliness in her blue eyes that spoke of something more than self-confidence.

'I've got two guys at the CCTV centre as we speak.' She reached for her envelope. 'If we're through with the tutorial, I'm off down there now.'

'I'm sorry. I thought I was here to help.'

'Help how?'

'Help with Munday. The company he kept. The people he pissed off.'

'The people who might have run him over?'

'Exactly. Does that sound outrageous?'

'Not at all.' She stood up and smoothed her skirt. 'So let's stay in touch, eh?'

Paul Winter instructed Scott Taylor to get off the train at the harbour terminus. Pompey's town station, at the foot of Commercial Road, had always struck him as faintly depressing, a jungle of iron beams to support the overhead tracks, and an awning on top that filtered a thin grey light over the two platforms. If you'd never been to Pompey in your life, and there was any prospect of you staying, then the harbour station – with its waterside views – offered a far gentler handshake.

On the phone Taylor had sounded enthusiastic about Tide Turn Trust. Small lean start-up charities, he'd said, could afford to take a risk or two, and after a decade at the coalface with various London local authorities he'd had more than enough of covering his arse. In the flesh, emerging from the station, he looked exactly the way Winter had pictured him. Tight jeans. Lean frame. Collarless shirt. A couple of days' stubble. And a hint of grey in his close-cropped hair.

Winter drove him to the Royal Trafalgar. Earlier, he'd reserved the best table in the big, ground-floor restaurant. Bazza would be joining them as soon as he was through in the office.

'So tell me more about this trust of yours.' Taylor was sitting beside the window, his chair half turned to enjoy the view across the Common to the sea.

Winter filled in the details. How Mackenzie had become involved in a kids' thrash in the house next door that had turned into a full-scale riot. How a couple of bodies had ended up beside his own swimming pool. How he and Winter, between them, had beaten the Old Bill in terms of finding the culprit. And how the whole experience had convinced Mackenzie that something had to be done about the state of the city's youth.

'*All* of them?'

'A handful. The hard core. I don't know how it is with you but we get real scrotes down here.'

'IC3s?'

'White boys mostly. IC1s.'

Taylor helped himself to a roll and reached for the butter dish. There was a smile on his face that Winter didn't much like.

'You used to be a copper. Am I right?'

'Yeah. Who told you that?'

'Nobody. It's obvious. My line of work, you're around coppers all the time.' He bit into the roll, smearing one side of his mouth with butter. 'So how come you link up with someone like Mackenzie?'

'Because he asked me.'

'And has it worked?'

'Definitely. The money's great and he doesn't believe in paperwork.'

'You're telling me you've got this trust thing going without *paperwork*?'

'That's not what I meant. I've been babysitting until someone who knows what they're doing comes along. Someone like you, maybe. You're right. The paperwork setting up the Trust has been a nightmare. Never again.'

Winter began to tally the kind of interventions he had in mind for Tide Turn, ways this infant organisation might pour oil on Pompey's troubled waters. Mentoring schemes for hardened ten-year-olds. Pathways to outward-bound weekends. Some kind of sports involvement. Computer courses.

Taylor, by the look of him, had heard it all before.

'Waste of time, mate.' He reached for his napkin and patted his mouth. 'Why not cut to the chase?'

'I'm not with you.'

'Teach them about the drugs biz. Sort out some kind of apprenticeship deal. Turn them into proper dealers. Make them *rich*.'

Winter stared at him. For once in his life, he didn't know what to say. Worse still, Bazza had just appeared, body-checking round the prettiest of the new waitresses, then pausing to murmur something in her ear. She began to laugh. Taylor was watching too.

'Doesn't change, does he? Old tosser.'

'You know him?'

'Of course I do.'

Bazza ended his tête-à-tête and headed for the table. The sight of Taylor put a huge smile on his face. He gestured him to his feet, then pumped the extended hand.

'Fuck me,' he said. 'What turned you legit?'

'Money. And marriage.'

'Kids?'

'Three, Baz. Another due next week.'

Mackenzie shook his head, holding Taylor at arm's length. Then he sank into the spare chair and turned to Winter.

'I never sussed it. You should have told me.'

'Told you what, Baz?'

'*The* Scott Taylor. You know what they called him at the Den? The Undertaker. We had a million rucks with the Millwall crew and they never let us down, not once. Waterloo, eight o'clock on a Saturday morning, they'd be waiting for us round the back of the concourse. Totally up for it, those animals. Totally reliable.'

Winter sat back as the two men reminisced. On one occasion Taylor had put Mackenzie in hospital. On another, barely weeks later, Bazza had trapped him at the end of a cul-de-sac and kicked the living shit out of him. Good sport. Great days.

The pretty waitress was waiting. Mackenzie told her to fetch champagne.

'How many bottles, Mr Mackenzie?'

'Bring two Krugs. Put another one on ice. Take a good look at this man, Kelly. He was famous once.'

She laughed again, turning on her heel, and Winter watched her leave the restaurant, knowing that this plan of his was heading for disaster. Scott Taylor had come down for a jolly.

He was right. They were talking drugs now, swapping stories from the late 80s. How Bazza had supplied industrial quantities of Ecstasy to an ever-widening circle of football hooligans. How clever he'd been, keeping the prices near-wholesale, letting guys like Taylor take their own profit along the supply chain. The summer of love, said Taylor, had turned into the winter of serious moolah. By the early 90s, before real life caught up with him, he was taking two-month holidays in the Caribbean and coming back with change in his pocket.

'So where did it all go wrong, mush?' Bazza wanted to know.

'I fell in love. She'd been to university, for fuck's sake. She'd got a law degree. Shagged me witless for a couple of years then made me get a proper job. Social work sounded a doss so I gave it a go.'

'And?'

'I was wrong about the doss but the rest of it was all right. Turned out I could get on with these kids, which isn't as common as you might think.'

'And now?'

'Three kids of our own and a fucking great mortgage.'

'Happy?'

'Pig in shit, mate. Love every minute of it.'

Winter's gloom deepened. No way would Taylor be spoiling his precious CV with any kind of association with the likes of Bazza Mackenzie.

The champagne arrived. For a moment or two Winter thought Mackenzie was going to neck it straight from the bottle but then the waitress turned up again with three glasses. She poured the Krug and headed for safety.

'Here's to crime.' Bazza winked at Taylor. 'Happy fucking days.'

The lunch lasted until four o'clock. Every time Winter got up and made his excuses Mackenzie waved him back into his chair.

Like Taylor, Baz had always loathed the Filth but Mr W had been far and away the best of them, much too streetwise to be a fucking *cop*, and Baz had finally squared the circle by making him an offer he couldn't refuse. By that time, he told Taylor, Winter himself had seen the light. The Old Bill in this city were shit, a bunch of total tossers, and it had been a pleasure to offer Mr W a proper home for his talents. Since then, despite a hitch or two, they'd had some great times. The business was turning over more dosh than he'd ever need and every last penny was legit. There was no one out there, *no one*, who could touch him.

'Eh, Paulie?'

They were standing on the front steps of the hotel. The waiting taxi would be taking Taylor back to the station. Any thought of discussing Tide Turn Trust had long gone. Winter was right. With the best of intentions he'd organised a tribute lunch dedicated to the memory of the 6.57 crew.

Bazza was giving Taylor a hug. Any time, mush. You know where we are. Bring the wife. Bring the fucking kids. Bring anyone.

Taylor stepped into the taxi. Like so many of Mackenzie's inner circle, he seemed to have a limitless capacity for alcohol. He gave them both a wave as the taxi sped away. Then Bazza turned to Winter.

'Brilliant, mush. Remind me ... why the fuck did he come down?'

Chapter three

Faraday gave up waiting for Suttle to appear at his office door.
He reached for the phone, dialled his home number. At length,
it answered.

'Jimmy?'

'Boss?'

'Are you ill?'

'I'm on a rest day. *Palliser.*'

Operation *Palliser* was investigating the slaughter of a Somali
drug dealer, found dead in a lavatory on the seafront. The killing had happened when Faraday was on leave and Jimmy Suttle
had probably worked both weekends.

Faraday was staring at his PC. An email from Sergeant Steph
Callan was tagged 'Urgent'. She wanted another meet. This
time, Faraday knew he had to play a stronger hand.

'We need to talk about *Melody,* Jimmy.'

'When?'

'As soon as.'

'We're off to Chichester this morning. Can't it wait?'

'No.' Faraday checked his watch. 'I'll be with you in ten
minutes.'

Jimmy Suttle lived in an area called Milton, street after street
of terraced houses that webbed the south-east corner of the
city. Recently promoted Detective Sergeant, he'd managed to
retain his desk in the Major Crime intelligence cell. This hadn't
gone down at all well with the long queue of other D/Ss eager
for a spell on Major Crime, but Faraday had put his case to
DCI Parsons, and Parsons – with some reluctance – had under-
taken to get the appointment past Willard. Strictly speaking,
Suttle should be transferred back to local CID work. Only his

very obvious intel talents kept him in Major Crime.

Suttle had the kettle on. For the best part of a year he'd been sharing the ground-floor flat with Lizzie Hodson, a reporter on the *News*. The moment Faraday stepped in through the front door she'd beaten a tactful retreat to the front room.

'Kyle Munday's dead.' Faraday explained the hit-and-run. 'Parsons thinks the investigation belongs to *Melody*. She might be right but it's down to me to argue the case. There's a sergeant on the Road Death team who doesn't see it our way. Surprise, surprise.'

Suttle was still digesting the news about Munday. Back in November, weeks of patient intelligence work had built profiles of the potential suspects who had crossed the dead teenager's path. It had been Suttle's job to rank these suspects and he'd never had a moment's doubt that Kyle Munday occupied pole position.

'You think there's linkage here? Someone paying off a debt?'

'That has to be our supposition.'

'Why?'

'Because Parsons wants the job in-house.'

'Sure. But who are we looking at? Tim Morrissey was a mouse. He never ran with the kind of guys who'd sort Munday out. In fact he never ran with *anyone*.'

It was true. Part of the tragedy of the Guy Fawkes night stabbing was the choice of victim. Morrissey, by all accounts, had led a blameless life. Quiet, studious, mad about modern jazz, he devoted most of his spare time to polishing his keyboard skills on a borrowed piano. His mother, Jeanette, kept recordings of his wilder riffs, and Faraday had heard them. The kid was seriously talented. He was also determined to make something of himself. Two reasons why he'd attracted Munday's attention.

Faraday watched Suttle hunting for the sugar bowl. Before he met Steph Callan again, he needed to be absolutely sure of the sequence of events that had preceded Morrissey's death. At forty-eight, his memory was beginning to let him down.

'Munday had been giving the lad a hard time ... right?'

'Absolutely. Morrissey was an easy target. Munday dominated a bunch of kids off the Paulsgrove estate. They thought he was God. A couple of them were in Morrissey's year at school. The kid was a boff. He read books. Loved his mum. Stayed in at night. Wanted to make something of his life. Big mistake.'

Faraday reached for his tea. One of the things about Munday that had stuck in his mind was the allegation that he and some of his scrote apprentices had cornered Morrissey behind the parade of shops at the heart of the estate. They'd forced the lad to the ground and Munday had stamped on his hands. The damage, mercifully, had been less severe than you might have expected but the message was clear. Think you're special on that fucking piano of yours? Think again.

'And we're saying Morrissey had no mates who might have fought back? You can't think of *anyone* who might have had it in for Munday?'

'No. That's why the lad came to us about the stamping incident. It was his mum's idea, had to be, but Morrissey named names. Which is probably what got him killed. Remember?'

'Yeah.' Faraday nodded. Munday's little gang had all been arrested and interviewed after the stamping, but denied any involvement. Forensic evidence from footware had later tied two of the kids to Morrissey but the case had gone nowhere.

Faraday was eyeing the cheerful chaos of Suttle's kitchen, last night's dirty dishes still piled on the draining board. One day back into the Job and already he felt knackered.

Suttle settled himself on a stool by the breakfast bar. In truth, he hadn't had a serious look at Munday since *Melody* began to wind down after Christmas. Early spring had taken him onto other killings, other jobs. Since then Munday could have got himself into all sorts of situations, pissed off trillions of people, probably had. If the hit-and-run had been deliberate, then the guy at the wheel might never have heard of Tim Morrissey.

'You're saying it needs more work, more intel?' Faraday said.

'Only if it gets sticky. And this Road Death skipper, he'll know that.'

'It's a woman. Steph Callan.'

'Her, then. These people deal with hit-and-runs all the time. You plough into someone, you've had a drink or two, there's no way you're going to hang around. A tenner says they'll crack it on the forensic. Trace the vehicle. Get an address. The bloke's been sitting there for days expecting the knock on the door. Bosh. Job done. Who needs intel when it's that simple?'

Faraday nodded. He was thinking of Steph Callan's face when she left his office. He'd treated her like some rookie probationer. He'd slipped effortlessly into Parsons' mindset, playing the Major Crime sleuth, assuming complications that simply weren't there. Suttle was doubtless right. A couple of beers too many. An empty road. A face in the windscreen. A bump or two underneath. A glance in the mirror. Foot on the throttle. Gone.

'Boss ...' Faraday became aware of Suttle looking at him.

'Yeah?'

'How was Montreal?'

'Crap.' Faraday drained his mug. 'But thanks for asking.'

Winter was late getting to the youth club. He'd had a ring round first thing, talking to mums, stepdads, brothers, sisters, occasionally even the kid himself. Conversations never got beyond a sleepy grunt but that didn't matter. In essence the message was simple. Somers Road. Half nine. Be there.

The minibus had been Marie's idea. Before Christmas, once Winter was sure the Tide Turn Trust would get the thumbs up from the Charity Commission, she'd leant on Bazza to acquire appropriate transport. At first, Winter had thought it was a neat idea. Appearances were important to kids and a decent set of wheels, badged with the Trust's logo, would give the operation a bit of class.

In the event, though, Bazza had talked to a couple of head-bangers who ran a forecourt operation in Fratton Road. They'd just taken a minibus in part-payment of a credit debt and were happy to offer it on extended lease. The fact that this loan was free remained Bazza's little secret, but the moment Winter set eyes on the vehicle he knew he'd been had. Almost 146,000 miles on the clock. An ominous rumbling from the prop shaft. And – worst of all – THE WEE GREEN BUS scrolled below the windows. In a former life this wreck had belonged to an infants' school in Aldershot. Winter's plea for a respray fell on deaf ears.

Now, he parked up outside the youth club in Somerstown. The plan was to ship half a dozen tearaways to the bowling alley in the city centre. These kids were serial truants, abandoned by their schools and by various welfare agencies, and in a more perfect world Winter would have dreamed up something vaguely educational to occupy their tiny minds. His experience over the last couple of months, though, had taught him a great deal. Anything that smacked of learning, or self-betterment, was a no-no. To produce even a flicker of interest, there had to be the promise of a laugh.

But even this, to Winter's intense irritation, sparked its own problems. He'd tried the swimming pool first, negotiating a one-month discount for his unruly flock on the strict promise of good behaviour. The first time they'd gone to Victoria Baths, a stormy Wednesday morning in March, one of the boys had hidden in the women's changing rooms, taking photos of the shower area on his phone. Shots of a naked middle-aged woman had made it onto Facebook, all the more regrettable because she happened to be a visiting fellow at the nearby university. Her lectures were packed out for weeks, but by that time the people who ran the swimming pool had given up on Tide Turn Trust. After the mobe shots had come an incident with the vending machine in the lobby, shaken to death by a couple of the handier lads, followed the next week by an enormous turd, deposited in the deep end by a promising young arsonist from Buckland. In his exit interview as the supervising adult, conducted in a windowless room at the Civic Centre, Winter had blamed unmanageable expectations. The phrase had meant fuck all but when it came to voluntary-sector bullshit, Winter was learning fast.

After the swimming pool there'd been other initiatives, equally disastrous. The outing to the Farlington Bird Reserve to stone a couple of mating swans. The canoeing expedition on the harbour that ended with a ride in the coastguard helicopter. The flick-knife initials gouged into an eighteenth-century mess table aboard HMS *Victory*. On each of these occasions Winter had once again carried the can, patiently explaining that these YPs were the victims of a society that neither understood nor cared about the loveless anarchy that passed as their home lives. They had to be brought inside society's tent. They had to be shown what a decent life could offer. They deserved a second chance.

YPs was social-worker-speak for Young People. As a cop, Winter had spent most of his adult life chasing these toerags around the estates and in his heart he knew exactly how to gain their attention, but brute force, sadly, was no longer an option. And so, like every other adult, he was obliged to shower them with treats and hope for the best. It didn't work. And more to the point, it was beginning to drive him insane.

By ten o'clock no one had shown up. Winter sat at the wheel, drumming his fingers to his favourite Neil Diamond CD, wondering how long he should give it. Part of the problem was the parents. In most cases the dads were long gone, leaving a small army of single mums desperate to make ends meet. Most of them worked at dead-end jobs, battling to stay afloat. A handful were on the game, pulling half-decent money. One or two had given up completely, shoplifting at lunch time to meet the smack bills. Winter was way past blaming any of these women. All he knew was that they'd long ago given up on their scrotey kids.

By ten fifteen, with nothing to show but a couple of drunks emerging from the bushes across the road, Winter had decided to call it a day. He'd drive the Wee Green Bus back to the Royal Trafalgar, park it outside Mackenzie's office window and leave him with the keys. The next time Bazza fancied solving the nation's social problems, he could fucking do it himself. Winter was reaching for the volume control on the CD machine when he caught a flicker of movement in the rear-view mirror. A yellow saloon had rounded a corner up the road. It looked like an Escort. The rear tyres spun as the driver accelerated hard and then it began to weave as the brakes came on. Winter twisted round in the seat, his heart sinking. In the car were kids, four of them. The driver was so small he probably needed a booster seat. Their silhouettes, all too familiar, explained why he'd been waiting so long.

The Escort squealed to a halt beside the minibus. Winter looked down at them, not bothering to open the window. His kids. All screaming with laughter, all giving him the finger. Winter took a deep breath, wondering where they'd nicked the car. Billy Lenahan, the midget at the wheel, was a legend for his hot-wiring skills. The girl sitting beside him, the girl he boasted about shagging every night, was allegedly his sister. Inbreds on wheels, thought Winter. Just what the fuck am I doing with my life?

Something snapped inside him. He'd had enough. More than enough. As the Escort roared off, he fired up the minibus's engine, hauled the beast away from the kerbside, set off in pursuit. Ahead, the Escort had slowed enough to let him catch up. Then it was off again, the rear tyres trailing little plumes of blue smoke, the matador's cloak trailed before the charging bull.

Winter fumbled for his mobile. Jimmy Suttle's number was on his directory. Driving at this speed with one hand wasn't easy. Suttle finally answered.

'Paul.' He sounded less than pleased.

'Listen, son. I'm in Somerstown. I'm following a bunch of twat kids in a yellow Escort. You gotta pen? G Golf. Four-five-two. X-Ray. Hotel. Delta.'

'I'm driving. I'm on a rest day. What's wrong with a treble nine?'

'Nothing, son. Except I don't want the attention. Just do us a favour, will you? Ring it in. Otherwise these little bastards are going to kill some poor fucker.'

'Shit, Paul, this is out of order. I'm with Lizzie. I'm doing seventy miles an hour. We're off for a nice day out. What's the problem with you?'

'It's not me, son. It's got fuck all to do with me. Are you still there?'

The line had gone dead. Winter looked at the phone in disbelief. He even shook it. Looking up, he just had time to register the Escort stopped at a T-junction ahead of him. His foot hit the brake and the van started to judder. Then came the splintering of glass as the Wee Green Bus rear-ended the Escort.

Winter sat motionless at the wheel. The seat belt, mercifully, had done its job. From somewhere below his feet he could hear the steady trickle of liquid onto the road. For a moment he wondered whether it was petrol then decided it was probably coolant. The thought that he'd just knackered the engine brought a smile to his face.

One by one, the kids were emerging from the Escort. Billy Lenahan was holding the back of his neck. The girl beside him was examining a bruise on her arm. The two kids in the back were staring up at Winter. One of them had gone white.

'Fuck me, Mr W. What did you do that for?'

Faraday had no problem agreeing to drive to Eastleigh, a red-brick railway town north of Southampton, for the meet with Steph Callan. After yesterday's encounter, the last thing she needed was another trip to Major Crime. The inquiry into the hit-and-run now had a name: Operation *Highfield*.

The sight of biscuits beside the Thermos of coffee brightened Faraday's morning. She, like him, must have seen the advantages of starting their relationship afresh.

She thanked him for driving over, poured the coffee.

'Scenes of Crime have recovered paint fragments from Munday's jeans. We're thinking red. We've also had a bit of a windfall.' She frowned. 'Or we think we have.'

She described the indicator recovered from the roadside after the crash. According to the stolen-vehicle examiner, the shape was distinctive. He'd accessed a series of websites and tied the item to a specific make and model. The shape of the indicator further offered a time window for the manufacture of the vehicle.

'So what are we looking for?'

'A VW van, or possibly camper van, built between 1980 and 1992.'

'Red?'

'Yes. And it gets better.'

Faraday found himself looking at a polythene evidence bag. Inside was a wiper blade.

'A woman handed this in. She found it a couple of hundred yards up the Southwick Hill Road yesterday morning and made the connection with Munday. According to the council schedule, the road was last swept on Friday. Guy from our FCIU thinks it might have come off the target vehicle.'

'FCIU?'

'Forensic Collision Investigation Unit. The guys who spend their lives piecing these accidents together. His name's Harry. He's a sweetie.' It was the first time Faraday had seen her smile. 'If Dodman was right about Munday getting hit full face, it's just possible his hands would have come out. It's an instinctive reaction. You're trying to ward off disaster.'

'Grasping at straws?'

'Exactly. In this case a wiper. It might not tear off at once but if the blade's weakened it might just drop off up the road.'

Faraday peered at the blade again. Callan anticipated his next question.

'It's a pretty standard make. There are millions of them around.'

'So why ...?'

'Turn it over.' Faraday did what he was told. 'See that tiny line where the rubber seats into the metal?'

'Yes.'

'That's probably a deposit from a tree. Put it in the hands of the right expert and we're looking at a specific make.'

'Make?'

'Sorry.' Another smile. '*Type* of tree. Think about it. Say it's a larch or an elm or whatever. Once we start talking TIE, something like that could be priceless.' TIE meant Trace, Interview, Eliminate.

Faraday nodded. She was right. Faced with a list of addresses, an elm tree overhanging a driveway or the road outside the house could put the vehicle owner in the dock for murder.

'What about CCTV?'

'Nothing. We established a window of thirty minutes before the treble nine and looked at cameras covering approach routes. No VW camper vans that fit the parameters.'

'So how could a camper van slip through?' Faraday was trying to remember the pattern of cameras that mapped the north of the city.

'Easy. The old A3 from the north isn't covered. Neither is Havant Road from the east. You can also get off the Paulsgrove estate and not be clocked.'

She came to a halt. Faraday swallowed the rest of his coffee.

'So what's your question?' he asked.

'I'm not with you.'

'Why did you want me over here? Why the meet?'

'Ah ...' A grin this time. 'I'm just wondering about the Volkswagen. Like I said, the colour of the paint flake is red, a deep red, red the colour of arterial blood, quite distinctive. On *Melody*, did you put anyone alongside a red VW? It might save us a bit of time.'

'Sure.' Faraday was thinking hard. Nothing came back to him in the way of vehicles and he was loath to phone Suttle again. 'Can it wait until tomorrow? The intel skipper on *Melody* is off today.'

'No problem. The stolen-vehicle bloke is due to send me a list of local red VW van registrations. I'll make sure he copies you in. A name might ring a bell.'

She offered more coffee. Faraday, checking his watch, said no. He got to his feet then sat down again, aware that there was something as yet unvoiced.

'Do you mind me asking you something personal?' she said.

'Not at all. Go ahead.'

'Someone told me you had a son.'

'That's true. That was me. Yesterday.' He paused. 'You were looking at the bird shots on my wallboard. Gannets.'

'Of course, I'm sorry. What I meant was a boy who's deaf and dumb.'

'That's him. His name's J-J.'

'He's the one who took the photo? The white birds diving into the sea?'

'Yeah.'

'Right ...'

She absorbed this information then told Faraday about her sister. She'd been married for a while now and desperately wanted kids but nothing was happening. She and her husband had been over in Thailand recently on a trek in the mountains and had made friends with a local family. One of their kids, a baby girl, was deaf and dumb. They were looking for someone to adopt her. They said she needed Western medicine, Western levels of care. Callan's sister had fallen in love with the child. But what did coping with that kind of handicap really entail?

Faraday changed his mind about the coffee, resisting the urge to ask where exactly this child lived. Thailand was where he'd first met Gabrielle, up in the mountains near the Burmese border. And she too in her more fanciful moments had occasionally wondered about adopting an Asian baby.

'It can be tough,' he said at once.

'How tough?'

'As tough as you make it. In my case I was on my own. My wife, J-J's mum, had died so that left us pretty much alone.'

'And you were a copper?'

'Yeah. A young probationer. This is some time ago. I was twenty, no ... twenty-one.'

'You were *married* at twenty-one?'

'Nineteen. Does that sound shameful?'

'I'd say reckless. Either that or you were in love.'

'Both. I'd settle for that.'

He told her about coping with J-J in the early days. Janna's parents, wealthy Americans, had written him a generous cheque for their new grandson, enabling Faraday to buy the Bargemaster's House, and there was enough left to afford to have someone look after the new baby when he was on shift. But from the start Faraday had detected something special in his infant son, something slightly odd, and by the time he'd hit his second birthday J-J had been diagnosed profoundly deaf.

'How did you feel?'

'I think it was a relief. I knew what the problem was, what the challenge was. And in a way that made it easier. I was his dad. He was my son, my boy. One way or another we had to start talking to each other.'

'But how could you do that?'

'Through the birds. I met someone having to cope with the same problem. We talked ... much like we're talking now. She'd done it through birds. You build a bridge. You learn sign language. You flap your arms around. You play games. You draw a lot. You make each other laugh. I happened to have this great house by the water. Look out of the window and the birds were everywhere. We were incredibly lucky.'

It was true. Looking back, Faraday could tally a thousand memories. Of J-J peering out of his buggy, kicking his plump little legs at the sight of a family of grebes in one of the nearby freshwater ponds. Of J-J years later, splashing around on the stony mudflats at low tide, building a nest of seaweed for a pair of oystercatchers that had taken his fancy. Without the gift of hearing, Faraday tried to explain, his son seemed to commune with the birds. He couldn't imagine birdsong because he had no experience of sound. Yet the world of these creatures was undoubtedly real. They connected. They spoke to him.

Steph was fascinated. She wanted to know more about the

house, about J-J. Did Faraday still live there? With this deaf mute son of his?

'Yes and no. Yes I still live there but J-J's up in London now.'

'And how is he?'

'Very good question.' Faraday glanced at his watch again. 'I had breakfast with him on Sunday morning. He's built a career. He's got a roof over his head. He does some pretty extraordinary things. Handicap's an ugly word. He'd kill you for using it.'

'He's grown up now?'

'Thirty this year, going on twelve. That's not arrested development. That's just mischief.'

Steph laughed as Faraday got to his feet. Then came the lightest of knocks on the door. In stepped a man in his early forties: jeans, a plaid shirt, and a smear or two of grease on his big hands. The way he looked at Steph, Faraday knew at once they were close.

'This is Harry,' she said, 'our star crash investigator. He's also my brother-in-law. He's the one who went to Thailand. I took the liberty of asking him to come up. Can you hang on another couple of minutes?'

'No problem at all.' Faraday sat down again. 'My pleasure.'

Chapter four

Winter phoned Mackenzie from the custody suite at the city's central police station. He'd locked the kids in the Wee Green Bus and belled 999. An area car had arrived in minutes, a decent response time, and at Winter's suggestion all four kids had been arrested on sus vehicle theft. Because they were so young, the booking-in process was taking an age. The custody Sergeant was a stickler for ticking every single box and laying hands on four Appropriate Adults was proving a bit of a nightmare.

Stepping into the fingerprint area, Winter waited for Mackenzie to answer. Tuesday mornings he normally reserved for an executive pow-wow with his new hotel manager, a heavily tanned forty-something who'd recently returned from running a block of self-catering apartments in Dubai. Her name was Chandelle and it turned out that Baz had first met her a couple of years back when he was investing a couple of million pounds in one of the Emirates' new shopping malls.

It wasn't immediately obvious why Chandelle should have wanted to swap Dubai for Southsea seafront, but Bazza was shrewd when it came to employing people and his new manager had certainly made an impact. Overnight bookings were up by a hefty percentage and Chandelle's looks, coupled with her schmoozing talents, had begun to change the hotel's clientele. In some ways she reminded Winter of Misty Gallagher, Bazza's long-term mistress. The same frank enjoyment of life. The same talent for convincing every man she met that they were inches away from scoring. No wonder some of the city's key players – the movers and shakers who always pushed their luck – were beginning to fill the restaurant at lunchtimes.

'How's it going?' It was Bazza.

'I'm down the Bridewell.'

'*Where?*'

Winter explained what had happened. Bazza dismissed the damage to the Wee Green Bus.

'What about the kids? You kill any?'

'No.'

'Shame. So how come the Old Bill got involved?'

'I belled them, Baz. It's called citizenship. Wins you lots of big brownie points. All they had to do was turn up and nick the little bastards. How sweet is that?'

Winter could tell Mackenzie wasn't convinced. He'd spent his entire adult life proving that crime paid, and collaboration with the Filth made him deeply uneasy. He wanted to know what would happen next.

'They'll get charged, then bailed. Sooner or later they'll appear in court. Some ditzy social worker will show up and we'll all agree they deserve a second chance. I give it a couple of months, Baz.'

'Before what?'

'Before they're at it again.'

One of the Bridewell's younger P/Cs, a face Winter didn't recognise, paused by the door. He'd caught the end of the conversation and he mimed applause. Winter gave him a wink, then turned his back to the door.

Mackenzie wanted to be sure there'd be no comeback from the men in blue.

'Comeback for what, Baz? Nicking cars is hot just now. The guys down here have to hit their performance targets. We just did them a big favour. Believe me, Baz, you'll be getting a letter from the Chief Constable. A couple more outings like this and you'll end up Lord Mayor. Result, eh?'

Mackenzie grunted, far from amused, and Winter tried to picture Chandelle gazing at him across the desk, playing with the beads she wore, her long scarlet fingernails straying across her permanently tanned chest. Bazza kept a suite of his own upstairs and Winter, like every other member of staff, assumed that room service on Tuesday lunchtimes meant exactly that. Bazza had never seen the point of being subtle.

'I had Stu on earlier,' he said. 'We need to talk.'

'Go on, then.'

'He's up in town for most of the week, had a gander at Ezzie's diary before he left.'

'And?'

'She's booked at the gym late this afternoon. You know the Tatchbury Mount Spa Hotel?'

'No.'

'Come round after lunch. Half two would be good. I'll talk you through it.'

The line went dead and Winter turned round to find the uniformed custody Inspector with a protective arm round the diminutive Billy Lenahan. The Inspector, a Scouse ex-submariner, had always had a soft spot for Winter.

'I'm locking up our little friend here,' he said. 'He just tried to nick the PDSA collection box.'

'Evidence?'

'Three witnesses, fingerprints, CCTV.' He held up a bloodied finger. 'Plus the little bastard bit me.'

Faraday ran into DCI Parsons in the car park behind Fratton nick. She was bustling towards her new Audi A5, already late for a lunch with the Head of CID over in Winchester.

'Somewhere nice, I hope.'

'Sandwiches, Joe, if I'm lucky. Have you talked to Callan again?'

'Yes.'

'And?'

'She says the investigation is ongoing.'

'Which means?'

'She's telling us to bugger off.'

'Really?' A frown signalled Parsons' displeasure. 'You briefed her on *Melody*? Registered our interest?'

'Of course, boss. But I don't think she's having it. She's read the small print. She knows her rights. She's standing her ground. And to be frank I don't blame her.'

Parsons shot Faraday a look. Later, locked in conference with Willard, she'd doubtless table her concerns about the veteran D/I. Major Crime needs new blood, she'd say. It needs youth, energy, 100 per cent commitment. Not some weary has-been unprepared to fight his corner.

'Take another look at the file, Joe. You've been away. Maybe something's slipped your mind. It'll be there, I guarantee it. Then you can phone her again and have a proper conversation.'

'And Mr Willard?'

'He's seeing it my way.' She smiled her little smile. 'We need to bring this in-house.'

In his office, Faraday fetched out the *Melody* file. The last couple of days, back on home turf, he'd realised just how easy it was to lose the plot. Effective detective work depended, above all, on total focus. On the Major Crime Team you were there to unleash the investigative machine, to trawl for evidence, to piece together a story, to weigh one probability against another, and to be aware all the time where this little boat of yours – so painstakingly assembled – might spring a leak.

Time after time, as a lowly D/C, he'd been astonished at how quickly a good defence barrister could demolish a case in court. A single flaw in the evidence, the merest hint of contradictory statements, the tiniest procedural oversight buried in the CPS file, could – within minutes – swing a jury against a stone-bonker case.

A stone-bonker case carried the virtual guarantee of a Guilty verdict. To anyone with half a brain it would be obvious where the blame lay. *Melody* was a brilliant example of a stone-bonker but the squad had struggled from the start with assembling lawyer-proof evidence.

Faraday opened the file and began to leaf through it. Jimmy Suttle, with his usual thoroughness, had assembled a timeline that began with the victim's mother, Jeanette Morrissey. She'd first become aware of Munday's interest in her son Tim when he'd arrived home in the early summer without the rucksack he used to carry his books. At first he claimed to have lost it. Then he said he'd left it on the bus. Only when she accused him of lying did he admit that kids from his class – one of them Munday's younger brother – had tossed the contents into one of the neighbourhood bottle banks and then used lighter fuel to set fire to the rucksack itself.

Three of the books had belonged to the school. Tim would have to foot the bill for replacements. But the fourth had been precious, a signed edition of a Terry Pratchett novel, and his obvious distress at its loss had delighted his tormentors. From that point on, said his mother, Tim had become the easiest of targets, and when word spread that he'd contacted the council to try and access the bottle bank the news simply whetted the kids' appetite for more wind-ups.

They'd begun to lay little traps on his way home, chasing him up the street, pelting him with stones nicked from a nearby rockery. They bribed the class minger to try and get inside his trousers on the back seat of the bus. They ambushed him outside his piano teacher's house, tearing up the sheet music she'd just given him and then videoing his frenzied attempts to prevent the wind scattering it all down the street. In a footnote Suttle had described this kind of behaviour as predatory, and he was right, but the months of bullying and abuse during the summer were merely a prelude to what followed.

The key, once again, was Kyle Munday. He'd just served ten months for assault, hospitalising a young Asian taxi driver who'd got on his nerves, and he was back on the estate, keen to re-establish himself at the top of the pecking order. Tim Morrissey, with his fancy ideas about becoming a jazz pianist, struck him as the perfect target. Munday's young lieutenants, the kids who trailed like comet dust in his wake, had made a decent enough start but Morrissey's obvious vulnerability justi-fied a step-change in the violence. Someone like that – bright, talented, hard-working – had to be taught a lesson. And Munday, with his bitten nails and dragon tats, was only too happy to oblige.

The hand-stamping had been his idea. On Friday evenings, like the good boy he was, Morrissey fetched fish and chips for his mum from the Happy Friar. Munday and half a dozen of the younger kids were already pissed on White Lightning from the corner shop up the road. They were hanging around outside the chippy but they let Morrissey through because that way they got a free meal as well as a laugh or two. When he came out, according to a woman who lived across the road, they followed him along the parade of shops, trying to trip him up, laughing and jeering as he began to run. Beyond the postbox, towards the end of the parade, she lost sight of what happened next but ten minutes later the kids and the tall one who was older were swaggering back along the parade, helping themselves to fish and chips from the two wrappers Morrissey had been carrying, treating passers-by to the usual volley of abuse.

By that time, according to Suttle's timeline, Tim Morrissey was taking the long route home, hugging the inside of the pavement, his head down, his arms crossed, his broken hands pressed against his ribcage. His mother, horrified, had driven him to A & E, demanding that the damage be photographed as well as X-rayed, dialling 999 on her mobile to bring a patrol car up to the hospital.

The photos and X-rays formed part of the file. As it turned out, Morrissey had been lucky. Four broken fingers, lacerations to both hands, but nothing that wouldn't – in the fullness of time – heal itself. That, though, wasn't the problem. An attack this organised, this vile, this vindictive, had shattered what little confidence the boy had left. He'd had enough of school, or study, of playing the piano. From now on, in his mother's phrase, he wanted to draw the curtains and spend the rest of his life in bed. Munday, in other words, had won.

The attending officer at A & E had got nothing out of Morrissey. Three days later, again at his mother's insistence, an area car called at the family address. This time he volunteered a statement. It turned out to be a death sentence.

Faraday leafed forward through the file until he found the statement. It was, as usual, transcribed by the interviewing officer but no amount of police-speak could disguise the boy's gathering sense of hopelessness and terror as he realised what lay in store for him. They'd taken the fish and chips off him. They'd pushed him to the ground, sat on his back, shoved his face into the wet gravel behind the parade of shops, given him a kick or two in the ribs and legs before Munday set about his hands. He'd jumped on them, rubber-soled Doc Martens, full force. Morrissey's hands were precious to him. He'd tried to scream, to struggle, to somehow get free, but there were too many of them and what few shouts he'd managed had gone unanswered. Then, all of a sudden, the weight on his back had disappeared and all he could hear was the thunder of his heart and the sound of footsteps on the gravel as they all ran away. It had taken him ages to get to his feet. He'd been frightened of them coming back. Getting home had been hard, really hard. He knew his fingers were broken.

At the end of the interview the attending officer had asked for names. Unusually, he'd got them. Dale Sapper. Casey Milligan. Roxanne Claridge. Jason Dominey. Ross McMurdo. And Kyle Munday. Four of the kids were in Morrissey's class. Roxanne had come along for the ride. Munday, said Morrissey, had been the worst of the lot.

All six had been pulled in for interview by local detectives. Four came voluntarily. Casey Milligan and Munday had to be arrested. All six denied having anything to do with an aggravated assault on Tim Morrissey. Three of them accused him of making it up. Faced with the evidence to the contrary – the X-rays, the photographs – only Dale Sapper showed any sign of changing his story.

The D/S holding the file, aware of the latest blitz on bullying, had seized footware and items of clothing. There was money in the operational budget for forensic analysis in a case like this and the results were back within a fortnight. The lab technicians had drawn a blank on Kyle Munday's boots – they showed signs of thorough cleaning – but they'd retrieved Morrissey's DNA from a brand-new pair of Nikes belonging to Casey Milligan, and matching bloodstains from jeans worn by Jason Dominey. Presented with the evidence, both Milligan and Dominey had gone No Comment. Dale Sapper, hauled in for a second interview, said he couldn't remember what happened. The CPS, in the absence of corroborating evidence, had profound doubts about taking the case to court. Then came the bombshell. Tim Morrissey phoned up one morning and told the D/S he wanted to withdraw his statement. Case closed.

Faraday sat back, staring out of the window. The first drops of rain were falling out of a grey sky, smearing his view of Stamshaw rooftops. A swirl of pigeons swooped low over the car park, then rose again, wheeling towards the ferry port and the harbour. These were Pompey racing pigeons, thought Faraday. And their big mistake was ever coming back.

If Morrissey thought the retraction of his statement would bring his torment to an end, he was wrong. Back at school for the winter term, he was labelled a grass. The harassment, if anything, got worse. Mrs Morrissey made arrangements to put her house on the market. They'd move somewhere else, somewhere half-civilised, somewhere her son might stand some small chance of getting his life back. It never happened.

On 5 November, in a corner of the playing fields half a mile from the celebratory bonfire, Tim Morrissey was stabbed to death. Four wounds to his back and upper chest. Deep slashes to the side of his throat and a single jabbing thrust through his right eye. In the pathologist's opinion, at least two blades had been used, possibly three. Faraday remembered Suttle's comment when he went through the post-mortem report. This isn't a homicide, boss, he'd said. It's an orgy.

Parsons, only too aware of the intensity of local press coverage, had thrown everything at *Melody*, and Faraday, as Deputy Senior Investigating Officer, had found himself with more D/Cs than he could remember in any previous case. He fired up the Major Incident Room and dispatched detectives to the four corners of the Paulsgrove estate. Media appeals for witnesses from the bonfire celebrations brought a flood of calls, all of them disappointing. Hundreds of people that night reported gangs of youths on the prowl, pissed, aggressive, lippy. Some, with long memories, even produced a name or two. But none of these lines of enquiry got any further than a bunch of revelling kids out for a laugh. Never carry a blade, mate. Not my style, know what I mean?

Within days, increasingly frustrated, Parsons was demanding progress. From the start, after a difficult interview with Morrissey's mum, Faraday was convinced the answer lay in the earlier file held by the detectives who'd investigated the stamping incident. The knife attack, while a clear escalation in violence, was clearly Munday's MO. Word on the estate suggested he'd lost it. The bloke had become psychotic. Too much White Lightning. Too many vodkas. Plus all the toot he could lay his hands on. A state like that, you start playing God. Which is precisely what he'd done. Morrissey, the cunt grass, needed a lesson in manners. And Munday had been happy to offer his services.

Faraday had pulled Munday in, plus all five of the kids named by Morrissey after the stamping incident. To no one's surprise, every single one of them had an alibi for bonfire night. The alibis, corroborated word for word, proved unbreakable. While individuals on the estate exchanged looks at the mention of Munday's name, no one was prepared to talk, let alone offer a statement. Stuff happens. None of my business. Shame about the kid.

Parsons, twisting Willard's arm, got clearance to put in Special Ops. *Melody* spent thousands of pounds plotting up surveillance on a series of addresses in Paulsgrove. Steps were taken to tap phone lines and plant bugs. But Munday, with his evil little ways, was streets ahead of them. People buttoned their lips, even behind closed doors. Not because they were clever, or even experienced, but because they were afraid of him. It was common knowledge that Munday had done the kid Morrissey. But common knowledge would cut no ice in court. Who wanted ten minutes in a locked room with Munday's pit bull?

Faraday read a little further, reliving those grim days of late November, then closed the file. He understood now why Parsons was so keen to extract a little something, *anything* for fuck's sake, from the shambles of Operation *Melody*. The fact was that Munday and his little band of helpers had humiliated the Major Crime Team. For all their investigative reach – dozens of detectives, thousands of man hours, every covert trick in the book – the sheer brutality of Munday's MO, his preparedness to maim, even to kill, had put him beyond reach. Here was a man, thought Faraday, who had pitched camp in the darkest corners of a society in free fall. He preyed on the weak and the vulnerable, and gloried in their pain. The fact that he'd got away with it was deeply shaming but the dawning realisation that younger kids were only too prepared to follow in his footsteps was frankly scary. Until, that is, Munday found himself looking at a pair of headlights at half past one in the morning, still playing God.

Faraday reached for his keyboard, glad he'd seen the post-mortem shots. Where Major Crime had failed, some nameless driver had done the world a favour. Tomorrow Jimmy Suttle would be back in harness. Faraday tapped out an email, enquiring whether a red VW had featured in *Melody*'s thousands of actions, knowing in his heart that the driver deserved a medal.

Chapter five

The Tatchbury Mount Spa Hotel lies on the eastern edge of the New Forest. Internet checks had already told Winter that it offered four-star accommodation, fine dining, a fitness centre, pool, beauty and health spa, two squash courts, plus complimentary membership of a nearby golf club. The accompanying photos showed a newish-looking three-storey building artfully timbered to blend into the surrounding trees. A night's stay in a double room, on the Spring Escape Package, would cost £184.00.

Winter followed the signs to the parking lot. Esme's new 4 x 4 occupied the space nearest to the exit and Winter slowed for a moment, gazing at the tinted windows. Why did people like Esme spend another grand or whatever hiding themselves away? Did she really think a sheet of glass would keep her safe?

He parked the Lexus on the far side of the compound. Bazza had lent him a golf umbrella to go with his surroundings and he stepped into the thin drizzle, setting off for a tour of the premises.

The health spa lay at the back of the hotel. A huge expanse of lawn fell away to a line of trees beside a small stream and the architect had glazed the side of the spa that faced the view. Winter was clueless when it came to exercise but imagined you'd be grateful for anything that took your mind off the drudgery of the treadmill. There was a small gazebo beside the health spa and he ducked inside, glad of the shelter. From here, he could see figures beyond the spa's rain-pebbled glass. Ezzie, in her black and white leotard, was easy to spot. Winter had seen this garment only last week, gatecrashing an impromptu modelling session in Marie's kitchen.

Winter grinned to himself. One of the pleasures of this new

life of his was the slow process of becoming part of someone else's family. Ezzie hadn't liked him at first. She had a good law degree from a decent university and had shared her husband's suspicions of an ex-cop who'd taken Bazza's shilling. But working for Bazza had forced them together, and when Winter returned from a spell babysitting Marie's residential development on the Costa Dorada, it was Esme who'd drawn up all the contracts for a raft of brand-new businesses. Between them, she and Winter had launched Mackenzie Confidential, Mackenzie Poolside and Mackenzie Courier, and to their mutual surprise they'd started to get on.

Esme, Winter quickly realised, was prone to sudden mood changes. One day, wildly extrovert, she'd be a walking exclamation mark. The next, moody and withdrawn, she'd barely bother with conversation. Winter, who didn't have to live with her, began to feel sorry for Stu Norcliffe. How would you cope with someone who was as volatile and headstrong as this? Blame her gangster dad and pray for quieter times? Or sit her down and tell her the facts of life?

As it turned out, Stu had probably done neither. Managing hedge funds gave you loads of scope to bury yourself in work, and if the wife ever complained about lack of personal attention you could shower her with goodies. An annual subscription to the Tatchbury Mount Health and Beauty Spa had probably been one peace offering. The gleaming BMW 4 x 4 doubtless another. Both had cheered up Ezzie no end.

The rain, if anything, was getting heavier. A nearby path ran the length of the spa, and Winter stepped out of the gazebo, the umbrella shielding his face. Walking slowly beside the glass, he had a perfect view of the blur of legs. Ezzie wore a thin gold chain around one ankle and favoured Nike runners. Today's choice were in silver with mauve laces. Beside the treadmill, he recognised her sports bag abandoned on the floor. On top of the bag was a squash racket.

Winter quickened his step. Somewhere, he told himself, there would be a reception area, a place where you could book a session on the squash court. And that meant there'd be a reservations schedule. With names.

Entrance to the spa took him into a lobby. A vending machine offered a range of isotonic drinks and there were glass cabinets stocked with expensive sports gear. The reception desk lay beside a pair of swing doors that led into the exercise area. Behind the desk, a striking-looking redhead was studying her PC screen. The name badge on her sports shirt read Dominika.

Winter asked her about court availability. He and his daughter were staying overnight. She was mad about squash and in the absence of a decent partner she was threatening to teach her dad the basic moves.

Dominika eyed Winter's bulk then smiled. Perfect English with a light Polish accent.

'You sure you're ready for this, sir?'

'Of course I'm not. Have you got anything in the next hour or so?'

Dominika bent to the keyboard, then studied the screen again.

'I'm afraid not. We're fully booked until nine o'clock.'

'Can I have a look?' Winter reached for the screen, angled it towards himself. The reservation was in Esme's name. Ms E. Norcliffe. Court Two. 18.30–19.10.

'Shame.' Winter didn't hide his disappointment.

'You want to give me your room number? We might get a cancellation.'

'No need. Tell you the truth, love, it's the perfect excuse.' He shot the receptionist a grin. 'I'll take her to the bar instead.'

He retreated to the car park and settled himself behind the wheel of the Lexus, resigned to a longish wait. A name for the new man in Ezzie's life would have been a flying start.

By now, it was gone six. Ezzie and her partner would be on court until way past seven. After that might come a sauna, or a swim, or maybe both. Followed, in all probability, by something more intimate. Stu was up in town. Back home, the babysitter would be putting the kids to bed. If lover boy had £184 to spare, they could shag all night.

Winter wondered whether to bell Mackenzie but knew it was pointless. Bazza paid him a great deal of money to look after his best interests. In the early days it had been a question of business. More recently the Tide Turn Trust. Tonight it happened to be his wayward daughter. Stick with it, mate. Get me a name, an address, a guarantee that this tosser will get out of our lives. Pretend you're back with the Old Bill, plotting up some poor bloody criminal. Time-wise, it takes what it takes.

Winter punched a button on the radio, then changed his mind. Anything was better than Chris Evans. He sorted through his collection of CDs, chose an early Elton John album, settled down to enjoy 'Bennie and the Jets'. The tracks slipped by. It began to get dark. After 'Yellow Brick Road' came 'Candle in the Wind'. By half eight, singing along to 'Don't Let the Sun Go Down on Me', Winter was suddenly aware of two figures heading for the car park. One of them was Ezzie. The other, taller, had his arm round her.

At Mackenzie's insistence, Winter had brought along a camera with a decent telephoto lens. It lay on the seat beside him. He picked it up, squinted through the viewfinder, anchored the auto-focus over the approaching couple. Ezzie was laughing. Then she nuzzled her head against her companion's shoulder. From this angle it was impossible to get a proper look at his face but Winter squirted off a couple of shots regardless. The tableau told its own story. A display of affection like this, in Bazza's book, would be quite enough to justify a spot or two of serious violence.

Ezzie got into the 4 x 4. Her bloke had his back to Winter's probing lens. Seconds later, the big BMW was pulling out of the car park. Winter gave it a moment or two, stowed the camera, and set off in pursuit. For Ezzie, the quickest way home was via the motorway but the BMW was heading west, deeper into the New Forest. Winter hung back, glad of the darkness, wondering quite what might happen next. Did this guy have a place of his own nearby? Somewhere they could get their heads down and enjoy some serious nooky?

It seemed the answer was yes. On the outskirts of a village called Bramshaw Ezzie suddenly indicated right. Winter slowed, then took the turn. Less than a hundred metres ahead the BMW had come to a halt. Then Ezzie was indicating right again, hauling the 4 x 4 into a driveway. Winter gunned the engine, sweeping by. There were no street lights but he had time to register a modern-looking bungalow, set back from the road, before the darkness swallowed him up again. He drove on for perhaps half a mile, then pulled onto an apron of mud in front of a farm gate. A three-point turn took him back down the road, moving very slowly. At length, round a couple of bends, the bungalow came into view. There were a pair of dormer windows set into the roof and a light was on in one of them. Ezzie's BMW was still in the drive.

Winter parked on the verge and took more photos. Later he'd confirm a house number and the name of the road but for the time being – once again – all he had to do was wait. He toyed with another helping or two of Elton John but settled for Carly Simon instead. By the end of the first album, he'd developed a serious respect for this bloke's stamina. By the end of the second, he was convinced Ezzie was staying the night. Then he realised that the light in the dormer window had been switched off. Moments later, the front door opened and two figures stepped out. Expecting a lingering farewell kiss, Winter watched the pair of them walk around the front of the bungalow to the driveway. For the first time, he realised that another vehicle was parked in front of the BMW. It was an estate car. It looked like a Renault or maybe a Vauxhall.

Ezzie kissed her lover goodnight, tossed her sports bag into the back of the BMW, got in behind the wheel. The bloke watched her for a moment or two, raised his hand in a farewell wave, then reached in his pocket for his car keys. Ezzie was already backing the big 4 x 4 into the road. The estate car followed. At the top of the road both cars signalled left, back towards the motorway. Winter stirred the Lexus into life. The next village was called Brook. Ezzie, as Winter expected, headed east while the estate car turned right, accelerating hard, plunging deeper into the forest.

Winter had left the village behind before he caught sight of a pair of red lights in the distance. He couldn't be sure it was the estate car but it was way past midnight and he had no choice but to find out. It had stopped raining by now but this part of the forest was virtually treeless, a vast plateau of heather and scrub, and despite the 40 mph speed limit the driver had his foot down. Slowly, Winter began to close the gap between them, pushing the Lexus past ninety on the faster stretches. From time to time, in the flare of the headlights, he caught a glimpse of ponies grazing at the roadside. Once, he saw a cow look up with a start as he swept past. What might happen if one of these animals ambled onto the tarmac didn't bear contemplation but Winter didn't care. He was back doing what twenty years in CID had trained him for: getting tighter to the target, plotting his next move, trying to assess the many possibilities that lay ahead. By now he'd closed the gap to a hundred metres. Definitely the estate car.

A signpost flashed by. FORDINGBRIDGE 3 MILES. Winter didn't know this part of the world but they seemed to have crossed the New Forest in no time at all. The road started to descend. Suddenly they were back in the trees. Then, for whatever reason, the hazard lights came on in the estate car. It began to slow. Winter did the same, his brain furiously computing his next move. Should he hit the indicator and overtake? Should he then find a spot down the road from which he could resume the chase? Seconds later, the mystery driver saved him having to make the decision. Slewed across the road, the estate car blocked his path. Right first time. A Renault.

Winter braked and came to a halt barely yards away. The driver's door opened and a tallish figure in a black tracksuit stepped out. In the throw of his headlights, Winter watched him approaching. There was something familiar in the way this man held himself, in the rigid upright posture, in the jut of his chin, but only when he bent to the Lexus' now-open window did Winter realise who he was looking at.

The recognition was mutual. The face from the darkness stared at Winter for a long moment, then the door was wrenched open.

'Out,' he said.

An evening with his new Mahler CD had lifted the worst of Faraday's gloom. Depression was too big a word, irritation too meagre. Somewhere in between lay the growing realisation that Gabrielle really had left him, that he was once again alone in the world.

As far as women were concerned, this had happened before. In fact Faraday had lost count of the times when he'd piled all his chips on a single square only to fall victim to a roll of the croupier's dice. Years ago it had been Ruth Potterne, the widow of a tormented soul who'd run an art gallery. Then had come Marta, a vivid, sexy IBM executive who'd remained, to the end, an enigma. An Australian video producer, Eadie Sykes, had stolen his heart for a while before she, too, had drifted away. And now there was Gabrielle. Immense promise. Total immersion. Real tenderness. Then, quite suddenly, an empty space. Was it a case of recklessness on his part? Of naivety? Was he expecting too much of human flesh and blood? Or might he, one day, stumble on a woman – a relationship – that lasted longer than a year or so?

In truth, he wasn't sure. If he'd shown judgement this flawed in the Job, he knew he'd never have made it into CID. With every justification, they'd have kept him in uniform and put him in charge of lost property. So how come he'd ended up on Major Crime, with a real talent for reading the criminal mind, if he was so hopeless when it came to making more personal judgements?

He shook his head, switching off the audio stack, happy that it was one o'clock in the morning and his body was at last ready to surrender to sleep. Upstairs, in the bathroom, he was looking for a new tube of toothpaste when the big framed etching of the naval dockyard caught his eye. The etching had been a present from Gabrielle. She'd spotted it in a local antiques shop and brought it home, wrapped in newspaper. Hanging it in the bathroom had been her idea. With its wealth of detail it was an extraordinary snapshot of mid-Victorian Portsmouth and she'd wanted it to become an everyday part of their lives.

Faraday gazed at it now. The tall brick chimneys belching smoke. The lines of horse-drawn wagons outside the Rigging House. The South Camber dock, brimming with navigational buoys. The comings and goings of thousands of men, tiny figures, perfectly realised. In that sense, these harbourside acres would have been the beating heart of the city, the very reason for its existence, but it was Gabrielle who'd pointed out something else. That this army of men, and all the generations before them, had helped build and protect the project that had become the British Empire. Without these skills, she said, the trade routes to the east would have been wide open. Without the sawmills, and the rope sheds, and the new machines for making blocks and pulleys, the French or the Dutch or the Portuguese would have feasted on India and Singapore, and those great pink-painted swathes of Africa. Without Pompey, in short, the cut and thrust of British imperial history would have been very different.

The truth of this had struck Faraday with some force and he thought about it again now. The Bargemaster's House was a relic of the same period and talking to Steph Callan had made him realise how much he owed to the place. It had become a friend as well as a refuge and at times like now it was something else as well. A solace.

With its sturdy red-brick construction it was a survivor from the days when energy and confidence were the only currencies that mattered. The navy's expansion had relied on keeping its supplies of raw materials out of reach of the marauding French, and so a canal had been dug to connect the dockyard on one side of the city to Langstone Harbour on the other. The old lock gates were still recognisable, a stone's throw away down the harbourside path, and further sections had been planned to take barges beyond Arundel to London. In the event, the spread of the railways had doomed canals nationwide but the Bargemaster's House remained, a souvenir from this extraordinary era, and Faraday felt eternally privileged to live in it. It connected him to something bigger than himself. It gave him a perspective untainted by the small disappointments of everyday life. And it was some consolation to know that Gabrielle had felt this too.

Before he finally turned in, Faraday stood at the bedroom window, gazing out at the blackness of the harbour, trying to picture the laden barges riding at anchor, waiting for dawn. Then he became aware of his own reflection in the glass: the bearded face, the greying hair, the hint of sag in his chest and belly. He managed a shrug, acknowledging the slow drip-drip of time, then turned to his PC, hearing the *ping* of an incoming email.

The message was tagged 'Urgent'. It had come from Jimmy Suttle. He clicked on the email and rubbed his eyes. Suttle was replying to his earlier enquiry about the red VW. *I remember a red camper van*, he'd written. *It belonged to Jeanette Morrissey.*

Winter sat in the Renault at the side of the road. Detective Chief Inspector Perry Madison had once been second in command on the Major Crime Team. The last time Winter had seen him was a couple of years ago. Now Madison sat behind the steering wheel, stripping the foil from another wafer of gum.

'It's true, then?' he said. 'About you and Mackenzie?'

'Yeah.'

'And you sleep easy with that? No regrets?'

'Not one.'

'Nothing you miss?'

'Fuck all.'

'*Nothing?* Not the blokes? Not the crack? Not jumping on the bad guys?'

'I don't miss any of it.' Winter shook his head. 'At the end they fucked me over. I get a sweeter deal from Mackenzie than I ever got from any of you lot.'

'I don't doubt it.'

'I'm not talking money; I'm talking support, back-up. I enjoy going to work, believe it or not. And that's something I'd given up on.'

Madison nodded, staring out into the darkness of the New Forest. He'd never been good at listening and nothing had changed since. He took what he wanted from every conversation and forgot about the rest. Winter had never met anyone so punchy, so totally dedicated to his own self-advancement.

'And you're telling me this is work?' Madison gestured at the distance between them. 'You're Stu Norcliffe's private eye?'

'Mackenzie's. There's a difference.'

'Yeah? Like how?'

'Mackenzie means it. She's his daughter. Norcliffe will kill you, believe me. But Mackenzie will do it slower.'

'That's bollocks.' Winter caught Madison's soft laugh. 'Esme's a grown-up. She's making a choice here. Mackenzie doesn't own her. Neither does her husband.'

'Meaning?'

'Meaning you ought to be talking to her, not me.'

'Maybe I have.'

Madison glanced across. For the first time Winter had caught his attention.

'Bullshit,' he said. 'I'd know.'

'You think she couldn't disguise it? Play you along? You think she's too thick for that?'

'I know when a woman's lying. Esme doesn't lie.'

Winter held his gaze a moment, then looked away. The thought that a woman having an affair never lied was a joke,

56

but Madison was way too thick to spot the irony. Winter could smell the spearmint on his breath. He's driving home, he thought. He's going back to the missus with his stage yawns and his complaints about the pressure at work. I'm fucked, sweetheart, he'd announce. Too right.

'Are you in love with her?'

'Who?'

'Ezzie.'

'That's none of your business.'

'Wrong, my friend. That's exactly what it is. In case you're wondering, I need to know.'

'And why might that be?'

'Because it affects the outcome. Tomorrow morning I have to report back to Mr M. He's going to want to know how serious all this is because that way he can come up with something sensible.'

'Sensible how?'

'Sensible in the way of a plan. Think of all those strategy meetings you must go to. It's the same principle. We have to scope the options. We have to weigh the odds.'

'What makes you think I'm still in the Job?'

'Your warrant card.' Winter nodded at the dashboard. 'I expect you swiped yourself out of the car park this evening. Major Crime, is it? Or are you somewhere else now? Either way, you're still a copper.'

There was a long silence. Winter wound down his window an inch or so. He could hear the stir of wind in the nearby trees.

Finally Madison turned to look at him.

'If you're trying to frighten me, forget it. I've seen off bigger people than Mackenzie.'

'Sure. It's tricky, though, isn't it? Whether you like it or not, Mackenzie's the closest Pompey comes to a proper Level Three. Screwing his daughter might not be a great career move.' Level Three was intel-speak for top criminal.

'My career's in fucking pieces already.' Madison shrugged.

'How come?'

'Too many people hate me.'

It was true. Winter had never met anyone with such a talent for making enemies.

'So how is it with Esme?'

'Fuck off.'

'I meant in terms of where we go next. You carry on? Keep screwing at your mate's house down the road? Only this is the point where it stops being covert. As of now, my friend, you have to make a decision.'

'And what might that be?'

'If you decide you can't stop, the shit hits the fan. In no particular order, a number of people come knocking at your door. One of them will be Stu. The guy's a brick shithouse. Another might be Mr M. Your missus won't be pleased. Neither will Professional Standards. Either way, you can kiss goodbye to your marriage, maybe the Job, maybe a whack of your pension, and probably Ezzie.'

'How's that?'

'Because the fairy tale's over. Think kids, for a start. She's got three of them.'

Madison didn't move. Just his jaws, chewing and chewing.

'And what's the other option?'

'You bin it. You call it a day.'

'*It* has a name.'

'I know. I've been there.'

'Not where I am, you haven't.'

'You're wrong. But you know the difference? Mine was legal. I had no wife to cheat on.'

'So what happened?' There was a hint of interest in Madison's question.

'Her name was Maddox. And if you're really interested I still get the odd postcard.'

'Was this the looker from the knocking shop in Old Portsmouth? The student you were shagging when you had the medical problem?'

'Yeah.'

'I heard about that. To be honest, I never believed a word.'

'Why not?'

'You?' He looked across at Winter again, then laughed and shook his head. 'Never.'

Winter let the insult pass. He checked his watch.

'I need a decision,' he said. 'Preferably before the fucking sun comes up.'

The silence stretched and stretched. Finally Madison reached for his keys and stirred the engine into life. Then he changed his mind. The engine coughed and stopped.

'Esme's been frank,' he said. 'That's one of the reasons I love her. We talk a lot. About pretty much everything. She trusts me completely. Maybe she shouldn't.'

'What are you saying?' Winter stared at him.

'I'm a copper. I know things.' Madison was smiling now. 'Where all this is concerned, your Mr M should mind his step.'

Chapter six

Jimmy Suttle settled himself in the spare chair beside Faraday's desk and flicked quickly through the file.

'Here, boss.' One finger was anchored halfway through a statement. 'She made a complaint about harassment. Kids had been round all hours. One of them had given her precious camper van a bit of a kicking.'

'And it was definitely a VW?'

'Yeah.'

'Red?'

'According to the PC who interviewed her, yeah.'

Faraday's hand strayed towards the phone. The obvious thing was to pass on this piece of information. He'd no idea how far Steph Callan had got but this might spare her budget a great deal of overtime.

Suttle hadn't finished. 'You want me to phone her, boss? Find out whether she's still the owner?'

'No.' Faraday reached for his car keys. 'Remind me where she lives.'

Paulsgrove is a part-privatised council estate that sprawls over the lower reaches of Portsdown Hill. Built to offer a new start for thousands of bombed-out Pompey families after the war, it was once a byword for peace and quiet, decent-sized gardens and fine views of the city below. Jeanette Morrissey occupied a house on the northern edges of the estate. Behind the property reared the upper slopes of the hill, gashed a startling white to reveal the chalk bones beneath.

Faraday pulled his ageing Mondeo to a halt to take a call. It was DCI Parsons. She'd just been talking to Jimmy Suttle.

'He tells me you've got a lead on the vehicle from the hit-and-run.'

'That's right.'

'Tying it to the woman Morrissey?'

'That's the supposition. Nothing's confirmed. She may have sold the thing, she may have moved, left the area, whatever. We just don't know.'

'Action it, Joe. Find her. Talk to her. You're working on *Melody* now. And I'm still the SIO, in case you'd forgotten.'

Faraday nodded. The phone had already gone dead. He looked across at the house. Suttle had given him 33 Harleston Road. There were flowers in the downstairs window and uncollected empty milk bottles on the front step. No sign of a red VW camper.

He got out of the car and pushed in through the gate. The garden had been recently tidied: neatly trimmed borders around a tiny oblong of grass and newly forked earth at the base of a rose bush. He rang the door bell, waited, rang again. Six months ago Jeanette Morrissey had been a practice nurse at the health centre in the middle of the estate. Maybe she was still at work.

He tried the bell one final time. Turning to leave, he became aware of a figure in the next-door garden. He was elderly, late sixties at least. With a chamois and a bucket he was about to clean his front windows.

'You after Mrs M?'

'That's right.'

'She's off out. You can catch her later.'

'Is she at work, do you happen to know?'

'No.' He shook his head. 'She's gone looking for a hire car.'

'Yeah?'

'Yeah.' He nodded. 'That camper van of hers got nicked, didn't it?'

Bazza Mackenzie had taken delivery of his new Bentley Continental only last week. The colour – Neptune Blue – was a nod to Marie to keep her sweet but everything else in the car told Winter that Bazza was turning yet another corner in his life. The bird's-eye maple veneer, the three-spoke hide-trimmed sports steering wheel, the six-litre engine that could haul several tons of motor car to 60 mph in less than five seconds. Even with the roof down, the Bentley smelled of power and money. For a hundred grand, Bazza assured Winter, you could buy the ride of your dreams.

They were purring north along the A3. At 90 mph, there was barely a whisper from the engine.

'Tell me more, mush.' Bazza was wearing a pair of Pirelli sunglasses against the brightness of the morning. They didn't suit him.

'About Madison?'

'Yeah.'

'Late forties, maybe a bit older. Fitness fanatic, always has been. Used to go fell running or whatever they do over mountains. Binned it after a bit of an incident in the Lake District.'

Fell runners, Winter explained, often ran with mates. That way, especially at night or in shit weather, they could keep an eye out for each other. Madison, though, would stop for no one.

'So what happened?'

'They were in some kind of race and his buddy dropped out. It was three o'clock in the morning pissing down with rain but Madison just kept going. The way I heard it he wanted to keep to his precious fucking schedule. Worked, too. I think he won in the end.'

'And this mate of his?'

'Turned out he'd broken his leg. Nearly died of exposure.'

'Nice.'

Bazza was brooding. On the phone, first thing, when Winter had broken the news about the new man in Ezzie's life, he'd been expecting a major ruck. Instead, Bazza had simply grunted. Stu was driving down to see a client near Guildford. He and Winter needed to meet up with him, have a pow-wow, decide what to do next. Earlier Winter had been impressed by the rare display of self-control. Maybe one-hundred-grand convertibles bought you a certain peace of mind. Fat chance.

'What did this guy Madison say about Ezzie?'

'He said he loved her. He said they were really tight.'

'Proper job, then?'

'Yeah.'

'Cunt.'

Winter, wondering which one Bazza meant, kept quiet. His only daughter shagging the Filth. Unthinkable.

'So how long has all this been kicking off?'

'He didn't say. Stu should know.'

'But what do you think?'

'A while. Has to be.'

'You're right, mush. She's been grinning fit to bust for months. Marriage doesn't make you *that* fucking happy.' He took the Bentley up to a hundred and ten. 'Stu must have had his head up his arse. Twat.'

Beddington Manor lay behind a pair of electronic gates in the rolling Surrey countryside north of Guildford. A long curve of gravelled drive led to an Elizabethan manor house, perfectly restored. Bazza pulled the Bentley into a half-circle and killed the engine. Beyond the helicopter pad, a peacock strutted the length of an ornamental lawn. Closer, in a fenced compound, were half a dozen animals.

Bazza took off his glasses, got out, had a proper look.

'What are they, mush?'

'No idea.'

They strolled down to the edge of the lawn until they were standing beside the fence. The animals, lazily cropping the grass, took no notice. Bazza was speculating about some fancy breed of goat when Winter heard footsteps behind them.

'Llamas, Baz. Pedigrees. There's more round the back. The guy's turning a hobby into a small fortune.'

It was Stuart Norcliffe. The last time Winter had seen him was a month or two back. Then, he'd been in the rudest of health, chasing his kids around Bazza's Craneswater garden. Now, he looked like one of life's windfalls, diminished, bruised, discarded.

They went into the house. Coffee was waiting in a sunny lounge overlooking a lake on the other side of the property. The owner, Stu explained, had already left for the executive airport at Biggin Hill. He was due to meet a couple of clients in Monaco for a late lunch.

Mackenzie made himself comfortable in an armchair by the window. Winter could tell by his body language that he felt at home here. Nice spread. His kind of people. Definite potential.

'Paul's got some news, Stu. You'd better sit down.'

Winter realised Norcliffe knew nothing of last night. Mackenzie had simply demanded a meet. Stu was still on his feet. He wanted to know what had happened. Badly.

Winter explained. When he got to the borrowed bungalow in the New Forest he was aware of Norcliffe looming over him, staring down.

'*How* long?'

'A couple of hours.'

'So what time was this?'

'Gone midnight when they left.'

'She phoned me at ten. Said she was out with a couple of girlfriends.' Norcliffe glanced at his father-in-law. 'You're sure about all this?'

'Paul's a copper, Stu, or he fucking used to be. I know they're a bunch of thick bastards but he definitely knows how to tell the time. Eh, Paulie?' There was an edge of irritation in Mackenzie's voice. He wasn't best pleased with any of this, thought Winter. Least of all a husband who couldn't keep his wife in line.

Norcliffe wanted to know about Madison. What kind of bloke was he? What was the big attraction?

'He probably looks after her, Stu.' It was Bazza again. 'Women like a bit of attention. You may have noticed.'

'You're telling me I've screwed up?'

'I'm telling you you've taken your eye off the ball. We all like the moolah, Stu, of course we fucking do, but there's a limit, old son. Ezzie can be a right handful and you're talking to someone who knows. She's a princess, always was. If you bugger off every week she's going to find someone else to tell her how wonderful she is. The fact that she's chosen a copper to shag is a fucking disgrace but that's not the point. Playing Ezzie's little game, you've got to be in the mood. If it wasn't this bloke Madison she'd probably have found someone else.'

'He's a *copper*?' More surprises.

'Yeah. According to Paul here. And he should know.'

Winter filled in the details. DCI. Used to be a high-flyer. Made enemies wherever he worked.

'So why did Ezzie pick him?' The question went to his father-in-law.

'Because she did, son. Because she was in that fancy gym, miles from home, miles from you lot, and I expect he said something nice to her, gave the eye, told her what great shape she was in, bought her a drink or two, played Prince Charming, did the same next time, and the time after that, and before Ez knows it she's having a bit of a think about what it might be like, no harm in trying him out, seeing where it might lead … Are you getting the picture here? Or do you need Paul to spell it out? You heard the man just now. The way he tells it they were in that shag pad the best part of a couple of hours. You think they were watching *telly*?'

Norcliffe said nothing. There wasn't enough money in the world to buy him out of this kind of humiliation.

'Another thing, son.' Mackenzie hadn't finished. 'According to Paul, this guy's Major Crime, or used to be. He's in a hole now, big time. And you know the stunt he's trying to pull? He's telling Paul that Loose Lips, your fucking wife, my own fucking *daughter*, has been speaking out of turn. About what we've been up to. About the business. About stuff that could hurt us badly. We need to know whether that's true, son, and I need to know whether you're the one who's gonna pop the question. *Comprende?*'

'You mean talk to Ezzie?'

'Yeah.'

'I'd kill her.' Norcliffe's voice was soft. 'The way I'm feeling at the moment.'

'I don't blame you, son. I'd probably do the same. So that leaves Paul here.' He glanced across at Winter. 'I'll drop you off at Ezzie's place on the way back. Golden Bollocks will have been onto her by now so I expect she'll be expecting a little visit. You happy to do the honours?'

Faraday was back in his office at Major Crime when Steph Callan phoned from the Road Death Investigation Team. He could sense at once it was going to be a tricky conversation.

'I've just belled the duty Inspector at Cosham. He says you were talking to him an hour or so ago.'

'That's true.'

'About Jeanette Morrissey's camper van.'

'Right again.'

'Reported stolen first thing Sunday morning.'

'Yeah.'

'Aren't we supposed to be part of this little game? Or is it true about you guys?'

'True, how?'

'That you're all cowboys. Always nicking the best jobs. Always on the bloody take.'

Faraday sat back, the phone loosely to his ear, letting her get it off her chest. How the stolen-vehicle examiner had come up with a list of local VW camper registrations. How one of them had belonged to Jeanette Morrissey. And how G467XBK had been ghosted away under cover of darkness last Saturday night.

'Jeanette Morrissey was the mother of a lad killed in the city here, back in November. I think I mentioned him the first time we met. Operation *Melody*,' said Faraday.

'The one where Munday was the prime suspect?'

'Yes.'

'And Jeanette Morrissey was the victim's mum?'

'That's right.'

'Well ...' she was close to losing control, 'thanks a bunch for telling me.'

Faraday began to defend himself, explaining about the intel dredged up by Suttle, then realised there was no point. Trying to argue his case with anyone in this kind of mood was hopeless.

'The *Melody* file's still open,' he said. 'My DCI is SIO. As far as she's concerned, the hit-and-run belongs to *Melody*. Her name's Gail Parsons. If you've got a problem with any of this, maybe you should be talking to her.'

He put the phone down and got to his feet. DCI Parsons was in her office down the corridor. She took one look at Faraday and waved him into the chair beside the desk.

Briefly, Faraday explained the situation. Jeanette Morrissey owned a red VW camper van. Early forensics seemed to be tying the same kind of vehicle to the hit-and-run. Morrissey had ample motivation for running Munday over and now she was claiming the camper had been nicked. So just who was going to run with this?

'You are, Joe.' Parsons nodded at her PC. 'I had a confirming email from Mr Willard this morning.'

'So no more grief from the Road Death lot?'

'Absolutely not. Mr Willard is arranging an attachment.'

'A what?'

'They'll be sending someone down to join us on *Melody*. Strictly in the interests of peace and quiet. I had their Inspector on the phone just now.'

'And?'

'It's Steph Callan again.' She glanced at her watch. 'Though I gather she hasn't been told yet.'

Bazza Mackenzie phoned ahead to tell his daughter to make sure she was at home for the next couple of hours. The au pair took the call and promised to pass the message on. When Mackenzie told her to get Ezzie to the phone she said she couldn't. Mrs Norcliffe was out riding. Back any time soon.

Heading south again in the Bentley, Winter seized his chance to pin Mackenzie down on the Tide Turn Trust. Nothing would be sweeter than turning his back on the whole caboodle but small start-up charities had a habit of generating endless day-to-day problems and already the stuff was piling up on his desk. If Bazza really wanted him to sort out this looming threat to the Mackenzie empire, then something had to be done about TTT.

Mackenzie, for once, saw the point.

'What do you need?'

'I need someone with a good track record with kids, someone who understands all the legal bollocks, someone who's been doing it a while, someone who's going to make us look good.'

The last phrase brought Mackenzie's head round.

'Someone like who?'

'I haven't a clue, Baz, but these things don't just happen. We have to advertise. We have to put the word around. We probably have to go through all sorts of fucking dramas. But it has to be done.'

Mackenzie nodded. A truck in the slow lane rapidly got bigger. Then it was gone. He glanced across at Winter again.

'You're right,' he said. 'Lippy kids aren't your game. Get someone in.'

*

67

Ezzie and Stuart lived in a seven-acre spread on a flank of the Meon Valley. The previous owner had knocked down a pair of cottages and built a rambling hacienda-style property in white stucco and black wrought iron, and several years later, despite the carefully tended Virginia creeper, it still reminded Winter of something that had been shipped up from Spain and dumped in the middle of rural Hampshire. The swimming pool that Stuart had commissioned, with its underwater lighting and quaintly thatched bar, didn't help. Neither did the recently built stable block where Esme kept her horses.

Mackenzie had no intention of staying. He dropped Winter outside the front door, pulled the Bentley into a tightish circle and disappeared down the drive. The au pair was trying to console the youngest of Esme's kids. Kate had just fallen off her plastic trike. Winter wondered whether four wasn't young for lipstick and lime-green nail varnish.

'Ezzie around?' Winter nodded past the open front door.

The au pair shook her head. She was a Czech girl with a name that no one seemed able to pronounce: Evzenie. Mrs Norcliffe was in the bottom field on her horse. Not in a good mood.

'The horse?'

'Mrs Norcliffe.' The girl laughed, scooping up the child and disappearing inside.

Winter took the path that skirted the house, stepping over a trail of discarded toys. In the distance he could see Esme driving the biggest of her horses at a series of jumps. As far as Winter could gather, she'd been in the saddle since she was a kid, part of her mum's plan to shield her from a Pompey adolescence. Getting close to animals, according to Marie, was altogether more healthy than hanging out in Southsea bars and clubs, though the way it turned out Esme had done plenty of both.

Winter paused, hugging the fence, waiting for Esme to finish her round. He'd never liked horses, never trusted them, and his certainty that Esme knew this was going to make the next half-hour even trickier.

She clipped the last hurdle, reined the horse in, and turned it towards Winter. The horse was huge: huge eyes, huge girth, huge everything. Esme brought it to a halt barely feet away from the fence. The horse stamped its feet, tossed its head, tried to rid itself of the bit between its yellow teeth.

'You getting off or what?'

'Say what you have to say, Paul. It's just a shame my dad didn't have the bottle to do this himself.'

'He's pissed off, love.'

'I bet. And what a little saint he's always been. Have you met the lovely Chandelle, by any chance?'

Winter let the dig pass. She was right, though. Bazza had never seen the point of monogamy, least of all when it came to his new hotel manager.

Winter peered up at Esme. The sun was in his eyes and all he could see was her silhouette on top of the horse. Clever.

'We need to talk, love. Here's not the place.'

'What is there to talk about?' Esme was still resentful. 'You seem to know everything already.'

'That's bollocks, love. Get off that fucking thing and act like a human being. I'm even less thrilled about this than you are. You're right. This is family. So how come I get the arse end of everything?'

The question, voiced with some feeling, drew the beginnings of a smile from Esme. She hesitated a moment, then bent to the horse's neck, gave it a pat and dismounted. Winter caught a perfume she'd never worn before, not to his knowledge. New man in her life, he thought, new scent on the pillow.

'Here ...' She gave him the reins and leant back against the fence to remove her boots. Winter gave the horse the eye. It began to back away.

'Be nice to him.' Esme was laughing again. 'Animals can smell fear. Here ...'

She gave Winter her boots and took the reins. Winter hadn't a clue why she wanted to walk barefoot back to the stables but was glad to be shot of the horse.

'Your dad's spitting nails,' he said.

'Yeah?'

'And Stu too.'

'You've seen him?'

'Couple of hours ago. He's gone back to London.'

He explained about the meet in the manor house. It turned out she'd spent a couple of weekends there.

'Stu fancies the guy's wife. Did he tell you that?'

'No.'

'She's German. I can't remember her name. We all got pissed the first evening and ended up in the jacuzzi. Stu speaks decent German. Had the woman in stitches.'

'A looker?'

'Yeah, big time. Body to die for and big-time fit. The husband bought her a gym for Christmas – treadmill, weights, rowing machine, the lot. Stu said she couldn't get enough of it. Funny that.'

'We're talking exercise?'

'I think so. You never know with Stu. He thinks I'm thick sometimes, I know he does. And that might turn out to be a big mistake.'

'You're blaming him?'

'Not at all. I'm blaming no one. We do what we do. Stuff happens. Que sera …'

They'd arrived at the stable block. Esme told Winter to sort out some feed while she got rid of the saddle and the rest of the tack. Kate had turned up by now, a plaster on her knee, and she led Winter to the empty stall where the oats were kept. Winter had seen a lot of the kids over the last couple of years. Esme brought them to his apartment in Gunwharf sometimes and he let them raid the fridge for Coke and banana smoothies. He liked their spirit and the way they all looked out for each other.

The horse stabled and fed, Esme called Evzenie on her mobile and asked her to take Kate back to the house. There was a pile of hay bales against one corner of the stable block and Esme made herself comfortable in the warm sunshine. The earlier hostility had gone. She'd decided to treat Winter as an ally.

'I think I'm in love,' she said. 'Does that make up for anything?'

'No.' Winter shook his head. 'I'm afraid not. Baz could probably wear the odd shag or two. It's who you're doing it with that matters.'

She nodded, reflective, and plucked a straw from the nearby bale. 'Do you know Perry at all?'

'Not well.'

'He's sweet. Really sweet. I know he's unpopular because he's told me, but you know something? Guys like him are often misunderstood. You blokes are always so macho. Perry's got a real feminine side, believe it or not.'

'Sure. If you know where to look.'

'That's cheap, Paul. I'm serious. Do you think I'd go through all this for any guy that happened along? He's got to be special. He's got to want to understand me. He's got to need me, trust me, become part of me. Perry does all that, has done from the start. That makes me lucky, doesn't it?'

'*Lucky?*' Winter gazed at her. 'You fuck off over to that hotel twice a week, you shag his brains out, you have a great time, all that I can understand. But why complicate it with all this *lucky* shit? Sex is one thing, love. Never complicate it by falling in love.'

'Why not?'

'Because you'll hurt people. And one of them, in the end, will be you.'

'You believe that?'

'I do.'

She sucked at the straw a moment, then wound it round her little finger.

'You sound like my mum,' she said at last.

'You've talked to her about all this?'

'This morning, on the phone. I think she sussed what you must have told Dad. She thinks I'm bonkers.'

'That's because you are.'

'No, Paul.' She shook her head. 'I'm not. I just told you. Perry does it for me. Big time. Every time. More and more. How can I turn my back on that? He knows who I am, Paul. He knows who I am inside.'

'Because you tell him?'

'Because he's clever, intuitive, just the way you are. Maybe it's a police thing, a CID thing, maybe it comes with the job. He's just brilliant at getting inside my head, inside my heart, getting me to open up, getting me to be *myself*.'

'So you tell him stuff?'

'Of course, all the time. No secrets, Paul. No hidey-hidey. That's not our style.'

'Right ...' Winter looked away. This was much, much worse than he'd imagined. Madison, true to form, had opened her up and helped himself. This was no longer a fishing expedition. This was damage limitation.

'I'm going to be blunt, love. Your dad is appalled at what you've done.'

'Because Perry's a copper.'

'Yeah. And that means you're sleeping with the enemy. Like I said, he probably wouldn't begrudge you the odd screw but this is way out of line.'

'Why?'

'Because people like Madison, people like I used to be, have an agenda. They can't help themselves. It's in their blood. It's what they do.'

'I'm not with you, Paul.'

'Think about it. Think about your dad. Think about how he made his money. Think about what paid for all this.' He nodded at the stables, at the pool, at the house, at the meadow. 'Perry Madison, like it or not, wants – *needs* – to have all that off you. Not least because it will do his career a power of good.'

'You're telling me he'd put his career before what we have?'

'I'm telling you he can't help himself. He's just programmed that way, Ez. Once a copper, always a copper.'

'So what does that make you?'

'A copper. Employed by your dad. Finding out stuff. Just like now.'

She was losing it again. Winter could see the flare of light in her eyes, the way her mouth had compressed. A princess, he thought. Exactly the way Bazza had said.

'You think he's set me up? You think he's using me? You think I couldn't see through something like that?'

'I think he may be as infatuated as you are. For the time being.'

'And then?'

'He'll screw you. Properly. And everyone else as well.'

'How do you mean?

'Your dad. Your mum. Me. And probably several hundred other people. All he needs is evidence.'

'Of what?'

'Of stuff that your dad's been up to. Of stuff that you'd know about. Fuck knows, he might have got enough already.'

'From me, you mean? You really think I'd tell him stuff like that?'

'You might. If you were pissed or silly enough.'

'Perry doesn't drink.'

'It's not Perry I'm worried about.'

'Thanks, thanks a lot. You think I'm some drunken old slut who can't keep her mouth shut?'

'No, it's much worse than that. I believe you. I think you're in love.'

She looked at Winter for a long moment, trying to find a way out of this conversation, trying – somehow – to turn it all around.

'And if I told you Perry's planning to chuck it all in? Resign? Call it a day?'

'I'd say he was lying.'

She shook her head very slowly, back in control. She even smiled.

'You're wrong, Paul. Perry doesn't lie. Not to me. Not now. Not ever. It's something we pledged to each other. No lies. Only the truth. Does that make sense to you?' The smile widened. 'Probably not.'

Chapter seven

Jeanette Morrissey was at home by the time Faraday returned to Paulsgrove. He'd met Steph Callan in the car park at the Marriott Hotel and they'd driven up together for the interview. The atmosphere in the Mondeo was icy.

It was a while before Mrs Morrissey came to the door. There was a new-looking Fiesta parked outside.

'Can I help you?'

Jeanette Morrissey was tall and slightly gaunt-looking. Her face seemed to have missed out on the recent spell of decent weather and there was a deadness in her eyes as she took in the strangers on her doorstep. She'd met Faraday over the death of her son but showed no signs of recognising him.

Faraday offered his warrant card and introduced Steph Callan. He knew at once that this woman had been expecting a knock on the door.

'Have you come about the camper? Have you found it?'

Faraday suggested they step inside for a chat. The front lounge was chilly. A cat was curled on one end of the sofa and Faraday saw Callan's attention caught by a line of photos on the mantelpiece above the flame-effect gas fire. The lad looked younger than his fifteen years. There was something slightly feminine about the softly curled hair and his face was lightly dusted with freckles. He wore a pair of heavy horn-rimmed glasses and in all four shots the smile had the same guileless innocence.

'This was your son?' Callan didn't hide her interest.

'Tim? Yes.'

'Lovely-looking boy. It must have been heartbreaking, what happened to him.'

'It was. It was horrible.'

The cat fled the sofa the moment Faraday sat down. In the car he'd agreed that Steph Callan would take the lead. She settled herself on the other end of the sofa and produced a notebook.

'You may be aware of an accident up on Southwick Hill Road ...' she began, 'last Saturday night.'

Mrs Morrissey said she'd heard about it. A man off the estate had been killed.

'May I ask you what you were doing on Saturday night?'

'Me?'

'Yes.'

'I was –' she frowned as if trying to remember '– I was here, at home.'

'Doing what?'

'Watching TV mostly. It's all rubbish on Saturday night, but to be honest I was exhausted. I work at the health centre. We're on the go all the time. It's just non-stop.'

'Was anyone with you?'

'No.'

'Did you make any phone calls?'

She looked up at the ceiling a moment, concentrating hard. Then she nodded.

'I phoned my friend Katie. She's just come back from Greece. We had a bit of a chat. She had a lovely time out there. It was nice talking again.'

'What time was that?'

'I don't know ...' She shrugged. 'Eight? Nine? I'm sure you can check if you want to.'

She gave Callan the number. She knew it by heart. Callan wanted to know what time she went to bed.

'Early. I watched the news at ten then went straight upstairs. Like I say, I was just exhausted.'

Callan glanced across at Faraday. He motioned for her to carry on. She turned back to Jeanette Morrissey.

'And you went straight to sleep that night?'

'Yes. Out like a light.'

Callan nodded, scribbled herself another note.

'Tell me about the following morning.'

'Sunday? I woke up as usual, had a bit of a wash, went downstairs, made myself a pot of tea. Just the usual things.'

'So when did you realise the camper had gone?'

'When I pulled back the curtains in the front room. I leave it right outside the house. At first I didn't believe it. In fact I got dressed and went out to check that I hadn't parked it somewhere else.'

'What time was this?'

'About nine o'clock. On Sundays I have a bit of a lie-in.'

'Was there any glass in the road outside? Any indication that someone might have broken a window to get into the van?'

'No.'

'You looked?'

'Yes.'

'And, thinking back, when you were lying in bed during the night, did you hear anything? A door closing? An engine starting?'

'My bedroom's at the back of the house. You get a lot of noise here at weekends, kids mainly. It's quieter at the back.'

'So you heard nothing?'

'Nothing at all. Then next morning I got up, just like normal, and like I say ... it had gone.'

'So what did you do?'

'I went to the police and told them what had happened.'

'You didn't phone first?'

'No.'

'Why not?'

'Because there's no point. We get lots of trouble up here. I'm not blaming the police. They must be really stretched. But a case like this –' she shrugged '– I just thought it would be quicker for me to come to you. The sooner you've got all the details, the quicker you might get it back. Isn't that right?'

Callan said nothing. Neither did Faraday. Over the course of an extremely difficult year this woman had been in touch with the local police on countless occasions. She'd have made personal contacts, even friends. So why not lift the phone?

It was Mrs Morrissey who broke the silence. She wanted to know why she was having to answer all these questions. Callan explained about the accident. Evidence recovered from the scene suggested that a red VW camper van might have been involved.

'You mean mine?'

'It's possible.' Callan glanced down at her notes. 'The man who died ... Kyle Munday. I understand you knew him.'

'*Of* him, certainly. He's notorious round here. Nothing but trouble. A horrible, horrible man.'

'He'd had dealings with your son ... is that right?'

'I wouldn't call it dealings. Munday bullied him, hurt him, made Tim's life a misery.'

'Can you prove that?'

'No. And neither could you lot. And you know why? Because everyone on this estate's terrified of him. Or was. And that's why no one had the courage to come forward and give evidence. He ruled the place with that dog of his. He just strutted around like no one could touch him. Decent kids, grown-ups, people who should have known better, they all kept their heads down. When something like that happens, you give up. It's anarchy. There's absolutely nothing you can do. I can't describe what that feels like. It's like living in the Dark Ages. You're totally, totally helpless.'

For the first time there was colour in her face. Faraday could sense the force of her anger. Callan too.

'I'm sorry, Mrs Morrissey,' she said. 'This must be very distressing.'

'Munday getting killed like that?' She shook her head. 'Not at all. If you want the truth, I was glad someone had the good sense to run him over.'

Another silence, longer this time. Then Callan cleared her throat.

'As a matter of interest,' she said, 'how do you know he was run over?'

'I don't. I just assume that was what happened. And you know something else? I hope he took a while to die.'

Carol Legge had always been one of Paul Winter's favourite contacts. A small, talkative Geordie, she'd become a legend in the city's Child Protection Team. People who knew her well spoke of her instinctive ability to recognise when a kid was in trouble and of the knack she had of cutting through all the bullshit and getting to the truth. In this respect, and many others, she'd never let Winter down.

They were sitting in a café in Fratton Road. Carol, who

adored cakes, had just demolished a hefty slice of Battenberg. Now she was showing Winter snaps of her latest grandchild. Winter went through the motions. What he really wanted to talk about was Tide Turn Trust.

Finally, he spotted an opening. Carol had spent most of the afternoon trying to sort out a feral seven-year-old who'd been squirting his kid sister with bleach. The mother, a career junkie, had given up, and the kids were currently in the care of the great-grandparents.

'This is a couple in their seventies, pet. They're that poor they can't afford the daytime tariff on the electric. In the middle of the night it's much cheaper so they do all their washing and cooking at three in the morning. Drives the bairns mad, especially when the lady of the house is getting up every hour to baste the chicken. It's old school, isn't it, pet? Mustn't let the Lidl bird dry out.'

Winter told her about Tide Turn Trust. He'd been trying to baste this particular broiler for nine months. He'd chalked up the odd success or two, keeping kids off the streets, but the truth was the thing was driving him barmy. Time for someone else to take their turn at the stove.

'This is Mackenzie's little party piece?'

'The same.'

'Still friends, are you?'

'Blood brothers. Inseparable.'

'No regrets about leaving the Job?'

'None.'

She gave him a look then asked how she could help. If Mackenzie was serious about sorting out wayward kids and had money to spare she'd be the last person to stand in his way.

'He's got loads of money. He practically invented the stuff. And he's happy to spend a decent whack on Tide Turn. In fact he insists.'

'Good. So what do you need from me?'

Winter explained that he was standing aside. The Trust needed a new Chief Executive, someone to drive it forward, someone who understood the real challenge that these kinds of kids were offering.

'I've been the midwife,' he said. 'I've brought it into the world. Now it needs someone who knows what they're doing.'

Carol was thinking hard. She knew exactly the hole that Winter had dug for himself. More importantly, she sensed the makings of a solution.

'You need someone with lots of local authority experience,' she said. 'That's going to be a man or a woman in their forties. They'll have been at the coalface as a social worker. They'll have climbed the ladder – Senior Practitioner, Deputy Team Leader, all that stuff. They might be a Service Manager by now. That's someone with real clout, believe me.'

'So why would they want to join us?'

'Because the higher you get, the tougher the frustrations become.' She beckoned Winter closer. 'In our little world, pet, we get short-changed all the time. Politicians are brilliant with the sound bites. Every child matters. Early intervention. Positive outcomes. The integration agenda. But every single one of these phrases comes with a price tag. And the truth is, no one's prepared to cough up. Now that's bad enough at the sharp end – people like me can give you chapter and verse on what we could do with more resources. But by the time you get towards the top of the tree you find people – good people, clever people – tearing their hair out. These guys are under siege. Wherever you look, society's falling apart. Whether it's booze or drugs or domestic violence or poverty, families can't cope any more. And so the bosses, my bosses, have got the world knocking on their door, demanding the impossible, and there's absolutely no way they can deliver. Not under the current lot. Probably not ever.' She leaned back again, spearing cake crumbs with a wettened fingertip. Then she looked up. 'Have you got the picture, pet, or am I going too fast for you?'

Winter shook his head. All that sounded fine. But how on earth could he lay hands on these people?

'You do what everyone else does, pet. You advertise. It costs a fortune but in the end it works.'

She named a handful of publications. The *Guardian*'s Wednesday supplement. *Community Care. Young People Today.*

Winter wasn't convinced. If advertising meant months of waiting for the right bunch of interviewees to turn up then it was a no-no. The last thing he had was time.

'I'm not with you.'

'I need someone now, love. Someone who's got the experience. Someone who knows the city. Someone who can turn up to work tomorrow, hand in their notice, and be with us by next month.'

'Why are you looking at me, pet?'

'Three guesses.'

'No way.' She smiled and shook her head. 'I'm an honest woman.'

'What are you on at the moment?'

'Don't be cheeky.'

'We'll double it.'

'No. Believe it or not, I like my job. Some days I even love it.' She broke off, checking her watch and then peering at the traffic outside. 'I'll have a little think tonight and give you a ring in the morning.'

'About whether to say yes or no?'

'About anyone else you might like to consider.'

Faraday drove Steph Callan back to the Marriott. In the interests of the coming days, maybe even weeks, he suggested a drink before she returned to Eastleigh. She hesitated a moment beside her car then said yes. Faraday had a glimpse of what looked like a lifejacket in the back of the estate.

'You go sailing?'

'Kite surfing. It's become an addiction.'

'Difficult?'

'Very. They warn you how hard it's going to be to begin with but no one ever tells you it gets tougher.' She pocketed her keys and shot him a wary grin. 'Bit like the Job, really.'

The bar in the Marriott was beginning to fill up. Men in jeans and sports shirts, newly pinked by a session in the hotel gym. Single women in business suits, bent over laptops. Faraday bought himself a pint of Guinness. Steph settled for lime and soda.

'It's yoga tonight,' she explained. 'I find it helps.'

'The soft drink?'

'The yoga.'

'Helps with what?'

'Pretty much everything really.' She reached for the drink. 'Cheers.'

Earlier, after they'd left Mrs Morrissey, they'd done a series of house-to-house calls up the road, asking whether anyone had seen the VW camper leaving late on Saturday night. This would normally have been the job of local CID but Faraday knew how pressed they were. At every address they'd drawn a blank. Yes, the big red van was often parked outside number 33. And no, they definitely hadn't seen some young scrote nicking it.

'She's lying, isn't she?'

'Definitely.' Faraday nodded. 'She's got the motivation. For some reason she must have been out late Saturday night, which means she probably had the opportunity. Plus we're looking at a red VW camper. This is someone who works in the medical field. She'll know about DNA. She'll realise what we can do with that vehicle. So once she's run the guy over, what's the first thing she does?'

'She bins it.'

'Sure. But where?'

First thing in the morning Faraday would task Jimmy Suttle to pay Mrs Morrissey another visit. They needed an association chart, a list of friends and relatives she might trust to look after her precious camper van. The front would have impact damage. Bits of Kyle Munday would still be hanging underneath. One way or another, she had to get rid of that evidence. Not easy.

Steph was worrying about the timeline. Once Mrs Morrissey had dumped the van, did she come home again? If the garage or lock-up was somewhere local, would she have made that journey on foot? Or if it turned out that the camper was secured miles away, should they be looking at a lift with a friend? Or a call to a taxi firm?

The questions went on and on, a net of suppositions designed to snare her alibi and test it to breaking point. DCI Parsons, meanwhile, would have to make a decision about applying for billing records on her mobile phone and landline. She may have made calls after the accident. If her mobile was switched on, cell site analysis might be able to track her movements. More questions for when they finally got Jeanette Morrissey down to the interview suite at the Bridewell.

'So what do you think?' Steph again. 'Three days? Four?

Longer than that? Only I'm off to Greece at the end of next week.'

Faraday was still musing about the first question. Guinness was something he hated to rush.

'I think it's a shame,' he said at last. 'I've read the file. I was at the *Melody* post-mortem back in November. I saw what Munday, if it was Munday, did to that kid. His mum was traumatised by what happened. Not just then but before, with all the bullying. Anyone would be. And for my money, for what it's worth, she'll never get over it. You heard her this afternoon. For once in her life she's looking at a result. The guy's dead. He died horribly. It wasn't pretty. You know that better than anyone. And if it turns out to be her that ran him over, and we can prove it, then ...' He shrugged. 'I'm not sure I'd blame her.'

'You're suggesting we pack it in? Turn a blind eye? Go through the motions?'

'Of course not.'

'Then this is all a bit of a wank, isn't it?'

The suggestion brought a smile to Faraday's face. 'You think I'm getting soft in the head?'

'I haven't a clue. I've only known you three days. But until someone tells me different I'm assuming I'm here to collect evidence. What a bunch of lawyers, or a jury, does with that evidence is down to them. Are we on the same page, boss, or am I missing something?'

Faraday shook his head. He felt, all of a sudden, unaccountably old.

'Somewhere nice in Greece?' he enquired, reaching for his glass.

Marie cooked that night while Mackenzie and Winter sat at the kitchen table, a bottle of decent malt between them. The big house in Craneswater's Sandown Road had become a second home to Winter over the course of the last nine months, a tacit thank you for sorting out the complicated homicide investigation that had begun with two dead bodies beside Bazza's pool, but this was the first time he'd seen Bazza's new souvenir corkboard.

It occupied half the back wall in the kitchen and was covered with pictures from the Wembley final. Bazza and his mates dismounting from the hired executive chopper. The same bunch of faces, arms linked, dancing up Olympic Way. A blur of blue and white from the Pompey end seconds before the ref got the first half going. Shots of the crowd erupting after Kanu slotted the winner. Shots of Calamity James lofting the Cup on the team's post-match lap of the stadium. A late-night snap of Bazza, pissed as a rat, at an undisclosed party somewhere in the depths of Southsea. This, Bazza told everyone who'd listen, had been the happiest day of his fucking life. *The* happiest day. No bullshit.

Now the mood was darker. Pompey's staunchest fan was trying to assess exactly how much damage his crazy daughter had inflicted on years of inspired criminality. Which meant, in turn, suppressing an urge to jump in his new motor, head for the Meon Valley, and throttle the life out of her.

'No point, Baz.' Winter had said it before. 'Absolutely none. Treat it like a business problem.'

'Sure. Easy as that.'

'Hard, Baz. But think about it. We know she's a goner as far as Madison is concerned. It doesn't matter how and it doesn't matter why. What matters is what she may have said already. She says she wouldn't and she hasn't. You know her better than me. What's that really worth?'

'A lot.' It was Marie. 'Esme can be a little witch but she's pretty straight when it comes to family.'

'You have to be fucking joking.' Mackenzie uncapped the Scotch. 'Have you tried to talking to Stu lately?'

'Stu's different.'

'You said family.'

'Stu's her husband. We're family. You and me. Maybe even Paul.'

'Great. And you really think that would keep her mouth shut? When this animal is crawling all over her? She's a woman, love. Women lose it totally, just piss it up against the wall then get all absent-minded afterwards.'

'You'd know that, would you?' Marie had stopped stirring the Béarnaise sauce.

'Of course I fucking would. You think I'm blind? Deaf? I'm telling you, Ezzie's lost it.' He threw an arm towards the darkness beyond the kitchen window. 'We may as well leave all the doors fucking open tonight. Let them help themselves.'

'Who's "them", Baz?' Winter was determined to head off a full-blown domestic.

'The Filth. The Old Bill. Madison's lot. Your lot.'

'But what, exactly, could she have told him?'

Mackenzie lowered his head, staring at the tattoo on the back of his right hand. This was the crux and he knew it.

'She could have told him lots, mush.'

'Like what?'

'Like what we got up to in the old days. The way we did it. The way we shipped the toot in. How we handled distribution. How we washed the money. All the fun and games we had getting all those old bastards out of all them houses we bought for development. She was part of all that, Ezzie. She saw it happen.'

'She was a kid, Baz.' It was Marie again. 'She was a teenager. All she was interested in was boys and crap music.'

Winter nodded. Laying the foundations of Mackenzie's empire had never been a pretty sight. Investing narco-loot in run-down property had been exactly the right decision but there'd been a lot of intimidation on the way, plus helping after helping of carefully applied violence. Yet Marie was right. The last thing on Ezzie's young mind had been where the money they all enjoyed might have come from.

'What about later?' Bazza was brooding again. 'What about Dubai? Spain? The yacht charter business in Gibraltar? What about all that?'

'All legit, Baz. As Ezzie well knows. Fuck me, she drew up most of the contracts.'

'Sure. But what about ...' Bazza frowned, hunting for the killer fact that would cement his argument. 'Westie?'

There was a long silence. Winter could smell burning.

'I know nothing about Westie,' he said.

'Yes you do, mush. You were fucking sitting there.'

'You're wrong, Baz. As far as Westie and me are concerned, it never happened.'

'What are you saying, mush? You didn't fly down to Spain with us? I didn't give you twenty-five grand in notes? You didn't wait for Westie in that building site of a fucking hotel? You didn't watch Tommy Peters blow his face off?'

'It never happened, Baz,' Winter said again. 'I'll deny everything. Not that Ezzie knows ...'

Both men fell silent while the tacit question hung in the air. Brett West had once been Bazza's favourite enforcer but last year he'd broken every rule in the book. And been killed for it.

Marie had abandoned the sauce.

'Esme doesn't know,' she said quietly.

'You're sure?' Bazza didn't believe her.

'Positive. She never liked Brett anyway, always did her best to avoid him.'

'Why's that?'

'He tried to come on to her one night. She'd bumped into him in some club or other. This was years back. She was silly enough to accept a lift home.'

'And?'

'You don't want to know.'

'The fuck I don't. Why didn't you tell me at the time?'

'Because there was no point, Baz. I had a word myself.'

'What did you say?'

'I told him never to go near her again. Otherwise you'd have him killed.'

'And I did too.' Bazza nodded, happy at last. 'Serves the cunt fucking right.'

He poured more Glenmorangie, toasting Tommy Peters. The twenty-five grand he'd paid for the hit? Cheap at the price.

Winter wanted to get back to Madison. All he could say on the evidence of this afternoon's conversation was that Ezzie was in deep.

'Meaning?'

'Meaning we have to think hard about how she relates to us from now on.'

'I'm not with you, mush. Relates? She's my daughter.'

'Of course, Baz. I'm thinking about the business. If she's off shagging a cop it might be wise to keep her at arm's length.'

The thought that this affair might still be alive and kicking seemed not to have occurred to Bazza. 'You're not serious. You can't be.'

'I am, Baz. She loves him.'

'But he's the Filth.'

'I know.'

'And he's there to screw us. Like they all are.'

'Sure. But she doesn't see it that way. Not yet.'

'You think she will?'

'Of course she will. These things never last. We're talking sell-by date, Baz. I give it a couple of months.'

'Marie?' he turned to his wife.

'I think Paul's being optimistic. Men are like that.'

'So what's your take?'

'I think this guy Madison does it for her. I think you have to accept that might be the case.'

'Never.' Mackenzie shook his head as if something had come loose inside. 'No ... not fucking ever.'

Marie shrugged. She seemed to have lost interest in cooking. She reached for a cloth and began to wipe the work surface.

Bazza swallowed the malt and reached for the bottle again. He was looking at Winter.

'There's another way of looking at this, mush. And right now I'm wondering why I didn't think of it before.'

'What's that then, Baz?'

'It's a set-up, the whole thing. Those bastards have put Madison into play. They've told him to cosy up to Ez. They're paying his gym bills and bar bills and what the fuck else he spends on her. And when the time is right, they'll get him to turn her against us.'

'How?'

'He'll get her to come looking, have a nose around. He'll tell her to start lifting stuff, photocopying stuff. Like I say, turn her against us. Evil bastards.'

Winter was looking at Marie. To his surprise, she appeared to be taking her husband seriously. Bazza hadn't finished. His forefinger was out, jabbing at Winter's face.

'It's Spit Bank all over again, mush. They're running an operation. I bet it's even got a fucking name.' He frowned. 'You remember last time? The fort? The scam they ran with the undercover guy? What was the name of the bloke in charge of the operation?'

'Faraday.'

'You know him at all?'

'Yeah.'

'You think he might be at it again? You think he might *know*?'

'I've no idea, Baz.' Winter sat back in his chair and gazed up at the ceiling. 'You want me to find out?'

Chapter eight

Faraday was still shaving when he took the call. It was Jimmy Suttle. He'd flagged Jeanette Morrissey's VW camper in case it raised a hit on an ANPR camera. Charlie One, the force control room, had been onto him first thing. ANPR means Automatic Number Plate Recognition.

'They've found the camper, boss.'

'Where?'

'It's in a car park up on Hundred Acres. Same registration. Burned out.'

Hundred Acres was an area of woodland ten miles inland from the city. It was popular with dog-walkers and Pompey families wanting a breath of country air. Faraday had been birding there a couple of times, with disappointing results.

Suttle had more details. A van driver delivering milk to the outlying villages had spotted the fire at around four in the morning. Appliances from Wickham had attended, followed by an area car from Fareham. The duty D/C, alerted by mention of a VW camper, had driven out for a look and matched the plate to Suttle's flag.

'The number plate was still in place?'

'So the guy says, boss. I talked to him a couple of minutes ago.'

Faraday was weighing the significance of this oversight. Professional criminals normally removed registration plates and filed off engine block numbers before torching vehicles. That way they muddied the investigative trail. In this case that hadn't happened.

'There's something else, boss. I've been talking to one or two people on the estate. One guy said Munday was supposed to be shagging some fifteen-year-old in the children's home in Skye Close.'

Faraday had his mobe tucked into one ear. With his other hand he was still trying to shave.

'So what?'

'Skye Close is close to the Scene, up on the other side of the road there. Munday was pissed. Say he wandered out of the estate, came up through the hospital site. Say he fancied it. Say he'd phoned ahead and got the girl out of bed to meet him somewhere.'

'And?'

'It's just a theory, boss. Maybe somebody else knew what was going on, somebody with an interest of their own in the girl, somebody who wanted Munday off the plot.'

'And ran him over?'

'Yeah.'

'Having nicked the camper?'

'Yeah.'

Faraday wiped his face with a flannel, thinking about the implications.

'We've got a name for the girl?'

'Hayley Burridge. Apparently she's still in pieces.'

'About what?'

'Munday.'

It took Winter a while to pick the bones from last night's conversation. He got up early, swallowing a couple of ibuprofen to still his thumping head. A second mug of tea took him out onto the balcony of his apartment. From here he had a third-floor view of the harbour and he stood at the rail, watching an early ferry emerging from the mist that coiled in from Spithead.

Five years ago his ex-bosses had mounted a covert bid to bring down his current employer. They'd done their sums, concluded that Bazza Mackenzie had netted at least seventeen million quid in narco-loot, and decided to get every penny back. To make that happen, they needed to snare him in serious criminality, something that would stand up in court, something that would open the doors of his ever-swelling empire to the avenging angels of the Serious and Organised Crime Agency.

It hadn't worked. Operation *Tumbril*, to the best of Winter's knowledge, had been run from offices within HMS *Excellent*, a navy training establishment on Whale Island. Undercover

officers had been brought in from London. A forensic account-
ant had been hired. And between them this little band of fanat-
ics had dreamed up a plan to entrap the city's most successful
criminal. The bait had been the chance for Bazza to buy one of
the offshore forts that guarded the approaches to Portsmouth.
They knew he loved profile. The fort was attractively priced.
And a rival bidder seemed – on the face of it – only too happy
to take part-payment in cocaine.

Tumbril, as far as the bosses were concerned, had been the
force's best-kept secret. But Bazza's connections reached deep
into every corner of the city and word of the covert operation
seeped out. Winter still remembered the rumours that had swept
across CID offices force-wide when *Tumbril* exploded and the
shit hit the fan. Geoff Willard, then an ambitious Detective
Superintendent, was one casualty. Joe Faraday, with day-to-day
operational control, was another.

The two men had weathered the storm in very different ways.
Willard – as bullish as ever – had dismissed the humiliation by
Mackenzie as a close-run thing and secretly vowed, one day, to
get even. His career, for reasons that Winter still didn't understand, seemed to have prospered in the aftermath and he was
now Head of CID. Faraday, on the other hand, hadn't. He was
still a D/I, still plodding from crime to crime, still dogged by a
reputation as a weirdo loner with a passion for birdwatching
and a deaf and dumb son.

Winter had never shared this take on Faraday. Over the
years, especially on division, he'd had his run-ins with the D/I.
Like any boss, Faraday had tried to control Winter's wilder
excesses – his impatience with paperwork, his over-reliance
on informants, his delight in playing one criminal off against
another – but despite their regular confrontations Winter had
sensed Faraday's grudging respect for his maverick D/C. Winter,
in the end, delivered. And Faraday, who was a bloody effective
copper, was canny enough to value that.

More recently, since Winter had binned the Job and crossed
to the Dark Side, there'd been occasions when the two men had
shared a drink or two. There'd always been a hint of mutual
advantage in these meets – especially over last year's double
homicide that had left a couple of bodies beside Mackenzie's
pool – and the fact remained that Faraday had been the only

cop who seemed to understand the logic of what Winter had done.

He was wise and damaged enough to recognise the kind of pressures that Winter had been under. And, like Winter, he seemed to have concluded that the Job was rapidly becoming impossible. The bad guys – proper criminals – were way ahead of the game. Families had given up trying to teach the difference between right and wrong. Kids ruled the streets. And all this while police trainees had their empty heads filled with nonsense about Proportionality, Human Rights and Victim Focus. No wonder Faraday was starting to look so old.

Winter stepped back into the kitchen to refill his mug. He knew the two of them would never be mates because Faraday didn't do mates. But even that was a kind of bond because Winter, like his ex-boss, was also a loner.

He poured the tea, eyeing the clock on the kitchen wall. Half eight. Way too early for a chat.

Faraday got to Hundred Acres by nine. The blackened shell of the VW camper stood in one corner of the gravelled car park. Most of the windows had shattered and the heat of the fire had melted all four tyres. A sharp, sour tang still hung in the air and shreds of charred fabric swam in the puddles of standing water left by the fire crew.

Steph Callan was deep in conversation with a uniformed patrolman beside a traffic car. She barely acknowledged Faraday's arrival. Faraday parked his Mondeo and walked across to the camper van. A single glance at the blackened front told him that the bumper was damaged at shin height and one of the wipers was missing. Inside, nothing had survived but the scorched metal framework of the seats and the remains of the oven and the sink in the back. There was a strong smell of petrol.

Callan finally came over. She was looking at the remains of the camper.

'Thanks for the call,' she said.

'D/S Suttle had it flagged. You were on the contacts list.'

'I know. That's why I'm here. Call me old-fashioned but in our neck of the woods we talk to each other.'

'You've got my number. Be my guest.'

She stared at him a moment, then shrugged and turned away. Moments later, she changed her mind.

'Jeanette Morrissey's got some relatives down the road. But I expect you know that already.'

Faraday said he didn't. How come Steph knew?

'I looked in the phone book. I'm nosey that way.'

'And you're sure they're relatives?'

'Not yet I'm not, but there are only two Morrisseys listed. One happens to be in Newtown. Our man in the traffic car there says it's a couple of miles away. I know you guys hate coincidence but right now it's all we've got.' The smile was icy. 'The Fire Investigation guys will sort this lot out. Shall we pay the Morrisseys a visit?'

Faraday wondered about mentioning Hayley Burridge, the girl in the children's home, but decided against it. Suttle was going to talk to her this morning. Better to wait.

They drove in convoy out of Hundred Acres. The road swooped left and right through miles of trees, then dropped down to the village of Newtown. The address from the phone book took them to a line of smallish bungalows overlooking a field of cows. Number 17 was on the end.

'How are we going to play this?' Faraday was gazing at the property. The pebbledash was stained a dirty yellow and the woodwork around the windows and front door badly needed a coat of paint.

'Up to you, boss.' She nodded at the garage tucked away on one side. 'I'd love to know what was in there over the last couple of days.'

They pushed in through the gate. There was a knocker on the front door but no bell. Faraday rapped three times. Nothing. He tried again, without success, then pushed the letterbox open and peered in. The narrow hall looked gloomy. There was an overpowering smell of urine. Cats, he thought. Or someone with a problem.

He turned to Callan but she'd stepped across to the adjacent window, her nose pressed against the glass, her eyes shaded against the glare of the sun.

'Here, boss. Don't quote me but I think she may be dead.'

Faraday took a look for himself. An old woman was curled in an armchair, angled away from the window. Her dress, crusted with food stains, looked several sizes too big. Her hands, small and bony, lay knotted in her lap, and her mouth hung open.

Callan knocked on the window, then managed to get the latch free. At this, the woman stirred, staring blankly at the wall.

'Mrs Morrissey?' Callan was shouting.

The woman tried to struggle to her feet, gave up. A cat padded in through the open door and jumped onto her lap. Callan glanced at Faraday, then nodded at the open window.

'Shall we?'

Faraday helped her clamber in, then followed. The smell here was even worse. Callan was looking down at the old lady, smoothing her uniform.

'We're police, my love.'

'You what, dear?'

'We're police. Coppers. Come to have a little chat.'

She peered up at Callan. Her eyes were milky in the gloom and the expression on her face spoke of nothing but confusion. Strangers coming in through the window? Whatever next?

Faraday took Callan into the hallway. The woman was old, possibly demented. There were special procedures here. Anything worthwhile in the way of evidence would have to be gathered in the presence of an Appropriate Adult. Otherwise it could be ruled inadmissible.

Callan didn't seem to be listening. She stepped past Faraday and went into the tiny kitchen at the back. Faraday watched from the open doorway as she began to go through the drawers in the dresser. The kitchen belonged in a museum. There was a scatter of potato peelings in the butler sink and a pair of woollen tights pegged to the length of binder twine strung over the gas stove.

'Bingo!'

Callan had found documents tying the property to the burned-out camper up the road. They included the registration certificate and a sheaf of service bills. She brought them back to the room at the front of the house and showed Faraday.

'You think she took them out of the van last last night? Meant to destroy them later?' She nodded at the old woman in the chair. 'You think this lady might be her mum?'

Mrs Morrissey appeared to have gone to sleep again but

responded when Faraday gave her bony shoulder a gentle nudge.

'Mr Perryman,' she said at once.

'Who?'

'Next door.' She gestured vaguely at the window. 'Ask him.'

Faraday and Callan exchanged glances. One more try. Callan knelt beside her, stroked her hand.

'We want to know about your daughter, Mrs Morrissey. Have you got a daughter?'

The woman looked blank.

'Mr Perryman,' she repeated. 'Next door.'

Faraday knew it was time to give up. Even if they managed to get this woman into court, the defence barrister would tear them to pieces. Oppressive behaviour. Inappropriate conduct. Objection upheld.

Back out in the sunshine, Callan rummaged in her bag for a tiny phial of perfume. She wrinkled her nose in disgust then dabbed some on her wrists and temples.

'Remind me never to get old,' she said. 'What now then, boss?'

Faraday was studying the bungalow next door. Flower beds around a newly mown lawn. UPVC double glazing. And a poster for the church bring-and-buy in one of the front windows.

'At least we've got a name,' he said.

Mr Perryman turned out to be a courtly, fit-looking man in his early seventies. He invited them into his bungalow. His wife, he said, was on flower-arranging duty at the local church. He himself was due at the chiropodist in Fareham. They were lucky to find anyone in.

Faraday wanted to know about his next-door neighbour. He needed to talk to her in connection with an incident over the weekend. How well did Mr Perryman know her?

'Very well. Mad as a coot, I'm afraid, but a sweet old thing really.'

'She lives alone?'

'Insists on it. I don't know whether you've seen the state of the place but for our money it's a health hazard. We do our best, of course, but these old folk have their pride. My wife's itching to get in there with the bleach but Elsie won't let us touch anything.'

'Does she have any relatives?' It was Callan.

'A daughter-in-law. She lives down in Portsmouth.'

'And does this daughter-in-law help out?'

'All the time. Margery and I sort out the daily shopping. We make sure she never goes short of something to eat. But it's Jeanette who does everything else. She's a bit of a saint that way.'

'That's her name? Jeanette?'

'Yes.'

'And she's up here a lot?'

'Couple of times a week. She's got her own problems, believe me, but Mum's always been a priority. These days that's good to see. Ideally, Jeanette would like to sell the place and get Mum into a home down in the city but Elsie won't hear of it.'

Faraday wanted to know about Elsie's garage. Did she have a car?

'She used to but it got too much for her. As a matter of fact we helped her sell it.'

'So the garage is empty?'

'Yes.' He glanced at his watch. Time was moving on. 'You should talk to Jeanette, really. She was here last night, funnily enough.'

He stepped towards the door, trying to bring the conversation to an end. It was Callan who stood in his way.

'You saw her? Last night?'

'Yes. There was a car I didn't recognise outside the bungalow so I popped across. It turned out to be Jeanette's. A hire car. Some problem with that old van of hers.'

'And what time did she leave? Did you happen to notice?'

'I've no idea. The car was still there the last time I looked. And that would have been – I don't know – ten o'clock.'

'Did you hear it leave at all? Hear it drive away? In the middle of the night maybe?'

'No go, I'm afraid. Margery and I both take sleeping tablets. One of the blessings of age. Now, if you don't mind ...' He was getting agitated about the time. His appointment was in half an hour. The parking in Fareham could be shocking.

Faraday signalled for Callan to let him go. His coat was on

a hook beside the door. All three of them stepped out into the sunshine. Faraday thanked him for his time, aware of Callan staring at the tree that overhung the driveway of the old lady's bungalow next door. As Perryman fumbled for his car keys, she turned back to him.

'Was Jeanette here first thing Sunday morning?' she asked. 'And did you give her a lift back to Portsmouth?'

Perryman paused a moment, buttoning his coat. Then he nodded.

'Yes to both,' he said. 'How on earth did you know that?'

Winter was thinking about getting in touch with Faraday when the phone went. It was Carol Legge. She was sitting in her big open-plan office with the rest of the Child Protection Team. They'd had a bit of a chat about Tide Turn Trust and someone had come up with a bright idea. Did Winter have a pen handy?

Winter found a pencil beside yesterday's Sudoku. The guy's name was Maurice Sturrock. Most people called him Mo. He'd spent the last eleven years on the Isle of Wight but had been a social worker in Portsmouth before that, which was when Carol had got to know him. Until very recently Mo been driving a desk as a senior manager at the Social Services HQ in Newport. He had a wealth of experience and a great reputation as someone who really cut it as far as the kids were concerned, but just now, to the best of anyone's knowledge, he was still on gardening leave. If Tide Turn Trust wanted to make a bit of a splash in the world of stroppy youth, she said, then Mo Sturrock would be near-perfect. Especially after his little outburst.

'His little what?'

'Google him, pet.' She was laughing. 'Fill your boots.'

Winter kept his computer in the spare bedroom. He googled Maurice Sturrock and found himself reading a feature article from the *Guardian*. The article was headed TELLING IT THE WAY IT IS? and appeared to be the text of a speech Sturrock had made to a London conference of senior Social Services managers.

A brief paragraph at the top explained that Sturrock had been standing in for his boss, who had evidently written a lengthy presentation about the miracles of integrated working.

Sturrock's job was simply to read the piece, acknowledge the applause and return to his seat. In the event, though, he'd done no such thing. After a brief tussle with his boss's prose he'd put the speech aside, eyeballed the audience, and gone totally off-piste.

Everyone in the business, he remarked, knew the truth about conferences like this. That they were an expensive jolly, dressed up to seem worthy and productive, but in essence just a chance to catch up with old mates, have a beer or two, eye the talent, spend the night in a decent hotel, and bugger off home. That might sound fine, he said, but do the sums. Two days of paid time for four hundred delegates on an average salary of around thirty-seven K. Conference fees at £450 a pop. Travel expenses. Hotel bills. Taxi fares. The whole caboodle. In total, you'd be lucky to see any change out of half a million quid.

Winter sat back for a moment, trying to imagine the atmosphere in the conference hall. For once a speaker would have had everyone's total attention. At last, someone with the bollocks to cut through all the bullshit.

Even on paper, Winter could sense Sturrock's anger. He'd challenged everyone in the audience to imagine what they could do with half a million pounds. A couple more youth workers on the action team. Access to paid mentors for difficult kids with artistic talents. Cash to hire expensive educational psychologists who might just make the difference. In Sturrock's own neck of the woods, help like this had become a luxury item, a fantasy, way beyond his overstretched budget. Just getting mainland experts across to the island, he'd pointed out, cost an arm and a leg. So what in God's name was he doing here? Turning his back on the kids who mattered? Watching half a million precious quid disappear down the plughole?

The speech came to an end. Evidently Sturrock had made no apologies, offered no analysis, no solutions. Wasting time, he concluded, was something we all did. It was a shame, and it mattered, but wasting this kind of time and this kind of money was criminal. Every social worker he'd ever met was trying to do more and more with less and less. And yet here we all were. Kissing goodbye to half a million quid.

Winter eyed the phone, a grin on his face, wondering whether he ought to read the *Guardian* more often. In the

Job, on countless occasions, he'd had to put up with the same kind of nonsense. Politicians turning *Daily Mail* editorials into bonkers legislation. Managers disappearing up their own arse with all the nonsense about Proportionality and Victim Focus. Fast-track guys on the make, fluent in bollock-speak. What a pleasure to find out that someone, at least, had seen through it all.

Carol Legge answered Winter's call on the first ring.

'Well?' she said.

'Brilliant, love. What happened when he got back to the office?'

'They suspended him. He's been on gardening leave ever since.'

Winter reached for the paper and checked the date: 17 November 2007.

'Since last *year*?'

'That's right. These things take a while. It could be another couple of months, easily.'

'On full pay?'

'Yes. This is local authority stuff, pet. There are lots of back-sides to cover.'

Winter was looking at the photo that accompanied the article. Mo Sturrock was a forty-something with tinted glasses and a mop of greying hair. In another life he might have been a rock star. No wonder he got on so well with the kids.

Carol was talking about Sturrock's bosses. They'd been crawling over his records since November and word from the Newport offices suggested that they'd failed to find any skeletons in his cupboard. Going on the record the way he'd done was definitely a sacking offence but in the nature of these things they always liked to find extra dirt.

'So what are you saying?' Winter's interest had quickened.

'I'm saying they might welcome an offer, pet.'

'Who might?'

'Mo's bosses. They may want him off their hands before it comes to a tribunal.'

'Excellent.' Winter reached for a pen. 'You've got a number?'

Chapter nine

Faraday and Steph Callan revisited Jeanette Morrissey towards the end of that same afternoon. Her hired Fiesta was outside the house in Paulsgrove and Faraday could see her shadow behind the net curtains in the front room. When she answered the door there was neither surprise nor alarm in her face. She's been waiting for us, Faraday thought. Mr Perryman up in Newtown has made a call and warned her to expect a visit. And here we are.

Faraday asked her to accompany them back to the Bridewell for a formal interview in connection with the death of Kyle Munday.

'Am I under arrest?'

'No.'

'So what happens if I refuse? Say I'm too busy? Say you have to wait?'

'Then I'm afraid we'd insist.'

'Will it take long?'

'It may do. That depends.'

She looked at him a moment. 'There are a couple of things I need to take with me. Do you mind?'

Without waiting for an answer she began to climb the stairs. Faraday was the nearest. He followed her. She paused on the top landing. Her bedroom door was open. There were more photos of her dead son on the dressing table.

'You'll give me a couple of minutes?'

'Of course. Just leave the door open, if you don't mind.'

She gave him another look, almost accusatory, then nodded at the room next door.

'That was Tim's bedroom. Help yourself.'

The invitation had the force of an order. Faraday pushed the door open. The bedroom looked west. A blaze of late-afternoon sunshine streamed through the half-curtained window. The single bed was unmade, the duvet thrown back, the pillow still dimpled with the imprint of a head. A pile of clothes lay on the floor beside it – jeans, a couple of T-shirts, a pair of black and white baseball boots – and there was a guitar propped against a chair in the corner. Beside the chair, on a music stand, a musical score.

Faraday stepped into the room. Motes of dust hung in the stale air. There was a smell of unwashed clothing. One corner of a poster for the Isle of Wight Bestival had come adrift from its little pebble of Blu Tack and the adjacent corkboard was covered with snaps, scribbled reminders and cuttings from various music magazines. Tim Morrissey had died on 5 November. This was his shrine.

'You know something very strange?' Jeanette Morrissey was standing in the open doorway. She was holding a sponge bag and what looked like a framed photograph.

'Tell me.'

'We've got a cat, a fat old thing. We called it Flopsy at first but Tim prefered Coltrane. It used to sleep with him every night – there, on that bed.'

'And?'

'It's never been in the room since. Not once. Not to my knowledge. Animals know, don't they? They know everything.'

Faraday followed her downstairs. The photo she was carrying showed mother and son at a function of some kind, a moment of time lifted from an earlier life. It had come from the dressing table.

Callan already had the front door open. The cat padded heavily down the hall and wound itself around Jeanette's ankles. Then it looked up, mewing.

She reached down, tickled it behind the ears, murmured something Faraday didn't catch. Then she was upright again, her eyes shiny.

'You see?' she said. 'They know.'

It took Winter most of the afternoon to track down Mo Sturrock. Carol Legge had given him a home number. The first couple of times there was no response. Around half past four, ringing yet again, Winter found himself talking to a youngish girl. Yes, this was the right number for her dad. But no, he wouldn't be back for at least half an hour. When Winter asked whether he was carrying a mobile she said yes but she wasn't allowed to give the number out. Finally, gone five, Winter made contact.

'Maurice Sturrock?'

'Yeah. Who are you?' He sounded gruff.

'The name's Winter. Friend of Carol Legge.'

'Leggie?' The voice softened. 'How is she?'

'Fine.' Winter explained his business. He was in the youth offending game. He ran a start-up charity across the water in Portsmouth. Tide Turn Trust was starting to make an impact. There might be room for new blood at the top.

'What are you telling me?'

'I'm telling you it might be in both our interests to meet.'

There was a long silence. Winter could hear the blare of a TV. Then Sturrock was back.

'Voluntary sector, you say? No local authority involvement?'

'None, my friend.'

'When?'

'As soon as.'

'Where?'

'Your choice.'

'Your end, then.' He named a pub in Albert Road. 'Tomorrow. Twelve thirty.'

Winter, surprised by the choice of pub, was about to agree but realised it was too late. Sturrock had hung up.

It was DCI Gail Parsons who chose the interview team for Operation *Highfield*. Normally, both Major Crime and the Road Death Investigation Team relied on specialist officers under the guidance of a Tactical Interview Manager. Road Death conducted hundreds of these interviews, all of them involving fatalities, and had won themselves a solid reputation for both thoroughness and results. On this occasion, given the sensitivities about turf and ownership, Parsons decided that Faraday and Callan should handle the interview between them. Faraday, because of his knowledge of Operation *Melody*. And Callan, because she was holding the RDIT file.

Already, in Parsons' office, both Faraday and Callan were anticipating a quick breakthrough. They could evidence motive. Morrissey's camper van, with its dented bumper and missing wiper blade, looked a dead ringer for the hit-and-run. Plus they could now tie the camper van to her mother-in-law's bungalow and prove she'd been lying about her movements over the Saturday night and Sunday morning. From here on in, according to Callan, you just had to find the right buttons to press.

Jeanette Morrissey had waived her right to phone for a solicitor of her choice, telling Faraday she'd be perfectly happy with the duty brief. Her name was Michelle Brinton, a plump freckle-faced solicitor in her late thirties. Eight years in Pompey had taught her a great deal about the realities of life on the estates but she was clearly having difficulty establishing any kind of rapport with her new client.

Jeanette Morrissey sat in the bare interview room across the table from Callan and Faraday. She looked detached, her face a mask, as if she'd become a spectator at a play for which she had little taste. It seemed there were few surprises in store, least of all for her.

Callan cued the audio tapes, introduced the faces around the table, added the date and time. At her elbow were notes from the earlier conversation. She studied them a moment then looked across at Jeanette.

'Yesterday you told us that you spent Saturday night at home in Paulsgrove. Am I right?'

'Yes.'

'So would you please take us through exactly what happened again?'

Something close to a smile ghosted across Jeanette's face. Then she turned her attention to Faraday.

'We first met in November,' she said softly. 'I don't know whether you remember.'

Faraday nodded. Contrary to his first impression, Jeanette Morrissey had perfect recall. He'd driven up to Paulsgrove with the Family Liaison Officer the morning after her son's murder. There'd been journalists waiting in the street outside. Later, a TV crew.

'You had a friend with you,' he said.

'Katie. The one who's just come back from Greece. She's

never let me down. Not once. Have you ever been in that situation, Mr Faraday? Depending on one individual, one human being, because you know that no one else really cares?'

'I'm afraid I'm not with you.'

'You're not? Why do I find that unsurprising?'

'I've no idea.'

'My son had died. He'd been killed. He'd been stabbed to death. Everyone on that estate knew who'd done it, knew who was responsible. You knew too. You all knew. And yet nothing happened. Nothing was done. And next day he was out there again, parading past my house with that horrible dog of his, stopping outside the gate, laughing at me, *laughing*, Mr Faraday. Have you any idea what that can do to you? Then? And ever since?'

'It was a question of evidence, Mrs Morrissey. We can't put people away without demonstrating why.'

'Then maybe you didn't look hard enough.'

'I think you'll find that's not true. If you have reason to make a formal complaint by all means go ahead.'

Faraday sat back, trying to steady the thunder in his head, aware of how wooden he must sound. The woman was right. They'd failed her.

'Another thing.' She hadn't finished. 'Before Tim died, before they stabbed him, they beat him up and broke his fingers. We gave you names, even addresses. Tim told you exactly what had happened, how they'd done it, everything you could possibly need. Yet still nothing happened. I know it wasn't your lot. I know it wasn't Major Crimes. But it makes no difference. You're all policemen as far as I'm concerned. Yet, like I said, nothing happened.'

'As I understand it, your son withdrew his evidence.'

'That's true. And you know why? Because they threatened to kill him. I said to Tim at the time that they were bluffing. I said it was his duty to go to court but he was simply too frightened. Looking back, I should have forced him because in the end it made no difference. He did what they wanted but they killed him anyway. You've lost it, Mr Faraday. My generation, we trusted people like you. We had some faith that you would put things right. We believed in justice. That's gone. It's gone totally. Today, we're at the mercy of people like Kyle Munday.

They can make our lives a misery. They even have the power of life and death. How do I know? Because he killed my son.'

Faraday held her gaze. It was tempting to enquire whether she could prove it, but he knew there was no point. Interviews like these were meant to establish matters of guilt and innocence. Hers, not his.

'We made sure you had access to a Family Liaison Officer, Mrs Morrissey. You chose to turn that offer down.'

'I didn't want a Family Liaison Officer, Mr Faraday. I wanted to see Kyle Munday in court. I wanted to know someone cared enough about Tim to make sure he was punished.'

'Punished how, Mrs Morrissey?' It was Callan.

The question took Jeanette by surprise. Michelle Brinton muttered something in her ear but Jeanette shook her head. Then, to Callan's irritation, she turned back to Faraday.

'You want the truth? I wanted that man dead.'

'That would never have been an option. You know that.'

'Of course I do. Life imprisonment would have been acceptable. Not perfect but better than the way it turned out. It wasn't just the next day, Mr Faraday. It wasn't just standing in my front room watching that horrible man leering at me. It was all the other times I'd bump into him and those pitiful kids he dragged around. It went on for months. It was still happening last week. Little comments. Little digs. They'd won, Mr Faraday. They'd driven me insane.'

Faraday nodded. He understood. The next question was only too obvious.

'So let's talk about last Saturday,' he began. 'What really happened?'

DCI Gail Parsons was still at her desk, bent over her PC, when Faraday and Callan returned to the Major Crime suite at Fratton. Faraday had talked to her earlier, prior to the start of the interview. She'd told him she'd be working late on a report for headquarters. She wanted an update before she packed it in for the night.

'Well?' Her fingers were still gliding over the keyboard.

'Full confession, boss. She hadn't lied about being at home on Saturday evening but she got a phone call from her mother-in-law way after midnight. The old lady was in a real state.

At that kind of hour there was no way Jeanette would phone the neighbour so she had to get out of bed and drive up there herself. She said she'd done it before. In fact it was becoming a bit of a habit.'

'So what happened?'

'She got in the camper, drove off the estate. The route she takes goes up the hill past the hospital. That time of night there wasn't much on the road. She says she was driving along, thirty-five, forty miles an hour, and saw someone crossing the road in front of her.'

'Which direction?'

'Right to left. Jimmy Suttle's spot on. That would put Munday up near the kids' home, sniffing around Hayley Burridge.'

'And she recognised Munday?'

'As she got closer, yes. She says he must have recognised her too, because he just stood in the middle of the road, swaying, obviously pissed, giving her the finger.'

Faraday paused, remembering Jeanette Morrissey in the interview room. At this stage her voice had hardened. At first Faraday had put this down to anger but quickly realised that it was something else. Excitement. After months of torment and frustration, she'd realised she finally had a chance to get even.

'So what happened?' Parsons was frowning, her fingers still anchored to the keyboard.

'She drove at him.'

'She said that?'

'Exactly those words. She said she put her foot down and drove straight at him. That's why there were no skid marks on the road. It wasn't an accident at all. It was an execution.'

'She said that too?' Parsons had finally abandoned the PC.

'No. But that's what it amounts to. She was convinced Munday had killed Tim. As we all know, she was probably right. Because we couldn't do anything about it, she'd decided to sort him out herself.'

'You're telling me she'd done something like this before?'

'She told us afterwards she'd thought about it. She knew where Munday lived. She'd driven past there a couple of times wondering how easy it might be to burn the place down but in the end she'd done nothing about it. On Saturday night it was much simpler. Munday was standing there asking for it. She could see him, see the smile on his face. So she obliged.'

Jeanette had described the moment of impact in minute detail. How, in the last second or so, it had begun to dawn on Munday that she wasn't going to stop. How his face had hung there in the lights, the frozen leer, the raised finger. And how, in an instant, inches from the windscreen, that same face had gone, swallowed up by the surrounding darkness. After the initial impact, she said, there'd been two big bumps, front wheel and back wheel, and then nothing but the empty road ahead.

'She didn't stop?'

'No. She said she checked the mirror but couldn't really see anything. Just a bundle of clothes in the road.'

'But why didn't she report it? She could have claimed it was an accident. We might have believed her.'

'No way, boss. She's a bitter woman. She's got no faith in us. She thinks we've let her down. Badly.'

Parsons said nothing. Callan was perched on the edge of the conference table.

'I think the woman's slightly unhinged,' she said. 'There was a definite pleasure in killing Munday. You could see it in her eyes. Once she'd taken that decision there was no turning back. She did it for her son and for herself and once she'd done it she wanted to be shot of the whole nightmare. Reporting it would mean months of hassle with the possibility of a court appearance. Another little victory for Mr Munday. What kind of closure would that be?'

Jeanette Morrissey had driven on to the bungalow in Newtown, Steph explained. Her job at the health clinic had made her forensically aware. She knew the front and underside of the van would be covered in Munday's DNA. So she decided to get rid of the van somehow and give herself an alibi.

'Yet she accepted a lift from the neighbour? Next day?' Parsons was frowning.

'Like I say, she was unhinged. She hadn't thought this thing through at all. But under those circumstances I guess you probably don't. It's a kind of madness. You think you've got the thing sorted but in reality you're stuffed. There's no way we're not going to nail her.'

Faraday nodded in agreement. Unlike Munday, Jeanette Morrissey was a sitting target. On Wednesday evening, after

Faraday and Callan had paid her a visit at home, she'd gone to Newtown. In the small hours she'd retrieved the camper van from her mum-in-law's garage, driven it up to the car park on Hundred Acres, and used a container of petrol to set it on fire. Returning to the bungalow on foot, she'd driven back to Paulsgrove in the hire car. Within hours, thanks to Steph Callan, the next-door neighbour had demolished her carefully constructed alibi. The rest, in Callan's phrase, had been a breeze.

Faraday's last glimpse of Jeanette, less than an hour ago, had stayed with him. Formally charged with murder, she'd been fingerprinted and subjected to a DNA mouth swab. Afterwards, her solicitor had fetched her a coffee from the machine. Ahead, over the months to come, lay the prospect of remand, trial and conviction. Doubtless there'd be many who would sympathise deeply with what she'd done. Her case might even spark an editorial or two in the national press. But her days of freedom were very definitely over. So how come, nursing her coffee, she seemed so suddenly relaxed?

Faraday had paused beside her. He'd wanted to wish her good luck but somehow the phrase had stuck in his throat. She'd looked up at him, ignoring the briefly comforting hand on her shoulder.

'Got what you wanted?' she'd asked.

The question, Faraday knew, would haunt him. Now Parsons was offering her congratulations. The pair of them, she said, had worked as a team, bringing complementary investigative skills to an inquiry that might easily have dragged on. As a template for future collaborations, Operation *Highfield* might offer some useful lessons. She'd certainly be saying something of the kind to Mr Willard and she was certain that he'd share her own satisfaction that Munday's death had been so speedily resolved. Well done to both of you.

Neither Callan nor Faraday said a word. Both knew that Jeanette Morrissey's story could never have survived an in-depth investigation. The neighbour's lift on Sunday morning had been a windfall, but one way or another she'd have ended up in the Bridewell, DNA swabbed and fingerprinted, just another crime statistic.

Minutes later, pausing outside Faraday's office, Callan had

said her goodbyes. Both of them knew that the relationship had been far from ideal but neither was in the mood to talk about it. Dutifully Faraday suggested a drink, but his heart wasn't in it. Maybe some other time. Maybe when they met again to finalise the file. Callan nodded, then laid her hand on Faraday's arm.

'You want a tip, boss?' The smile seemed genuine. 'Don't let it get to you.'

Back home, late, Faraday knew that wasn't an option. He went upstairs and settled at the desk in the window of his bedroom. For several minutes he did nothing except stare into the darkness beyond. The moon was full and torn shreds of cloud threw ragged shadows across the silvered brilliance of the harbour. The top sash of the window was open, and beyond the chatter of ducks along the foreshore Faraday could hear the haunting call of a distant curlew. The curlew, especially at night, had always spoken to the very depths of his soul. It summed up a hollowness, even a vacuum, that he suspected lay at the heart of modern life. In this mood he knew he was treading the very edges of the abyss.

At length he began to scroll through his emails. A message from a birder caught his eye and he followed the prompts to an article from an environmental agency in Scotland. The article was brief, but by the time he got to the end the accompanying photo was a blur. A box of tissues lay on the floor beside his chair. He blew his nose, still gazing at the screen, wondering who to talk to. No Gabrielle. No soulmate. *Personne.* Not for the first time in his life, he was totally alone.

He opened the Create Mail box and typed in the first three letters of Gabrielle's name. Then he began to write. *In the Firth of Forth there's a colony of guillemots. They're tough birds. They nest on cliffs and get together in vast huddles to protect themselves from gulls which prey on their eggs and chicks. Mating pairs rear one chick a year and take it in turns to stand guard on the nest while the other hunts at sea. Lately, food has become so scarce that both parents have to go hunting otherwise the whole family will starve, but that leaves the chick on its own. It would be nice to think that neighbouring guillemots take care of these temporary orphans but that's far from the case. In reality, if the undefended chicks come looking for food, they find themselves under attack. These attacks can be savage. Sometimes they're even pushed off the cliff ledge to certain death on the rocks below.*

Faraday sat back a moment, wondering how far to take the parallels. Tim Morrissey, in some respects, had been an undefended chick, but the likes of Munday and his little gang had sensed weakness and had come looking for him. That wouldn't have happened on the cliffs beside the Firth of Forth – and there lay the essential difference. The attacking guillemots were simply defending their territory. Munday was a predator.

He bent to the keyboard again. *You know Paulsgrove. As estates go, it's better than most. Decent people struggling through. Plus a hard core of delinquents, sadists and assorted psychos who do nothing to make life easy. Just now, society being the way it is, these guys (and women) have the whip hand. Violence speaks louder than small (or large) acts of kindness. People frighten easily. And when that happens on a large enough scale, people like me have a problem.*

Faraday gazed at the final sentence. He'd spent the last hour or so mentally reviewing his role in Operation *Melody*. Given the lack of clinching forensic evidence – no murder weapon, no clothing, nothing of any value recovered from the scene or the body – he and the rest of the squad had relied on witness statements, hearsay and phone billings. In every respect, Munday had the estate bound and gagged. As far as Tim Morrissey was concerned, people were simply too scared to talk.

Last year, for months on end, Gabrielle had researched gang culture on the city's estates. She'd done countless interviews with kids of all ages, trying to map the web of loyalties which so often replaced family structures that – for one reason or another – had simply disintegrated. Some of her findings had taken her by surprise. She was an anthropologist by training and she recognised that membership of a gang was a godsend for kids who had simply run out of people who might love them. In the absence of functioning mums or dads, belonging to a gang offered very welcome shelter from what Gabrielle had come to refer to as *la tempête qui vient*.

Quite what this gathering storm might bring she'd never made clear but day by day, week by week, Faraday was beginning to recognise the symptoms. The nineteen-year-old smackhead who'd had her third miscarriage on the steps of the magistrates' court. The estate mums with no previous record who regularly shoplifted from the corner store to feed their kids. The boyfriend with an anger management problem who punched his girlfriend's granny in the face over a ten-pound debt and then set her on fire. And now the dead Kyle Munday, whose party piece was training his pit bull to kill swans on Great Salterns lake. Some of these horror stories were down to simple inadequacy. Others were the product of hard times. But some, including Munday, spoke of a deep well of something else. Evil was a word that Faraday had always tried to avoid but some days, like now, it was staring him in the face.

Your name is Jeanette. Someone has killed your only child. Months later, you haven't touched anything in his bedroom. He's still with you, in your head, in your heart. And his killer is still out there, gloating, goading you, knowing all the time that he's put himself beyond the law. We do nothing because our hands are tied. With all our cleverness, all our budget, all those man-hours in overtime, we still can't prove the case against him. We haven't given up, and we never would, but none of that matters any more because Jeanette has done it for us. By sheer luck, nothing more, the chance came and she took it. She ran her tormentor over and killed him. When we challenged her after she'd confessed she said she was glad. Glad to have got it off her chest. And glad to have done it in the first place. The world, she told me, was a better place without Kyle Munday. Do you blame her? Wouldn't you have done the same thing?

Faraday wondered what Gabrielle would make of a message like this then decided that it didn't matter. Better, like Jeanette Morrissey, to get it off his chest. Better to ping it into that other vacuum, the emptiness that had once been a relationship he'd cherished. As ever, he thought, he was talking to himself. The mouse arrow lingered briefly over the Send command. His forefinger left-clicked.

Gone.

Chapter ten

Winter had been in the pub less than ten minutes when Mo Sturrock walked in through the door. The photo in the *Guardian* hadn't done him justice. He was tall and carried himself with an air of easy command. The tangle of greying hair was secured at the back by a twist of green ribbon and there was a whiff of roll-ups as he folded himself onto the stool at the bar. Scuffed cowboy boots. Frayed 501s. Faded Levi jacket. At first glance, Winter knew he'd be perfect. Looked right. Dressed right. Even smelled right.

'Paul Winter?' The voice came as a surprise, lighter than Winter had expected, no trace of the gruffness on the phone. The handshake too was soft. 'I used this place when I was a student. Practically lived here when I could afford it.'

'Is that right?'

'Yeah. It was busier then, mind you. Hard times, love?'

The question was addressed to a thin woman in her late forties who'd just appeared behind the bar. Sturrock's wink softened the abruptness of the enquiry.

'Terrible,' she said. 'What can I get you?'

He settled for Guinness. Winter swallowed a mouthful of Stella and pushed his glass forward for a top-up. Sturrock was studying the menu.

'Hungry?' Winter had seen it already.

'Starving.' He was still looking at the barmaid. 'I'm a veggie, love. What can you sort me out?'

'Cheese roll. It's on the next page.'

'You've got onion? Pickle? Mustard?'

'Just cheese. Who's paying?'

Winter gave her a ten-pound note. Sturrock settled for a bowl of chips. He wanted to know more about Tide Turn Trust.

'I googled you lot,' he said. 'Very impressive.'

The website had been Marie's idea. Winter hadn't been sure about some of the copy. Promises to glue fractured lives back together sounded wonderful in theory, and so did the line about turning long-term liabilities into society's assets, but Bazza loved bullshit phrases like these so Winter's scope for protest had been strictly limited.

'So what do you think?'

'About Tide Turn? Honestly?'

'Yeah.'

'I think it's fucking hard. In fact I *know* it's fucking hard. But if you're telling me you've found a way then fair play to you. These little commando raids are often better value than the big set-piece battles.'

'Commando raids?' Winter was lost.

'Take a few hostages. Work hard on them. Turn the little bastards round. The problem guys like me had was volume. Join a local authority and the client base just gets bigger and bigger. Why? Because we *have* to sort these buggers out. It's statutory. It says so in black and white. And the longer you do it, the more of them appear. Now that may be a sign of the times, God knows, but they were fucking all over us come the finish.'

'Were?'

'Yeah.' He frowned. 'How much do you know about me?'

Winter shrugged, said he knew very little. In these situations it was always better to feign ignorance.

'That's kosher? You don't know about the conference? Everything that's gone down since?'

Winter hesitated. Carol Legge may have primed him. Better to cover his arse.

'I know you had some kind of run-in up in London. In fact I read the speech.'

'And?'

'Brilliant. I used to be a cop until I knew better. If I had a quid for every day I had to wade through all that managerial bollocks I'd be a rich man.'

'Is that why you quit the job?'

'No.'

'But you saw what I was driving at?'

'Completely. Brave boy. They must have loved you.'

'They did, most of them. Not the bosses of course. The bloke who'd given me the speech to read went ape.'

'What did he say?'

'He didn't. Next day, back at the office, I got suspended by email. Fifteen minutes to clear my desk. I even had to lean on the security guard for a couple of cardboard boxes.'

'And now?'

'Nothing's changed. I'm in limbo. I'm a non-person. I've been banished. They call it gardening leave but maybe the joke's on them. We're out in the country, me and the good lady, and we've got a fair spread. Last time I looked, we had enough veg to feed half the village. I go door to door, flogging the stuff. The local kids can't work out why my van hasn't got Tesco on the side. Big learning curve.'

'You?'

'Them. Life should be more than fucking supermarkets. The more I do it, the more I love it.'

'So why would you need Tide Turn?'

'Because it's not enough, my friend. You have to get real here. I've spent most of my working life with problem kids and the truth is I miss them. Just how challenging is a row of parsnips? Even ones as knobbly as mine?'

For the first time Winter caught a whiff of bitterness. What little he knew about life on the Isle of Wight told him it was claustrophobic. Everyone knew your business. And if word spread about your so-called disgrace then you were probably doomed.

'Does your wife work?'

'Partner. And the answer's yes.'

'Same line of business?'

'She's a psychotherapist. She deals with kids occasionally but mostly it's adults.'

'Grown-ups?'

'Adults.'

Winter liked the distinction. His laughter brought a grin to Sturrock's face. Winter was starting to wonder how often that happened.

'It must have been tough,' he said. A statement, not a question.

Sturrock studied him a moment. He hadn't touched his Guinness.

'You're right.' He nodded. 'It is.'

'Still?'

'More and more in some ways, less so in others. I don't miss the meetings. I don't really miss the culture if I'm honest. But the blokes down at the coalface, the social workers, the teams we were putting out there, all that was great. You're in the business of constant challenge. You've got to know how to press people's buttons, how to get the very best out of them. It's the same with the clients, the kids you have to deal with. None of them are monsters, they've just come unstuck, and once you realise that then everything else follows. We live all the time with the instant fix. It's everywhere. Dream up some new fucking initiative, wave a magic wand, and everything's sorted. Problem is, that never works. You have to get to know these kids. That takes time. And time takes money. To put someone from my team alongside an individual kid for – say – nine months costs the earth, and scoring that kind of funding isn't easy. But I've managed it a couple of times and, believe me, it works. These kids trust nobody. Building that trust, keeping it, is what really matters.'

At last, he reached for his glass. Winter watched him take a couple of swallows then wipe his mouth with the back of his hand. He'd known from the start that Bazza would take to this guy. He was authentic. He was rough around the edges. Beyond the macho bluster he was a bit of a dreamer as well, but he obviously had the bollocks to speak his mind.

'There are kids in this city who might put all that to the test.'

'I know. I worked here.'

'And you think you could hack it?'

'I know I could. I'm not talking about the job now, if there is a job; I'm talking about my own experience. What works on the island works in Pompey. If you don't believe that then you might as well chuck it in.'

'Tesco's? Stacking shelves?'

'Never.' He laughed again. 'I haven't got the brain.'

*

Detective Chief Superintendent Willard descended on the Major Crime suite shortly after lunch. Faraday, summoned from his office, found the Head of CID in conference with Gail Parsons.

Willard was a big man, physically imposing. He'd earned a career-long reputation as a copper's copper and now found himself in charge of Hantspol's detectives. Promotion had given Willard a taste for expensive suits plus the beginnings of a national profile and Faraday knew that he now had his eye on an ACPO job. Assistant Chief Constable in a decent force could open all kinds of interesting doors once he'd done his thirty years.

For now, though, he was preoccupied with *Melody*. Major Crime had taken a great deal of stick from the media when the hunt for Tim Morrissey's killer had stalled and now was the time to put the record straight. Willard had always been extremely sensitive to criticism of any kind, especially from the press.

'Well done for boxing off the hit-and-run, Joe.' He waved Faraday into a seat at the conference table. 'Tell me about Munday's mother.'

'She lives up on the estate. Munday was there pretty much when it suited him.'

'You think they were close?'

'I've no idea, sir. She's a smackhead. Most of the time she's out of it.'

'Who broke the news?'

'Steph Callan sent a FLO round. Three in the morning.'

'One of ours?'

'No. She's on the Road Death team.'

'So what happened?'

'She went to the mother's address with the death message but couldn't get any sense out of her. She went back next morning to pick the woman up for the ID but she was all over the place, totally strung out. It got so bad that the FLO was tempted to try and score some morphine from the one of the techies.'

'At the hospital, you mean?'

'Yes. She had to drive her over to Winchester to ID the body.'

Willard shot a glance at Parsons, digesting the news. Then he turned back to Faraday.

'So who was supplying the gear on the estate?'

'I've no idea, sir.'

'You think it might have been her son? Munday?'

'It's possible. I don't know.'

'But she's vulnerable? Is that what you're saying?'

'Definitely.'

At last Faraday sensed where all this was leading. Willard wanted more names for *Melody*, more kids who might have helped take Tim Morrissey to the grave, more evidence to fuel a round of high-profile arrests to counter the impression that Major Crimes were off the pace. And, in her current state, some of that information might well come from Munday's mother.

'You need to talk to the FLO, Joe. Get her back in there. Shake a few trees. Tell her to have a poke around.'

'What happens if the Road Death lot kick up? I get the impression they're under the cosh just now.'

'Put in one of our own FLOs. In that kind of state, Mrs Munday won't notice the difference.' He paused, then bent to his briefcase and pulled out a file. Faraday caught sight of an operational name on the cover – S-something. 'Gail tells me you've just come back from leave. Montreal? Am I right?'

'Yes.'

'Good time?'

'Wonderful.'

Willard caught the heaviness in Faraday's voice but let it pass. His fingers toyed with the file for a moment then he pushed it across the table.

'Gail also says you've got time on your hands, Joe, so this one's for you. Cold case. Operation *Sangster*. Take a look and tell me what you think. I'm back in the office on Monday. Ring me.'

Winter found Marie at the Royal Trafalgar. Mackenzie had recently installed a modest gym in the hotel's basement and Marie, who rarely bothered with lunch, was working out on a second-hand rowing machine Bazza claimed to have acquired from a health spa in Albert Road that had gone bust.

Like her daughter, Marie put a lot of thought into what she wore for these sessions. Now in her late forties, she'd managed to keep her figure, and the tan leotard clung to the firm swell of her breasts as she pushed hard against the footplate at the end of the slide. Winter stood beside the open door a moment, wondering why Bazza would ever waste a second with anyone else. Even Misty Gallagher couldn't hold a candle to this woman.

The gym was empty. One entire wall was mirrored and Winter was aware of Marie watching him as he walked across towards her. She slowed on the machine and then stopped completely, her head down, the leotard blotched dark with sweat. It was a second or two before she found the breath to talk. Her face was pinked with effort.

'You want to be careful, my love.' Winter settled on the wooden bench beside her. 'I'd hate you to go pop.'

'You would?' She reached for a towel and mopped her face. As she did so Winter caught the hint of lemons, a fragrance so subtle Bazza would never have noticed.

'I just met the man,' Winter said. 'And I think we've scored a winner.'

He told her about Mo Sturrock. The guy was under professional sentence of death. Sooner or later, once they'd given up trying to nail him on countless other charges, his bosses would be giving him the boot for bringing the organisation into disrepute. Before that happened, it might be in everyone's interests to put the man back to work.

'Disrepute?'

Winter explained about the conference. In the six months that followed, Sturrock had received upwards of a hundred emails, all of them confidential, all of them applauding his impromptu speech.

'Says who?'

'Sturrock.'

'And we believe him?'

'We do.'

'On what basis?'

'Intuition, love.' Winter tapped the side of his nose. 'I might be a fat old bastard but not much gets past, believe me.'

Marie studied him a moment. Winter thought she was fond of him and he wasn't wrong. Very slowly, she began to move herself up and down the slide.

'Great,' she said. 'That makes three of you, then.'

'Three what?'

'Three mavericks. You, Baz and now this other guy.'

'His name's Sturrock.'

'Sturrock.' She nodded. 'And you really think he can hack it?'

'I do, my love. And you know what? We've struck lucky. A word in the right ear and he can start pretty much immediately. All we have to do is talk nicely to his boss.'

'How much does he want?'

'He was on forty-seven K come the finish.'

'How much did you offer?'

'Twenty-five for starters. Plus a performance review after six months.'

'How do we measure performance?'

'Body count. He gets a five-grand bonus for each of the little bastards he kills. Girls count extra.' Winter shot her a grin. 'Do I hear a yes?'

'I'll have to run it past Baz. The way he is at the moment, he won't even listen. I've never seen him like this. Even that bloody woman upstairs can't sort him out.'

Winter ducked his head, aware that Marie was watching him in the mirror again. Marie had never stooped to mentioning Chandelle before. Something must have really got to her, he thought.

'Listen ...' he began. 'What's Bazza not telling us?'

There was a long silence. Then a soft laugh.

'You want a list?'

'I'm talking about the business.'

'I know you are, Paul. I think about it all the time. That and one or two other things. But you're right. I can read him like a book, believe it or not, and he's definitely hiding something, something to do with Esme.'

'Which she might have shared with lover boy?'

'Yes.'

'And which might screw us?'

'Yes. Personally, I think that's unlikely. I probably know Esme better than she knows herself. She can be far too emotional for her own good sometimes, just like her dad, but there's something rock solid inside that no amount of booze or sex can ever reach.'

'Just like her dad?'

'Yeah ... if only.' She shook her head then extended a hand. 'Help me up?'

Winter got to his feet and took her weight. She was tall for a woman, barely a couple of inches shorter than Winter. Lemons, Winter thought again.

'You know where he is at the moment?' Her eyes had a frankness he'd never seen before.

'No idea, my love.'

'Can't even guess?'

'No point.'

'Then I'll tell you.'

'Don't.' Winter's face was inches from hers. Over her shoulder, reflected in the mirrored wall, he had a perfect view of the door. The door had opened. Silhouetted against the harsh neon of the corridor outside was the familiar stocky figure, totally immobile. Mackenzie.

'Fuck me. Not you as well, Marie.' There was a cackle of laughter. He'd obviously been watching them.

Marie's eyes had closed. There was something infinitely secret about her smile and for a split second Winter thought he'd been set up. Then he recognised that this was for real. He turned round. Bazza was picking his way between pieces of gym equipment, his eyes fixed on Winter. At moments of extreme tension the blood seemed to drain from his face. Just now he was the colour of death.

His finger came out, jabbing and jabbing. 'I don't know what you're fucking up to, mush, but don't. You understand that? Not now. Not here. Not ever. You lay a finger on my missus and you'll never walk again.'

'Baz—'

'Don't Baz me. And don't think I'm just blaming you.' He spun round to find Marie stooping to pick up her towel. 'Where the fuck do you think you're going?'

'Home.'

'Not yet, you're not. Not until we've had a little sort-out.' He turned back to Winter. 'You cushty with what I just said, mush? Only it might get fucking messy if you're not. Just say yes or no.'

'Yes, Baz.'

'Good. Something else. Last time we talked like human

fucking beings you said you were going to get hold of a bloke called Faraday. About Madison. *Comprende?*'

'Yes, Baz.'

'And?'

'He's not been around.'

'Well fucking find him, mush. Like now. Like this afternoon. Like tonight. You got that?'

'Yes, Baz.'

'Good. Then fuck off and leave us alone.'

Winter stole a look at Marie. In moods like this Mackenzie could be truly frightening but she seemed perfectly calm, weathering a storm that must have happened countless times before.

She began to say something placatory, oil on troubled waters, but Bazza wasn't having it. As she tried to step over the rowing machine, putting distance between them, he grabbed her upper arm. She froze for a second, then turned on him.

'I'm going to count to three,' she said softly. 'One ... two ...'

Bazza's grip slackened. Free, she began to rub her arm. The flesh was reddening already. Then she took a tiny step forward and slapped Bazza hard across the face.

'That's what you should do to kids who cross the line,' she hissed. 'Just ask Paul.'

As Faraday had anticipated, the Road Death Investigation Team wanted no further involvement with Operation *Melody*. In Steph Callan's judgement their Family Liaison Officer had done her best with Avril Munday and now she was deployed elsewhere. Since the weekend, the team had been involved in two more fatalities and their list of must-do actions was lengthening by the hour.

Faraday toyed briefly about some kind of appeal to Callan's boss but knew she'd probably briefed him already. The turf war was over as far as Munday was concerned and it gave Faraday no pleasure to acknowledge that he'd been woefully off the pace. He could imagine the conversation the next time Steph and her mates found themselves in a bar. Headquarters made me tag along with an old dosser from Major Crime. Grumpy old bugger who couldn't tell his arse from his elbow.

He lifted the phone again and passed the news on to Gail

Parsons. They needed another FLO. She gave him a name he didn't recognise.

'Hannah who?'

'Miles. She's on attachment from Lyndhurst. Country girl. Be gentle, Joe.' Faraday was left with the sound of laughter before the line went dead. He stared at the phone. Parsons seldom laughed.

Hannah Miles appeared at Faraday's door within minutes. She was an elf-like blonde with a smile that warmed him the moment she stepped into the office. She was wearing a nicely cut linen jacket over a sky-blue T-shirt. In a world of deepening shadows, she seemed almost luminous.

'D/I Faraday?'

'Hannah Miles?'

They shook hands. Faraday nudged the door shut with his foot and found her a chair. She said no to coffee. DCI Parsons had given her the impression she was to babysit a junkie on one of the estates. True or false?

'True, I'm afraid.'

Faraday explained the status of Operation *Melody*. Kyle Munday, the prime suspect for the killing of Tim Morrissey, was dead. Staying close to his mother might, in every sense, be a bit of a culture shock. Parsons' cunning plan called for a degree of manipulation. This woman's waking life was governed by heroin. Like every smackhead, she struggled to get by on a couple of fixes a day. Until last weekend she'd probably relied on her son to source the gear. She'd now have to find it from somewhere else. By playing the compassionate FLO, by getting in her face, Hannah could make life extremely difficult for Mrs Munday.

'So what are we after?'

'Intel on who did Tim Morrissey. Our best guess is her son, but Mrs Munday is going to be in the business of denial. To stand that up she's going to put other names in the frame, bound to. It may well be that these other names were complicit. It took half a dozen of them to break Tim's fingers so there's no reason why they weren't around for the stabbing as well.'

'Just names, then? Is that it?'

'No. In the end we're obviously thinking court so we need evidence. We've looked already and we've found nothing but we may have been looking in the wrong places. Realistically, we can put you alongside Mrs M until the funeral. After that it starts looking dodgy.'

'So when's the funeral?'

'I've no idea. Ask D/S Suttle. He's down the corridor.' He sat back, the day's first smile on his face. 'Happy?'

'Always.' She turned towards the door, then paused. 'What's with this culture shock?'

'I understand you're a country girl. Somewhere in the New Forest?'

'Yeah.' She grinned at him, reaching for the door handle. 'But that makes me a natural with animals, doesn't it?'

Faraday was still reflecting on the conversation when his phone went. It took him a couple of seconds to recognise the voice at the other end. Paul Winter.

'What can I do for you?'

He bent to the phone, listening to Winter, trying to sieve something half-sensible from all the bullshit. Tide Turn Trust. Busy days sorting out the city's wayward youth. Blow-your-mind conversations with infant drug dealers. Finally, Winter popped the question. He wanted a meet.

'When?'

'As soon as.'

'Why?'

'I'll tell you later.'

Faraday sat back, glanced at his watch. No cop in his right mind would risk being seen in public with the likes of Winter, but since Gabrielle's departure Friday nights had been especially bleak. The last thing he wanted was an evening tucked up with the Operation *Sangster* file.

'My place,' he said. 'Make it around eight.'

Chapter eleven

Winter took a cab to the Bargemaster's House. Knowing Faraday's affection for decent wine, he'd lingered long enough in Thresher's to take advice on a choice of bottle. A 2003 Rioja, fingers crossed, should do the trick.

The moment Faraday opened the front door, Winter knew he was in with a shout. Something on the stove was laced with garlic. Classical music played in the background. Either Faraday was expecting other company or the pair of them would be settling in for a cosy evening.

Winter stepped into the house, shaking the rain from his jacket. The jacket, in soft Italian leather, had been a Christmas present to him from Marie, the first time Bazza had begun to take any interest in the possibilities of a relationship. Since this afternoon's confrontation in the hotel gym, Winter had heard nothing more. The fact that he'd never touched Marie in his life should have been a comfort, but he knew Bazza had never been much interested in hard facts. If it looks like a dog, he'd often say, it *is* a fucking dog.

Faraday glanced at the wine. He had a bottle already open. 'Côtes-du-Rhône OK?'

'Love it.'

Winter was standing at the big picture window in the lounge. The view across the harbour was pebbled with rain but with the aid of Faraday's binos he could just make out Misty Gallagher's place on Hayling Island. He and Misty had been meeting regularly for some time now, an arrangement largely ignored by Bazza, who'd bought her the waterside house in the first place. His latest passion for the winsome Chandelle had left Misty at a loose end, a situation Winter had gleefully exploited. You could always rely on Bazza jumping to the wrong conclusion, he thought. Not the wife at all, but the ex-mistress.

'Cheers.' Faraday handed him a glass of red.

'Cheers, boss.' Winter raised the glass in salute. 'Where's your lady?'

'Don't ask.'

'Gone?'

'Yep.'

'Bad?'

'Yep.'

In the grey evening light from the window, Faraday looked exhausted, thinner, almost ill. Now Winter knew why. Years ago, when he discovered his wife was dying from cancer, he'd come to this very house on some mad pretext. That night, over the best part of a bottle of Scotch, Faraday had done his best to ease the pain. Maybe now was the time to return the favour.

'You want to talk about it?'

'Not really.'

'Might help.'

'Yeah? You think so?' Faraday sank onto the sofa, reaching for the remote to lower the volume on the audio stack. Music like this, thought Winter, would turn anyone into a depressive.

'Mahler.' Faraday seemed to read his mind. 'Not to everyone's taste.'

'Each to his own, boss. Neil Diamond does it for me.'

'I bet.'

Winter caught an edge in Faraday's voice but the expression on his face seemed benign enough. His glass was already empty. Winter wondered whether this was the first bottle.

'So how's it going then, boss?'

Faraday eyed him for a moment or two, said nothing. Winter put the question again. These days his only connection with the Job was Jimmy Suttle, though even at the level of gossip the young D/S was reluctant to risk a conversation.

'It's crap,' Faraday said at last. 'If you really want to know.'

'Crap how?'

'Crap everywhere. We live in a swamp of our own making. We're going backwards. We're sinking. Maybe this happens with every civilisation. Maybe the Romans got there first. God knows.'

It dawned on Winter that this wasn't about the Job at all.

For reasons he didn't understand, Faraday appeared to have thrown in the towel.

'I'm not with you, boss.' Winter was still on his feet. 'You're telling me we're doomed?'

'I'm telling you it's crap.' Faraday gestured vaguely towards the window. 'All of it.'

From the kitchen came the smell of burning. Winter got there in time to rescue a pan of onions. The air was blue with smoke. He opened a window and flapped around with a tea towel to get rid of the smell. Then he spotted the open bottle of wine and returned to the lounge. Faraday hadn't moved. He watched Winter splashing wine into both their glasses.

'You miss it?'

'What?'

'The Job?'

'Never.'

'I don't believe you. It was in your bones. I watched you. You could be bloody good when you made the effort. Difficult but bloody effective.'

'Difficult as in bent?'

'Difficult as in –' Faraday frowned '– stroppy. Difficult as in devious. You any good with onions? Only we need to start again.'

Winter went back to the kitchen. Faraday had told him where to find the veggie basket. Half a dozen onions nestled amongst a collection of other produce. The new potatoes were still caked with soil. Maybe he grew this stuff himself, Winter thought. Maybe he had an allotment or a veggie patch out in the garden. Another solace. Another refuge.

Winter peeled a couple of onions and then looked for a chopping board, unaware that Faraday had joined him. He was standing in the open doorway, leaning against the jamb, staring glassily in. Winter knew he'd been right. Pissed as a rat.

'Any garlic, boss?' Winter was looking round the kitchen.

'Cupboard above the stove.'

Winter reached up. On the back of the cupboard door was a photo of Faraday sharing a hammock with a slender woman in a red bikini. She had a cap of black hair and a generous mouth. She must have taken the photo herself because Winter could see her thin arm stretching towards the camera lens.

'That's her?' Winter stood aside.

'Yeah.'

'Name?'

'Gabrielle.'

'Lovely.'

'You're right. Too lovely.'

'Impossible, boss. You know something about life? You can never get too much of it. Never. And you're looking at someone who knows. If it feels good, enjoy it. The rest is bollocks.'

Faraday was still gazing at the photo. He appeared to agree. Winter shut the cupboard door and scraped the wreckage in the saucepan into the waste bin. He hadn't come here to cook a meal but under the circumstances he was happy to oblige. He'd never seen any man this lost, this vulnerable.

In the absence of further instructions, he sliced the garlic, raided the fridge for a tube of tomato paste, primed the saucepan with a generous splash of olive oil, and started again. There were herbs in a rack beside the cooker. Salt too. A glance into the lounge told him that Faraday had returned to the sofa. The music, thank Christ, had come to an end.

On the windowsill behind the sink was an ancient radio. Winter helped himself, retuning to BBC Radio Two. *Friday Night Is Music Night.* Perfect.

He found a packet of pasta, a tin of tuna, half a dozen eggs. He filled another saucepan with water and turned the gas up high. Then he had second thoughts, adjusting the flame to a low simmer. Food might return Faraday to sobriety. He didn't want that. Not yet.

'I can't vouch for this, boss, but the woman in the offie swore by it.'

Winter had appeared at Faraday's elbow with the Rioja. The other bottle in the kitchen was empty. Faraday was stretched full length on the sofa, his eyes closed.

'You awake, boss?' Winter gave him a nudge.

'Yeah.'

'Fancy a drop more?'

'Silly question.'

His hand strayed to the carpet, fumbled for the glass. Winter did the honours.

'There's a DCI called Perry Madison,' he said. 'Used to be on Major Crime.'

'Complete arsehole.'

'You're right. Horrible man.'

'Gets up everyone's nose. Ego the size of a planet.'

'Yeah.'

'And?' Faraday's eyes were open now.

Winter perched himself on the arm of the sofa. He wanted to keep this casual, matey, matter-of-fact. He also needed Faraday's total attention.

'He's shagging Bazza's daughter,' he said. 'Big time.'

Faraday blinked, struggled up on one elbow.

'How do you know?'

'She told me. Her name's Esme. She's tucked up with a City banker, nice bloke, Stu. She's got kids, horses, money, the lot, but for whatever reason she's binned all that for Madison.'

'She's walked out?'

'Good as. Stu's up in town most of the time but comes back at weekends. The shit hit the fan on Monday. A tenner says she'll bail out tonight, find somewhere else to go, maybe Bazza's place, maybe Madison's.'

'He's married.'

'I know.'

Winter went back to the kitchen and took both saucepans off the heat. By the time he was back in the lounge Faraday was standing by the window, staring out. His wine glass was still beside the sofa. He hadn't touched it.

'What about Mackenzie?'

'The man's spitting nails. He'd like to fill Madison in but something tells him that wouldn't be clever.'

'He knows Madison's a copper?'

'Of course. I told him.'

'And?'

'He's convinced there's more to it.'

Faraday at last turned round. His balance wasn't perfect but the vagueness in his eyes had gone.

'You're telling me we're trying to fit him up again?'

'I dunno, boss.' He shot Faraday an easy smile. 'What do you think?'

Chapter twelve

Nights when Faraday drank too much, he sometimes left his mobile downstairs. It woke him next morning just before ten. By the time he found it the thing had stopped ringing. Faraday checked caller ID. Jimmy Suttle.

'We've got a problem, boss. Hannah Miles.'

Faraday rubbed his eyes. To his amazement, he felt OK. Suttle had just taken a call from the new FLO. She was in deep shit.

'What's happened?'

'She's at Munday's place up in Paulsgrove. She went round there last night and again this morning, just the way you asked her. Apparently some of the scrote kids arrived. One of them's got Munday's dog.'

'And?'

'She can't get out of the loo.'

Faraday fought the temptation to laugh. 'This is a wind-up, right?'

'No, boss. She's scared shitless. I can hear it in her voice. She went up to use the loo and the moment she tried to get out the dog had a go at her. Her only option was to stay put and lock the door. This is a hostage situation. Or that's what Parsons is calling it.'

'She knows?'

'Yeah. I belled you a couple of minutes ago but there wasn't an answer. I had no choice.'

'So what did she say?'

'She said she's going to sort it. I told her a uniform car would probably do the trick but you know the way she kicks off.'

'So?'

'She's thinking FSU.'

Faraday's heart sank. The Force Support Unit meant full

house entry: shields, stun guns, ninja gear, the works. All because of Munday's dog.

'Get back to her. Tell her we're onto it.'

'It may be too late, boss.'

'Doesn't matter. I'm at home. Pick me up as soon as you can. OK?'

He ended the conversation and headed for the bathroom. Suttle lived less than five minutes away. He filled the handbasin with cold water, doused his face, rinsed his mouth. By the time Suttle appeared in his Impreza Faraday was waiting at the kerbside, enjoying the warm spring sunshine.

'What did she say?'

They were heading north on the main road that skirted Langstone Harbour. Traffic was heavy coming into the city, many of the cars still sporting Pompey scarves from last weekend's Cup final triumph.

'She said she'd spoken to the duty skipper on the FSU. They're getting themselves together. She's going to meet them up there.'

'Terrific.' Faraday foresaw nothing but trouble. He checked his watch. 'Faster, son.'

Avril Munday lived at the back end of Paulsgrove, the scruffy half of a council house that had never been sold. There were curls of dogshit on the pavement outside the property and an abandoned mattress folded against the front wall. Hannah Miles had left her unmarked Fiesta at the kerb. Suttle paused beside it to take a look.

'Someone's trashed it, boss.' He called Faraday back.

Both front tyres had been slashed and the bodywork was dented around the passenger door. Faraday nodded, told him to note the damage, then returned to Avril Munday's house. A broken line of paving stones led around the side of the property, still puddled with water from the overnight rain. Body-checking past a couple of supermarket trolleys, he finally made it to the back garden. A car tyre was suspended on a rope from the rusting frame of a child's swing. The earth was beaten flat beneath the tyre and an empty steel mesh cage lay against the fence. Faraday turned back to the house. The loo window was on the first floor. It was open.

'Hannah?' He heard a noise, someone moving, then the shape of a face appeared behind the ribbed glass. 'Are you OK?'

'Yes.' Her voice was faint.

'Where's the dog?'

'I don't know.'

'You think it's still outside the door? Have you heard it at all?'

'No.'

Faraday hesitated a moment. The kitchen lay at the back of the property. Beside the window was a door. He rapped twice, called Mrs Munday's name, waited for a dog to bark. Nothing happened. He called again then tried the door. It opened. Inside, the smell was overpowering. He thought briefly about Jeanette Morrissey's mother, banged up in her bungalow with an incontinent tabby. Animals, he thought. Who'd ever bother?

A narrow hall led from the kitchen to the front door. He moved carefully, still wondering about the dog.

'Mrs Munday?'

No response. On the right, a door opened into a curtained lounge. In the gloom he could make out a couple of bikes lying against the far wall and a new-looking stroller parked beneath the window. The air, still tainted with dog shit, smelled stale. He pulled the curtains, flooding the room with sunlight. A woman of uncertain age lay on a mattress behind the door. Faraday bent long enough to make sure she was still alive then stepped back into the hall and opened the front door. DCI Parsons had arrived. Still in her Audi at the kerbside, she was talking on her mobile.

Faraday gestured for Suttle to step inside. He nodded in the direction of the lounge.

'Take a look,' he said. 'Give me a name.'

Suttle was back in seconds. 'Avril Munday.'

'Check upstairs, will you? Then sort Miles out. She's still in the loo.'

Outside in the street Faraday waited for Parsons to finish her call. He'd no idea how long it normally took for the FSU to deploy but was glad they'd managed to head the ninjas off. Nothing attracted trouble quicker than the sight of policemen in full riot gear.

'Joe?'

Faraday bent to the Audi and told Parsons that the property was probably secure. The kids appeared to have fled. Along with the dog.

'What about the FLO?'

'She's still in the loo. Suttle should have got her out by now.'

'And Mrs Munday?'

'Blitzed. You want me to call off the FSU?'

'No.' She seemed disappointed. 'I'll do it.'

Faraday returned to the house. He found Suttle and Hannah Miles sitting on the back step, enjoying the sunshine. Miles, if anything, looked sheepish. She'd called for the cavalry. Now this.

'So what happened?'

She did her best to explain. Last night she'd driven up from the city to introduce herself to Avril Munday. The woman had shut the door in her face and only after lengthy negotiations through the letterbox had Hannah been able to talk her way in. The place, as Faraday could see, was a tip. Dog shit and stolen goods everywhere. She'd explained the benefits of having a FLO around, smoothing out Mrs Munday's various traumas, but the woman hadn't been interested. She was expecting visitors. Her life was her own affair. Fuck off.

This morning, first thing, Hannah had tried again. This time, mistaking the FLO for someone else, the door had opened. Inside, Hannah had talked her way into the kitchen. Avril Munday, she said, was a wreck, a bag of nerves, strung out, pacing up and down, scratching herself, checking her watch time and again. Hannah had asked her how she was coping with Kyle's death, and in reply, as voluble as ever, Avril had gone on about arrangements for her son's funeral. His mates, she said, were planning something really special. They wanted to give her boy a proper send-off, bless them, and they were pulling out all the stops. Horse-drawn hearse. Walnut coffin. Black plumes for the gee-gee. Maybe even a bugler from the Boy Scouts to sound the last post outside the crem. It was all getting sorted, all getting arranged. The estate would never have seen nothing like it, never.

'You were still alone?' It was Suttle.

'I was then, yes, but pretty soon a bunch of kids appeared, really rough. One of them had the dog.'

'Munday's dog?'

'I assume so. Black thing. Really vicious. They knew I was Filth from the start because she told them. That's when the trouble started.'

One of the kids, she said, disappeared outside. The others started taking the piss. The dog was on a chain but they kept creeping it closer and closer, pretending it was too strong for them. One of them seemed to be in charge. He'd say something and the dog would lunge at her, teeth bared, mad as you like, while all the time the other kids were winding her up.

'Like how?'

'Like saying how young I was to be Filth, and – you know – how pretty I was, and what a shame if the dog ever got really close. They did all this in the third person as if I wasn't there. To tell you the truth, it was really scary. I don't like dogs at the best of times but this one was totally evil.'

She decided to do a runner. When she tried the back door it was locked.

'No key?'

'No.'

'The front door?'

'That was locked too. Big mortise lock. That's when I went upstairs. There must have been at least half a dozen of them plus the dog. I know it's pathetic but the loo was the only option.'

Faraday nodded. In terms of risk assessment he should have seen this coming. As DCI Parsons would doubtless point out.

Suttle was thinking about the car outside.

'The kid who went out must have done the Fiesta,' he said. 'You remember what he looked like?'

'Yeah. Grey hoodie. Baseball cap. Trackie bottoms. New trainers. Take your pick.'

Faraday eyed her a moment then shook his head. Any one of a million city kids. He nodded at the tyre hanging in the garden then looked at Suttle.

'Munday strung it up for his dog,' Suttle explained. 'The pooch leaps up at it, bites it, then sinks his teeth in. Does wonders for the little bastard's jaw muscles. Think gym.'

'And the cage?'

'That's where the dog lives. The longer you bang it up the madder it becomes.'

'Think jail.'

'Exactly.'

DCI Parsons appeared around the side of the property. The sight of Suttle and Hannah Miles sitting on the doorstep put a frown on her face.

'Debrief, boss,' Faraday announced. 'PTSD.'

PTSD meant post-traumatic stress disorder. Parsons didn't think it was the least bit funny.

'I've just been talking to Mr Willard,' she said. 'Like me, he's taking this incident extremely seriously.'

Faraday could only agree. The problem, he said, was deciding what to do. The kids had been canny. None of them had made any direct threats. Neither would any neighbours have the bottle to make a statement about vehicle damage. A proper search of the property would doubtless yield a tidy pile of stolen goods, and if they were clever they might snare the local smack dealer. But nothing, he said, would really adjust the balance between law and disorder. The fact was that anarchy had got the upper hand. Again.

Parsons looked shocked. She had no time for home truths. She beckoned Faraday around the side of the building and followed him back to the street. Beside the Audi he turned to face her. She nodded back towards the house.

'That was totally inappropriate.'

'What was?'

'What you said just now. In front of junior officers. We're in this to win, Joe. If you don't think that's possible, then maybe you're in the wrong job.' She stared at him a moment then got in the car. Moments later, the window purred down. 'Do we have a date for the funeral?'

'Not yet.'

'Then I suggest we find out. Can you manage that?'

It took Winter less than a minute to coax a decision about Mo Sturrock from Bazza Mackenzie. Badly hungover, or during periods of personal crisis, Mackenzie sought refuge in Giardino's, his favourite Gunwharf café-bar. Winter, summoned by phone, found him nursing a cappuccino in the sunshine.

'Do it,' he said briskly. 'Just give the man a contract. Three months for starters. Then we'll look again.'

'I told him six.'

'Six then. Whatever. But not a penny over twenty-five grand, OK?'

'Sure. And you want Ezzie to draw the thing up?'

'Good question. It's nothing that could hurt us so why not? The little tart's staying the weekend. I was thinking of moving in with you, mush.'

'You're welcome, Baz. I'll tell Mist to pack her bags.'

'Is that some kind of joke?'

'Yeah.'

'Good. What did Faraday say?'

Winter had been expecting the question. He'd left the Barge-master's House close to midnight. Faraday, for reasons no amount of Rioja could explain, had opened up about Operation *Tumbril*. How his little team had been determined to set a trap for Mackenzie. How cleverly they thought they'd prepared the bait. And how, with an arrest team in the wings, they'd watched Pompey's most successful criminal demolish their little fantasy. Mackenzie, he'd admitted, was a class operator. Faraday had no time for greed and no taste for violence. Much of what Mackenzie had been up to over the years had disgusted him. But the fact remained that – when it came to the final curtain – he'd stolen all the applause. It wasn't necessary to respect that. But you did yourself no favours if you didn't admit it.

'He was surprised,' Winter said carefully.

'About Madison?'

'Yeah. He hates the man. They had a run-in a couple of years back. You remember that double killing? The property developer and then the government minister? Faraday was playing a blinder on both jobs before Madison stepped in and tried to steal the glory.'

'So what happened?'

'Faraday screwed him in the end, got a result on both jobs. The thing about Faraday is you never underestimate the man, not if you've got a brain in your head. That's why he can't stand Madison. He thinks the bloke's thick, as well as a cunt.'

Mackenzie was warming to this conversation. Winter could sense it.

'Have I ever met this Faraday?'

'Not to my knowledge.'

'Does he fancy a life outside the Old Bill?'

'I doubt it.'

'Shame. What floats his boat then? Money?'

'Definitely not. He dresses like a dosser, drives a Mondeo that should have been put out of its misery years ago. He's unusual that way. He genuinely doesn't care a toss about any of that consumer bollocks.'

'So how do we get to him?'

'We don't, Baz. I've planted the seed. Now happens to be a good time. He's pissed off with pretty much everything. He'll start having a nose around about Madison, I know he will. And if it suits him to get back in touch then he might do just that.'

'But what happens if he doesn't? What happens if we never hear from him again?'

Winter shrugged. He said he didn't know. Mackenzie wasn't having it.

'You *have* to know, mush. I *need* you to know. I don't give a fuck about all this softly-softly nonsense. Get in there. Give the man a shake. Make it worth his while. Sort fucking Madison out.'

Winter rolled his eyes. Mackenzie in a mood like this was impossible. He sieved every conversation, hearing only what he wanted to hear. Subtle wasn't a proposition he understood.

'Baz, there's something I need too.'

'Yeah? Like what?'

'Like some kind of steer on why we're doing this.'

'I'm not with you, mush. Doing what?'

'Getting so uptight about Madison.'

Mackenzie stared at him. He was outraged. 'You don't think I should? You think that's a bit of a surprise? A copper – Filth – taking liberties with my own daughter? You think that's something I should just keep to myself? Grin and bear it? Send the happy couple a bunch of fucking roses?'

'There's something else. I know there is.'

'Like what?'

'I've no idea. Otherwise I wouldn't ask. There's something else you haven't told me, and unless you do then I'm afraid this whole thing's pointless. You pay me for results, Baz. Why waste good money?'

Mackenzie hated it when conversations took this kind of turn. He lowered himself in the chair, withdrew physically, reached for his coffee, eyed Winter over the edge of the cup. He owed much of his success to keeping his cards close to his chest. Information, after all, was power.

'Say you're right,' he said at last, 'how far would all this go?'

'As far as you wanted, Baz.'

'I don't want it to go anywhere, mush.'

'Then no further than me.'

'Marie?'

'Not unless you said.'

'You mean that? Only you fucking better had.'

'I mean it, Baz. And while we're at it forget whatever fantasies you've had about her and me. I think she's great, Baz. And I think you're the luckiest fanny rat on the planet. That's for the record.'

Mackenzie said nothing. At moments like these he brooded. Finally Winter got a nod.

'OK,' he grunted. 'Let's say I believe you.'

The silence between them stretched and stretched. A woman in a loose cotton dress sauntered past. She was beautiful and she knew it, but for once Mackenzie didn't spare her a second glance. Winter was watching him carefully. Waiting was becoming a chore.

'It's something about Ezzie, isn't it?'

'How do you know?'

'Because she's pressing your buttons. It's not just Madison being a copper. It's what she might have told him.'

'Very clever.' He mimed applause. 'No wonder you potted all those low-life villains.'

'So what is it?'

The head went down again. He took another sip of coffee. Whiskers of milky froth appeared beneath his mouth. Then he shrugged.

'It may be nothing,' he said.

'That's not an answer, Baz. Try me. Trust me.'

'OK.' He frowned. 'You won't believe this but I meant it as a present for Ezzie and Stu. What a fucking joke.'

'Meant what?'

'The project.'

'And does Ezzie know about it? This project?'

'Of course she fucking does. She has to because she's done most of the negotiations. What she doesn't know is that the whole deal will end up in her name.'

At last he put the cup aside and beckoned Winter closer. Last year, he said, he'd been contacted by a mate in Spain. This was a guy who lived out in Galicia on the Atlantic Coast. He had plenty of useful connections and wanted Señor Mackenzie to know about an investment opportunity in a place called Baiona.

'Where's that?'

'Down near the Portuguese border. Bang on the coast. Big with Spanish tourists who know a thing or two. Pretty as you like.'

This guy's brother, he said, had a stake in a big apartment development. The thing was half built already and six of the apartments had been sold off plan, but the consortium in charge had hit rough water and were now looking for an injection of fresh capital.

'And you were interested?'

'Not in a deal like that. Not in a million years. But I went down there with Ezzie to check it out. You might remember.'

Winter nodded. Last year Bazza and his daughter had disappeared in a hurry to Spain. At the time Winter had assumed they'd gone to the Costa del Sol. He'd been wrong.

'So what happened?'

'It turned out the spics had fucked up big time. No one in his right mind would buy into their consortium. They were totally over-leveraged. What had to happen was a fire sale. It took Ez about half a day to sniff that out. She's got real talent, that girl. Sharp as you like.'

Between them, Mackenzie and his daughter had put together a business plan. They knew they had the Spaniards over a barrel. They knew the consortium was facing a banking deadline only weeks away. They could drive the bargain of their dreams. And so it proved.

'You bought the apartments?'

'Yeah. For a song. Then it got a bit more complicated.'

The land for the apartments had once belonged to a local businessman who also owned a hotel in the resort. This too was for sale.

'Cheap?'

'Not especially. He was much cannier than the guys in the consortium. He knew he was sitting on something pretty valuable. You should see the place. The views, the rooms, the potential, every fucking thing. We were staying there. Ezzie fell in love with it.'

'How much did he want?'

'A lot of money. We got him down a bit but it still wasn't cheap.'

'So you decided to spread the risk?'

'Yeah, too right. Like you wouldn't.'

Winter looked away a moment. Bazza had learned a great deal over the past couple of years, and one of the more important lessons had been about risk. No matter how wealthy you might be, always minimise your exposure.

'You cut someone else in on the deal?'

'Yeah.'

'Who?'

'It doesn't matter.'

'How much?'

'A million. Euros, not pounds.'

'And where does this money come from?'

'Toot.' He winced. 'As it turns out.'

Chapter thirteen

Live by the powder, die by the powder. Winter knew the Proceeds of Crime Act backwards. If Mackenzie was ever silly enough to get himself involved with tainted money, and the subsequent case was proved in court, then the authorities could turn up the next day, seize cash and other assets, and start tearing his empire apart. This was the evil bit of legislation that had driven Operation *Tumbril*. This was what top cops dreamed about in the small hours of the night. The prospect of returning Bazza Mackenzie to his Copnor roots was the crock of gold at the end of Willard's rainbow.

Just how serious a threat was Mackenzie facing? Winter knew it was hard to say. Bazza's still-nameless partner had evidently acquired much of his wealth from the cocaine trade. That was no surprise, especially in the kind of social circles Mackenzie still occasionally frequented, but amongst serious players there was always an unspoken assumption that your money was properly laundered. You never came to the party, as Bazza had once observed, without having a good scrub-up first.

In this case, to Bazza's alarm, that hadn't happened. The guy had excellent connections. His reputation as a major wholesaler, importing huge quantities of Colombian cocaine, was second to none. Like Bazza himself, he'd invested wisely, residential property first, then commercial developments. Awash with profits, all of them legit, there'd been no need to keep dabbling in the Dark Side. And yet the sheer size of the mark-up on good-quality toot had been irresistible. Cocaine addiction went way beyond chemistry.

The man, it turned out, was in deep shit. A couple of weeks back, Bazza had taken a call from a Spanish-domiciled Colombian dealer called Riquelme. He lived near Cambados, north of Baiona, and Baz had never had any reason to doubt his word. Riquelme told him that Mackenzie's new partner, who was in and out of Spain every week on narco-business, was being shadowed by English cops. He knew this because one of them had totalled his hire car in a collision with a lorry. The hire car had ended up in a Cambados garage, where a mechanic had discovered a New Scotland Yard expenses form in the glove box. Word had reached Riquelme. With interests of his own to protect, he'd instructed a couple of local guys to sit on the cops and within days he knew the garage mechanic had been right. Bazza's new partner was under investigation. Big time.

This morning, at the café-bar, Winter had done his best to squeeze out more information. Was this bloke home-grown? Was he English? Did he operate out of London? Had Bazza been asking around, making guarded enquiries, trying to suss whether he was as reckless and brain-dead as Riquelme seemed to suggest? To all these questions, Bazza had no answer. Like the rabbit in the onrushing headlights, he seemed paralysed. Bad stuff was happening. And he didn't know what to do.

To Winter the latter realisation was deeply troubling. It meant that Bazza had surrendered more of this project to his daughter than might have been wise. With a thousand other deals on his mind he'd given Ezzie free rein. He had trusted her completely. He knew she was bloody good. But then she'd met Madison and slipped the leash. It was, as Bazza freely admitted, a fucking disaster.

Not necessarily. Back in his apartment Winter stood on the balcony, mobe to his ear, waiting for Ezzie to answer. A couple of dickhead canoeists were out on the harbour, riding the wake from the Gosport ferry, and Winter watched as one of them dug deep with his paddle, executing a neat U-turn. There was still time, he thought, for a word or two with Bazza's daughter. He knew she respected him. He'd suggest a spot of lunch. She might even listen.

Finally her number answered. It was the au pair. Mrs Norcliffe had packed her bags that very morning. A taxi had arrived a couple of hours ago. She'd gone.

'Gone where?'

'I don't know. I have an envelope here. For Mr Norcliffe.'

'Open it.'

'I can't.'

There was a thump in the background then the wail of a child in floods of tears. Winter tried again, telling her to open the envelope, telling her he'd square it with Stu, telling her it was really *really* important, but all he could hear was the child. After a while, knowing it was hopeless, he gave up. Out on the harbour, one of the canoeists had capsized.

Faraday spent the rest of the day on Farlington marshes. There'd been reports of a pectoral sandpiper on a local birding site and a glance at the tide tables told Faraday that late afternoon, with a big spring tide, would give him a decent chance of enjoying this shy little bird.

The marshes lay at the northern end of Langstone Harbour, an hour's walk from the Bargemaster's House. A tongue of land reached deep into the mudflats, accessible from a scruffy car park beside the motorway. The best pickings at this state of the tide were to be found on a small lake at the western side of the bird reserve. Here there was every chance of settling down with black-tailed godwits and with luck the pectoral sandpiper. Further out on the harbour hundreds of waders would be gathered on their island roosts, waiting for the water to fall, but with the exception of the big oystercatchers sheer distance turned solid identification into guesswork.

Faraday found a perch beside the lake and made himself comfortable. He'd brought a Thermos of coffee and sat back, enjoying the warmth of the sunshine. An initial sweep with his binos had already confirmed the godwits in decent numbers, many of them dousing themselves in the lake's fresh water to rid themselves of salt.

He steadied the binos for a more methodical search. The pectoral sandpiper was a vagrant from North America. It normally appeared in late summer and Faraday loved its cape of mottled brown and the way it stalked amongst the tangles of seaweed, alert, erect, like a patrolling dowager cursed to be in less elevated company. Quite what it might be doing here in May was anybody's guess but global warming was starting to play havoc with migration patterns and the big frontal troughs across the Atlantic were depositing all kind of surprises on European shores.

After a while, disappointed by the absence of the sandpiper, he put the binos to one side, lay back and closed his eyes. This expedition had offered the possibility of an escape from all the nonsense up in Paulsgrove but the memory of the brief kerbside head-to-head with Gail Parsons was still with him. He'd long begun to suspect that the battle to preserve law and order was – to use Winter's mocking word – doomed. Society had changed. The glue that stuck everything together was disintegrating. It was commonplace now to keep your head down, your fingers crossed, and ignore the mounting evidence that life was getting nastier. All that was true, and Munday's tyro psychopaths were the living evidence, but Parsons was right to demand that Faraday kept his pessimism to himself. It was one thing to find your FLO entombed in a Paulsgrove lavatory by a bunch of predatory kids, quite another to assure her that things could only get worse.

He stifled a yawn, his eyes still closed, letting his mind drift back to last night. Winter, in some strange instinctive way, must have seen this coming. With his matey smile and his devious little ways he'd spent twenty years carving a path of his own through all the procedural bullshit. The sheer number of scalps hanging from his belt, some of them much-prized, had kept the Professional Standards Department at arm's length for most of the time, but in the end even Winter had been forced to raise his hands and call it a day. Why? Because the Job had changed as much as the society it served.

Gone were the evenings when the Fratton bar would fill with a CID squad celebrating a trophy result. Gone were the wild nights on the piss. Faraday himself had no time for the cruder excesses of the canteen culture but even he missed the camaraderie that went with it. These days you watched your back, had salad for lunch, drank sensibly and got home in time to put the kids to bed. Not Winter's style at all.

He struggled upright and reached for the binos again, wondering where Perry Madison fitted into the squeaky-clean world of modern policing. Faraday had never liked him, never got on. He was brisk to the point of abruptness and took a savage pleasure in belittling subordinates. He'd never bothered to hide his burning ambition and had stepped over a number of bodies on his way up the promotional ladder. Madison wasn't bright enough to get any further than DCI but what had always struck Faraday was his recklessness. At life's table, the man had always been a gambler. He played for high stakes and took it hard when he lost. Was Mackenzie's daughter his latest throw of the dice? Or might Winter have a point in suspecting a darker agenda?

Faraday took a last sweep across the lake, searching in vain for the sandpiper, knowing that the answer was probably beyond him. Then he got to his feet, bending to retrieve a half-crushed can of Stella before turning for a last long look at the harbour. A low mist had hung over the water all day, impervious to the sun, and in the far distance, for a split second, he thought he made out the shape of a sailing barge. Bringing the binos to his eyes, he racked the focus in a bid to resolve the image but it disappeared into the greyness like a phantom. Something snagged in his mind, something recent, and he was still trying to resolve the thought when his mobile rang.

It was Jimmy Suttle. More drama. Faraday checked his watch. Gone six.

'What's happened?'

'There's a Chinese restaurant in Paulsgrove. Something horrible kicked off about half an hour ago. Uniforms have got the place secured. I think it's Munday's lot again. I'm on my way up there now, boss.'

Faraday told him to detour via Farlington marshes. He'd be waiting in the car park. Suttle gone, Faraday looked seawards again. He'd got it now. The sailing barge was a throwback, a ghost. It had slipped in from the nineteenth century, en route to Pompey dockyard, and now – after a taste of the shiny new millennium – it had simply vanished. He paused, treasuring this private moment. Gabrielle, he thought. Her kind of fantasy.

In Paulsgrove, the entire parade of shops had been sealed off. Mums with buggies and clusters of kids stood behind the flapping lines of blue and white tape while paramedics hurried between the restaurant and the line of waiting ambulances at the kerbside. Faraday, stepping out of Suttle's Impreza, counted three uniform cars. The white Transit from the Force Support Unit was parked round the corner.

DCI Parsons was locked in conversation with a uniformed

inspector. Faraday was beginning to wonder whether she ever left the estate. Maybe she lived here now, kept her ear to the ground, patrolled the streets at night.

Suttle intercepted a uniformed sergeant whom he evidently knew. His name was Dave Kenyon. He threw Faraday a nod.

'A bunch of kids turned up around five,' he told Suttle. 'It seems they were after money for some funeral or other. They went to every shop along here but it was the Chinese who really stuck it to them.'

The boss, he said, had been behind the till sorting out a cash float for the night. When the kids walked in and demanded fifty quid he told them to get lost. One of the kids set a dog on him. A guy from the kitchen waded in with a meat cleaver and took the dog's head off. At that point, it started getting serious.

'How serious?' It was Faraday.

'There were two more guys in the kitchen. They both had knives. The kids waded in, the way you do, and three of them got stabbed. One of them's dead, another's looking extremely dodgy.'

'And the Chinese?'

'The kids had knives of their own. One of the Chinese got stabbed in the throat but they seem to think he'll live. Another one took a blade in the arse but he's still standing.'

'Any customers?'

'Half a dozen, max. They do a half-price offer before seven. The ones who couldn't get out ended up standing on the tables.'

The sergeant broke off, beckoned by his inspector. Parsons joined Faraday.

'We should have got a grip of this,' she said at once.

'I'm not with you.'

'I understand the FLO warned you about the funeral arrangements, what they were planning, the sheer bloody scale of the thing. We should have anticipated something like this, we should have thought it through.'

'You mean I should have thought it through.'

'Yes.'

It was a direct challenge. Later, they'd doubtless have a longer conversation. In the meantime, Faraday was to organise retrieval of the CCTV footage.

'It exists?'

'It does, Joe. Thank Christ one of us still has some kind of interest.'

Access to the restaurant was limited to the paramedics. A couple of the kids and one of the Chinese were still receiving attention inside. Parsons handed Faraday a number.

'What's this?'

'That's the guy who runs the place. Don't ask me his name. He's probably up at the hospital by now but he'll know how to access the CCTV.'

She was right. Mr Hua was in a cubicle at A & E having wounds in his thigh stitched up. The dog had taken a chunk out of his lower leg as well. Faraday asked him about the CCTV.

'In my office,' he said. 'You want the recording?'

'Yes please.'

'Machine behind the door. Take it, my friend.'

Suttle was at the kerbside, talking to an investigator from Scenes of Crime. Another CSI was en route, plus a Crime Scene Co-ordinator. According to one of the attending uniforms, the interior of the restaurant was a mess.

'Real DNA-fest.' He was struggling into a one-piece forensic suit. 'Blood everywhere.'

Faraday explained about the CCTV footage. It was by no means certain that all the kids were in custody. A couple may have legged it.

'Not the dog, though, eh?' Mr Cheerful zipped up the suit and left to sort out the CCTV.

Faraday rejoined Suttle. Parsons was back in her Audi, shouting at her mobile. Willard, Faraday thought. Poor bastard.

Suttle wanted to know how Faraday was going to play this.

'Are we still talking *Melody,* boss? Or *Highfield*? Or what?'

It was a good question. Did a couple of homicides and a riot qualify for a new operational code name? Or was this an extension of Tim Morrissey's death? And of Munday's?

'Ask Parsons,' Faraday told him. 'I'll organise the troops.'

Faraday got a lift with a uniform back to Fratton. A procedure existed for moments like these. He rang the on-call D/I, briefly described what had happened, and then found himself a DVD player. The first trawl through the CCTV footage was normally an intel responsibility but Suttle was still in Paulsgrove and Faraday needed a fix on exactly what had happened.

According to the time printout, the kids entered the restaurant at 17.13. The resolution on the pictures was excellent and Faraday recognised the faces from the *Melody* file. Casey Milligan. Jason Dominey. Ross McMurdo. A girl was with them too, and the moment she turned round he knew it was Roxanne Claridge. The same determination to share her chest with anyone who might be looking. The same instinct to find the only mirror in the room. Dominey had Munday's pit bull.

The camera was positioned high up behind the serving counter. In the foreground the restaurant's owner was shaking bags of change into the till. He looked up as the kids came in. The thin scatter of diners did likewise. Dominey approached the counter. At sixteen he'd perfected the rolling Pompey swagger, hands dug into the pockets of his shell suit. He had a hoodie pulled forward over his baseball cap and his face was in shadow. There was no soundtrack with the pictures but it didn't take much to imagine the dialogue.

Awright, mush? We needs some money off yer.

The Chinese shook his head. He must have said something forceful because another of the kids pushed forward, alongside Dominey, and reached for the man's throat. The Chinese stepped back and Faraday saw his right hand find the panic button. Dominey had rounded the counter by now and Faraday got his first proper look at the dog. All those nights caged up in Munday's garden had worked a treat. He couldn't wait to get stuck in.

Dominey must have demanded money again. The cash register was still open. Faraday watched the Chinese shake his head and push the drawer shut. Dominey bent to the dog and let it off the chain. The dog hurled itself at the Chinese, who did his best to fight it off. Faraday slowed the action. Had the dog jumped any higher the Chinese would have been in real trouble but as it was the damage was bad enough. Clamped to the man's thigh, its legs flailing, the pit bull shook its massive head left and right, tearing at the flesh. Blood began to pump through tears in the cloth of the trousers while the kids looked on, laughing.

Then, from nowhere, a thin figure in a pair of blue track

bottoms appeared. He was a Chinese from the kitchen. Naked above the waist, he was holding a meat cleaver. He pulled hard on the dog's back legs before bringing the cleaver down across the back of the animal's neck. It was a beautiful blow, perfectly judged, and the sharpness of the glittering blade neatly severed the pit bull's head from its body. Nobody moved. Not even the owner. Then one of the other kids, Casey Milligan, pulled a knife and lunged at the half-naked Chinese across the counter.

By now, a couple of the diners were making for the door to the street but they were too late. Another Chinese had decided to surprise the kids. He must have raced round from the rear entrance. He pushed in through the front door, locked it, and plunged into the melee around the counter. Faraday saw his arm rising and falling. He had a long kitchen knife and knew exactly how to use it. A couple of the diners, unaware that the dog was no longer a threat, had climbed onto their tables.

Faraday paused the action. He'd lost track of the developing pattern of the fight. Yet another Chinese had emerged from the kitchen. He too was armed with a knife, holding the kids at bay while he helped his limping boss to safety. His face, frozen on the screen, told its own story. Hatred, Faraday thought. Salted with an implacable desire for revenge.

His finger found the Play button and the carnage resumed. Dominey was lying behind the counter, blood pouring from a wound in his chest. McMurdo was on his knees, begging for mercy. Only Casey Milligan and the girl Roxanne were left standing. Milligan, braver than the rest, tried to go to McMurdo's aid, slashing at thin air with what looked like a sheath knife, big showy widescreen moves. The bare-chested Chinese let him come, chose his moment, then drove the cleaver deep into his face. Milligan's mouth dropped open. He doubt-less screamed. Then he fell, clutching the gaping wound in his cheek, his hand scarlet with his own blood. The Chinese struck again, taking him in the throat this time before stepping back and eyeballing the girl.

The fight was over. Faraday, in a moment that would stay with him forever, stopped the action a second time, knowing he was glad. Not that the violence was over. But because people, at last, were taking a stand. A week ago Jeanette Morrissey had killed Kyle Munday. Now this.

Chapter fourteen

It was early evening before Winter got through to Mackenzie. His mobile had been on divert for hours. Now Bazza picked up on his landline.

'Been out with Marie, mush. Spot of shopping.'

'Somewhere nice, I hope.'

'Salisbury. She loves it there. Can't get enough of the place. You know what? Give her half a chance and we'd start looking for a house.'

He sounded relaxed and cheerful, the spat in the gym forgotten. They'd probably toured the shops together, had a cosy lunch, buried their differences with a decent bottle of wine. Winter was about to change all that.

'Ezzie's disappeared,' he said. 'She packed her bags this morning.'

'You're fucking joking.'

There was a *clunk* as Mackenzie dropped the phone. Winter heard the slam of a door in the background. Then he was back again.

'Where's she gone?'

'No one knows.'

'You've talked to Stu?'

'Yeah. She left him a note. Said she'd be back next week sometime. She put a kiss at the bottom. He couldn't work out whether she was taking the piss or not.'

'A kiss? What the fuck does that mean?'

'That's exactly what he said. I told him she's probably having second thoughts.'

'About?'

'Lover boy. I told you it wouldn't last, Baz. All you have to do is listen.'

Mackenzie grunted. Irony, Winter knew, was a waste of breath.

'Listen, mush. You at home? Give me five minutes, yeah?' He hung up.

Winter waited. Outside, beyond the harbour, he could make out the beginnings of a glorious sunset. Moments later, the phone rang. Baz seemed to have forgotten about Salisbury.

'Get over here, mush. We've got a huge fucking problem.'

By the time DCI Gail Parsons got back to the Major Crime Department, Jason Dominey had died. Faraday had taken the call from Jimmy Suttle. He put his head round Parsons' office door and gave her the news. She was crouched over her desk, intent on her PC screen, exactly the way she sometimes drove the Audi.

'How many's that then, Joe?'

'Two. Casey Milligan died in the restaurant. Dominey made it as far as the QA.' The Queen Alexandra was the city's biggest hospital.

'What about the rest of them?'

'McMurdo's got stab wounds to his shoulder and arm. Mr Hua's still at A & E with the Chinese who got it in the arse and they're operating on the other guy. It's a throat wound but they don't think it's life-threatening.'

'And the girl?'

'Unmarked. Apparently her mum's already talking to the *News of the World*.'

'Brilliant. That's all we need.'

Parsons pushed her chair back from the desk. Word about the Blue Dragon had spread across the city. Radio and TV were using the word 'massacre'. Parsons was still awaiting confirmation but she understood that a couple of other Chinese restaurants in the city had already received death threats.

'This is a disaster, Joe. Normally I'd be talking damage limitation but I suspect it's a bit late for that. We need a coping policy. Fast.'

Faraday nodded. These situations always called for a fall guy and he had absolutely no doubt who that was going to be. He could see it in her eyes, in the way she was almost measuring him for the drop. This year's buzzword was Community

Policing and a double killing with this kind of exposure would do nothing for the feel-good factor. Parsons was right. They were looking at a disaster.

Faraday studied her a moment.

'I'm a copper, boss. Four kids go into a restaurant. They're known to us. They have previous. They demand money with menaces. The owner has a perfect right to say no. They set the dog on him. The thing kicks off.'

'Is that some kind of defence?'

'Only if you think I've got a case to answer.'

She returned his look but denied him the satisfaction of a reply. Instead, she nodded at her phone.

'Mr Willard was on just now. He wants to know we're on top of this thing.'

She meant the investigation. Faraday ran through the steps the duty D/I had already taken. A D/C had arrested McMurdo and Claridge at the hospital on suspicion of blackmail. Their clothing had been seized for forensic analysis and they'd both be swabbed for DNA and subjected to a full medical examination. Another D/C was waiting for an interpreter at the hospital before taking statements from the Chinese. A couple of FLOs, meanwhile, had been dispatched to deliver the death message to the parents of the slain teenagers.

Later, while Scenes of Crime sorted out the carnage in the restaurant, a smallish squad would do house-to-house calls to plot the kids' movements. Other shopkeepers along the parade had already come forward, volunteering statements. These same kids, they said, had tried it on with them as well, demanding money, saying it was a contribution to a worthy cause, trying to pretend they had a duty to honour one of Paulsgrove's finest.

Even Parsons laughed. 'They actually *said* that? Kyle Munday? Paulgrove's *finest*?'

'According to Suttle, yes.'

'That's bizarre.'

'Exactly, boss. And that's my point. This whole thing's bizarre. It's a no-brainer. The kids were in the wrong.'

'You're telling me they stabbed themselves?'

'Of course not. The Chinese went way over the top. No one's defending what they did, but under the circumstances you can see why it happened. And so will a jury. A couple of years for manslaughter, max.'

Parsons shook her head. Faraday thought he detected a hint of pity in her eyes, as well as impatience.

'You don't get it do you, Joe?'

'Get what, boss?'

'This whole thing. The Blue Dragon. The death threats. The girl's mother talking to the press. We're into something else now. We're into pressure groups, politics, media coverage. I can name you dozens of people in the city that are going to make a real meal of this. They're going to tell us that things are out of control. They're going to be using words like chaos and anarchy, and you know who's going to carry the can for all that? Us. They're going to say we've lost our grip. They're going to tell us we've sold them short. We live in a democracy, God help us. He who shouts loudest wins. It's perception that counts, Joe. As Mr Willard has already pointed out.'

He who shouts loudest wins. Faraday, for once, was impressed.

'Maybe they're right,' he said softly.

'About what?'

'About the anarchy and the chaos. It's not the big things. It's not the Blue Dragon. It's everything else.'

'Low-level social disorder? Kids mouthing off in the street?' She dismissed him with a shake of her head. 'That's ASBO territory. People accept that now. It's mood music. It's what you put up with.'

'Sure. And it leads to this.'

'Wrong. It leads to lots of people, decent people, getting into a state about the way times have changed. We can do nothing about that, Joe. Absolutely nothing. No one breaks the law by leaving school without a clue about anything. No one comes to our attention because they're foul-mouthed yobs who wouldn't know a waste-paper bin from a hole in the road. No one goes to court because they push past old people in the bus queue. That's just the way things are. But tonight was different, Joe. Tonight upped the ante. And you don't need me to tell that there will be consequences.' She raised her hands, a gesture that was both a warning and an apology.

Faraday fought to contain his temper. Seldom had he felt so angry.

'You mentioned a coping policy,' he said carefully.

'That's right. It's Mr Willard's phrase, not mine. He's driving down from London.' She offered Faraday a cold smile. 'I'm afraid you'll need to make yourself available.'

Marie answered the door to Winter's knock. Bazza, she said, was in his den. Apart from a demand for a bottle of Scotch, she'd heard nothing from him all evening. Bad sign.

'He told you about Ezzie?'

'Yes.'

'And?'

'I think the kiss is interesting.'

Winter knew the way to the den. Mackenzie was sitting in his favourite recliner, watching last weekend's Cup Final. Thousands of copies of the souvenir DVD had been snapped up across the city. Pompey's moment in the Wembley sun.

'Good for the blood pressure, mush.' He nodded at the screen. 'There's Black Label on the side there.'

Winter helped himself. He tried to avoid alcohol at moments like these but knew that Bazza wouldn't have it. Sharing the secret of the Baiona project was a big step for a man who trusted nobody. The least he owed him was a drink.

'Cheers, Baz.' Winter made himself comfortable in the other chair. Sylvain Distin had just scythed down a Cardiff attacker. In due course, when it suited him, Mackenzie would raise the issue of business. Until then, Winter's sole responsibility was to wait.

It came sooner than he'd expected. David James was flat on his arse in the Pompey goal.

'Just after we talked, mush, I went through the paperwork.'

'On the project?'

'Yeah. There's a whole bunch of stuff but the key to it all is the contract. That's the one Ez drafted herself. It went through umpteen fucking versions but we ended up with pretty much what we wanted.'

'Is it signed?'

'No, but that's not the point. It's gone, mush. She must have lifted it.'

'Doesn't she have a copy herself?'

'No. I insisted everything was kept here.' He nodded at the safe in the corner of the room. 'But she knows the combination so she could help herself any time. Marie says she was over yesterday. They had a little chat. She must have nicked it then.'

'Why?'

'You tell me. She's got power of signature. Worst case, she's trying to close the deal.'

He glanced across at Winter and nodded. A third of a bottle of Scotch couldn't disguise the anxiety in his eyes. Mackenzie seldom panicked. You didn't build a twenty-million-pound business by being a wuss. But now was different.

Winter was trying to compute the possibilities.

'Who else needs to sign?'

'The hotel owner and our new friend. Plus witnesses, lawyers, all the usual shit.'

'So where are they?'

'Good question. I've belled our friend twice this evening. No answer from his mobe or his landline. The owner is a spic. He lives in Vigo. Half an hour ago his wife said he was having dinner in town with a couple of buddies.'

'Might your new friend be down there with him?'

'In Spain, you mean?'

'Yeah.'

'Sure. It's possible.'

'And Ezzie?'

'You're right. She might be there too. Fuck, she might be one of them. Little get-together. Little ceremony. Couple of bottles of bubbly. Contracts on the table. Pens at the ready. Just sign on the dotted line. Done.' He closed his eyes and shook his head. 'Shit ...'

There was a long silence, broken by a roar from the Wembley crowd. Kanu had just slipped the ball into the Cardiff net. Mackenzie watched the Pompey fans erupt, fields of blue shirts swept by the sweet anticipation of victory. Then he turned to Winter again. 'That would be enough, wouldn't it? That's all they'd need? Her name on the contract?'

'Yeah. Ezzie's a co-director of the company. She's assisting your new friend to retain his benefit from criminal conduct. She's supposed to have checked out where that money came from. So should you. The money's dirty, Baz. Under the money-laundering laws, you're wide open to prosecution.'

'And then what? Assuming they got a result in court?'

'They come looking. You're connected with a criminal life-style offence. They crawl all over you. If the court convicts, then every penny, every brick, is dodgy and it's down to you to prove it's not. Even if you're acquitted, or the CPS bottle out on a prosecution, SOCA can still have you through civil recovery proceedings.'

'*Everything?* The whole fucking caboodle?'

'The lot.'

'That could *all* go?'

'Yeah.'

Mackenzie returned his attention to the screen but Winter wasn't fooled for a second. It was moments like these that he missed the reach he'd had in the Job. The ability to lift a phone and initiate checks on the airlines. The chance to put together a target's movements before they even arrived at their destination. Then a thought occurred to him.

'Ezzie went this afternoon?'

'Yeah.'

'How did she get to the airport?'

Mackenzie stared at him a moment, then blinked. 'She'd have called a cab. She'd have used Speedy. Bound to have done. How fucking thick am I?'

Speedy was a Pompey cab company, the much-loved child of a 6.57 stalwart called Grant Percy. Since Christmas it had belonged to Mackenzie.

He reached for the phone. The dispatcher worked from premises above a chemist in Fratton. Mackenzie recognised her voice.

'Cheryl? Baz. You got today's fares handy?' He waited for her to access the tally of bookings, his eyes still glued to the Cup Final. It took her several minutes to find Esme's name. Then she was back on the line.

'Where, love?' He was frowning. 'OK ... cheers.'

He put the phone down then let his head sink back against the softness of the leather squab. Winter knew already that it was bad news.

'Heathrow?' he suggested.

'Gatwick, mush. The driver's name is Gerri Madeley. 33a Wallace Road. Get round there. See what Ez had to say for herself.'

Willard was in the worst of moods. He'd been en route to a private dinner in Kingston upon Thames when Gail Parsons phoned him with the news from Paulsgrove. At first he'd driven on, telling her to keep him briefed. Only when he tuned to BBC Five Live and picked up the breaking news reports did he stop the car and turn round.

Now, he stepped into Faraday's office and shut the door. At the weekend the Major Crime Department was virtually empty. Normally, Willard seized control of every meeting he attended, laying down an agenda, flagging a path forward. This occasion was evidently different.

'So where do we go from here, Joe?'

'We sort it, sir.'

Faraday had just had an update from Jimmy Suttle. Both the Chinese who'd gone to the rescue of their boss had been arrested at the hospital on suspicion of murder. One of them had refused to give a name and it was thought that he was probably an illegal. The other one, a relative of the owner, had been in the country for a number of years. Ample evidence existed in the shape of the CCTV, and in statements taken from the terrified diners who'd witnessed the whole thing. Operation *Adelaide*, as it was now known, would barely make the status of a three-day event. The Chinese would be up before the magistrates on Monday morning. Remanded after that.

'What about the kids?'

'We're charging both of them for blackmail. There's no soundtrack on the CCTV but the owner's claiming they demanded a couple of hundred quid and the pictures would tend to support that.'

'Witnesses?'

'The woman who was nearest definitely heard Dominey demand money. She's not prepared to say how much. She says the kid's voice was muffled.'

'What about threats to kill?'

'She heard Milligan say, "I'll have yer." That's as far as she's prepared to go.'

'And the owner?'

'He's saying they all wanted to kill him.'

'I'm not surprised. DCI Parsons just showed me the CCTV tape. What have we done, Joe? How did we ever get here?'

The question took Faraday by surprise. At the very least, he'd been expecting a major bollocking for not keeping tabs on Munday's funeral arrangements. Instead Willard seemed to be voicing a little of Faraday's own despair.

'I've no idea, sir. And if I had I'm not sure anyone would listen.'

'I think you're wrong, Joe. I suspect it's time we faced up to some home truths. We see more of this stuff than most people because that's our job. But when it really kicks off, like this evening, we need to be on the front foot when the shit hits the fan. This isn't just our problem, it's everyone's. We have to be forceful. We have to make people acknowledge that we've pretty much lost it.'

Faraday nodded. Willard, he knew, was rehearsing his line for all the media interviews to come. He'd done something similar only last year, in the immediate aftermath of a Craneswater party that had got totally out of hand. That occasion had also produced a double murder – two more young lives – and Willard had derived a grim satisfaction from the press and TV coverage that followed. For a couple of days he'd found himself quoted in both the broadsheets and on *Newsnight*. The thin blue line, he'd warned, was no insurance against the simmering violence that threatened to boil over. And here, all too sadly, was the evidence.

Willard hadn't finished. DCI Parsons had suggested that the on-call D/I should take over Operation *Adelaide* as Deputy Senior Investigating Officer under her own overall leadership. In view of the sheer number of crime scenes, plus the possibility of retribution offences over the coming days, the investigation needed careful supervision, but the persons responsible were either under guard in hospital or already in custody at the Bridewell. And so the immediate challenge lay in strategising a response to the inevitable public reaction.

'We're going to get shat on, Joe. I could give you a list of names at headquarters who've been praying for an opportunity like this. And that's just people on our own side. Factor in all those other bastards just itching to shaft us and you can sense what's coming our way. The loonies and the green ink brigade will be frothing at the mouth. The cleverer ones, the ones who can read, will say we're too reactive. They may have a point. We weren't on our toes in Paulsgrove, Joe, and we should have been. We need to be watching the forward radar. What we don't need are surprises like this.'

Faraday nodded. The word 'reactive' had struck a chord with him. 'Reactive' meant letting events take control. 'Reactive' meant surrendering the initiative.

'You think we should be in charge?'

'I know we should be in charge.'

'Scoping situations out? Anticipating developments? Making our own luck?'

'Precisely. Intel-led policing. Never fails.'

'What about *Tumbril*?'

There was a long silence. Willard was staring at him. Faraday knew he'd scored a direct hit.

'*Tumbril*?' Willard said at last.

'Yes.'

'Why *Tumbril*?'

'Because the thing was intel-led. And it failed.'

'But that was different, Joe. *Tumbril* got us screwed, I admit it. But the last thing I anticipated was getting shafted by one of our own.'

Faraday said nothing. The plot to bring down Bazza Mackenzie had crashed and burned because a disaffected officer had blown it. Willard had recovered his poise. He was back in charge. He was looking impatient, wanting to know what relevance any of this had. They were here to discuss a murderous affray in a Paulsgrove Chinky, not a long-term covert operation against the city's top face.

Faraday took his time. He wasn't at all sure where this conversation would go next but he was determined to find out.

'Perry Madison is shagging Mackenzie's daughter,' he said slowly. 'Mackenzie thinks it's *Tumbril* all over again.'

Willard showed no sign of surprise. For a long moment he said nothing. Only his eyes gave him away.

'How do you know?'

'Winter told me.'

'*Winter?*'

'Yes.'

'You've spoken to him about this?'

'Yes.'

'Do you speak to him often, as a matter of interest?'

'Very rarely.'

'But it happens?'

'Obviously.'

'On what terms?'

'Strictly social. We're friends … of a kind.'

'Do you think that's wise? Given the company he now keeps?'

'Of course not. But he was a copper for twenty years and we worked together from time to time, and nothing's going to change that. We compare notes occasionally, have a few drinks. I know Winter well. Nothing he does ever happens by accident. We only meet because he wants something.'

'And now he's telling you that Mackenzie's daughter is over the side with Madison? Is that it?'

'Yes. And like I just said, he thinks there may be another agenda.'

'So why tell me, Joe?'

'Because he may be right. And if he *is* right then you might spare yourself a great deal of grief. Again.'

Willard nodded. Then he stood up and checked his watch. At the door he paused and turned round.

'This conversation never happened, Joe. You understand that?'

Gerri Madeley was on the point of going to bed when Winter knocked at her door. He'd phoned a couple of minutes ago as the cab left Mackenzie's Craneswater house. They'd never met but Marie had marked his card. Like her daughter, she often asked the dispatcher for Gerri by name. 'She's been through the mill a bit,' she'd told Winter. 'But she's got a heart of gold.'

No one had warned him about the scar. It ran down the side of her face, a livid slash that puckered the flesh and seemed to staple the corner of her mouth shut. Try as he did, Winter couldn't take his eyes off it.

She invited him into the downstairs flat. She was wearing a

dressing gown that was several sizes too big and a pair of fluffy pink slippers.

'I won't keep you, love. It's about Esme Norcliffe. You took her to Gatwick this morning, am I right?'

'Yeah.'

'And you know her well?'

'I drives for her, yeah.'

'Any idea where she was going?'

'Who wants to know?'

'Her dad.'

'Mr M?'

'Yeah.'

'He's a mate of yours?'

'I work for him.'

'Prove it. You look like the Old Bill to me.'

Winter laughed. Driving cabs all day certainly wised you up. He produced his mobile and called Bazza's number. When he answered Winter gave her the mobe. She had a brief conversation, eyed Winter, nodded, and then returned the phone.

'Ez was going to Spain,' she said.

'Any idea where?'

'Same place as last time. When Mr M went too.'

'Vigo?'

'That's it. She really likes it down there. Told me how different it is – you know, not full of bloody English. That's why she's learning Spanish.'

'Since when?' This was news to Winter.

'Since Christmas. Her old man bought her one of them quick-learning courses. She tried bits out on me this morning. Sounded all right like. *Viva España*. All that crap.' She threw back her head and laughed. 'You would though, wouldn't you?'

'What?'

'Learn the bloody language. If you were going to live out there.'

Minutes later, back in his car, Winter passed the news to Mackenzie.

'*Live* out there? Who says?'

'She did – Ez – this morning. She told Gerri she was going to move out there, make a new start. She said she was doing it for her kids. She thinks this country's gone down the khazi. No way does she want to bring them up here.'

'So where does Stu figure in all this?'

'She didn't say. Gerri knows Stu. She thinks he's lovely.'

'And Madison?'

'She'd never heard of him. Ez never said a word about any of that.'

There was a long silence. Then Mackenzie was back. He said he'd been on the Internet, checking flights. He wanted Winter at Heathrow by half past eight next morning to get the ten o'clock departure for Madrid. A domestic connection would take him to Vigo.

'Hire a car at the airport or take a cab. Baiona's just down the coast. I've booked you into the hotel. It's called the Fonda Perla de Cuba. You got that?'

Winter was trying to find something to write on. Mackenzie went through it again.

'The guy's name is Casimiro Fresnada,' he added. 'Proper old school, charming as you like. Watch him like a fucking hawk.'

'Which guy's this?' Winter was lost.

'The guy who owns the hotel.'

'The Perla de whatever?'

'Yeah. Pound to a penny, that's where Ezzie's gone. To get this thing signed she needs Fresnada and the other guy.'

'Your new partner?'

'*Our* new partner.'

'He's got a name? Only that might be really useful.'

Another silence, even longer.

'Garfield,' he said at last. 'Al Garfield. Fat little guy. He's got a squint. You can't miss him. When you get down there, mush, just head Ezzie off.'

'How?'

'Tell her not to sign anything. Tell her from me. If she kicks up, give her a cuddle, give her a slapping, any fucking thing. Just make sure her signature gets nowhere near that contract, OK?'

Something was bothering Winter. He sat back in the Lexus, eyeing a couple of students weaving their way down the street towards him. One swung a foot at a can on the pavement and missed.

'Why don't *you* go, Baz? You know these guys. You understand the deal. And she's your bloody daughter, after all.'

'No can do, mush. I'm in London first thing Monday morning. Big meet at the Dorchester. Raghead from Dubai. There's no way I can stand him up. Just get down there and tell bloody Ez to behave herself for once. I'll owe you big time.'

'What about Mo Sturrock?'

'Who?'

'The Tide Turn guy I want to bring on board. You said yes when we met this morning. Just tell me you meant it.'

'Of course I meant it. Marie's been in touch with him already. They're having a meet tomorrow. Tide Turn's history, mush, as far as you're concerned. You're OK with that? Happy now, my friend?'

Winter watched the students roll past the car. The downstairs lights in Gerri Madeley's flat were out.

'That cab driver I just met, Baz. What happened to her face?'

'She came off a motorbike, mush, a couple of years back. Bloke in a van hit her from the side. You know what they say? You never see it coming until it's too late.' Mackenzie barked with laughter. 'Let's hope they're wrong, eh?'

Faraday was home by ten. He'd worked late at Major Crime, making sure the *Melody* and *Highfield* files were ready for the D/I who'd be driving Operation *Adelaide*. What struck him as he leafed through the paperwork was the way the three investigations dovetailed so seamlessly together.

First Tim Morrissey had been bullied to death, in all probability by Kyle Munday and his little gang. Then, six months later, in a settling of accounts, Tim's mother had run Munday over. And now, within days, two of those same kids running with Munday had in turn been killed. The theme that ran through all three incidents, the message in the Pompey stick of rock, was a deep undercurrent of violence, the kind of violence that suddenly erupted in wild spasms of bloodletting: ungovernable, reckless and often fatal.

The tariff, Faraday thought, was going up all the time. A generation ago differences would have been settled with fists. There was an intent to hurt, of course there was, but far fewer brawls ended in the mortuary. Nowadays, though, that restraint, that respect for some kind of unspoken code, had gone. When people fought, for whatever reason, they really meant it. Welcome to the world of the one-punch homicide.

At the Bargemaster's House Faraday poured himself a lager and carried it upstairs. Both Parsons and Willard had made it plain that they were standing Faraday down from sharp-end investigations pending some kind of review. This wasn't, as yet, a transfer out of Major Crime, but Faraday sensed that his days at Kingston Crescent were probably numbered. They were right in looking for energy, appetite and total commitment. Experience was a huge asset but the last thing they needed was a D/I who'd begun to suspect that the ongoing war they were all fighting was probably unwinnable. Hence the decision to move Faraday aside from today's double murder. And hence the small, time-filling consolations of a cold case.

The buff Operation *Sangster* file lay beside his PC. Faraday settled himself behind the desk, fighting the temptation to open it. Instead, he fired up the computer and opened his email account. Below the usual list of birding updates and miscellaneous spam was a message from Gabrielle. The time in Montreal was late afternoon. He toyed with the mouse, trying to picture her in the rented flat, hunched over her laptop. Before he'd left, barely a week ago, she'd been thinking of getting herself a kitten. There was a guy downstairs who had to find a home for a whole litter. Otherwise he was threatening to drown them.

Had she found space for one? Two? The whole lot? Faraday hovered the pointer over her email, glad that she'd got in touch at last, but bracing himself for disappointment. Since getting back from Canada, his own emails had gone unanswered, even unacknowledged. The worst week he could remember could yet have a last bitter twist.

He swallowed the rest of the lager and opened the email. His French was beginning to suffer from lack of use but the sheer length of the message gave him some small encouragement.

He quickly scanned it, jumping from sentence to sentence, hearing Gabrielle's voice, recognising the mood she was in, understanding with a little jolt of pleasure that loneliness was something you could share. On the face of it, she said, she had nothing but good news. The university had offered her a permanent post. She'd been hauled away to various social get-togethers. She'd fought off a Russian Fine Arts lecturer who was determined to talk her into bed. She'd eaten and quaffed her way from restaurant to restaurant, fêted by her fellow academics, adopted by their pretty wives, made hugely welcome. All this, in their phrase, was fine and dandy, but something was missing, something had gone, and it wasn't until she'd dropped Faraday at the airport and waved him *au revoir* that she'd realised what it was. She couldn't wait to get back home. Home, she said, was the Bargemaster's House. Happiness, she said, was an evening in the kitchen with a bottle or two of Côtes-du-Rhône and some decent conversation. The future, if Faraday was still interested, was theirs for the taking. *On ne sait jamais ce qu'on a jusqu'à on le perde.* You never know what you've got until you lose it.

Faraday stared at the screen, aware of the print blurring in front of his eyes. Then he sat back, flooded with warmth and with hope, staring out at the darkness on the harbour.

Chapter fifteen

Vigo airport was busier than Winter had expected. He carried his only bag through the customs channel and paused for a moment in the arrivals hall. The flight down from Heathrow had been packed, mainly retired Brit couples on late-spring package deals, and Winter let them plod past while he got his bearings. He spotted the Avis counter at the far end of the concourse. A rental car, he'd decided, would be better than a cab.

A small queue had already formed. Winter was still deciding whether Hertz would be quicker when he became aware of a presence at his elbow. The lightest touch on his arm, barely perceptible. Then a voice in his ear, almost a whisper.

'Señor Winter? You remember me?'

Winter glanced round. The tall slim Latino was wearing a faded Jim Morrison T-shirt. The fall of plaited hair was greyer than he remembered but the eyes still held a laid-back curiosity you might associate with a younger man. Winter shook the extended hand. A moment later the man's name came back to him.

'Riquelme,' he said. 'From Cambados.'

'Rikki. I have a car outside. You must come. Quickly.'

Winter stood his ground. He wanted to know why this man had been waiting for him. And what would happen next.

'We have no time. Not now. Not here. You come with me. Otherwise it will be hard for you.' He nodded towards one of the exit doors. A pair of policemen were eyeing passengers as they headed for the line of coaches waiting outside in the sunshine.

Winter wondered whether to argue the toss but decided against it. This man knew something he didn't.

'You come?'

'Yeah.'

They walked to the far end of the concourse. A security door opened to Riquelme's touch. Beyond lay a car park.

'The red Megane. Walk slowly. No hurry.'

Winter did what he was told. The last time he'd seen this man was a couple of years back. Mackenzie's stepbrother, Mark, had been killed in a jet ski accident off Cambados, and at Bazza's invitation Winter had joined the funeral party, a volatile mix of family, friends and prominent Pompey faces. Mourning the departed in this kind of company had been a novelty for Winter but he'd flown out to Cambados nonetheless. Everything had been fine until the second evening, when Riquelme had invited himself to Winter's table on a café terrace overlooking the harbour. Riquelme was a main player in the cocaine biz. And he'd known at once that Winter was a cop.

'How is Señor Mackenzie?'

'He's fine. You've talked to him?'

'Last night. He told me which plane to meet. I drove down this morning.'

'Why?'

'He didn't tell you?'

'No.'

'No kidding?'

'No.'

Riquelme began to laugh. He opened the doors of the Renault. Winter got in. When Riquelme gunned the engine and checked round for the exit Winter reached across and removed the keys.

'Tell me where we're going,' he said. 'And why.'

Riquelme wanted the keys back. Winter held his gaze.

'Last time we met you thought I was a cop,' he said.

'You tell me I was wrong?'

'No.' Winter shook his head. 'I'm asking you what you think now.'

'Now I know you work for Señor Mackenzie.'

'You're sure about that?'

'Of course, my friend. Otherwise I'd leave them to do their business with you.'

'Who? The police?'

'*Sí.*'

'Why would they bother with me?'

'You don't know? You don't remember last year? Rincon de la Vittoria? Las Puertas de Paraiso?'

Winter said nothing. The temptation was to step out of the car, retrieve his bag, go back to the terminal, and get the next plane out. Bazza must have known, he told himself. This man, or maybe someone else, must have told him. Don't set foot in Spain for a while. Or maybe ever.

'Who told you about last year?'

'I have good contacts in the police. They have a watch list at all our airports. Your name is on the list, my friend. You were lucky to get through.'

Lucky to get through. Winter shut his eyes. Bazza *had* known, he told himself again. He'd definitely fucking known.

'So what happens next?'

'We go to Baiona. You do your business. Señor Mackenzie asks me to look after you. That way –' he shrugged '– *no problema.*'

'And you know what happened last year? The way it went?'

'*Sí. Una lástima, verdad?*'

Winter shrugged. He hadn't a clue what this man was saying but he'd caught the tiny ironic inflection in his voice. Westie and his new girlfriend blown away in an unfinished bar in the hills behind the coast. Two more bodies heading for the foundations of the latest Costa del Sol development. An event like that, profoundly shocking, will always come back to haunt you. Always.

They were out on the main road now, heading south. To the right, beyond the advertising hoardings and the odd stand of trees, Winter caught sight of the blueness of the sea.

'Esme?' he queried.

'She's at the hotel.'

'And a man called Garfield?'

'He hasn't come.'

'He was due?'

'Yesterday. He comes here many times. You know about Señor Garfield?'

'No. Tell me.'

Riquelme said nothing, dropping a gear and easing the Megane past a huge petrol tanker. According to Mackenzie,

Riquelme controlled a sizeable chunk of the Colombian toot shipping into Spain's Atlantic coastline. If anyone knew the workings of the cocaine business in these parts it would be Rikki.

'Señor Garfield buys from people, friends of mine. He pays a good price. We like his business. But he takes risks. Risks give you trouble. Risks give everybody trouble. This we don't like.'

'So why hasn't he turned up?'

'*Qué?*'

'Why isn't he here? Doing more business with Esme?'

'*No sé?* You don't know?' The smile again.

'No. So just fucking tell me, OK?' Winter knew he was beginning to lose it. Most Sundays he stayed in bed late, read the *Telegraph*, took a leisurely stroll with Misty if she was in the mood, tucked into a roast at one of the Gunwharf eateries. Now he was fleeing the Spanish police and trying to head off a London gangster who'd evidently taken one risk too many.

'He's been arrested. Is that what you're telling me?'

'*Qué?*'

'Arrested. Crashed and burned. Gone. Potted. Off the plot.'

'*Sí.* By your police.'

'Where?'

'In London. Two days ago.'

'Does Mackenzie know that?'

'Sure. He tells me on the phone. He checks up that I'm meeting you. He tells me to keep you safe. He says for me to take you to Baiona, to the hotel, to his daughter. A pleasure, my friend.'

'Why the drama? If Garfield's not coming?'

'His wife is here. She arrive last night at the airport. She comes to see Esme.'

'Why?'

'*No sé.*'

'You don't know?'

'No.'

'Mackenzie didn't tell you?'

'No. Like I say he tells me to look after you. He tells me to keep you safe. I have men in Baiona. Esme?' He glanced across. 'She speaks Spanish?'

'Yeah.'

'*Bueno.*' He nodded. 'Good.'

The last person Esme expected to see was Winter. She was sitting in the sunshine on the hotel's terrace. The hotel itself was a wonderful confection of wrought-iron balconies and peeling wooden shutters. A Spanish flag fluttered over the ornate entrance and the fading pink of the stucco was streaked with seagull shit. The terrace formed part of the restaurant and the remains of a meal for three had yet to be cleared away. Winter eyed the mountain of discarded oyster shells and crab claws. There were two wine bottles upended in the ice bucket and a folded copy of the *Financial Times* lying on one of the empty seats. Esme's guests had clearly gone.

He stood behind her, wondering where Madison fitted into all this.

'Some kind of celebration, Ez?'

She looked up. She was wearing a pair of Ralph Lauren sunglasses and must have spent most of last week on the tanning bed but nothing could hide the fact that she was pissed.

'You,' she said.

'Me,' Winter agreed. 'Your dad sends his best. Hopes you're having a nice time. Where's lover boy?'

Esme looked at him for a long time then tried to get to her feet. Winter pushed her gently back.

'I want you to meet a couple of friends of mine,' he said. 'This is Juan. The other guy's name I didn't catch. They're mates of a guy called Riquelme, big fan of your dad. Problem is, they don't speak English.'

He waved the two Spaniards into the empty chairs and requisitioned a fourth from a neighbouring table. Esme was looking from one face to the other, clearly lost. Riquelme, after the lightest of handshakes, had disappeared back to Cambados.

'So ...' Winter nodded at the debris on the table. 'Who had the pleasure?'

'Of what?'

'Your company, Ez. One of them, I assume, was Madison. The other?'

Esme gazed at him a moment then shook her head.

'This is none of your business.'

'Wrong, love. It *is* my business. And you know why? Because it's also your dad's business. And just now you're in fucking disgrace. How do I know that? Because he told me.'

Esme's shoulder bag lay beside her chair. Winter bent quickly and retrieved it. The two Spaniards were watching his every move.

'Tell them it's cool, Ez.' Winter was going through the bag. 'What's the Spanish for damage limitation?'

Esme tried to seize the bag. Winter pushed her off. Then the edge of his shoe found her shin under the table. She swore and pushed her chair back. She was wearing a short cotton skirt. Her legs were as tanned as the rest of her. She began to rub the hurt, still cursing.

'Put ice cubes on it, Ez.' Winter nodded at the bucket. 'Brings out the bruising.'

He'd found what he was looking for. He cleared a space on the table, mopped it with a napkin and laid the document flat. It was in English. It appeared to be a contract for the sale of the hotel. There were ten pages, each initialled at the bottom. Three signatures, one belonging to Ezzie.

'So who are these people?' Winter tapped the other signatures.

Esme took off her sunglasses. Pain appeared to have sobered her up.

'One of them's the owner.'

'Fresnada?'

'Yeah. He signed first thing this morning.'

'And the other?' Winter peered closer at the name.

'That's our partner.' She frowned. 'Dad's partner.'

'You mean his wife.'

'Yeah. How did you know that?'

Winter ignored the question. He'd turned to the final page. Each of the signatures had been separately witnessed. Damage limitation had ceased to be a joke.

'Who did you get as a witness, Ez?'

Something in Winter's tone of voice had caught her full attention. She'd never seen him this businesslike.

'A local guy. Dad and me met him last time we were down here. He's a *notario,* a lawyer. He's handling our side of the deal.'

'And Mrs Garfield?'

'She brought her own, a London guy, Christopher some-one.'

'He was here? At the table?'

'Yeah.'

'So where are they now?'

'En route back to the airport.'

'With the contracts?'

'Of course.'

'Shit.' He nodded at the Spaniards. 'Ask these guys if they have wheels.'

'Why?'

'Don't fuck around, Ez. Just trust me. Just do it.'

She turned to them and said something in Spanish. Juan, the older of the two men, nodded.

Winter asked her what time Garfield's flight went. She frowned. She thought early evening. It was a direct flight back to Gatwick. They had some call or other to make in Vigo first. Winter reached for her bag. Her mobile was at the bottom. He passed it across the table and told her to check the flight's departure time.

She stared at the mobile, not knowing what to do.

'Ask at reception,' he told her. 'They'll have a number.'

She got to her feet and limped inside. The younger of the two Spaniards couldn't keep his eyes off her.

'*Guapa*,' he muttered.

Winter had returned to the contract. As far as he could make out, Bazza had just parted with two million euros for the hotel. Garfield was in for a million. His wife's signature was indecipherable.

Esme had reappeared at his elbow.

'The flight goes at seven forty-five local.' She appeared to be getting a grip at last. 'They'd have to be there at half six.'

Winter checked his watch. Just gone four. The airport was an hour away, max.

'Do we know what they're driving?'

'It'll be in the hotel register. They had a hire car.'

'You know which company?'

'Hertz. I saw the key fob.'

'Good girl.' Hertz was allocated spaces for hire cars in the airport car park. He'd seen them this morning. This was getting better. He nodded at Juan. 'Tell our man we need to get back to the airport.' He grinned at her for the first time. '*Pronto*.'

Winter could tell that Esme wasn't keen on joining them for the trip to the airport. When he accused her of hiding Madison upstairs she took him to her room. Only one of the twin beds had been slept in and there was no sign of any other luggage but her own. She'd flown down here, she insisted, to complete the deal that she and her dad had been negotiating for months. None of that had anything to do with Perry Madison.

'But you want to move out here. Is that right?'

'Who told you that?'

'It doesn't matter, love. Just tell me whether it's true or not.'

She shrugged. Spain was nice. She'd always liked it. This particular area was wonderful, so green and unspoiled after all the crappy developments along the Mediterranean coast, and yes she could see herself spending a bit of time out here. As far as the hotel was concerned, her dad was right. She'd fallen in love with the place at first sight and nothing that had happened since would change that.

'Not even Madison?'

'Fuck off, Paul. Perry's my affair, not yours.'

'Wrong again, Ez. Shagging coppers is a crap idea. Especially in our line of business.'

'He's a human being not a copper. Why can't men see that?'

'Because you're potty about him. Because he might be more devious than you think. And because you've just put your dad in bed with a cocaine dealer.'

The latter news brought Esme to a halt. She was standing by the window, enjoying the sun on her face.

'A what?'

'A drug baron. A toot peddler. A bugle merchant. This guy's money is dirty. And now some of it will soon be sharing an account with your dad's. You're a lawyer, Ez. You know the way POCA works.'

'The Proceeds of Crime Act?'

'Yeah. Garfield's money taints everything. Including us. Where is he, as a matter of interest?'

'Garfield?'

'Yeah.'

'In the States. On business.'

'Who told you that?'

'His wife.'

'Great. You want the bad news or the bad news? Number one, his wife's lying. Number two, Garfield was arrested a couple of days ago on supply charges. We're talking millions and millions of quid, Ez. I checked with your dad on the way down from the airport. He's put some calls in. The Met don't do these things lightly. They wouldn't touch a face like Garfield unless they were sure of a result. Once that happens, your dad is history. And so are you.'

'Shit.'

'Exactly.'

'I didn't know.'

'Why the fuck not? You're a lawyer, Ez. You're supposed to understand all this money-laundering bollocks. It's your job to check out Garfield's stake. It's there in the legislation. In fact it's your responsibility. You can go down for this, easily. So why didn't you look? Why didn't you start asking questions?'

'Dad said there was no problem.'

'Dad was wrong.'

'Yeah, but –' she shrugged '– Dad's Dad.'

Winter held her gaze. She was right. Bazza Mackenzie had always believed what suited him at the time. It was part of his charm, part of his MO.

'We have to get that contract back, Ez. What's Garfield's wife's Christian name?'

'Nikki. She's really nice.'

'I bet she is. You've just let her bury a million euros offshore. They'll get it back in the end but if that lawyer's smart he could make it very difficult for them. A million buys a lot of sangria. *Comprende?*'

Esme nodded. Then she sank into a chair and put her head in her hands. Winter stood over her, waiting. Finally her head came up, her eyes shiny with tears.

'So what do we do, Paul?'

*

They were at the airport car park by half past five. Winter fetched take-out coffees from the terminal while Esme briefed Riquelme's heavies on the way they were going to play the interception. By the time Winter got back the atmosphere in the car was almost festive.

'They don't see a problem,' Esme told him. 'Under the circumstances they say there's no way Garfield will go running to the police. They're shit hot on money laundering down here.'

'Glad to hear it.'

They sipped their double espressos in silence for a while. Juan found a local station on the radio. The sun began to dip towards the west. By the time the Hertz Seat turned up, Winter was wondering about the possibility of a nap.

'They're here.' Esme gave him a nudge. 'That's them.'

The Seat circled the car park. The woman was driving, a younger man beside her. The Spaniards were watching him too, making their assessments. The car pulled into one of the Hertz reserved spaces, no more than twenty metres away. The Spaniards were already out of the car, moving across to the Seat. Jeans and T-shirts. Obviously fit. They stationed themselves on either side of the Seat, making it impossible to open either door. Winter and Esme joined them.

Nikki Garfield wound down her window. She was a sleek middle-aged woman with a salon tan. Plainly irritated, she wanted to know what was going on.

Esme told her she'd had a change of heart over the purchase of the apartments and the hotel. She'd decided to ditch the project. She wanted the contract back.

'Why?'

'Commercial reasons.'

'Like what?'

'I'm not prepared to say.'

Her companion leaned over. He was younger, looked in good shape. There was no warmth in his smile.

'Why the pressure?' He gestured at his door. 'What's with the heavies?'

'They're friends of ours.' Winter this time. 'They're looking after our interests.'

'Is that right?'

The lawyer whispered something to Nikki Garfield. The key

was still in the ignition but Winter got there first. He yanked it out then slipped it into his pocket.

At this, the lawyer pushed hard on his door and got out. Winter admired his courage but knew he was doomed. Juan, the older of the two Spaniards, must have been in the military or maybe the police. He spun the lawyer round in a neat arm-lock and slammed him against the side of the car before kicking his legs apart.

Esme told him to go easy. She still wanted the contract.

'This is totally out of order.' Nikki stared up at her, outraged. 'We negotiated in good faith. We're civilised people. A contract is a contract. You pledged your word. It's done, signed, sorted. So now, if you don't mind, we'll be on our way.'

She too tried to get out of the car but couldn't shift the weight of the younger Spaniard against the door.

Winter went round to the back of the car and unlocked the boot. A briefcase lay between three pieces of luggage, two of them in matching pink. He pulled it out. It was locked.

'You've got a choice here, Nikki.' He was back beside her door. 'Either we take the briefcase or you unlock it.'

'That's theft.'

'Wrong. It's negotiation. I expect your tickets are in here too. If you want to get home tonight, maybe you should give me the key.'

The car park was covered by CCTV. One of the Spaniards was looking at the nearest camera. The terminal was a couple of hundred metres away. The last thing Winter needed was a visit from security.

'The key,' he repeated.

The woman shook her head. She too had realised that time was on her side.

The lawyer made his move. Lashing out with his foot, he caught his captor below the knee. The Spaniard grunted with pain but maintained the armlock. The lawyer did the same thing again. This time he missed but the Spaniard's patience had run out. He reached forward with his spare hand, smash-ing the lawyer's face against the edge of the roof. The lawyer's body sagged. His hand went to his face. Sitting on the warm tarmac, his back against the car, he stared at the blood dripping into his lap.

Nikki had produced a mobile. Winter had no idea who she was phoning but knew this was getting out of hand. Seizing the mobile he told Esme they were off. Any minute now security would arrive. Worse still, the police.

'What about the contract?'

'We take their luggage.'

'All of it?'

'Yeah. Plus the briefcase.'

She stared at him a moment then shrugged. Winter had already removed the luggage from the boot. The Spaniards carried the bags back to their car. The lawyer, watching, made no attempt to stop them. Seconds later, they were on their way out of the car park.

Esme was sitting in the back, nursing the briefcase. The other bags were in the boot. She stole a look over her shoulder. Nikki Garfield was bent over her lawyer beside the hire car, a tissue in her hand.

'She's right.' Esme was shaking her head in disbelief. 'That was definitely theft.'

Chapter sixteen

It had taken Jimmy Suttle two minutes to brief Faraday on the latest developments over the Blue Dragon murders. Faraday had come in early, wanting to clarify his own role on Major Crime, only to find DCI Parsons already chairing an Operation *Adelaide* meet. Peering round her office door, Faraday counted half a dozen faces at the conference table before beating a retreat. Now, more than an hour later, Suttle appeared to give him an update.

The surviving kids, he said, had both been charged with blackmail. After a brief appearance before the magistrates they'd been released on police bail, stepping out of the court buildings to find themselves mobbed by a huge bunch of supporters who'd taken the bus down from Paulsgrove. The Chinese, meanwhile, had both been remanded on murder charges. Their solicitor was already talking about a defence of provocation and in all likelihood they'd be looking at a couple of years for manslaughter. It was now confirmed that one of the Chinese was an illegal but he'd still be facing an initial stretch inside before the Home Office got round to deporting him. Mr Hua, the owner, was back at the Blue Dragon, contemplating the ruin of his business.

'What happened?'

'Someone put a brick through his window first thing this morning. He's also had stuff through the letterbox, dog shit mainly.'

'Weren't uniforms supposed to be keeping an eye on the property?'

'They had a bloke on all Saturday night. Then they relied on car patrols. It obviously wasn't enough.'

Feelings on the estate, he said, were running high. One of

the witnesses in the restaurant had filmed the whole thing on his phone and posted the result on YouTube. The movie had become an overnight sensation. Two and a half million hits and counting.

'We didn't seize mobes in the restaurant?'

'Not this one, obviously. We've got names, though. We might push for an aid and abet. That's up to Parsons.'

Faraday nodded. *Adelaide* might end up expending more investigative effort nailing the owner of the rogue mobile than on any other element in the inquiry.

'So what's the word from the top?' Faraday nodded at the corridor.

'Control and containment. They're bricking themselves in case this turns into another paedo-fest. They need to lock Paulsgrove down, big time.'

Quite how you'd do that with the resources available was anyone's guess but Faraday saw the point. Eight years ago Paulsgrove had made the national news after days of rioting over alleged paedophiles living in the community. Some of the stories from officers policing the front line had stayed with him.

'Vulgarity and ignorance.' Faraday glanced up. 'What do you think?'

'I'm not with you, boss.'

'Vulgarity and ignorance. I was listening to an interview on the radio this morning. They were talking to a social worker. She used the word "epidemic". She said Vicky Pollard had a great deal to answer for. You agree?'

'Yeah. They got her dead right, fat old slag.'

'But in the wider context ...'

'You mean real life? It's been that way forever, boss. It's just fashionable now, that's the only difference. Actually, it's worse. People *want* to be Vicky Pollard. She's become aspirational. That way you get yourself on telly.'

Suttle caught sight of the Operation *Sangster* file on the emptiness of Faraday's desk.

'What's *Sangster*?'

'Cold case. I'm the pigeon, Jimmy. *Sangster*'s the crumbs. They're definitely sending me a message here. Problem is, I haven't a clue what they're trying to say.'

It was rare for Faraday to let anyone so close. Suttle helped himself to the spare chair.

'It's quiet just now,' he pointed out. 'Maybe they're just trying to keep you out of mischief.'

'Yeah. And maybe they're not. Spend too long in this job and it can get difficult to keep your mouth shut. There are real people out there, real issues. The law's always been a blunt instrument but lately ... I don't know ...' He turned to the window and stared out, leaving the sentence unfinished.

'Jeanette Morrissey got refused bail, boss, if that's what this is about.'

'I know. I checked. She'll go down and she knows it.'

'Of course she'll go down. She killed someone. Did you ever read the bit about intent when you were a probationer or did that pass you by?'

Faraday shot him a look, aware that he was wide open to this kind of mockery. A policeman's worst friend was his conscience. Stick strictly to the letter of the law and you couldn't afford to look too hard at the consequences. Jeanette Morrissey deserved better from Operation *Melody*. As had the memory of her son.

'We failed her, Jimmy. Munday paid for it in the end but that was her doing not ours.'

'So what are you suggesting, boss? Should we have drawn our own conclusions and knocked him off? Saved on the budget? Spared Mrs Morrissey all those years inside?'

'I don't know, Jimmy, but it doesn't stop with her. You know what I felt when I watched that CCTV from the restaurant? Those scrote kids on the wrong end of a blade?'

'Happy, I hope.'

'Yeah.' Faraday nodded, surprised. 'That's right, that's exactly right. Happy. Glad. Someone had stuck it to them the way they'd been sticking it to everyone else. In my book that's a result.'

'And you think no one else feels that way?'

'I don't know.' He blinked. 'Do you?'

'Of course I do. Do I tell some rookie D/C? No bloody way. As far as they're concerned it's all in the line of duty. Killing people is wrong. It's bad stuff. Whether you're Jeanette Morrissey or a pair of Chinese psychos you get nicked. Us lot do the business, muster the evidence, and away you go. Good fucking riddance. Job done.'

'But in the small hours?'

'In the small hours I roll over and give Lizzie a cuddle. She knows. And she knows I know. And there it stops.'

Faraday was oddly touched, one confidence prompting another. After years of claiming she was lesbian Lizzie Hodson had evidently changed her mind. Hence the fact they were living together.

'You're lucky, son.'

'Because I've got someone to talk to? Someone sane? Someone who cares?'

'Yeah, all those things.'

Suttle nodded. He was far too tactful to take this conversation any further so Faraday spared him the trouble. Suttle had met Gabrielle. He'd liked her a lot.

'She's only out there for another couple of months, Jimmy. Then she's coming home.'

Suttle nodded, then got to his feet.

'Thank Christ for that,' he said.

Mackenzie picked up Winter at Gatwick Airport, summoned first thing by an abrupt text message. It was a couple of minutes past one o'clock in the afternoon. Winter was standing outside South Terminal surrounded by luggage. Mackenzie brought the Bentley to a halt, staring at a pair of pink suitcases.

'Whose the fuck are those?'

'Long story, Baz. Unlock the boot.'

Winter dumped the luggage in the back and got in. Mackenzie wanted to know about the contract.

'Did Ez sign it?'

'Yes.'

'Witnessed?'

'Yes.'

'And Garfield's missus signed as well?'

'I'm afraid so, Baz.'

They were still at the kerbside. Mackenzie gave an approaching security guard the finger and purred away. For a moment Winter thought he was going to drive round the block and drop him off at Departures. Get back there, mush. Try again.

Sort it out. Instead, they were heading for the exit road to the motorway.

'Before I forget, Baz, why didn't you tell me about your mate Riquelme?'

'Rikki? Guy who saw you right at the airport?'

'Yeah.'

'Because you'd have been up all night Saturday fretting about it.'

'About what?'

'About the spic police. They're clueless, mush. Take it from me. Once Rikki was on the case I knew you'd never have a problem. That guy knows how to look after people. Plus he's got half the police force on his payroll. In my book that's called insurance. You were safe as houses, mush. I guarantee it.'

'But why would I have a problem?'

'Because the spics think they've got a lead on what happened to Westie.'

'What kind of a lead?'

'I've no idea. Maybe the geezer in that bar where it happened spoke out of turn. Maybe bits of Westie turned up where they shouldn't have. Maybe Tommy Peters has been bigging himself up to the wrong people. Fuck knows. All that matters is that you're back in one piece.'

Winter said nothing. Last summer's hit had taken place in a half-finished bar inside a deserted hotel development. One minute he'd been enjoying an ice-cold beer. The next he was looking at gobbets of Westie's brain spattered across his favourite suit. Shock, real shock, would always taste of San Miguel and newly poured cement.

'The spic police will be talking to our lot.' Winter was fighting to contain his temper. 'Has that occurred to you yet?'

'So what?' Mackenzie couldn't care less. 'We took a trip out there, we had a nice time, we had a look round Malaga, the boys were off the leash for the night, we came home again next morning. Who can prove otherwise?'

'The Spanish probably can. Otherwise they wouldn't have been looking for me.'

'You're kidding yourself. All they'd have is a bunch of names off the manifest.'

'Including yours, Baz. Is that why you didn't go out yourself? Is it? Just make it easy for me. Just say fucking yes.'

Mackenzie glanced across at him. They were on the motorway by now, nudging 95 mph.

'You sound upset, mush.'

'I *am* fucking upset. You spin me some line about a meet at the Dorchester, you never say a word about the spic police or your mate Rikki. Next thing I know I'm standing on the concourse and some bloke's whispering in my ear. You know what he says? If I don't get out in the car park pronto I'll be spending the rest of my life in some khazi of a Spanish jail. Great career move, Baz. The best.'

Mackenzie nodded, saying nothing. Then he wanted to know about the Dorchester. How come Winter thought he hadn't been up there?

'Because Marie told me.'

'When?'

'I phoned her last night.'

'She never mentioned it.'

'That's because I asked her not to. When I wondered about getting a lift back from Gatwick today she said there was no problem. You'd got a clear diary, fuck all else to do. You know what, Baz? I sweated my bollocks off trying to do right by you, trying to do the best job, and just now I'm wondering why I bothered.'

The first whiff of good news brought a grin to Mackenzie's face. He turned to Winter again.

'You're telling me the contract's going to be OK?'

'It's in the boot.'

'All of them? All the signed copies?'

'Ours and Garfield's. Ez is still out there waiting for Fresnada to come back from Madrid. She thinks it won't be a problem getting it back off him. Apparently there's another buyer for the hotel in the wings.'

'So the contract's back with us?'

'Yeah. Like I say, Ez will sort Fresnada.'

'Result, mush. Total fucking result.' The Bentley lurched to the right as Mackenzie thumped the wheel. 'So how did you manage it?'

Winter described the stake-out in the airport car park. By the time he'd arrived in Baiona, the deal was done. His only option was to unpick it.

'Messy?'

'Very. We left the lawyer in a bit of a state and the wife without her luggage. Good job, as it turned out. The contract was in the suitcase with her knickers. You won't believe how many sex toys that woman travels with. She must be repping on the side.'

Mackenzie was laughing now. They were off the motorway and onto the dual carriageway that funnelled traffic down towards Brighton. Spotting a pub, Mackenzie abruptly signalled left. Winter heard the squeal of rubber behind them as the line of drivers in their wake fought for control. The pub was called the Three Ravens. Lunch, Mackenzie announced, was on him. First, a drink or two.

Winter settled for a large whisky. Rikki's boys, he said, had been brilliant. Once they were back in the hotel in Baiona, they'd summoned the boss for a council of war. Riquelme had driven up from Cambados and decided to smuggle Winter over the nearby Portuguese border in the boot of his Megane. From the border, they could be in Lisbon in time for the mid-morning flight to Gatwick.

'Worked a treat, Baz. I'm not sure Rikki even stopped at the border. I think they just waved him through.'

'EU, mush. Bad boys' charter. We're all Europeans now.' He still couldn't get over the scene in the car park. Maybe, after all, he ought to have gone. Just for the crack.

'There'll be consequences, Baz. The lawyer bloke will have taken it hard. So will she. And so will her husband. How well do you know this guy?'

'Barely at all. It was Rikki who mentioned him in the first place. Said the geezer was sniffing round for somewhere handy to invest his money.'

'And you never thought cocaine? Even then?'

'Never occurred to me. The first time I met him he said it all came from gambling. He runs a casino operation in Richmond upon Thames. He showed me the brochures. Classy. I was impressed. Seemed a nice enough guy, obviously had the dosh, so who was I to worry?'

Winter eyed his empty glass then pushed it towards

Mackenzie. Rikki, he told himself, would have felt guilty about introducing Garfield. Hence the string of favours over the last couple of days.

Mackenzie returned from the bar. A treble, at least.

'What about Madison?'

'He wasn't there. Not as far as I could see.'

'What did Ez say?'

'She wouldn't say anything. Not about him. You're right about the hotel, though. She's crazy about the place.'

'Too fucking bad. You know what I was going to do with it? Once it was ours? Give it to her and Stu as an anniversary present. It's their tenth coming up. How sick is that?'

'Nice gesture, Baz.' Winter reached for his glass. 'Here's to marriage.'

Mackenzie ignored him. He had some news about Tide Turn. Winter's heart sank.

'Like what?'

'Like Marie's meeting your bloke this morning. I'm surprised she didn't mention it.'

'Mo Sturrock?'

'Yeah. She showed me that article you gave her. The speech he made at the conference.'

'And?'

'I loved it, mush. Showed the bloke's got bollocks. If we're serious about sorting out these little scrotes it's guys like him we need. The only problem is the money.'

'He told me twenty-five K was fine.'

'Yeah. What he didn't say was that only buys three days a week. He says he was on forty-seven. For twenty-five we get a part-timer in charge. Won't fly, mush. You'll have to sort it.' He nodded at the menu. 'Are we eating or what?'

Chapter seventeen

By mid-afternoon, Faraday had been through the *Sangster* file. At Parsons' suggestion, he'd bailed out of the office and taken it home. This sudden concern for his peace of mind had done nothing to quieten his suspicion that he was being readied for a transfer out of Major Crime but he told himself that there was nothing, at the moment, he could do about it. Better to take advantage of the dusty sunlight in the Bargemaster's House and concentrate on the task in hand.

He opened the French doors out to the garden, took a precautionary sweep across the glistening mudflats with his binos, and settled down on the sofa with the file. *Sangster* dated back to 1984. On 6 June a Poly student, Tessa Fogle, had spent the evening partying. Her exams were over and she was about to graduate. She lived in a bedsit in Southsea. The house was shared with five other students. Past midnight, after finishing up at the Student Union, she'd gone home and fallen into bed.

The room had a window that looked onto the garden at the back. It was a hot night and the window, according to Fogle's statement, had been wide open. She'd woken up with someone on top of her. Because of the heat she was sleeping naked on the duvet. She'd tried to fight him off but he'd been too strong. Partially penetrated, she'd managed to wriggle free. When she screamed for help he'd put a pillow over her face. After that she must have passed out because the next thing she knew she was awake, groggy, still drunk and still trembling. Her attacker had disappeared. The window was open. There was a payphone in the hall. She'd dialled 999 and then waited in her room for the police to appear.

Faraday turned to the attending officer's statement. He and his oppo had found Ms Fogle in a state of some distress. They'd searched the garden, secured the house and questioned other students in the property. The duty D/C had arrived and taken a full statement from Fogle. Her room had been sealed pending a visit from Scenes of Crime and she'd been driven to the Bridewell for medical examination by a police doctor. He'd found no evidence of semen in her vagina but confirmed mild bruising around her vaginal orifice consistent with attempted penetration. He'd also noted her own admission that she'd consumed at least three pints of lager and a bottle of wine that evening.

Next morning, Scenes of Crime had boshed her room. Faraday flicked through the attending officer's report. Soil on the carpet had indicated entry through the window. Blood had been retrieved from the duvet and sent for analysis. The grouping hadn't been hers. Semen samples had also been recovered from the duvet, as had skin scrapings from Fogle's fingernails, but DNA analysis was still a miracle waiting to happen and so the exhibits had been lodged in the Exhibits Store at Highland Road nick.

A smallish squad of detectives, meanwhile, had done house-to-house calls in the immediate area enquiring about possible sightings of a lone male. Nothing. Interviews with a current and previous boyfriends had likewise drawn a blank. Checks on local weirdos went nowhere. By the end of the week, with the *Sangster* file still open, the SIO had concluded that they were dealing with stranger rape.

Faraday made himself a pot of tea and returned to the file. Stranger rape had always been a priority crime not least because the offender was still out there. He'd done it once; he might plausibly do it again. The leads in the *Sangster* case, though, were non-existent. Given the SIO's conviction that the crime was genuine, that the sex hadn't been consensual, then the squad had no option but to wait for the next attack.

Mercifully, nothing similar had happened. Tessa Fogle would have graduated, her peace of mind shattered. In the nature of these incidents, she'd have gradually picked up the pieces, tried to learn how to trust men again, done her best to lock the memories away. A year after the incident, a member of the investigative team had been in touch, assuring her that *Sangster* was far from over. By then, according to his entry on the file, Fogle was living with her parents in Petersfield.

In 1995 the national DNA database had been established. An attempt had been made to tease a DNA profile from one of the *Sangster* blood samples but the science was still crude and it had failed. Four years later, a different technique had yielded better results and a procedure known as Low Copy Number had produced a full profile. This profile, indexed against the national database, failed to raise a name. This was progress of a kind. *Sangster*'s SIO now knew that Tessa Fogle's attacker had no criminal record.

Another four years later, in the wake of a Home Office forensic review of undetected serious rapes, Hampshire Police had launched Operation *Alverston*. A Cold Case core team had been formed and more than thirty cases had been identified for re-investigation. One of those cases was Operation *Sangster*.

Alverston's D/I had been tasked to contact each of the raped women to check whether or not they were prepared to step through the doors that the new DNA techniques might open. Tessa Fogle by then was living in Chalton, a village south of Petersfield. She had three kids. She told the D/I that she'd never mentioned the rape to her partner, and probably never would, but she still nursed a grudge against her attacker and was happy for any investigation to proceed. In the event of an arrest she would, of course, have to prepare herself for the trauma of a court appearance but she decided to face that possibility if and when it happened. Her partner, in the meantime, would remain in a state of blissful ignorance.

Faraday poured himself another cup of tea. *Alverston*'s Cold Case unit drew heavily on DNA familial search techniques introduced a couple of years earlier. These offered the possibility of matching a tiny fragment of anonymous DNA – a bare handful of cells – against profiles sharing the same family characteristics. An operation like this might flag the path to literally hundreds of other samples on the national database, amongst which could be the fathers, mothers, brothers or sisters of the unknown target. Amongst this harvest of criminal names, investigators might find a lead that would take them to the perpetrator. Detectives on cold case units couldn't believe their luck. This was the golden key. They started knocking on doors nationwide.

Within months, though, there were huge problems. Many of

those contacted through the national database had never shared the secret of their criminal conviction with their partners. Their only crime with respect to the Cold Case was a familial DNA match and the last thing they wanted was this unwelcome echo of a long-forgotten past. Representations were made through lawyers. There was an agreement that familial DNA searches raised profound human rights issues. And very quickly the Home Office was obliged to rein in the Cold Case investigators. Henceforth, the authority of an Assistant Chief Constable was required for the pursuit of enquiries.

Faraday put the file to one side to take a phone call. It was Jimmy Suttle. He'd just had Paul Winter on the phone.

'He says you and he have been having a little chat. This has to be bollocks, doesn't it, boss?'

Faraday refused to answer the question. A cosy evening with Winter had never been a good idea but the least he'd expected was a degree of discretion.

'What did he want?'

'He wants you to bell him.'

'So why didn't he just phone me?'

'No idea, boss. Maybe you should ask him yourself.'

Of all the detectives in Pompey, Suttle probably knew Winter best. At times it seemed to Faraday that they'd enjoyed almost a father-and-son relationship. Winter had taught the young Suttle everything he'd known and as a consequence, like now, Suttle had become an extremely shrewd operator. The subtext of this little chat was all too obvious. Be careful.

'I'm grateful, Jimmy. Leave it to me.'

Faraday pocketed his mobile and returned to the file. *Sangster* had been a low priority for the Cold Case squad. They'd concentrated on higher-profile cases, successfully putting names against decades of individual trauma. Just now, the list of undetected stranger rapes numbered seven. Tessa Fogle was the next in line.

Where was she now? How many kids did she have? How big a scar had her mystery attacker really left? There were no clues in the file. Her last known address dated back four years. There was a decent chance she still lived in Chalton but equally she could have moved on. Fragments of DNA left on her duvet had not, so far, been submitted for familial search but Faraday knew that this, logically, would be *Sangster*'s next step.

The front door bell rang. Faraday got to his feet, putting the *Sangster* file to one side. To his surprise, it was Willard. The Head of CID wasn't in the habit of making house calls. Faraday stood aside, inviting him in. Then he realised that Parsons must have known about this little visitation. That's why he'd been sent home in the first place.

'Tea? Coffee?'

Willard didn't want either. He took a brief glance at the view then suggested they sat down.

'Nice place.'

'You're right.'

'Had it long?'

'Thirty years.'

Willard nodded. He had perfectly manicured hands and he'd developed a habit of leaving them on display, the way that photographers suggest when taking an official portrait. Just now, one trailed along the back of the sofa while the other plucked at a stray thread in the piping.

Faraday was waiting for the bad news. Willard was about to sack him from Major Crime, he knew he was.

'Perry Madison, Joe. We owe you.'

'Sir?'

'It can't have been easy, passing on that kind of information. I know he can be a difficult bugger and you've probably had your fair share of grief from the man but even so …'

'You think I grassed him up?'

'Yes. And like I say, Joe, thank God you did.'

He'd had a private word with the DCI, he said, and the man had been big enough to come clean. He'd been giving Mackenzie's daughter a seeing-to for months now but had done his best to box it off from everything else. He'd known it was crazy from the start but the thing had got a bit out of hand. He wasn't just shagging her; he'd fallen in love.

'Unfortunate.'

'Very. Though that isn't the word his wife's using.'

'She knows?'

'Madison told her. As of now he's living in some poxy flat in Romsey. The man's always been a bit of a liability, Joe, but now it's a whole lot worse than that. Frankly, he's a disgrace.'

Willard was right. Falling in love with a Level Three's only child was career suicide. By losing his heart to Mackenzie's daughter, Madison had opened himself up to all kinds of pressure.

'Shame,' Faraday said.

'Shame how?'

'Shame he's lost it like that.'

Willard nodded, said nothing. Then his fingers began to drum on the back of the sofa. Faraday braced himself for a change of subject. Madison had been the hors d'oeuvre. Now for the main course.

'You mentioned *Tumbril* the other day. No one's suggesting that was our finest hour, least of all me, but the fact remains that strategically we were right to mount the operation. The day we stop making it hard for people like Mackenzie is the day we should pack our bags and find something else to do.'

'I agree, sir. And next time we might have better luck.'

'I'm not sure luck comes into it, Joe. We fucked up because we didn't spot the enemy in the camp. That was an oversight. That should never have happened.'

Faraday couldn't work out if the blame was his. He decided to say nothing. Willard had gone back to Madison. The man was still in post. As far as Willard could judge, no one else knew about the wreckage of his private life.

'Madison has no friends,' he said. 'Which turns out to be a blessing.'

'Why?'

'Because they'd know about Mackenzie's daughter and I'd have to sack the man. As it is –' he shrugged '– Madison may still have his uses.'

'With respect to Mackenzie?'

'Exactly. The daughter's in as deep as he is. From our point of view that could be promising.'

'Could be?'

'Is.'

'You're telling me Madison's become part of the family?'

'Far from it. Mackenzie's gone ape shit as you probably know. But women in these situations do strange things, Joe. She's the keeper of the crown jewels. Love knows no secrets.

Fuck knows what she sees in Madison but that's not the question that concerns me just now. She trusts him. She talks to him. She tells him things.' He smiled. 'Are we getting the drift?'

'Of course.' Faraday held his gaze. 'So what do you want me to do about it?'

'Nothing, Joe. I just came to say thank you.'

'I really liked him, Paul. I thought he was fabulous.'

Marie had summoned Winter to tea in the Tenth Hole, a wooden shack, handsomely refurbished, that looked onto the Craneswater pitch-and-putt course. Mo Sturrock, it turned out, had been here to meet his new employer.

'We had the most brilliant lunch. You know the way some men can put you at your ease? Make you laugh? Make you feel you've known them half your life? Mo's got that ... and you have too. Except he's better-looking.'

'And younger.'

'Quite.' She put a warm hand over his. 'Don't take offence, Paul. If anything, I'm thanking you. That man's an inspired choice. Truly. I mean it.'

Sturrock, it seemed, had shared a great deal of his past six months with Marie. Suspension from the Social Services directorate had forced him into taking a long hard look at his life. All communication with the office was forbidden: no phone calls, no emails, not even the chance to natter with a colleague you might bump into at the weekend. Twice he'd met friends, *friends* for God's sake, at the big Tesco in Ryde, and both times they'd fled. If you were thin-skinned or vulnerable enough, he said, this kind of back-turning and isolation would drive you nuts. It was exile. It was like being sent to the Gulag except worse because you had no one to talk to.

'What about his missus?'

'That was the point really. She works part time as a counsellor but just now they're obviously spending a lot of time together. Mo says that's been brilliant. You get the feeling the relationship's always been pretty sound but now he says he never realised what he was missing.'

'Wonderful. So why is he interested in us?'

'That was my question. I get the impression they might need the money.'

'But he's on full pay.'

'Sure, but that won't last forever and if he ends up losing his registration then he'll have to leave social work entirely. So things might get tough for a while.'

Winter nodded. Social workers couldn't practise without being registered with the General Social Care Council, just one of the reasons why Winter had tried to convince Bazza that he was a trespasser in the field.

'What else did Sturrock say?'

'He told me about his kids. He's got three: Temple, Poppy and Fleur. They've been on the island a while now. Mo says they love it.'

Temple, she said, had just got himself a motor scooter. Fleur, the youngest child, was Down's syndrome but like her sister she was mad about horses. It sounded idyllic.

'Is she bad? Fleur?'

'Mo was cagey about her. I get the impression she can be a bit of a handful sometimes but Mo says she just loves having her dad back full time. I can imagine. The guy's really good news.'

Winter helped himself to another scone. As far as he could gather, Mo Sturrock had been invited across so Marie could check him out. In which case he'd somehow managed to turn an interview into a blind date.

'Bit of a star, then, our Mo?'

'Absolutely, and I'll tell you why. These days people just lose it with each other. They haven't got the patience to keep the relationship, the marriage, whatever it is, together. Maybe they expect too much, I don't know, but it's really refreshing to meet someone who still fancies their other half.'

Winter, contemplating another spoonful of clotted cream, wondered whether she was talking about her own marriage. If he were to enquire further he had a feeling he'd probably be here for the rest of the afternoon so instead he told her about Esme.

'She took Bazza's word about Garfield. Which is why we nearly screwed up.'

'I know. We all take Baz's word. Old habits die hard.'

'Too right. Bazza needs someone to watch him, someone to put the harder questions. That someone should be a lawyer.'

'Esme *is* a lawyer. She just happens to be family too.'

'Of course. And that's exactly the way Baz likes to play it. Apart from anything else, it's cheaper. Plus it gives him an easy ride. He just follows his nose and hopes everything will turn out dandy. In this case he could have ended up inside, Ezzie too. When it comes to money like Garfield's, lawyers have a responsibility. It's all spelled out in the act. Ezzie wasn't even on the same page.'

Marie looked chastened. When she asked what happened over the contract Winter described the scene in the airport car park. It had done the job, he warned her, but they hadn't parted friends. Marie watched Winter demolish the last of his scone, licking the cream from his fingertips.

'You're right about Baz needing someone on his case. I've been thinking that for years.' She smiled at him. 'And you know who that someone should be?'

'I do my best.' Winter looked up at her. 'But he never listens.' He sat back, gazing out at the sunshine. A plump couple in cargo pants were poking around in the border, looking for a golf ball. 'What's with Madison?' he said at last. 'He wasn't out in Spain. At least not yesterday.'

'I've no idea, Paul. My daughter's love life is a closed book. Since we had words about this whole shambles she's refused to talk to me. How come she's so headstrong? Does she get it from Baz, do you think? Or me?'

'Baz, definitely. What about Stu?'

'He's back in London but he phones me most evenings. We have long chats, which is strange because we were never especially close before. He's really hurt, Paul, he really is. And I worry about those kids. Evzenie seems able to cope OK and Stuart hasn't said a word about what's going on but kids are canny, they can smell trouble. It's all such a bloody mess, Paul. It's just so bloody *sad*.'

'And Bazza? What's his take?'

'Nothing changes. He'd gladly throttle Madison and there are nights when he's had a few to drink and then he blames Stuart too. Baz is no angel, I know that, but I've never felt neglected, not the way Esme says she has.'

Winter smiled then changed the subject, asking again about Sturrock. Marie said she'd hire him tomorrow.

'Baz wants him full time.'

'I know.'

'You think he'll do it?'

'Yes.' She nodded. 'The other thing we talked about was what he'll actually be doing. To be frank I don't think he realised quite how much scope there is in TTT. He can take it wherever he wants. There are enough problem kids in this city to keep him busy 24/7. He's got total carte blanche.'

'And that fired him up?'

'Yes.' Her eyes were gleaming. 'It most certainly did.'

Faraday knew it was nonsense. Willard hadn't come to say thank you, nor anything of the sort. Willard had come to leave a message. He'd never compromise himself by spelling it out but he'd rely on Faraday to do the necessary. Get hold of Winter. Tell him Mackenzie's in the shit. And let's see what happens.

The *ping* of an incoming email took Faraday upstairs. It wasn't that he had anything against another attempt to bring down Bazza Mackenzie. On the contrary, the man's success was a beacon for every work-shy adolescent in the city. Better a career in drug dealing, went the word on the street, than the chore of staying in every night mugging for a bunch of exams that would probably get you nowhere. No, Willard was right to keep Mackenzie in his sights. Faraday supported that. But what angered him was this latest bid, poorly disguised, to use Faraday as some kind of back channel. Just what was he supposed to say to Winter? How kosher was the threat to his boss? What did Madison really have on Bazza Mackenzie?

The fact that Willard had volunteered nothing in the way of detail was hardly surprising. Covert operations relied on the thinnest possible spread of information. But keeping Faraday in the dark simply added to his sense of embattlement. First he'd been removed from the Blue Dragon inquiry. No apology. No explanation. Now he'd become the messenger boy in Willard's latest bid to settle a long-standing debt. Was he really interested? He thought not. Would he bother to lift the phone and help cast Willard's net? Unlikely.

Upstairs, he bent to the PC. The message was from Gabrielle. *Tu as probablement pensé que j'étais bourré samedi soir. Comme on peut se tromper?* Faraday grinned. You probably think I was drunk on Saturday night, she'd written. How wrong can you get?

He gazed down at the screen for a moment, framing a reply. Then he had second thoughts, knowing how much more fluent he'd be after a glass or two of wine. The *Sangster* file was waiting for him in the kitchen. He'd yet to read the various appendices but knew it could wait. Time, quite suddenly, was the least of his problems.

Chapter eighteen

Marie took the call. It was four in the morning. She recognised the voice. It was Esme's au pair, Evzenie. She was sobbing.

'What is it? What's happened?' Marie rolled over in bed, shielding the conversation from her slumbering husband.

'The police ...' Evzenie broke down again.

'What about them?'

'They're here. Everywhere. Please come. Quickly.'

The line went dead. Marie got out of bed. With the light on, Mackenzie sat up, rubbing his eyes. Automatically, his hand went down to the carpet. Under the bed he kept a baseball bat.

'What the fuck ...?'

'We've got to go, Baz. It's Evzenie. Something's happened.'

'Where?'

'Esme's.' She looked round for something to wear. Tracksuit bottoms. A sweater. Anything. Mackenzie was standing beside the bed, still naked. Befuddlement was giving way to anger. He watched Marie stabbing a number into her mobile.

'What now? Who are you phoning?'

'Paul. We'll pick him up on the way out.'

Winter was waiting for them outside Blake House. He got into the back of the Bentley and gave Marie's shoulder a little squeeze.

'It'll be fine,' he said. 'We'll sort it.'

'Sort what?' Mackenzie had jumped the lights outside Gunwharf.

'Whatever's happened. Maybe the girl's had a bad dream. Maybe she's got stuff all out of proportion.'

'Sure, Paul.' It was Marie. 'And maybe she hasn't.'

It took less than half an hour to drive deep into the Meon Valley. Esme's property lay up a narrow country lane. From the main road on the valley floor, Winter could see lights on. At the final bend before the house itself, a traffic car blocked the lane.

Mackenzie's window purred down. A face appeared from the darkness.

'And you are?'

'The name's Mackenzie. My daughter lives here. What's going on?'

The officer didn't answer. His torch had settled on Winter's face.

'Well, well ...' A soft laugh. 'Mr Winter.'

'Yeah. The gentleman here asked you a question. What's happened?'

The officer told Mackenzie to follow him up to the house. The two vehicles drove in convoy. There were two more cars and a white van parked on the big semicircle of gravel outside Esme's front door. Winter recognised the van. Scenes of Crime, he thought. Something horrible had definitely kicked off.

Marie was out of the Bentley first. Another uniform managed to intercept her before she made it to the front door. Only then did she spot the au pair in the passenger seat of the unmarked Escort. Two of Esme's kids were in the back, their pale faces pressed against the glass.

A tall figure got out of the Escort and extended a hand.

'D/C Yates. Evzenie tells me you're Mrs Mackenzie.'

'That's right. What's going on? What's happened?'

Marie had been joined by Bazza. Winter was still in the Bentley. Yates spared Mackenzie a nod.

'There's been a bit of an incident,' he said. 'I wish we could do this inside but Scenes of Crime have the place secured.'

Mackenzie stepped very close. His patience had run out. He spoke very slowly, the way you might address a child.

'Just ... tell ... me ... what ... happened.'

'I'm trying, Mr Mackenzie.'

'Good, son. So?'

'The au pair belled 999 about an hour ago. She'd had an intruder in the house. The long and short of it is the oldest boy. The intruder took him. He's gone.'

'Guy?' Marie let out a gasp, a small animal noise. Winter had joined them by now. He squeezed her arm.

'*Took* him?' Mackenzie wanted to know more.

'We're assuming he broke in. A noise woke the au pair. She found him in Guy's bedroom. He had the boy out of bed, hands bound behind his back, mouth taped, blindfold, the lot. She says he'd even sorted some clothes for the lad.'

'And?'

'He gave Evzenie a bit of a shove. The next thing she knew, he was carrying the lad out of the house. They must have had a car outside. She heard it drive away.'

'They?'

'She says she heard voices, just a snatch of conversation. She was pretty upset, as you might imagine.'

'Yeah?' Mackenzie wasn't listening. 'So who'd want to do a thing like that?'

'Very good question. I'm sure we'll find out.'

'You're not wrong, son.' Mackenzie turned round and shot Winter a look. 'You know any of these clowns, Paul?'

Winter and Yates exchanged glances. They'd worked together on countless jobs over the years. Now this.

Marie was squatting beside the Escort. One of the rear doors was open and she was talking to the kids. One of them clambered out, bare feet on the cold gravel, and put her arms round her. She was still wearing her pyjamas. Marie carried the child to the Bentley and wrapped her in a blanket from the boot.

Winter wanted to know about descriptions. First, the intruder. Yates pulled a face.

'She says jeans, army-style sweater, socks, no shoes. He was also wearing a black balaclava. Apparently the guy didn't say a word inside the house.'

'And the motor outside?'

'She never saw it. Just heard it driving away. Control have put out an alert but don't hold your breath. The guy cut the landline and nicked the au pair's mobile. She knew the owners keep a spare but it took her a while to find it.' Yates turned back to Mackenzie. 'Where are the parents, sir?'

'Ezzie's in Spain. Stu's in London.'

'You want to tell them? Or shall we do it? Either way we need to talk to them. Sharpish.'

'I'll sort it,' said Winter. He caught Mackenzie's eye and they stepped away from the house into the darkness.

'What happens now, mush?'

'They'll want statements. Evzenie, obviously. Then you and Marie, and Ezzie and Stu, and anyone else they can lay their hands on. They need to build a picture, Baz. They need to try and put some names in the frame.'

'But it's obvious, isn't it? Big house? Money? Take a hostage? Earn yourself a few bob?'

'Not necessarily.'

'No?'

'No.' Winter looked him in the eye. If anyone was prime suspect here he knew exactly who it was. Mackenzie didn't get it.

'Tell me, mush. Tell me what I'm missing.'

'Who have we pissed off recently?'

'Is that a serious question? You want the full list?'

'Very recently.'

'You mean Spain?' It was beginning to dawn on him. 'The contract? That silly fucking woman?'

Winter nodded. 'I've been here, Baz. I know how these guys work.'

'You mean Garfield?'

'No.' He shook his head. 'The Bill. They'll be looking for motive. Garfield's perfect.'

'But you only did the lawyer a couple of days ago ... and Garfield's inside on bloody remand. You think they're *that* organised?'

'I've no idea, Baz, but it smells right. Ez had dinner with the wife on Saturday night. She says they got on really well, had a proper chat, all that bollocks. Ez might have told her about the kids, the house, the horses, the whole set-up. Fuck knows, if she had a few to drink she might even have told her about – you know – the situation ... about what's going on with lover boy and about Stu being up in London all week. The place was wide open, Baz, as you can see.'

Mackenzie nodded, thoughtful. Then his gaze returned to the house.

'You're right,' he said quietly.

Winter went across to the Escort. Yates was back behind the

wheel making a phone call. Catching Winter's eye he gestured for him to hang on. He nodded a couple of times and muttered something Winter didn't catch. Then the conversation was over.

'Good news, mate.' He was still looking at Winter. 'The duty D/I from Major Crimes is still dealing with a murder in Waterlooville. Guess who's picking this lot up?'

Winter gazed at him a moment. 'Faraday?'

After the phone call Faraday took a moment to get his bearings. A stripe of grey light at the edge of the curtained window suggested it was dawn. He reached for the mobile again. 04.51. DCI Parsons wanted a meet in half an hour at Kingston Crescent. Faraday headed for the bathroom. A kidnap?

Parsons was already at her desk by the time he finally got to Major Crimes. She must have made him the coffee a while ago because it was nearly cold.

'It's Mackenzie, Joe. I don't know whether I told you on the phone. One of the grandchildren. A little boy called Guy.'

She briefly recounted what had happened. The property would be in the hands of Scenes of Crime for a while yet. They were starting at the front entrance and working slowly towards the boy's bedroom.

'Professional job?'

'Definitely.'

'How many people in the property?'

'Four. Three kids and an au pair.'

Parsons explained about Esme and Stuart being away and Faraday nodded, wondering how much she knew about Perry Madison. Maybe Willard really was keeping the info under wraps.

'Was the property alarmed?'

'Apparently there's an alarm installed but it doesn't seemed to have functioned. The au pair only woke up when the intruder was in the next bedroom.'

'So the place was unprotected?'

'It would seem so.'

Faraday scribbled himself a note. Only hours ago Willard had been doing his best to point Faraday in Winter's direction. Now he had no choice but to lift the phone.

'So how do we play this, boss?'

'I'm SIO, Joe, for the time being. You're Deputy. SOCU will end up managing it, of course, assuming it runs and runs.'

The Serious Organised Crime Unit worked from three centres across the county. Normally, they'd have taken ownership from the off. So why were he and Parsons in the driving seat?

'It's Mr Willard's decision, Joe.' Parsons reached for a notepad. 'Maybe you should ask him.'

Ten minutes later, Faraday was back in his office. Between them, he and Parsons had agreed the ground rules for Operation *Causeway*. A total media blackout, pending developments. Examination of traffic cameras along the various approach routes to the Meon Valley. House-to-house calls in the surrounding villages. A trawl through the Sex Offenders Register to chase up local paedos. And, most important of all, an in-depth examination of the family's lifestyle. Friends. Enemies. Feuds. Debts. Anything, in short, that might trigger a post-midnight visit to the family home.

While it was true that some kidnaps were the work of predatory strangers attracted by rumours of wealth or paedophiles after the fuck of their dreams, most – in the parlance – were Bad on Bad: drug dealers after outstanding debts, criminals using flesh and blood to settle old scores. This, Faraday quickly realised, was why Willard had decided to retain *Causeway* within Major Crimes, at least for the time being. Faced with the loss of his grandchild, Mackenzie could hardly complain about intrusive questioning in the bid to get the lad back. And given his relationship with Winter, Faraday was the obvious choice to ask those questions. Willard had also stipulated that D/S Jimmy Suttle would head the intel cell over the coming days. Suttle, of course, had been very close to Winter while the disgraced ex-cop was still in the Job. Another piece of inspired casting on Willard's part.

Faraday checked his watch. Half six was early to be phoning Suttle and so he found a pad in the desk drawer and began to list his immediate lines of enquiry. Top of that list was a single name. Perry Madison.

*

Mackenzie, back home in Craneswater, had the same thought. Marie was upstairs, trying to get the kids to sleep. In the kitchen Winter had made a pot of tea.

'Do you think it's a runner, mush? Do you think he's that crazy?'

Winter wasn't convinced. 'He hates kids, always has done. He and his missus never had any of their own and that's why.'

'So what's he doing with my fucking daughter? Didn't she ever mention she had three of them?'

'I've no idea, Baz. But why would he nick Guy?'

'Maybe Ez put him up to it. New life in Spain. Trophy kid to remind her of the old times.'

'Then why not take all three? Just put them in the car and head for the ferry?'

'Fuck knows. You're right, though. Doesn't fly, does it?'

Winter found a loaf and fed the toaster with slices of Hovis. To his surprise, he was famished. Mackenzie wanted to know about the FLO mentioned back at Esme's place. What the fuck was an FLO?

'Family Liaison Officer, Baz. She'll turn up first thing, probably with Faraday.'

'But what's her game?'

'She's there to hold your hand. These days they call it Victim Support.'

'Fuck that.'

'Play along, Baz. Number one, you want Guy back. Number two, we want to keep these people at arm's length. That's not going to be easy. There are blokes I know in the Job who'll be creaming themselves at an opportunity like this. They'll be crawling all over you, Baz. We have to plan for that. We have to be ahead of their game.'

'Yeah?' Mackenzie was watching the curl of blue smoke from the toaster. 'So what about Spain?'

'We tell them.'

'Tell them what?'

'Tell them about the hotel, about the apartment block, about the deal with Garfield. Either we do that upfront or they'll find out anyway.'

'You're off your head, mush.' Mackenzie was staring at him.

'We've just bust a gut making sure that bloody deal never happens. Why make it easy for them?'

'Because, like I say, they're bound to find out. Faraday's no fool and if he's working with a bloke called Jimmy Suttle there's no way they won't put the deal together.'

'So we just own up? Is that what you're saying?'

'Yeah. You and Ez negotiated the deal. You took Garfield at face value. Then you realised it was dirty money and you pulled out. You're horrified, Baz. You feel betrayed, but thank God you've got the bollocks to do the right thing. You're a businessman. You depend on your reputation. The last thing you can afford is to lose it.'

'I *tell* them all that?'

'Word for word, Baz. You grit your teeth and you do it.'

'They'll piss themselves laughing, mush. They know me. They know what I'm like.' He rescued the toast and left it on the worktop. 'What about the lawyer you smacked around? The luggage you nicked?'

'That too. That was how much pressure we were under. That was how much we *cared*.'

Mackenzie sat down again. He wasn't convinced. Winter put more bread in the toaster and binned the first lot. Mackenzie watched his every move.

'You really think this is all down to Garfield? Nicking my fucking grandson? Just to get even?'

'It's more than possible, Baz. The guy's minted, he's well connected, and being inside won't make any difference. On remand you can have all kinds of visits, make phone calls, the lot, plus that missus of his might turn out to wear the trousers. Maybe there's something going on between her and the toy-boy lawyer. Whichever way you cut it, the woman was humiliated.'

'Yeah. By you, mush.'

'By me. Too right. To save your bacon.'

'Yeah. And look where we are now.'

Winter was sorting out some plates for the toast. He stopped. Turned round.

'Are you serious? Am I hearing what I think I'm hearing? Only if I am you can stick your fucking job up your arse. Who sent me out there in the first place? Who never bothered to check out Garfield's money?'

Mackenzie stared at him. In the spill of early sunshine through the window he looked suddenly exhausted.

'Sorry, mush.' He shook his head. 'That was totally out of order. You know what? I think I'm fucking losing it. What we really need to do is sort this cunt out, big time.'

'Which cunt?'

'Garfield. A stroke like that? Un-fucking-forgivable.'

'Forget it, Baz. Sorting Garfield out is down to the Bill. That's their job. That's why you pay your taxes.'

'Yeah ... but it doesn't feel right, none of it. A *kid* for Chrissakes, a game little nipper like Guy. If anyone lifts a finger to him, I swear to God ...' He left the sentence unfinished, staring into nowhere.

There was a long silence. Winter could hear footsteps descending the stairs. Then Marie appeared at the open kitchen door. She gazed at them both. Winter knew she'd been crying.

'They're asleep, poor lambs,' she said. 'Is anyone going to tell me what happens next?'

Chapter nineteen

The FLO's name was Helen Christian. She was a local girl, early forties, Pompey born and bred, slightly overweight. She, more than anyone on the *Causeway* squad, knew exactly the kind of challenge that lay ahead.

'You won't believe this, Jimmy, but I went out with him once. He won't remember but it's true.'

'Who?' Suttle was sitting at Faraday's desk waiting for his boss to return.

'Mackenzie. He was an estate agent in the early days, Jack the Lad, really funny, really good company. We used to go to those all-nighters out in the country. He always got the best drugs, even then.'

'You knew his missus too? The lovely Marie?' Suttle was looking impressed.

'Yeah, she was a High School girl. Posh but a bit of a wild child. If I remember right, her dad was an architect. Mackenzie was all over her until she fell pregnant.'

'And then?'

'He ran a mile, took up with loads of other women.'

'Including you?'

'Yeah. I really liked him, to tell you the truth. He was different to the other layabouts. He knew what he wanted. He was going places, you could tell.'

'Sure ... and look where it took him.'

'Trillionaire? Nice car? Pretty wife? Big house? Am I missing something here, Jimmy?'

Faraday stepped back into the office with a tray of coffees. He'd been in conference with Parsons. Word from the scene so far offered nothing in the way of a decent lead.

'The guy forced an entry through the front door. He must

have left his shoes outside because they can't raise any soil samples or prints from the carpet, and the girl says he was wandering around in socks. He was wearing gloves too, so prints are another no-no.'

'Alarm?'

'It didn't work. No one knows why.'

'You think he might have disabled it?'

'It's possible.'

'Tyre marks?'

'It's a gravel drive. No chance.'

'Neat job, then.'

'Very.'

'Skin colour?'

'IC1 as far as she could make out. He was wearing a balaclava.' IC1 meant white male.

'Accent?'

'He never said a word until he got outside. The au pair's not great on regional accents and all she heard were murmurs. But there were definitely two of them, maybe more.'

'This mobile of hers, the one he nicked. It wasn't on by any chance?'

'She says not. We've got the number. That's something you might chase.'

Suttle made a note. Cell site analysis, providing the phone was live, could track its whereabouts.

Faraday handed Christian a coffee. Suttle mentioned her fling with Mackenzie. Faraday turned to the FLO.

'Does DCI Parsons know about that?'

'Yeah ...' Christian nodded. 'I gather she phoned Mr Willard just to check whether it was appropriate. He must have said yes.'

Faraday nodded, amused. 'He'll think it might play to our advantage. He's probably right too. Mackenzie's going to be vulnerable, his missus as well. The tighter you get ... You know the way it goes.'

'Of course, boss.'

'There's something else I ought to mention. The daughter's been over the side recently. With Perry Madison.'

Suttle's head came up. Like more or less everyone else, he loathed the DCI.

'Madison? You have to be joking.'

'Far from it.'

'But why him? Why beat yourself up with someone like that? The man's an arsehole.'

'Sure.' It was Helen Christian. 'But he's *her* arsehole. Some women can't wait to get themselves abused. Don't ask me why.'

Suttle was still getting to grips with this latest news. From Esme's point of view, he said, it seemed an inexplicable choice. From Madison's too. Any kind of involvement with the Mackenzie brood was a kamikaze move. As Suttle himself knew only too well.

'How come?' Christian was intrigued.

'I got it on with a girl called Trudy a while ago. She wasn't the sharpest pencil in the box but we had a good time. Then it turned out that her mum was Mackenzie's long-term shag and when the Man found out I got a toeing. Couple of heavies outside Tiger Tiger one night. Fucking painful if you're asking.' Tiger Tiger was a nightclub in Gunwharf. The attack had put Suttle in hospital for a couple of days.

'Nasty.' Christian was looking at Faraday. 'So that's two of us with previous as far as Mackenzie's concerned.'

It was gone ten by the time Faraday and Christian made it to 13 Sandown Road. Marie opened the front door. Faraday could smell fresh coffee and the lingering scent of burned toast. Two tiny faces peered out at him from the depths of the hall.

Mackenzie and Winter were sitting at the kitchen table. There was an exchange of nods. Faraday said yes to coffee. Christian declined.

'Old times, eh?' Winter was looking up at Faraday, then Christian. 'Who'd have guessed?'

Christian was explaining her role to Marie. She and her husband were to treat her as part of the family. It was important that she won the confidence of the kids.

'Part of the family?' Mackenzie's head came up, immediately suspicious, staring at Faraday. 'How does that work?' He rounded on Christian, provoked by the very thought. Then he took another look at her, harder this time. 'What's your first name again?'

'Helen'

'Helen?' He was frowning now, trying to match the face to some long-ago memory. 'Do I know you?'

'Maybe.'

'How?'

'We went out a couple of times. Ages ago.'

'We did?' He was fighting hard to keep focus. Last night's events didn't help. 'Like when?'

'Back in the 80s. 83? 84? I can't remember.'

Mackenzie stared at her a moment or two longer. She was on the point of giving him another clue when his hand closed on hers.

'Iron Maiden T-shirt? Big fucking poster on that bedroom wall of yours?'

'Yes.'

'We went to the Reading festival, right?'

'Right.'

'Black Sabbath? The Stranglers?'

'Yeah.'

'So what are you doing with this lot?'

Christian glanced at Marie. Maybe this hadn't been such a good idea. Mackenzie hadn't finished. Curiosity had given way to bewilderment. First someone nicks his favourite grandchild, then an old shag turns out to be working with the Filth. Faraday was watching him carefully. He almost felt sorry for the man.

'She's a copper, Mr Mackenzie,' he said. 'She's come to lend a hand.'

Marie left the room without a word. Helen went after her, leaving the three men at the table. Mackenzie was still trying to make sense of it all. He looked sideways at Winter.

'This is totally out of order, isn't it? This is taking the fucking piss.'

'Ignore it, Baz. She's a lovely girl.'

'You're right, mush, but what's lovely got to do with it? This is a kidnap not an 80s fucking reunion. Am I right Mr F?'

Faraday ignored the question, aware of the sudden force of Mackenzie's anger. Putting Helen Christian into play had been a deliberately provocative ploy. Best now to move on. He outlined some of the steps Operation *Causeway* had already taken.

When he got to the Sexual Offenders Register, Mackenzie interrupted. He seemed to have forgotten about Helen Christian.

'You think the boy might have been nonced?'

'I doubt it. The MO's all wrong. Nonces don't break into houses like Esme's.'

'But you think it might be possible?'

'We have to bear it in mind.'

There was a silence around the table. Then Faraday assured Mackenzie that everything possible was being done to progress the investigation. For the time being they were imposing a media blackout but this decision might change later. Mackenzie wanted to know why.

'Because it might be in our interests to make some kind of appeal. They'll be expecting that. They'll be tuned in.'

'But these cunts will get in touch, won't they? Isn't that the way it works? Gimme the moolah? Or fucking else?'

'It's possible,' Faraday admitted, 'but we try and plan for every eventuality.'

He asked about Esme. It was important to talk to her. When was she coming back?

'I've been trying to phone her all morning. Silly cow's got her mobile switched off. I've left a message at the hotel too. She'll get in touch in the end.'

'And her husband? Stuart?'

'He's on the way down. He should be here in an hour or so.'

'Good. So how are the kids?'

'Upset. Guy's always been the big brother. Big brothers don't just fuck off like that.'

Faraday nodded, turning his attention to Winter.

'Perry Madison?' he enquired.

'Haven't got a clue, boss.' The 'boss' was deliberate, Faraday knew it. Winter's role here was to muddy the waters. Faraday looked at Mackenzie again.

'Is Madison still with your daughter, Mr Mackenzie?'

'No idea. I've never discussed it with her, to tell you the truth. No offence, mate, but how could she pull a stroke like that? With the Filth?'

Faraday, unsmiling, made a note. When he asked whether either of them could think of any possible reason why anyone would want to kidnap young Guy, Mackenzie was the first to answer.

'Money,' he said. 'Stands to reason.'

'Nothing else?'

'No.'

'No vendettas? No one you've upset recently? No one trying to settle a debt?'

'No way.' Mackenzie shook his head. 'I'm a businessman, mush. I watch my manners. Reputation's everything in my game, especially in a city like this.'

'I don't doubt it.' Faraday turned to Winter. 'How about you?'

'I work for Mr Mackenzie.'

'I know. You've been in the Job though. You know the way these things work. Can you think of anything, *anything*, that might account for last night?'

Winter held his gaze, aware of Mackenzie trying to catch his eye. This, he knew, was the fork in the investigative road. For whatever reason, Bazza had decided to bluff it out. Was it really Winter's job to grass him up?

'Offhand, the answer has to be no,' he said carefully. 'It's been a long night. If anything comes back to me you'll be the first to know.'

Winter watched Faraday scribbling himself another note. Already he felt like a hostage, bound hand and foot by a boss who paid him a great deal of money and then refused to listen to sensible advice.

Faraday hadn't finished. He was still looking at Winter.

'We'll need a full account of your movements over the past week or so.'

'Why?' It was Mackenzie.

'Any of you may have been watched. It's unlikely you'd be aware of something like that but there are steps we can take to check these things out. We look for patterns, as Mr Winter will doubtless explain.'

'Fine.' Mackenzie shrugged. 'Ask away.'

'It won't be me, Mr Mackenzie. We have a D/S on the team. His name's Suttle. He'll be along later. If you can give him – say – an hour of your time, I'd be grateful.'

'No problem. Paul's the one with the heavy schedule.'

'Oh?' Faraday cocked an eyebrow.

'Yeah, he's up to London on the one o'clock – important meeting with clients. Back tomorrow, eh Paulie?'

'Yeah.' Winter offered him a weary nod, already aware that Faraday didn't believe a word.

Faraday was back in his office by eleven, summoning Jimmy Suttle for an update.

'Winter's lying, Jimmy. Mackenzie too. I've no idea what's been going on but the daughter will know, Marie too probably – if she ever talks to us again.'

Faraday described the scene in the kitchen, with Mackenzie raking the ashes of a long-ago fling. Before he'd left the house Faraday had snatched a quiet word with the FLO. According to Helen Christian, Marie had been appalled to find one of her husband's old girlfriends in the house and it was going to take a while to get her onside.

'You think that's going to be possible?'

'Helen does, and that's all that matters. She's playing the sisterhood card. They both know the man, they've both had to cope with him. She's a good girl, Helen, and the fact that she's so local might even help in the end. God knows, they'll probably end up mates.'

Suttle nodded. Parsons had organised a squad of detectives for *Causeway* and fired up the Major Incident Room. A D/I from the Serious Organised Crime Unit had arrived with a watching brief but the returns from the initial actions had so far been disappointing. Nothing hugely significant from the traffic cameras. No reports of anything out of the ordinary from neighbouring properties. Four local entries on the Sex Offenders Register, all of them with alibis that would probably check out.

'Early days though, boss, eh?'

Faraday nodded. He wanted Suttle to get across to Craneswater as soon as possible. Mackenzie, his wife and Winter would have had ample chance to get their stories straight by now but Helen Christian had been right to flag up Marie's distress. The rift between her and her husband was doubtless what Willard had planned, and in the nature of these incidents Faraday knew that the sheer emotional impact of losing the child would deepen that divide.

'The son-in-law will probably be there too. Get a full account off him, the last week or so – pin him down.'

'And Winter?'

'He's off to London. Back tomorrow. Good luck, son.'

Suttle left the office, followed by Faraday. Down the corridor, Parsons' door was open. She was on the phone. Faraday stepped inside and closed the door. His earlier request had given the Surveillance Unit barely an hour to get themselves together.

Parsons ended her call and looked across at Faraday.

'Well, boss?'

'Sorted.' Parsons rarely grinned. 'He'll be on the one o'clock, you say?'

Mackenzie insisted on having the confrontation in the den. He didn't want Marie in on this. No way.

Winter told him to sit down. He rarely lost his temper but now was different. He literally had no choice.

'You know your problem, Baz? You've started to believe your own publicity. You think you're smarter than they are. You think they're stupid. Ten years in clover and you think you're home free. Money's bought you all this. Money's even bought you *me*, for fuck's sake. But you know something? The hole you're looking at now is deeper than even your fucking pockets. They'll have it off you, Baz. Every last fucking penny.'

'I know, mush.'

'So why fanny around? Why try and pull the wool? Why not do as I suggested? Try and turn the thing to our advantage? Prove what a load of born-again do-gooders we really are? Marie tells me you want to go into politics. Fat fucking chance. Politics takes a bit of wit, Baz. You have to listen to people. You have to suss their weaknesses, their strengths, their funny little ways. Not just march on as if the rest of the fucking world doesn't exist.'

'So what was I supposed to say? That we were that close to signing a deal? That we sussed the guy? That we pulled out?'

'Exactly. All you had to do was make a little drama out of it. All we had to stand up was our own integrity. We could have signed that contract but we didn't, and there's no way they can disprove that. These guys are into evidence, Baz. That's what they collect for a living. In this case there isn't any. Why? Because we've got it all back off them.'

'Wrong, mush.'

'What?'

'I said you're wrong. I got through to Ez just before they arrived. Told her what had happened.'

'And?'

'She's taking the next plane home but that's not the point. It's about the contract.'

'You're telling me the hotelier won't play ball? Won't give us the contract back?'

'No, it's not that. Fresnada's fine about his copy but he had a little chat to the receptionist who was on duty on Sunday. The lawyer guy apparently asked her to send a fax to the UK just after they signed the contract. Guess how many pages?'

'Ten?'

'Yeah.'

'Shit.'

'Exactly. Fresnada got me the details. It's a London number.'

Winter sank into one of the big leather recliners. Suttle was due any minute. They had to work this out, had to.

'Tell him, Baz.'

'Tell him what?'

'Tell him everything. It's called disclosure and it's still not too late. The fact that Ez signed the contract needn't land us completely in the shit. It's a mistake, sure, but no one's perfect in this world. We got it wrong. End of.'

Mackenzie shook his head.

'They'll screw me, mush, I know it.'

'So what are you suggesting? What choice do we have?'

'You go to London. I've got Garfield's address. He won't be there, of course, but his missus will. Get that contract back off her, the faxed copy plus any others. Then put her in front of a lawyer and get her to sign an affadavit saying that the deal's off. Do whatever it takes. Be sweet to her. Apologise. Say you're really, really sorry. Blame what happened on Rikki's boys. Tell her we're as pissed off as they are. The thing was totally out of order. If it's money she's after she can talk to me. We'll call it compensation. We'll call it *any* fucking thing. But she has to see it our way, mush, before these animals get on your case.'

'*My* case?'

'Yeah. You're right about the Filth but you're in as deep as me, mate. And I'm not just talking money laundering.' He checked his watch. 'I'll phone for a cab. You can still make the one o'clock.'

Perry Madison didn't bother to knock. Faraday looked up from his desk to find the DCI shutting the office door behind him. As ever, he was wearing a sharply cut grey suit with the kind of fuck-off tie that drew your attention. Today's was scarlet with yellow blobs. Look at me.

'Are we making this official or what?'

He stood over Faraday and glowered down at him. This was less than subtle but on a good day he could turn intimidation into an art form.

'Like it or not you're part of this thing.' Faraday reached for his pad. 'I take it we both want the kid safely back?'

'Of course we fucking do. Don't be a twat, Faraday. You know exactly what I'm talking about.'

'I do?'

'Yeah. Even you can't be that thick.' He was on the balls of his feet now, the classic boxer's pose, and Faraday wondered whether there was a reasonable chance of violence. Oddly enough, the prospect didn't worry him in the slightest. He'd long considered Madison to be a headcase and this simply confirmed it. He looked up at him, holding the man's gaze, then suggested that he sit down.

'You think I told Willard about you and Mackenzie's daughter? Is that it?'

'Yeah.'

'Then you're right for once. That's exactly what I did.'

'Then you're a grassing cunt.'

'Maybe.' Faraday shrugged. 'But what does that make you? Apart from stupid?'

'I could have you for this, Faraday. I can't think of anyone else who would have done what you've done. There's a code in this job in case you're wondering, things you do and things you don't do. Grassing up a colleague is fucking outrageous and climbing up Willard's arse is even worse. You smell of shit, Faraday. I don't know how people like you sleep at night.'

'With ease, if you're asking. And I'll tell you something else. I spent the worst six months of my professional life trying to nail Mackenzie and he pissed all over us. You know why? Because he's smarter than we are. But hey, you might have cracked it. Shag his daughter? Have her fall in love with you? Smart move. That may have legs. That may do it.'

Madison at last lowered himself into the spare chair. He crossed one leg over the other, his eyes never leaving Faraday's face. Whoever was doing his ironing knew a thing or two about knife-edge creases.

'You really think that?'

'Think what?'

'Think that I'm doing some kind of number on her? Charging her up to overtime?'

'Yeah. And like I say, that may do it for you. This job loves legends. You could just become one of them. The guy that screwed the Mackenzies. Not just the father but the daughter too. Bold, Perry. It's good to see guys like you thinking outside the box.' Faraday reached for his pad and took his time sorting a pen. 'I hate to lower the tone but what have you been doing these last few days? Care to give me a full account?'

'You're twisted, you know that?'

'No, Perry, I'm just a simple cop. And right now I'd like to know what you've been up to. Let's start with Esme. When did you last see her?'

The question drew a frown from Madison. For a moment, Faraday thought he was about to walk out. He was wrong.

'Five days ago.'

'Really? Is this self-denial or have you had a tiff?'

'She's not around.'

'Then where is she?'

'Spain. Place called Baiona.'

'And what's she doing there?'

'I've no idea.'

'I don't believe you.'

'Well fucking try. She works for her dad. It's something commercial. I haven't a clue what.'

'She doesn't tell you?'

'No.' He shook his head, studied his bitten nails. 'We've got better things to talk about, believe it or not.'

'Like getting it on properly? Divorce? New life? All that?'

'Like getting out of this khazi, for a start. And like rejoining the rest of the human race.'

'With her?'

'Yes.'

'Abroad? Spain?'

'Whatever it takes.'

'So what has she told you? About this place Baiona?'

'Nothing, except it's beautiful. She loves it.'

'And she says you will too. Am I right?'

Faraday knew he wouldn't get the satisfaction of an answer. For the first time it began to occur to him that Madison might be telling the truth. There really was no covert subplot. He'd met the woman, talked her into bed, and good sex or chronic loneliness had done the rest. After years in the marital desert, the oasis of his dreams.

'Would it be easier for you to talk to my intel skipper?' Faraday gestured at his pad. 'Only I don't want this to get personal.'

Madison looked up. For once, he'd spotted the irony.

'Fuck off, Faraday,' he said softly.

Chapter twenty

Jimmy Suttle's interview with Mackenzie was nearly over. They were talking in the front room. Stuart Norcliffe drove a black Porsche Carrera. He parked it outside the big square bay window and let himself into the house. Suttle heard him greeting Marie in the hall. Then the door burst open.

Norcliffe was a big man, shorn scalp, jeans and an open-necked pink shirt under a white linen jacket. He'd driven down from London. He wanted to know just what the hell was going on.

Mackenzie told him. When he'd finished, he introduced Suttle.

'This guy's on the case, Stu. He wants to know what we've all been up to lately. Isn't that right, son?'

'Yeah. Maybe a bit later, Mr Norcliffe? As soon as we're through?'

'Whatever will help. Just give me a shout.'

He looked uncertainly at Mackenzie for a moment then left the room. Suttle heard Marie asking whether he'd eaten or not. The kids were upstairs. They'd love to see him.

Suttle turned back to Mackenzie. His notebook was virtually empty. As Faraday had warned, his interviewee was playing the innocent.

'So nothing that you can think of? Nothing personal? Nothing connected with your business?'

'Nothing. *Nada*. That's Spanish, by the way.'

'And your daughter?'

'Back this afternoon.'

'From Spain, you say?'

'Yeah.'

'Business or pleasure?'

'Neither. Needs must, son. She's had a coupla problems at home, needed a little break, needed to be by herself, have a bit of a think about things. Stu's pretty much the same except he still needs to work, poor bastard. You probably know about all this over-the-side bollocks, don't you? From that nice Mr Faraday?'

'I do. I'm sorry.'

'Don't be, mush. Happens all the time, more and more.'

'I meant the kids.'

'Yeah? Well there's that, of course, big time. You know what my dad would have done if my mum had been knobbed by some other bloke? He'd have done them both, slowly, one after the other. We're too polite these days. Ever thought about that?'

The interview was at an end, Suttle knew. Mackenzie got to his feet and said he'd send Stu in.

'Must be like an audition for you, eh, son? Putting us through our paces, see if we measure up? Go easy on Stu, though. Bloke's in a bit of a state.'

Mackenzie left the room. Seconds later Helen Christian came in. She'd been upstairs with the kids but beat a discreet retreat when their dad appeared. The kids, she said, were a real credit.

'You sound surprised.'

'I am. I never had Mackenzie down as a family man. Turns out they worship him ... and her of course – Marie.'

'He's upset, isn't he? You can sense it.'

'Yeah, definitely. That's exactly what Marie says too. Normally he plays stuff pretty close to his chest. Since last night he's been all over the place. She's worried for him, she's worried for them all.'

'I'm sure she is. You want to sit in when I talk to Norcliffe?'

'Please.'

Stu appeared minutes later carrying a tray laden with snacks. Marie thought they might be hungry. Suttle helped himself to a chicken salad sandwich. Stu didn't want anything.

'This must be tough for you, Mr Norcliffe. I hope it goes without saying that we're really sorry. It won't last forever. We normally sort these things out within days.'

Stu nodded but he looked far from convinced. He wanted

to know what would happen next. Surely there'd be a ransom demand of some kind?

'That's possible, Mr Norcliffe.' Suttle wiped his mouth with a napkin. 'That's one of the things we have to discuss.'

Briefly he explained that with Mackenzie's consent they'd be monitoring calls to the house.

'Yours too. With your permission.'

'Of course. How do you do that?'

'We get them diverted here. We have techies to sort all that out. As far as mobiles are concerned, we'll be relying on you.'

Suttle explained about Helen's role. She'd be on the premises most of the time. Once the kidnappers made contact it was obviously important to be listening in.

'And getting some kind of number from them?'

'Of course. In these situations they normally use call boxes but we can locate those too. Whatever it takes, Mr Norcliffe. Patience, I'm afraid, is what we're all going to need.'

Stu was studying his hands. Then he shook his head.

'Nightmare. Total nightmare. This is stuff that happens to other people, stuff you see in the movies.' He looked up, his eyes brimming. 'Have either of you got kids?'

Suttle shook his head. Christian said she had three.

'How old?'

'Adolescents.'

'Then you'd know. Guy's six. He's a tough little bugger but he's vulnerable too. Some things really freak him. Not at night, funnily enough, but other things. I took him on the London Eye recently, just by himself for a treat. It was part of his birthday present and sometimes you know that you don't get enough time on your own. I asked him whether he wanted to bring some mates along but he said no. Just him and me. I'm sorry ...' His head went down again. Christian and Suttle exchanged glances, then Christian went to sit beside him on the sofa, her arm around his heaving shoulders.

Finally he looked up, accepting the proffered tissue. 'I'm sorry, I'm really sorry. Doing the job I do you never lose control, never. This whole thing is just so ...' he shook his head again '... weird. To think of taking a boy that age. What kind of person does that?'

'You were telling us about the Eye,' Suttle reminded him. 'Something freaked Guy out.'

'Yeah, that's right, it did. Down on the embankment there you get these guys who paint themselves in silver and dress up in costume and stuff and just stand there like statues. Guy was fascinated. Absolutely fascinated. Then the man winked at him. That threw him completely. He physically jumped. I swear it. Now, whenever he passes a statue, you know, a *real* statue, he crosses the road to get away from the thing. Maybe it's to do with trust. He really thought the man was a statue. But kids are like that, aren't they? They trust completely. Until we let them down.'

'We?'

'Adults. Mums and dads. I understand you know about Guy's mother and me.'

'Yeah. That can't be easy either.'

'It's not, believe me. And it isn't for the kids.'

There was a long silence. Suttle decided against another sandwich. Instead, he asked Stu whether he'd noticed anyone hanging around the house recently, maybe a strange car driving slowly past, unexplained phone calls with no one at the other end.

'No.' Stu was staring at the opposite wall. 'But then I'm away during the week.'

'What about the alarm?'

'The what?' He didn't seem to have heard.

'The house alarm, Mr Norcliffe. It doesn't seem to have worked. Has there been a problem?'

'Yes, there has. On Saturday, funnily enough.'

'What happened?'

'I was coming back from London. The kids were down here with Marie and Baz. I had to drop some stuff off at the house before picking them up. I tried using the remote to disable the security system, as usual, but it didn't seem to work. Then I did it again, and again after that, and the fifth or sixth time it let me in. It's never done that before. Christ knows why.'

'Did you report it?'

'Yeah. A guy came out that same night, once I was back with the kids. He couldn't find anything wrong, of course, so he just told me to keep an eye on it.'

'And since?'

'It was fine on Sunday and I assumed it was just a one-off glitch, but then when you really need the thing –' he shrugged hopelessly '– it lets you down.'

He wanted clarification on exactly what would happen if he took a call on his mobile from the kidnappers.

'If it happens here, alert Helen. She'll be alongside you. If it happens somewhere else, then fix a time when these guys can phone you back. And try and make sure you're here with one of us. Are you OK with that?'

'Of course. Anything you say. I'm totally in your hands. Help yourself.' He frowned. 'How would they know my number?'

'Mrs Mackenzie tells me Guy knows it by heart.'

'That's right. Of course he does. It was a party piece of his. Typical.' He blinked, reached for the tissues. 'So you think they'll be in touch? Whoever they are?'

'That's our assumption. It's not a guarantee but that's normally what happens.'

'So what do I say?'

'You say nothing. Just that you want your son back. Try and get them to put him on the line if he's there. If that's impossible ask for proof that he's still alive.'

'*Alive?*'

'I'm sorry, Mr Norcliffe, I didn't mean to spring that on you. It's a remote possibility but it's something we have to bear in mind. What you're going into is a negotiation. I know it's difficult but it might be wise to bear that in mind.'

'Negotiation? That's what I do every day of my working life.'

'Sure. But not for your son, I imagine.'

'No.' He looked at Suttle for a long moment. 'He's worth everything to me, that boy. Whatever they ask for, I'm happy to pay.'

'It might not come to that, Mr Norcliffe. Let's hope it doesn't.'

'What do you mean? I don't understand.'

'It means that we use certain techniques, sneaky-beaky stuff, pretty high-tech most of it. Actually paying the ransom is pretty rare, at least in this country.'

'But would he be at risk? Guy? Because if there's the slightest question of that, then … like I say … I'll just pay up. I want him back. And I don't care what it costs.'

Suttle nodded and then made a note. Christian tried to reassure him. He seemed to have little faith in high-tech gizmos.

'I'm in hedge funds. I'm surrounded by ace-bright back-room boys, kids straight out of uni who write the most amazing software programs for tracking stocks and shares, for predicting what's going to go up and come down, and you know something? I just know that in the end they'll get too clever. Most of the time I trust my instincts. And most of the time I'm proved right. So as far as Guy's concerned –' he spread his hands wide '– why don't we just keep it simple?'

'Of course.' Suttle made another note. 'I'll talk to my bosses, see what they say. These may be early days, Mr Norcliffe.'

'Christ, I hope not.'

'So do we. But it might be best to be patient, like I say.'

They talked for a while about people who'd have some shrewd idea about Norcliffe's net worth. The list of names was endless. Every client, for a start, though in Stu's view these were hardly the kind of people who'd be remotely interested in kidnapping.

Suttle said he wanted a list.

'You're serious? A client list?'

'Yes.'

'With contact details?'

'I'm afraid so.'

'OK.' It was Norcliffe's turn to write himself a note. 'I'll have my secretary email something through. Anything else?'

Suttle mentioned friends, casual or otherwise, individuals Stu played squash with, drank with, even met on holiday. People can be strange, Suttle said. You think you know them yet something happens and you realise you don't.

Norcliffe nodded. His eyes were shiny again.

'Too right,' he said. 'Have you met my wife?'

Winter belled Esme from the train. She said she was sitting on a trolley beside a luggage carousel at Gatwick Airport, waiting for her bags to appear. Her dad had been too busy to drive across and pick her up. She hoped he'd have a sense of humour about the cab fare.

'You should have phoned Speedy, Ez.'

'I forgot. And I don't need the lecture, thanks. Where's Stu?'

'At your dad's place, as far as I know.'

'Great, that's all I need. How about the kids?'

'They're there too.'

'They're OK?'

'Of course they're not. What do you expect? Losing your big brother's bad enough. Having both parents on the blink's probably worse.'

'So that's my fault is it? Is that what you're saying?'

'Yeah. Talk to you later, love.'

Winter snapped his mobile shut, glad he'd got it off his chest. The sight of the kids at Bazza's place had seriously upset him. She hasn't got a clue, he told himself. Not the first fucking idea.

The address Mackenzie had given him for Garfield turned out to be a leafy Richmond crescent within walking distance of the Thames. Winter changed trains at Waterloo, pausing to buy himself a burger, and walked the half-mile from Richmond station. The area reminded him of Craneswater – lots of trees, no litter, every house badged with expensive security alarm systems – and Garfield's property, like Bazza's, also featured a high brick wall and electronic gates. An address like this, thought Winter, would put a smile on anyone's face.

There was an entryphone beside the gates. Winter waited while a motorbike roared by then announced himself. When nothing happened he did it again. Finally, a woman's voice.

'Mr who?'

'The name's Winter. We met in Spain. At the weekend.'

'At the airport?'

'Yes. I've come to apologise. Were you the lady in the hire car?'

There was a long silence. It was hot in the sunshine and Winter wondered whether to shed his coat. Then he heard footsteps. Moments later, the gates swung open. There were two of them. They were both minders, both black. One stepped out onto the pavement, checking in both directions.

'You got a car, man?'

'I walked.'

'*Walked?* Shit ...'

He accompanied Winter into the drive. His colleague gestured for Winter to raise his arms the way they do in the security line at airports. Winter complied, eyeing the nearby vehicles while he got the full body check. One of them was a new-looking Mercedes saloon, black, top-of-the-range. The other was a van, rusting around the sills, white. Close to, the minder stank richly of aftershave.

'What's this?' He opened Winter's jacket and extracted his wallet then resumed the search. Finally he stepped back, satisfied.

'You're going to give me that back?' Winter nodded at the wallet.

'When it's over, man. Not before.'

'Over?'

'You and Mrs G. Good luck, baby.' He swapped glances with his buddy and began to laugh.

The house was even bigger than Winter had expected. He could hear the *tock-tock* of a sprinkler watering the lawn at the rear of the property and he caught a glimpse of sunbeds on a terrace. Blinds shielded windows on the sunny side of the house and there was a warning about guard dogs on a plaque beside the front door.

The door was open. Winter stepped inside. For a moment, in the gloom, he could see nothing. Then came a woman's voice from a room on the right.

'In here, Mr Winter. I must say I admire your nerve.'

She looked younger and thinner than Winter remembered from the airport. A fall of blonde hair softened the boniness of her shoulders and her legs were bare beneath the loose cotton shift. The scent of coconut in the room told Winter that she must have been out on the terrace, creaming herself up.

'Nice weather.'

'Lovely. And totally unexpected.' She cocked her head, looking him up and down. 'What can I do for you?'

Winter said again that he was sorry about the incident in the car park. The locals, he said, had no manners and his own boss had been horrified to hear about what had happened. The fault, he said, was entirely his.

'I agree.'

'You'll pass that on to your lawyer friend?'

'That won't be necessary. I understand he's preparing a writ.'

'Against?'

'You.' She sweetened the news with a smile. 'Assault and aggravated robbery. I'm no lawyer, Mr Winter, but I imagine that pretty much covers it.'

'This is in Spain?'

'Of course. Associates out there have managed to identify the actual assailant. No doubt he'll be co-defending the action.'

Winter nodded. He sensed at once that the woman was bluffing. No way would she or her lawyer want to attract any kind of police attention. Nonetheless, Winter did his best to look contrite.

'I'm not sure I blame him,' he said carefully. 'But do we really have to make this official?'

'I'm afraid that's Christopher's decision, not mine. Was there anything else?'

'Yes. As you probably gathered, we've pulled out of the deal.'

'You have?'

'Yes. That's why we wanted the contracts back. That's why ...' Winter was struggling ' ... it all kicked off.'

'But why didn't you ask nicely? Why didn't we talk about it?'

Good question. For once in his life Winter was robbed of an answer.

'You're right,' he said. 'We should have handled it differently.'

'So why didn't you?'

'I don't know. Time, I suppose. Like I say, I'm sorry.'

On a low table beside the long curve of the sofa Winter caught sight of a pile of magazines. Someone was crazy about Morocco.

'We have problems with the money,' Winter said.

'I'm sorry about that.'

'Your money, not ours.'

'Oh?'

'Yeah.' Winter nodded. 'My understanding is that your

224

husband, if he is your husband, has been arrested on supply charges. Is that right?'

'Go on.'

'If it is right, then – like I say – we have a problem.'

'And why might that be?'

'Because we'd end up tainted. Where I come from you have to be very careful about getting into bed with the wrong people. Washing money was never our game.'

'But you think it's ours?'

'That's our supposition. Mr Garfield told my boss his money came from a casino. Now it turns out that might not be true. To be honest, we can't afford to fanny around. That's why we needed to step away from the deal. If Mr Garfield was here I'm sure he'd understand.'

The woman held his gaze. She had the greenest eyes. At length she nodded at the tall French doors at the other end of the room and turned on her heel. Winter followed her out into the sunshine. Only one of the four sun beds was occupied. She gestured down at a plump, pale figure deep in the pages of the *Financial Times*. He was wearing designer shorts and a pair of expensive-looking sunglasses.

'This is my husband, Mr Winter. Maybe you ought to be talking to him.'

'Al Garfield?'

The man glanced up, then nodded. No trace of a smile.

'I take it you've come for the contract,' he said. 'We rather thought you might.'

An hour later, Winter phoned Mackenzie on his mobile from the garden of a pub beside the river. When he asked whether the kidnap squad was monitoring the conversation, Mackenzie said no. There was a techie camped out in the lounge to record incoming calls on the landline but mobes were unaffected.

Winter gave the news some thought. Setting up intercepts without the owner's consent required authorisation by the Home Secretary. He'd done a few himself in the Job and knew they could be a nightmare. Maybe Faraday was still working his way up the food chain with his intercept application. Maybe.

'You've still got that pay-as-you-go?'

'Yeah.'

'Give me the number.'

Seconds later, Winter began the conversation again. Pay-as-you-go was as secure as it ever got. Mackenzie wanted to know whether he'd got the contract back from Garfield's missus.

'No.'

'Why the fuck not?'

'Garfield's there. There's no way we're going to get anywhere near that contract. Not unless you bung him.'

'He's supposed to be inside. They're supposed to have arrested him.'

'He says not. He says he's a businessman just like he's said all along.'

'You think he's lying?'

'Definitely. My guess is he's out on police bail. Unless your mate Riquelme makes these things up.'

'So how much does he want?'

'A million sterling.'

'That's not far beyond what he kicked into the hotel deal.'

'You're right. Now he's calling it compensation. With a bit on top for expenses.'

There was a pause. Winter realised Mackenzie was giving the demand serious thought.

'So what would he settle for, mush? Five hundred thousand? Half that?'

'Forget it, Baz.'

'You're joking. Half a mill to get a decent night's sleep? Half a mill to keep it all together? I call that a bargain.'

'So what happens when it turns out he's made a trillion copies of that fucking contract? This isn't rocket science, Baz. It's called a photocopier.'

'You think he'd do that? From where I'm sitting, mush, the guy has a huge problem. If he's under the cosh like Rikki says then he knows they're probably going to nail him in the end. You'll tell me how these things work but if they've frozen all his assets, or whatever else they do, then he needs to start thinking hard about bailing out. Am I getting warm here?'

'Yeah, spot on, Baz.' Winter was thinking about the van. In Garfield's place you'd start moving stuff out regardless. And Morocco might not be a bad place to take it.

'OK.' Mackenzie hadn't finished. 'So he's got a plan,

somewhere hot and sunny where they can't touch him, but to make all that work he needs moolah. Mine, as it turns out.'

'So what do you do?'

'I pony up, give him the dosh, get the contract back, buy the guy's silence. Then we're home free.'

Winter shook his head. A lone sculler slipped past on the ebbing tide, drawing low whistles from a pair of women at a nearby table.

'You'd be mad, Baz. You and Ez are already in the shit over the Baiona deal. Spending a fortune on a faxed contract doesn't solve any of that. In fact it makes it worse.'

'How?'

'You know the guy's bent. I know the guy's bent. By giving him money, by buying his silence, we've committed yet another fucking offence. Same piece of law, Baz. And it lays you wide open to confiscation, imprisonment, the whole nine yards. You're right about Garfield. If there's an investigation under way, the first thing they'll do is issue a restraint order to freeze all his assets. That's why he was desperate to buy into the Baiona deal and that's why he's playing hardball with us. He's trying it on, Baz. And he's relying on the fact that we're stupid.'

'We?'

'Yeah, Baz, you and me. If we give the guy a penny, they can have us. Just believe me for once.'

'So what do we do?'

'We do what I've said we should be doing all along.'

'Tell them everything? Lay it all out? Sweet as you like?'

'Yeah. And then you tell them you're sorry.'

'The *Filth*? Tell the Filth I'm *sorry*? What the fuck else do they want?'

Another silence, longer this time. Winter was beginning to lose patience. In these situations, as far as Bazza was concerned, logic was useless. Winter was no closer to making the man see sense.

'Did you mention Guy at all? Any of that?'

'No.'

'You still think it might be down to Garfield?'

Winter hesitated. He'd asked himself exactly the same question.

'I doubt it,' he said. 'They're too classy for that.'

'*Classy?* How does that work?'

'It turns out the story about the casino was true. He inherited it from his dad. Garfield's mum was Spanish. That's what took him out to that coast in the first place. He's got relatives there and my guess is he saw the potential with all the toot coming in. He's like any businessman, Baz. He wants to make his own fortune his own way. That's obviously what he's done and now he's discovered he's not quite as clever as he thought.'

'But credible, yeah?'

'Definitely.'

'Which is how he fooled me.'

'Absolutely, Baz. But let's call it a day, eh? This guy's fucked us over once already. There's no way we should be giving him a second chance. Do I hear a yes?'

Faraday settled himself in Parsons' office, summoned by a breathless phone call. Moments of high excitement put colour in her face.

'I just had the Surveillance D/I on.' She nodded at the phone.

'And?'

'Winter went to an address in Richmond. It belongs to a man called Alan Garfield ... and guess what? According to the Met he was released on police bail yesterday. They've got him down as a major importer, cocaine mostly. The investigation's ongoing. They say it's just a question of time.'

'Did they mention Spain at all?'

'Yes, they did.' She failed to mask her surprise. 'They wouldn't give me any details but he seems to have business interests out there. Why do you ask?'

'Because, according to Mackenzie, his daughter flew back this morning.'

'Where from?'

'Spain.'

Chapter twenty-one

Stepping into the kitchen, Winter knew at once that something had happened. Mackenzie and Stu were sitting at one end of the big table, Esme at the other. Marie was busy at the stove while Helen Christian was sorting out cutlery for a meal. Looking at the faces, Winter thought at first that someone must have died. He wasn't far wrong.

'He's been in touch.' It was Mackenzie.

'Who has?'

'The bloke who lifted Guy. He says we've got twenty-four hours.'

'When did this happen?'

'Teatime. Six o'clock. He wants ten million quid.'

'*What?*'

Mackenzie shrugged, turned away. There it was. Ten million quid or the nipper gets it.

'Who took the call?'

'I did.' Stu was drinking lager straight from the can. Stella could bind a multitude of wounds but not this one. He looked pale and drained, and Winter noticed a tiny shake when he lifted the tinny again.

'So what happened?'

'I was upstairs with the kids. The phone went and there was this voice I'd never heard before in my life. I knew it was him, I just knew it.'

'What did he say?'

'He said I had twenty-four hours to find ten million quid. I told him that was a joke, had to be, but he just kept saying it, ten million quid, ten million quid.'

'Did you ask him about Guy?'

'Of course I did.'

'And?'

'He just said he was OK.'

'Nothing else?'

'No, just that. I asked what OK meant and he just laughed. Can you imagine that? A situation like this? And the guy just laughs?' He nodded to himself, pushed the chair back from the table and stared up at the ceiling. 'Bastard,' he said softly.

Esme watched, totally dispassionate. She was drinking coffee.

'And what are you supposed to do with this money?' Winter was still looking at Stu. 'Assuming you can lay hands on it?'

'He didn't tell me. All he said was he'd be in touch again. Once the money was confirmed he'd explain exactly how to play it.'

'And that was it?'

'Yeah. I asked whether there was any way I could speak to Guy, just hear his voice, anything, but the bloke hung up on me. Jeez ...' He shook his head and reached for the can.

Winter was looking at Mackenzie.

'It's a joke, mush. Who's got ten million quid?'

'You have, dad.' It was Esme.

'Readies? Ten million notes I can peel off and stuff in an envelope? You have to be kidding. Even if I've got it, you're looking at months and months before I could get that kind of money together.'

'Borrow it then.'

'Just like that? Four per cent over bank rate? That's nearly a million in interest before you even blink.'

'You're telling me Guy's not worth it?' she said hotly. 'Your own grandson?'

'I'm telling you none of this would have bloody happened if you'd stayed at home.'

'I had to go to Spain on business. You know that.'

'That's not what I meant, love. You should listen a bit harder.'

Esme abandoned her coffee and left the room. Winter listened to her footsteps thumping up the stairs. Then came the slam of a door and the sigh of bedsprings.

'Helen seems to think we can negotiate.' Marie was stirring something in a saucepan.

'That's right.' Christian nodded. 'Ten million's obviously an opening bid.'

There was a silence. Everyone was still conscious of Esme upstairs. Families were like this, Winter thought. At exactly the moment you'd think they'd hang together, they often fell apart. Not that Esme hadn't done her best to wreck it already.

'Did the techie trace the number?' Winter was still looking at Christian.

'Yes. He was using a call box in Woking.'

'Do we know where in Woking?'

'We do.'

'CCTV?'

'No.'

'But someone's up there having a poke around? Scenes of Crime? Guys in the grey suits?'

'What do you think?'

'Sorry. Just asking.'

The silence returned, broken by Christian. She wanted to confirm that negotiations were still possible. It was in everyone's interests to string this thing out as long as possible. The longer it went on the greater the chance the kidnapper would make a mistake.

Stu shook his head. 'You're playing with my son's life. I hope you understand that.'

'That's a factor, Stu, of course it is, but the moment we think there's any direct threat to his well-being then we'll take appropriate action.'

'Like?'

'Like advising you to pay up.'

Mackenzie loved the word 'well-being'. 'I'd say there was a big fucking threat to his *well-being*, Helen. I bet he's chuffed to death being banged up with some psycho maniac. I bet he can't get enough of that. Well-being, bollocks. Call it the way you mean it, love. It's his fucking life we're talking about.'

'Of course. I'm sorry.'

Mackenzie dismissed her apology with a wave of his hand and looking at him Winter realised how strange this conversation around the table must feel. He'd spent his entire life keeping the Filth at arm's length. Now it was the Filth – here in his own house – who were doing their best to minimise the damage to his fortune. Odd.

Stu got up and went to the fridge for another tinny. 'If we get the bid down to a reasonable sum I'll pay up,' he said.

Mackenzie wanted to know what he had in mind.

'Say a million.'

'You've got that kind of money?'

'I can find it.'

'Quickly?'

'Yes.'

'Fingers crossed then. Eh?'

There was a ring at the front door. Marie was still busy at the stove so Winter, who was nearest, stepped out into the hall. A tall figure was visible through the pebbled-glass panels at the end of the hall. Winter opened the door. It was Mo Sturrock.

'I'm just passing,' he said at once. 'There was just a couple of things I wanted to check out with Mrs Mackenzie. Is now a bad time?'

'Not at all.' It was Marie. She was drying her hands on a cloth. She invited Sturrock in.

Winter lingered a moment, watching the pair of them disappearing into the lounge at the front of the house. Now was very definitely a bad time but he sensed a neediness in Marie that Sturrock, with his easy smile, might be able to address. The guy had built an entire career out of coping with impossible situations. Welcome to Craneswater.

Back in the kitchen, Mackenzie wanted to know who'd been at the door. Winter told him.

'The Tide Trust bloke?'

'Yeah.'

'This time of night?'

'Yeah. He needs a couple of things off Marie.' Winter looked Mackenzie in the eye. 'You think we ought to have a little chat as well?'

Mackenzie gazed up at him and for the first time Winter realised he was drunk.

'No, mush.' His eyes strayed to the cupboard where Marie kept an emergency bottle of malt. 'I'm nicely settled in.'

*

Willard drove down from Winchester for the council of war in the Major Crime suite of offices. Faraday couldn't remember when he'd last seen him this lively. There was a lightness in his step, and as he strode down the central corridor past Faraday's open door he was even humming. There was a tune in there somewhere but Faraday was struggling to name it. Maybe Tchaikovsky, he thought. Maybe the climax of the 1812 *Overture*. Napoleon about to be sent packing. Very apt.

The call to Parsons' office came minutes later. Operation *Causeway* was up to speed now and there was a scatter of detectives in the Major Incident Room at the end of the corridor, trying to tease some kind of lead from the latest development. Faraday had listened to the kidnapper's opening salvo in the war for Mackenzie's grandson and recognised the start of what might prove to be a lengthy negotiation. The voice – flat, Home Counties – gave little away. A bloke in a call box in Woking. Big deal.

To Faraday's surprise, Jimmy Suttle was already at the conference table in Parsons' office. The last time Faraday had seen him was a couple of hours ago. Then he'd been on the point of calling it a day. She must have kept him on specially, Faraday thought.

Willard took the chair at the head of the table and kicked off. Expecting a review of Operation *Causeway*, Faraday found himself listening to Willard's take on something very different.

'This is about Mackenzie,' he said at once. 'We need to be sure about exactly where we are. D/S Suttle?'

Suttle had obviously been charged with pulling together the day's intelligence. He bent to his notepad, flipped through a couple of pages, then looked up.

'This is what we know for sure,' he began. 'Mackenzie's daughter flew to Vigo on Saturday. I've got the flight details. I've also been working through Interplod and they put a local cop into the airport this afternoon and talked to the rental companies. Interplod are saying that Mackenzie's daughter hired a car at the airport and mentioned she was going to a place called Baiona. Their bloke did a quick check on the big hotels there and struck lucky. She was staying at –' he looked down at his pad to check the name '– the Fonda Perla de Cuba. That same Saturday night a Nikki Garfield also checked in. That has to

233

be Garfield's wife. She and Mackenzie's daughter had dinner together and Esme put the bill on her tab. Garfield checked out on Sunday afternoon, Esme flew back today.'

'And who else was there?' Willard was enjoying this.

'Winter, sir. He booked in on Sunday. Booked out yesterday. One of the waiters saw Winter and Esme on the terrace with a couple of other guys on Sunday. These guys were Spanish. That's all we know.'

'But there was something else, wasn't there?' Willard was looking at Parsons. Parsons told him to be patient. The best was evidently yet to come.

'Jimmy?' she said.

'The Interplod guy picked up something else at the airport. He hasn't had a chance to check the CCTV yet but he thinks something might have kicked off in one of the car parks. Apparently the girl on the rental desk told him that when Nikki Garfield returned the car she had blood on her dress. There was a guy with her too. And he was in a right mess.'

'So what does this tell us?' Willard again.

'I can't be sure, sir. The waiter at the Baiona hotel is pissed off with the management because everybody knows the place is up for sale and he thinks the owner's going to screw him out of redundancy money. According to him, Garfield and Mackenzie's daughter are buying it between them. We can't prove that, not yet, but the daughter's been there before, at least a couple of times according to the waiter, so that would make sense.'

Willard nodded.

'We've got contact details for the waiter and the rental girl?'

'Yeah. Interplod have been brilliant. Textbook stuff.'

'How about airport security?'

'They're onto that. My man says he'll bell me first thing tomorrow.'

'Excellent. What about Garfield?' Willard was looking at Parsons now.

'I talked to the Met again this evening. To be frank they're not that helpful but they confirmed again that Garfield's the subject of a major investigation. They pulled him in at the end of last week and managed one extension but got knocked back on the other.'

Willard nodded. A uniformed Superintendent could extend twenty-four-hour custody by a further twelve hours. After that it was in the hands of the magistrates.

'What happened?'

'He's got a shit-hot lawyer and he managed to keep them at arm's length but reading between the lines they're obviously light on evidence. I ended up talking to the Detective Superintendent in charge. They've bailed Garfield until the end of June. As far as he's concerned it's just a matter of time.'

'So the investigation's definitely under way?'

'Big time. They've thrown lots of resource at it, surveillance teams in Spain, lots of covert, lots of sneaky-beaky. Garfield's high priority, no question.'

Mention of covert had sharpened Willard's interest still further. 'Has Mackenzie's name come up?'

'They're aware of our interest. When I put it to them straight, tabled Mackenzie's name, they refused to comment, but the answer's yes, I'd put my life on it. He's in there with Garfield on the hotel deal, and probably all kinds of other stuff as well.'

'Knowing Garfield's bent?' It was Faraday this time, the first tiny hint of dissent. 'Why on earth would he take the risk?'

'Because he's reckless, Joe. And because we might have overestimated him. He's a Copnor boy, through and through. Once a scrote ...' Willard shrugged, leaving the sentence unfinished.

Parsons wanted to know where Willard wanted to take this inquiry next. For the sake of keeping everything neat and tidy it was important to maintain a clear focus. Operation *Causeway* had been mounted to resolve the kidnapping of Mackenzie's grandchild. This latest flurry of enquiries, whilst an offshoot of *Causeway*, would presumably lead somewhere else.

'Of course.'

'Where, exactly?'

'To Mackenzie's arrest. And his daughter. And Winter, for that matter. This is prima facie, Gail. We have evidence, or near-evidence, that Mackenzie has gone into some kind of partnership with Garfield. Garfield is already under active investigation. That means grounds exist for believing that he leads a criminal lifestyle. Anyone who does business with him is tainted by that lifestyle. Mackenzie, for whatever reason, has done exactly that. Game, set and fucking match.' He beamed at Faraday, a fellow survivor from *Tumbril*. 'Right, Joe?'

'Right, sir. So what do we do?'

'We pull him in tomorrow. Early doors. In fact we pull the lot of them in. All three. That launches the investigation. And by doing that we can trigger the restraint order and freeze his assets.'

'He's just had his grandson kidnapped.' It was Suttle. 'Aren't we being a bit hasty, sir?'

Willard waved the consideration away. 'This is about crime, son. Not hearts and minds. Mackenzie's been taking the piss for far too long. Winter as well. There's no way we're going to nail them in interview, not first time round, but we have to get the ball rolling. Joe? You agree?'

Faraday was gazing at Parsons. Early doors meant dawn arrests.

'So who's going to organise this?'

'You are, Joe.' She smiled. 'You're happy with that?'

Winter, despairing, took himself off for a walk. The danger, he knew, was acute. Ever since he'd started to work for Bazza Mackenzie he'd recognised the sheer scale of the challenge that lay ahead. The very things that so often made the man a joy to be with – his instinct for the killer move, his delight in running rings round the competition, his contempt for the boring and the ordinary – were equally a handicap when it came to taking advice. He never listened. He always assumed – *knew* – that he was in the right. Winter, with a lifetime of manipulation behind him, had quickly sussed how to channel Bazza's wild energy, how to torpedo some of his crazier schemes, but he'd always been aware that something enormous might suddenly turn up and swamp them both. That something had arrived and yet Bazza still couldn't see it.

At the kitchen table Winter had done his best. They were up against classy opposition. Faraday and Suttle knew what they were about. The Met were definitely crawling all over Garfield. He and Bazza, and Esme too, had precious little time to block the holes in their little stockade and keep the Apaches at bay. Bazza didn't begin to see this, partly because it wasn't in his nature to do the Filth any kind of favour, but mostly because he couldn't stop thinking about his grandson. He'd always been especially proud of Guy. The boy was gutsy, a bit of a scrapper. He was bright too, and funny. If it was true that the better genes jumped a whole generation then there was no one prouder than Bazza Mackenzie.

Winter looked back at the house before he stepped out onto the pavement. Marie, he knew, had introduced Mo Sturrock to the kids, and as far as he was aware Mo was still up with them. Half nine was late for five-year-olds but just now time seemed to have lost any meaning. He thought of Stu in the kitchen, nursing yet another can of Stella, of Esme still sulking in the spare room upstairs, of Bazza drinking himself insensible in his den, and wondered whether every family enterprise was doomed to end this way, in a car wreck of blame and recrimination, any hope of rescue slipping remorselessly away.

He wandered down the road and headed for the seafront. The last embers of a decent sunset were dying in the west and a thin grey mist hung over the Solent. There were strings of coloured lights on the promenade and the warmth of the evening had drawn couples out for an evening stroll. Winter paused for a moment at the seawall, smelling the heat still rising from the pebbles, knowing how much this city meant to him. He'd spent most of his working life policing the battlefield. Lately, he'd had a lot of fun on the other side of no-man's-land. He understood the place. He spoke its many languages. He was totally fluent in Pompey. And, perhaps for that reason, he had absolutely no illusions about what lay ahead. Unless someone took the initiative, he was fucked.

Faraday was on the point of retiring early when the doorbell went. Between them, he and Jimmy Suttle had put together a couple of D/Cs and a WPC for tomorrow's expedition to Craneswater. They were to meet at Kingston Crescent at half past three in the morning to be at Mackenzie's place by four. Now, barefoot, he opened the front door. It was Winter.

Faraday stared at him. In six hours he'd have this man under arrest.

'Inviting me in, boss? Or shall we do it here?'

'Do what?'

Winter didn't answer. After a moment's hesitation Faraday

stepped aside and let him in. Winter walked through to the lounge and made himself comfortable on the sofa.

'You'll need a pad and paper, boss,' he said. 'I want to keep this thing official.'

Faraday didn't quite believe it. 'What thing?'

'I want to make a disclosure under the provisions of the Proceeds of Crime Act, 2002. That OK with you, boss?'

'You're talking like a lawyer.'

'Funny that. You remember Nelly Tien?'

'I do.'

'I've asked her to drive down.'

'Now? At this time of night?'

'Yeah.' Winter checked his watch. 'She's just moved to a big place in Petersfield. She should have been here by now.'

Nelly Tien was Mackenzie's lawyer, a ferocious Hong Kong Chinese who defended his interests with considerable guile. She arrived minutes later, a busy swirl of expensive Italian leather behind a bow wave of Coco Chanel. She extracted an audio recorder from her briefcase and stationed it carefully on the low table in front of the sofa. Faraday gazed at her in wonderment.

'This is totally inappropriate,' he said. 'I could do you both for invasion of privacy.'

'You invited me in, boss,' Winter pointed out. 'You should have told me to fuck off.'

'Good idea. So why don't you?'

'Because we have a pressing need to make an authorised disclosure, Mr Faraday.' It was Tien. She'd pressed the Record button. 'My clients are under extreme pressure, as you know. Naturally you want to limit knowledge of the kidnapping. Making this disclosure in the normal way is therefore not an option. We could go to the Bridewell and make a statement but that might jeopardise your handling of the kidnap.'

Faraday gazed at her. This was nonsense but it was clever nonsense.

'We're still talking the Proceeds of Crime Act?'

'We are.'

'With regard to money laundering?'

'Indeed.'

'Then I don't understand. If you're anticipating some kind of action on our part with regard to money laundering what does that have to do with the kidnap?'

'It has everything to do with it, Mr Faraday. My clients are in no state to make rational decisions. In Mr Winter's judgement, and in mine, there have been business oversights on their part that require addressing.'

'But why the urgency? Why now?'

'Because we don't wish to add to their problems. And neither, I assume, do you.'

This was doubly clever. Nelly Tien was playing the human rights card. Faraday turned his attention to Winter. Either he'd got wind of tomorrow morning's arrests or he'd simply worked it out for himself. The latter was by no means beyond him. As ever, he was ahead of the game.

Faraday told her to carry on. Under the circumstances, short of throwing them out he could do little else. She pulled a notepad from her briefcase, announced the date, time and persons present for the benefit of the tape, and invited Winter to make his report on the family's behalf. Faraday's living room had become an interview suite.

Winter went through the Baiona property deal. How, in good faith, Mackenzie and his daughter had mounted a bid for a hotel in the Galician resort of Baiona. How the agreed price had obliged Mackenzie to seek a partner to spread his risk. And how a local introduction had brought another British businessman to the table. His name was Alan Garfield and he'd put up a million euros.

'You'll want to know where that money came from, Mr Faraday.' Tien turned to Winter. 'Paul?'

'Garfield has a casino in Richmond upon Thames. We checked it out. It exists. He owns it.'

'So the money came from there, as far as my clients were aware. Are you clear about that, Mr Faraday?'

Faraday nodded. He was still looking at Winter.

'Go on,' he said.

Winter obliged. 'As far as we were concerned, the deal was done. Then Mr Mackenzie heard a whisper that Garfield had been arrested on Class A supply charges. This was Saturday.'

'Whisper?'

'Information. Intel. From our point of view, of course, we

couldn't afford to ignore it. It's a sweet deal on offer in Baiona but the last thing we need is tainted money to make it work.'

'So what happened?'

'Mr Mackenzie's daughter was already down there. For reasons you know about, her private life's a bit of a mess just now. Communication with her dad isn't all it should be. She didn't know about Garfield's arrest, about the possibility of dirty money, and there was every chance she'd signed the deal.'

Winter described his own mad dash to Baiona. His boss wanted nothing more to do with Garfield. Winter's job was to torpedo the deal.

'And?'

'It was messy. The contracts had been signed. It was a question of getting them back.'

'From whom?'

'Garfield's missus and their lawyer.'

'So what happened?'

'We recovered the property.' Winter shot a look at Nelly Tien. She gestured for him to carry on. 'Like I say, it was messy. We had a couple of blokes with us. We caught up with Garfield's missus at the airport. The lawyer took a bit of a slapping, I admit, but there you go ...'

Faraday could picture the scene only too clearly. No wonder the lawyer had turned up at the rental desk in a bit of a state.

'This is standard business practice?' Faraday enquired drily.

'Not at all, Mr Faraday.' Tien shook her head. 'What my client is trying to establish are the lengths to which he and his colleagues will go to stay within the law. In this case they were acutely aware of their disclosure responsibilities under the money-laundering regulations and were doing their very best to comply.'

'Assault is a crime,' Faraday pointed out. 'You're telling me they broke one law to comply with another?'

'That's your interpretation, Mr Faraday. I need hardly add that we don't agree. Means serve ends, in this case the right ends.'

'So why didn't you make a report?' Faraday had returned to Winter.

'About what?'

'About the dodgy money?'

'This was Sunday night, boss. We had to be sure about Garfield being under arrest. That took most of Monday. That night, which was last night, the boy got lifted.' He lifted his hands in a gesture of helplessness. 'And since then it's been chaos.'

'So here you are?'

'Yeah.'

'Playing it by the book?'

'Yeah, and doing our bit for law and order.' He sat back and grinned. 'Any chance of a drink?'

It was gone midnight when Faraday got through to Willard. His mobile was on divert. The third call to the landline at his Winchester address brought him to the phone. He'd obviously been asleep. Faraday had to go through parts of the story twice.

'So what are you telling me, Joe?'

'I'm telling you they've complied, sir. A day late, they admit, but the brief is pleading extenuating circumstances. We could still arrest them first thing but there might be consequences.'

'Like?'

'Like the brief would probably go public. Oppressive behaviour on our part. She used the word "vindictive" before she left. You can imagine the headlines – FAMILY IN TORMENT ARRESTED AT DAWN.'

'Fuck the headlines. What do we do?'

'That's your call, sir, not mine.'

'Have you been in touch with DCI Parsons?'

'Yes. She told me to talk to you.'

Willard grunted something Faraday didn't catch. The full implications of this latest news were beginning to catch up with him. Winter appeared to have admitted everything. What was there left to talk about?

'They've committed an offence, Joe. We can have them for that.'

'Early doors, then? The way we've planned it?'

'No. You're right. We need something else.'

Chapter twenty-two

To Winter's surprise, Bazza turned up for breakfast. He'd raided the fridge at home and presented Winter with eggs, half a pound of Waitrose bacon, a tin of baked beans and fresh croissants from a bakery in Southsea. Expecting a major hangover from last night, Winter found himself trying to cope with Bazza at his most cheerful. Another surprise.

'I had Nelly on the mobe, mush. She told me how savvy you'd been.'

Winter had yet to break the news about his late-night visit to the Bargemaster's House. The fact that Nelly Tien had spared him the trouble came as a bit of a relief. Bazza hated his staff going off-piste.

'You OK with that, Baz?' Winter was breaking eggs into the frying pan.

'Totally. Nelly said we just snuck in under the wire. I told her to blame it on you.'

'Cheers.'

'Seriously, mush, I owe you.' He picked up Winter's copy of the *Daily Telegraph* and turned to the sports pages but quickly got bored. Sport wasn't sport without football.

Winter gave one of the eggs a poke. 'How's things at home?'

'Crap. Stu's moping around like a five-year-old and Ezzie's still got the hump. I tell you something, mush. Grown-ups these days are like kids. Life gives you a smack or two and you stay on your feet. I'm surprised about Stu. I thought there was more to him.'

'He's had a bit of a shock, Baz. Can't be easy, all this.'

'Yeah, but you fight it, don't you? Get in there. Try and sort something out.'

'Like what?'

'Like his bloody missus for a start. He's got a problem there. He says he's still crazy about her and I believe him. But no way will he get Ez back by playing the wuss. He's looking for sympathy, I can see it, but he hasn't got a prayer. Ez doesn't do sympathy, never has, and if Stu thinks otherwise then he must have his head even further up his arse than I thought.'

'What's happened to Madison?'

'No idea. She won't talk about him.'

'You think he's still around?'

'Yeah. She makes a lot of fucking calls on that mobe of hers.' He folded the paper and tossed it onto the windowsill. From the kitchen there was a fine view of the Spinnaker Tower. 'Tell you something, mush.'

'What?'

'That Mo Sturrock's a find. Marie says the kids have fallen in love with him.'

'How long did he stay last night?'

'He never went. Marie made a bed up and he kipped over. He's the only sane one left standing. Good bloke. Fucking sound.' He turned back from the view. His breakfast was nearly ready. 'So what about Garfield, then? You think we've got all that squared away?'

Winter hoisted an egg onto a wedge of toast. He loved the 'we'. Half a day ago Mackenzie wouldn't listen to a word he was saying. Now, for whatever reason, they were suddenly on the same wavelength.

'No, Baz. They've had a knock-back. They'll still be keen to nail us. None of that will go away.'

'Ever?'

Something in his voice brought Winter's head up. He returned the frying pan to the hob.

'That's right, Baz. They'll never give up.'

'On Garfield, you mean?'

'Of course. And what happened with Westie too.'

'Westie's nothing. We had the guy shot.'

'You had the guy shot.'

'We, mush. But the spics have got fuck all. They're playing games. Ignore them. It'll all go away.'

Winter knew this was bullshit. You didn't end up on an

airport watch list without good reason. He put the laden plate on the breakfast bar and found Mackenzie a stool. Baz was standing by the window, staring out. Something else was bothering him.

'What's the matter, Baz? What else haven't you told me?'

'Nothing, mush.' Mackenzie did his best to look shocked. 'Nothing at all.'

Faraday had organised a conference in Craneswater for ten o'clock. He picked up Suttle from his office and drove to Sandown Road. Stu's Porsche was still in the drive. There was no sign of Mackenzie's Bentley.

Marie met them at the door. Stu was waiting in the lounge, talking to Helen Christian. When Faraday said he wanted Esme to join them, Marie went upstairs to fetch her. She'd had a rotten night, Marie said, and was trying to catch up on her sleep.

She took an age to appear. Marie served coffee, and when one of the kids wandered in Suttle got down on the carpet with her and started leafing through her picture book. The child was finally rescued by a tall, lean stranger Faraday had never met before. His feet were bare and his long hair, threaded with grey, was secured with a twist of scarlet ribbon.

Helen Christian did the introductions.

'This is Mo Sturrock,' she said. 'He's a friend of the family.'

'Employee more like.' Sturrock extended a hand towards Faraday. 'You've heard of Tide Turn Trust?'

Faraday nodded. In the wake of last year's double homicide the Trust had been Mackenzie's gift to the community, a bid to rein in the city's wilder youth.

'You're part of all that?'

'I'm down to run it.'

'As of when?'

'Pretty much now. Give or take.'

'And you've been in the field a while?'

'All my working life.'

'Not fed up?'

'Never.'

Faraday wished him luck. Esme had appeared at the door. She'd thrown on a pair of jeans and an old Pompey top that was much too big for her. Her hair was tousled and there were flecks of last night's mascara in the pouches under her eyes.

'I know. I look a wreck.' She shrugged. 'Too bad.'

Faraday asked Sturrock to leave. He waited for Marie to return with fresh coffee from the kitchen then got down to business. One or two leads had presented themselves. He was going to hand over to D/S Suttle for more details.

Suttle described the operation they'd been mounting in the villages close to Stu and Esme's property. In the small hours of Tuesday morning, traffic on the A32, which ran the length of the valley, had been light. From four CCTV cameras they'd recovered details of every vehicle on the road between midnight and 3 a.m. Follow-up checks were virtually complete and in every case the *Causeway* team had ruled out any connection with the kidnap. This, said Suttle, was itself significant.

'Why?' It was Stu.

'Because it suggests that the kidnappers knew the area really well. They knew where the cameras were. They knew which roads to avoid.'

'But a decent recce would tell you that.'

'You're right, it would. But if we're looking to eliminate Al Garfield then this would be a major pointer.'

Esme began to take an interest. How come Suttle knew about Garfield?

'Mr Faraday had a long conversation with Paul Winter last night. It seems you had something of a run-in with the guy.'

'That was Paul, not me.'

'So it's true?'

'Yes.'

'That's what we assumed. In these cases we look for motive. Garfield's wife and lawyer would have been pretty upset. Garfield himself is out on police bail. He might be looking for payback, sure, but to organise a kidnap like this and miss all those cameras he'd need more than a day to sort it. Are you with me?'

Esme nodded. For once, she glanced at Stu, who was studying his hands.

'What else have you got for us?' he muttered.

'We've been doing checks on the Sex Offenders Register. I'm afraid it's standard procedure in cases like this.'

'You think this guy might be a paedophile?' Stu looked up.

'It's possible. Unlikely but possible.'

'Why unlikely?'

'Because of the way he handled the abduction. The man we're dealing with is extremely organised. Sex offenders tend to be more impulsive. They'll spot an opportunity and go for it. That's not what's happened here.'

'So no chance of it being a paedo?'

'I doubt it.'

'Is that a guarantee?'

'Of course not. There are no guarantees in these situations, Mr Norcliffe. We can't rule anything out until the child's back home.'

'Christ.' Stu stole a look at Esme. 'This just gets worse.'

There was a long silence. When Marie asked if there'd been any other developments Suttle shook his head. Enquiries were ongoing. He'd make sure they stayed briefed. In the meantime he was still waiting for a list of clients from Mr Norcliffe.

Stu was looking at the carpet again. He didn't react.

'Mr Norcliffe?'

'I haven't done it yet. Haven't had a chance. I need to talk to my secretary. I'm sorry.'

Faraday took over. The twenty-four-hour deadline would expire at around six. They should anticipate another call by then, and another conversation. In his experience a prior decision on the ransom always helped. If the kidnapper was still asking for ten million pounds what did Stu plan to say?

Stu at last looked up. 'Baz and I were talking about this just now. On the phone.'

'And?'

'Ten million might just be possible.'

'Are you serious?'

'Yes. Baz needs to make some calls of course, but … yes.'

'And you're telling me you're both prepared to pay that kind of money?'

'If we have to, yes. What choice do we have?'

'We string it out. Or more precisely *you* string it out. We'll get to him in the end, believe me.'

'But what if he starts making threats? Against Guy?'

'Then we have to assess whether he's bluffing or not.'

'And if he isn't?'

'Then we're in a whole different ball game.'

'I see.' Stu knotted his hands, staring at Faraday. 'Have you got the call box covered? The one in Woking?'

'Yes.'

'But he wouldn't be stupid enough to use it again?'

'No.' Faraday reached for his coffee. 'I very much doubt it.'

Mackenzie spent the rest of the morning in his office at the Royal Trafalgar, making phone call after phone call. The last couple of years had taught him a great deal about running a successful business and it hurt him deeply to be involved in a fire sale of his own assets. Nevertheless, he told himself, it had to be done.

He started with the hotel itself. He'd bought the freehold from an old Pompey family who'd had the place for years. He'd got it for a song, leant on a series of mates in the building trade to refurbish the place, thrown a huge party at the end, and had recently turned down a handsome offer from an American-owned operation looking for prime sites in English seaside resorts. He pulled a pad towards him, drew a heavy black line down the middle of the page and scribbled the hotel's name at the top. Beside it, a figure: £5 million.

Next came the list of Pompey houses he'd hung on to through thick and thin. These were relics from the old days when he'd first realised the potential for turning drug money into bricks and mortar. Most of them were terraced houses, deep in Fratton and Copnor, and all of them were still let to students. Chasing the kids out would never be a problem, especially not at this time of year, but property was getting hard to move in the city and only silly prices would guarantee a quick sale. From memory, he wrote down a list of addresses. They numbered sixteen. At a conservative price of – say – £150K he was looking at another £2.4 million.

After liquidating his modest residential holdings Mackenzie started on the other parts of his Pompey empire. He owned the leasehold on three café-bars in Southsea and Old Portsmouth. All the leases were new and had a minimum of eighty-six years to run. Add fixtures and fittings, plus decent trading histories, and even in this market you had to be looking at a minimum of – say – a million quid between them. On top of the café-bars, there was a tanning salon, a two-branch estate agency, a gaming arcade, two garages, a 51 per cent stake in a taxi firm, plus a fun investment in a Fratton shop specialising in exotic reptiles. Another million. At least.

Mackenzie lifted the phone and told the girl in reception to send more coffee in. For a moment, while she was still on the line, he wondered whether to add a bottle of Moët to the order but then decided against it. Already he'd got within a whisker of ten million quid. Why celebrate losing it?

Beside his UK assets, Mackenzie made another list – of holdings abroad. He'd begun with a ruined manor house in the depths of the Normandy countryside. The place was barely an hour's drive from the ferry port at Le Havre and a Pompey builder who'd hit hard times had fallen in love with the place. The best part of three years' work had restored the property to its former glory and Baz had taken Marie there on a surprise Valentine's outing. She'd also adored it and so Baz had instructed the builder to hunt down similar properties, all within reach of the coast. The builder, who by now spoke half-decent French, had done him proud. Under various nominees Mackenzie now owned nine rural properties in Normandy, Picardy and Brittany. The smallest of them had seven bedrooms.

In the wake of this adventure, Mackenzie had extended his interests still further, applying the same business model to Spain. Word of earning opportunities abroad had spread amongst Pompey builders and those eager to flee impending divorces had been only too happy to sign up. To date, after a slow start, Mackenzie Abroad had twenty-seven Spanish properties on its books, not counting a separate retirement development on the Costa Dorada, which was Marie's baby. Most of them were more modest than the holdings in northern France, and all of them were in the hands of Spanish rental agencies. It was one of these agencies that had first alerted Mackenzie to the apartment block on offer in Baiona.

Now, still waiting for the coffee, he sat back and tried to do the sums. His UK empire was big enough to make ten million quid and there was no need to liquidate the stuff abroad. All these properties, in any case, were held by nominees to put them beyond the reach of the taxman but ownership, in the end, was his. He gazed at the list and experimented with a sum or two.

By the time he heard the knock at the door, he was grinning. Another £15 million. Easy.

The girl left the coffee on his desk. He sat back, gorging on a pile of Jammie Dodgers, wiping the crumbs from his jeans. He had no idea where the next few days might lead but he knew he'd have to start unravelling the Pompey end of his empire. One day, probably soon, he might do the same thing with the properties in France and Spain. These days the real money was to be made in Dubai. There were canny blokes in Portsmouth, some of them ex-6.57, making huge fortunes in shopping centres and real estate out there. All it took was a bit of patience, a lot of nerve and a tame Arab to act as a frontman. After that, all you needed was the ability to count.

Mackenzie swallowed the last of his coffee and reached for the phone. He held his business accounts at the local branch of a national clearing bank and kept a sizeable cash reserve on deposit. The sums involved entitled him to preferential treatment. After a moment or two a voice answered.

'Terri? ' The voice had put a smile on Mackenzie's face. 'It's me.'

Stu Norcliffe took the call at half past four in the afternoon. He was sitting in the lounge in Sandown Road, staring out of the window. Faraday was on the sofa, deep in Winter's *Daily Telegraph*, when the phone rang.

Stu lifted the receiver. He recognised the voice at once and nodded at Faraday. Faraday picked up the extension.

'Put my son on,' Stu said.

'I can't. He's not here. Listen to me. Ten million, right?'

'We never agreed that.'

'I don't care a fuck. It's ten million or nothing.'

'Meaning what?'

'Meaning you get hold of the money or never see your kid again. I said twenty-four hours. This isn't a game.'

'Ten million is a fortune. Where am I supposed to get that sort of money?'

'You can find it if you have to.'

'How?'

Faraday had instructed him to keep the guy talking. Hence all the questions.

'Listen to me ...' the voice was saying now. 'The next time I call we discuss delivery arrangements. You got that? I'm not into hanging around, believe me.'

The phone went dead. Stu looked up, aware of the sweat pouring down his face. Suttle was upstairs in a spare room. He'd been listening on another extension. Faraday knew he'd be talking to the Comms techie who'd also monitored the call.

Minutes went by. Stu was still in the armchair, his head back, his eyes closed. Then Suttle appeared at the door. Faraday looked across at him.

'Well?'

'Payphone at Waterloo station, boss. We never had a prayer.'

Metropolitan Police Special Ops was headquartered in a bleak office block in the depths of Lambeth. On the phone, Willard had fixed a five o'clock meeting with the Detective Superintendent in charge. He was ten minutes late.

Special Ops worked out of a suite of offices on the fifth floor. Det-Supt Blake Aaron was a lightly-coloured thirty-something who reminded Willard of Barack Obama. The same ease and grace in his physical movements. The same uncanny ability to spin a thought or mint a phrase. Here was someone who'd spent a great deal of time and effort on the dark arts of presentation. In a force as politicised as the Met, thought Willard, Blake Aaron was heading for the top.

'Traffic's like weather, Geoff. All you need is patience.' He shrugged aside Willard's apologies for being late. 'You want something to drink? A coffee or something?'

Willard shook his head. Time was regrettably short. He had to be back in Winchester by half seven. What he needed was a steer on the Alan Garfield operation.

'So I gather. Can you be a little more specific?'

'Certainly. There's a Pompey Level Three we have an interest in.'

'Pompey?'

'Portsmouth. His name's Mackenzie. Aka Bazza. If you've been plotting up Garfield in Spain you may have come across him. The pair of them were about to close a property deal in a town called Baiona. Am I getting warm?'

Aaron said nothing. Then he gestured for Willard to carry on.

'We suspect Mackenzie may be in deep with this Garfield but we can't prove it. Experience tells me you might be able to.'

'Prove it?'

'Yes.'

'Prove what exactly?'

'Prove that Mackenzie has put himself alongside Garfield. And we're not just talking property.'

'You think they're at it across the board?'

'I think they may be.'

'Class A drugs?'

'Yes.'

'Specifically cocaine?'

'Yes.'

Aaron nodded, reflective, taking his time. Willard, watching him, knew that cooperation between forces was often a minefield, especially when Covert Ops were involved. Both sides in any of these negotiations were extremely reluctant to reveal their investigative hands in case the information went further. A slip of the tongue, two counties away, could wreck six months of painstaking fieldwork.

'Where exactly do you think we are with Garfield?' Aaron had a question of his own.

'I know you pulled him in for interview. And I know he was released on police bail. I'm obviously assuming you haven't got enough.'

'You're right.'

'But the operation's ongoing?'

'Very much so.'

'And the prospects?'

'Extremely good. I'd give it a couple of weeks, max.'

'And Mackenzie?'

'Mackenzie?' Aaron's smile looked genuine. 'Like I say, a couple of weeks.'

Chapter twenty-three

Gail Parsons summoned a *Causeway* meet first thing next morning. The core squad managing the kidnap was growing by the day. As well as the attached D/I from the Serious Organised Crime Unit and the Family Liaison Officer, Helen Christian, the cast list included Jimmy Suttle, a tech adviser from Scientific Services' Comms Intelligence Unit and a Crime Scene Co-ordinator to advise on the forensics.

It was Faraday's job to offer an update on developments. He briefed the meeting on yesterday's call from Waterloo. Voice analysis had established a match with the previous Woking call and there seemed little doubt that room for negotiation on the ransom sum was extremely limited.

Parsons was frowning.

'Do we assume the family can raise that kind of money?'

'Between them, yes.' Faraday nodded. 'We did a full audit on Mackenzie's holdings four years ago for *Tumbril* and came out with a figure not far short of twenty million. Since then he's gone from strength to strength. This isn't a man who lets money lie idle. In my judgement I think it's likely he could raise ten million very quickly.'

'How?'

'By raising a loan against properties.'

'But *would* he, Joe?'

'That's a different question. Mackenzie hates paying for anything. That's partly why he's made it. Buying his grandson's life might be different. He'll be under the cosh, like everyone else.'

'And you're saying he'd wear ten million?'

'I'm saying he might have no choice.'

There was an exchange of glances around the table. Most of these people knew Mackenzie, either personally or by reputation. The last thing you ever did was assume you had the measure of the man.

The D/I from the Serious Organised Crime Unit had previously worked in Portsmouth. His name was Dalton.

'Joe's right,' he said. 'People like Mackenzie hate being pushed into a corner. If there's a way out of paying that sort of money, Mackenzie will find it.'

'How?'

'I've no idea. He may have a line on the guy he thinks did it. At this level of criminality, that's not a name he's going to be sharing with us. We're guests at his table. He decides the menu. We do what we're told.'

Parsons had no time for this kind of admission. Collectively, the people round this table were in the business of returning the child to its parents. Every tool in *Causeway*'s box was available to make sure that happened.

'Like what, boss?' Dalton was decidedly punchy.

'Like comms. We need to be listening to everything that goes into and out of that house.'

'We're doing our best, boss.' It was Jimmy Suttle. 'Helen and the techie between them are monitoring all the landline calls. Plus we've got a divert on the landline into Stu Norcliffe's place.'

'What about Mackenzie's mobe? The daughter? The wife? What about any undeclared mobes they might have hanging around? What about Mackenzie's line at the hotel?'

Dalton's eyes rolled. 'Are you rippered up for that?'

'No, but we can put a bid in. This is a high-risk Misper. We're talking a Grade One life in danger. Are you telling me we can't stretch to a couple more RIPAs?'

The Regulation of Investigatory Powers Act demanded top-level authorisation for comms intercepts without the owner's permission. Dalton shrugged. He had a great deal of experience in this field. Every authorisation for a comms intercept had to meet extremely tight criteria. The RIPA bar was always set higher than you expected.

Suttle said he'd set the wheels in motion, talk to the uniformed Superintendent downstairs, see how far he was prepared to push it.

Helen Christian caught Parsons' eye. 'I was talking to

Mackenzie first thing just now,' she said. 'He phoned in. I don't know what it's worth but he's come up with a name.'

'Who is it?'

'Cesar Dobroslaw.' She was reading from her notepad. 'Apparently Mackenzie has had some dealings with him recently. He's saying there's no love lost. The guy's been pushing to set some kind of operation up in Pompey and Mackenzie wouldn't have it.'

'What kind of operation?'

'He didn't say, boss, but Mackenzie was playing the vigilante – you know, Citizen Joe – so it must have been dodgy. His point was that the guy was extremely pissed off with him so in Mackenzie's view anything might be possible.'

'Even a kidnapping?'

'Even that. Stu Norcliffe told him about the way we got knocked back on the traffic cameras and how we're starting to think someone with local knowledge and Mackenzie says that's this bloke Cesar.'

'Anyone know him?' Parsons was looking round the table. Dalton nodded.

'Dobroslaw's a major face in Southampton,' he said. 'He runs most of the brothels in the city, imports Belarusian toms by the truckload from Minsk, and my guess is he's pushing to get into Pompey. He's got a lovely place up Chilworth way. We've been trying to take him out for years.' He glanced across at Christian. 'How come he knows the Meon Valley so well?'

'Mackenzie claims he goes shooting on an estate round there,' Christian said. 'He's mates with the guy who owns it. He thinks we ought to check him out.'

'The guy's a Scummer.' Suttle was looking at Parsons. 'That'd be enough for Mackenzie.' 'Scummer' was Pompey for anyone from Southampton.

'You're telling me we take it no further?'

'I'm saying he's blowing smoke up our arse.'

'But what happens if he turns out to be right?'

'Then we'd have a problem, boss. You're absolutely right.'

Parsons turned back to Faraday. 'You'll action it? This morning?'

'Sure.' Faraday nodded at Suttle. Suttle scribbled a note, checking the spelling of Dobroslaw's name with Christian.

Parsons asked Faraday about the paedophiles culled from the Sex Offenders Register.

'All the alibis checked out, boss. The kid goes to primary school in Droxford and his mum takes them all swimming at the pool in Fareham. We widened the search parameters to include Fareham but still no joy. This doesn't feel like a paedophile, not this MO.'

'I agree.' Parsons glanced across at the Crime Scene Co-ordinator. She wanted to know about the public payphones used by the kidnapper. Both had been declared crime scenes.

'We had them boshed but I wouldn't hold your breath. We're talking hundreds of fragments of DNA and if chummy's the same guy who did the kid's house there's no way he wouldn't be wearing gloves.'

'And the house itself? Anything new?'

'Nothing. The guy left his shoes outside. He wore gloves the whole time. According to the au pair, the balaclava didn't even have a hole for his mouth. He was that aware.'

'No possibility of DNA?'

'None. No saliva, no dribbles, nothing. The only DNA we took was from the young lad's toothbrush. I'm sorry but there it is. The preliminary report's ready. I'll get it sent over this afternoon.'

Faraday sat back. DNA from Guy's toothbrush would identify him in the event of a body being found.

'Not great,' he said softly. 'Not great at all.'

The meeting came to an end twenty minutes later. Faraday asked Helen Christian to come back to his office. The incident room at the end of the corridor was filling up. Another day to cast the *Causeway* net still wider.

Faraday shut the door. Christian took a seat.

'Tell me about the family,' he said. 'How are they bearing up?'

'It's difficult to call, boss. You've been there. You must have felt the atmosphere. It's not just the kidnap, it's the maritals as well. I know I shouldn't say it, but the mother, Esme, is a nightmare.'

Faraday was watching her carefully. 'Nightmare how?'

'She's spoiled to death, for a start. She's obviously been used to getting her own way, probably her whole life, and nothing's changed. To tell you the truth I'm really surprised, especially as far as Mackenzie is concerned. I never had him down as a soft touch.'

'She's his only child. You make all kinds of mistakes, believe me.'

'I know, but she doesn't seem to have grown up. She's a very attractive lady and she's got the money to make the best of herself, but the way she treats people is beyond belief. What she wants she gets, and if that doesn't happen you certainly know about it.'

'Madison?'

'She wanted him. She got him.'

'And now?'

'The jury's out, boss. They're certainly still in touch, but for my money, knowing Madison, that's a relationship she bossed completely. There's another thing. Esme's still a kid at heart and I get the sense she bores easily. That's something our Perry should have seen coming.'

'Maybe he did.'

'I doubt it. She has quite an effect on men. I've seen it.'

'Stu?'

'The perfect example. He's a puppy. He wants to be all over her, even now. You can see it. In a way it's quite sweet.'

'So what's the secret? Have you sussed it yet?'

'She's very challenging. She looks you in the eye. She's beautiful too, and rich, and I expect she's brilliant in bed. Any one of those would be enough for most men. Put it all together, like Stu must have done, and the poor man hasn't got a chance.'

'So you think he'd have her back?'

'Tomorrow. This afternoon. Now. No question. He's dotty about her.'

Faraday stepped across and opened the window. There was a rumble of rush-hour traffic from the nearby motorway. Families, he thought. How fragile they are. How easily dropped and broken.

'And Mackenzie?' He turned round.

'He's as rough as a badger's arse but he's still a charmer.' She shook her head. 'Poor woman.'

'Who?'

'Marie. She's really nice. She knows how to behave, how to treat people. That man doesn't know how lucky he is.'

'Maybe he does. And maybe she likes him that way. How is he coping though?'

'With Guy? The kidnap? This whole thing?'

'Yes.'

'Badly at first. It's twenty years since I had anything to do with him but people don't change, not that much. Yesterday morning he was all over the place – couldn't make a decision to save his life, huge mood swings, totally manic.'

'And now?'

'He seems to have got a grip. Maybe it's the fact that Stu's heard from the kidnapper. Maybe it's the fact that there's someone out there, a voice, something tangible, something he can *work* with. Do you know what I mean, boss? Mackenzie, in the end, is like the rest of us. He hates a vacuum. He loathes not knowing where he is. Give him a challenge, just that bloke's voice on the phone, and he gets stuck in.'

'You're telling me he's freelancing it?'

'It wouldn't surprise me in the least.'

'Keeping us out of the loop?'

'Could be.'

'What makes you think that?'

'I went out with the man. I *know* him.'

Faraday held her gaze for a moment, then his phone began to ring. It was Parsons. She needed a word in his ear. Urgently. Faraday signalled for Christian to leave the office. Then he turned back to the phone.

'Go ahead, boss.'

'I've had Mr Willard on. SOCA have received a clearing-bank disclosure. Notice from guess who to withdraw guess what.'

'How much?'

'A million. In cash. Mr Willard has authorised it on condition the bank marks the notes.'

Faraday nodded. The Serious and Organised Crimes Agency ran a database, known as ELMER, for all financial disclosures nationwide. This latest heads-up would have pinged down to Hantspol within minutes.

'When did this happen?'

'This morning, first thing.'

'And when is Mackenzie picking it up?'

'Around now. And the answer's yes, we've got the bank plotted up.'

'You want this to run?'

'Of course. It's the old story, Joe. We follow the money.'

Winter met Mackenzie outside the bank in Commercial Road. Early shoppers were watching a gelled young assistant dressing a window in Debenhams while a passing drunk attempted a tune on a battered harmonica.

Mackenzie was carrying a rucksack, pink, with a picture of a kangaroo on it.

'Yours, mush.' He gave it to Winter.

Winter followed him into the bank. The summons had come by phone half an hour earlier. Apart from a worried-looking woman waiting for an appointment, the bank was empty. Mackenzie went to the nearest service point and asked for Terri.

'Tell her it's Aladdin,' he said. 'Quick as you like, love.'

Moments later a tall, attractive-looking woman emerged from a side office. She stepped across to Mackenzie and offered her cheek for a kiss. Winter, still holding the rucksack, was impressed.

'Mate of mine.' Mackenzie nodded at Winter. 'Best I could find.'

'Your mate?'

'The rucksack.'

Terri led them through to an office deep in the bowels of the building. Thick pile carpet and a big crescent of desk.

'Has anyone offered you gentlemen coffee?'

Mackenzie shook his head. A percolator was bubbling softly on the glass-fronted cabinet behind the door. Beside a plate piled with croissants was a choice of marmalades. Mackenzie helped himself while Terri bent to a safe set into the wall behind the desk.

'How's that race of yours coming on?' he wanted to know.

'It doesn't happen until October, thank God. Me and my friend are still up for it but we've been a bit lax lately. I can't remember the last time we got out for a decent run.'

'You go along the seafront?'

'Yeah.'

'I'd better look out for you.' He passed Winter a coffee. 'What about the sponsorship?'

'Thirty quid so far and most of that's from my nan. Are you up for this? Only we might as well start.'

Winter turned round to find himself looking at thick piles of banknotes, all fifties. Terri had sorted out a couple of chairs and gestured for Mackenzie and Winter to sit down. Unless Mackenzie had any objection she'd leave them to it.

'No problem.' Mackenzie licked his fingers, then eyed the notes and glanced up at Winter. 'Half each, mush. If we're fifty quid long or fifty quid short we have to do the whole fucking thing again.'

'Short of how much, Baz?'

'A million.'

'Really?' Winter was doing the sums. 'That's two thousand notes.'

'Spot on, mush. A grand each. Race you?'

It took the best part of half an hour to count the notes. Winter had never seen so much money in his life but after the first £100,000 it became a chore.

'I've had more fun playing Monopoly, Baz.'

'Yeah. She does a nice croissant though, eh?'

'I'm sure.' He paused a moment, looking at the money. 'So why do you need all this?'

'Doesn't matter, mush. Just keep counting.'

Terri returned to find twenty neat piles across her desk.

'Are we done?'

'Yeah.'

'Happy?'

'Spot on. Paulie here's thinking of becoming an ATM. Got a real talent for it.'

The rucksack was lying on the carpet. Mackenzie picked it up and tossed it across to Winter, telling him to stuff it with the money while he sorted out the paperwork. Terri had a form for him to sign. A million quid cash, thought Winter. At the stroke of a pen.

The rucksack was barely big enough. Terri suggested she find a thick manila envelope for the rest but Mackenzie told

Winter to use the pockets on the side. Bulging with banknotes, the rucksack was surprisingly heavy.

They all shook hands. Winter put the bag over his shoulder and headed for the door. Then Mackenzie called him back. He unzipped the nearest pocket, extracted a fifty-pound note and gave it to Terri.

'Call it sponsorship, Tel.' He shot her a grin. 'Now you've *got* to do that fucking race.'

Back in the precinct outside the bank Mackenzie was wondering about a coffee. Winter, who had profound doubts about walking around with a million quid in cash, persuaded him to wait until they got back to Craneswater. En route to the Bentley, he had another thought.

'Why Aladdin, Baz?'

'She thinks I'm a genius, mush. She thinks I magic this stuff up.'

Faraday took Suttle to Southampton. He'd asked the intel D/S to phone ahead and arrange a meeting with Cesar Dobroslaw. Today, it turned out, Dobroslaw was working from his office at home. He'd be delighted to give them half an hour of his time. Should he ask his lawyer to attend?

'I told him no, boss. We're just after a chat.'

Faraday nodded. His new TomTom had taken them to a leafy avenue on the northern edge of Southampton. Chilworth was the favoured address of the city's high-flyers, big handsome houses in an acre or two of garden. Think Craneswater, he'd said, without the sea views. The same quiet dependence on space and a decent security system. The same glimpses of spoiled children and cosseted wives.

They found Cesar Dobroslaw up a ladder having an argument with his roofer. The house was clad in scaffolding and the roofer was reseating tiles around a new dormer window. Dobroslaw clambered down the ladder and apologised for the lack of a handshake. He was a big man, heavy-jowled, with a mane of jet-black hair swept back from his forehead. He looked like a retired boxer, Faraday thought, or someone who was considering a new career in undertaking.

They went indoors. The house was warm with shafts of late-spring sunshine panelling the carpet in the big lounge at the back. Looking round, Faraday detected a woman's hand everywhere: in the subtleness of the paint tones, in the gold-threaded tapestries, in the choice of paintings. One in particular caught his eye, a glorious watercolour of a landscape he didn't recognise. A huge tumble of clouds shadowed a water meadow. Cows grazed in the distance. A peasant leant on a gate, watching a pair of swans drifting on the river which dominated the canvas.

'The Vistula.' Dobroslaw had appeared at his elbow. 'Near my home town.'

The voice belonged to a life-long smoker. Roll-ups to begin with, thought Faraday; these days more likely cigars.

Dobroslaw offered them a drink. He'd washed his hands in the kitchen, returning with a bottle of vodka. Faraday turned the offer down. This needn't take long.

He asked Dobroslaw to account for his movements on Monday night. The Pole settled on the sofa.

'I was in London,' he said.

'In a hotel?'

'In a hospital. I have a mild heart condition. I was there for tests and they kept me in overnight.'

He gave Suttle the details of the hospital and the consultant. He'd come home yesterday afternoon and wouldn't be returning to work until next week.

'Doctor's orders.' He smiled. 'Does that answer your question?'

Faraday nodded.

'Do you know a Mr Mackenzie?'

'Bazza Mackenzie? From Portsmouth?' He slapped his knees, roaring with laughter. 'Is this why you come here?'

'Yes.'

'He's done something? He's made a complaint? Is that it?'

'An allegation, Mr Dobroslaw.'

'About what?'

'I'm afraid I'm not at liberty to tell you.'

'You're not? You want me to tell you something about this man? Here ...' He beckoned Faraday closer. 'At the end of this road is a small hotel. It's run by friends of mine. It does very well. Excellent food, nice rooms if you have people who want a recommendation, good clean family business. Your Mr

Mackenzie, he wants to buy it from them. He makes them offers. He has plans. He wants to expand, to build an extension, many more rooms. This place is perfect for the motorway, for visiting businessmen, and your Mr Mackenzie, he's not stupid. I tell my friends, don't sell. And then I tell them also, if you do sell I shall fight Mr Mackenzie on the planning. I know everyone round here. We don't want Mr Mackenzie. And we don't want his hotel. So … an allegation … What a surprise, eh?'

Minutes later, heading east again, it was Suttle who voiced the obvious.

'Dalton was right, boss. Smoke up our arse. I wonder how many other accounts Bazza wants us to settle?'

Chapter twenty-four

Mackenzie and Winter were back in Sandown Road in time to catch Esme eating her breakfast. Stu was sitting beside her at the big kitchen table cutting thin slices of white toast into soldiers. Lucy and Kate were resisting their mother's attempts to make them sit down. The boiled eggs, Esme said, would be getting cold. Up to you.

'Christ.' Mackenzie took the rucksack from Winter and tossed it into the corner by the window. 'You lot want to be careful. This looks almost normal.'

Marie was at the Aga. She glanced round, trying to smile, trying to add something extra to this tiny flicker of returning warmth, but Winter could see the effort she had to make. Alone in this broken family she seemed to understand the enormity of what was going on.

Lucy, perched on her wooden stool at the table, waited while her father peeled fragments of shell from the top of her egg. He spooned a generous dollop of yolk onto one of the soldiers, just the way Lucy liked it, but when he turned back to her, she'd gone.

'That's mine!' She'd dived onto the pink rucksack.

Winter moved quickly to retrieve it but he was too late. As soon as Lucy unzipped the top, a cascade of fifty-pound notes fell out. She stared at them, delighted, then shook the rucksack until it was empty. A million pounds lay on Marie's kitchen floor. No one moved. Even Esme, for once, looked impressed.

'Where did that come from?'

'The bank,' Mackenzie told her. 'You think we keep this stuff under the mattress?'

Winter was watching Lucy grab handfuls of the banknotes and throw them up in the air. Then, barefoot, she started dancing on them, more flurries of pink as she did stagey little pirouettes, kicking out sideways with her tiny feet. Her sister wanted to dance too but Lucy pushed her away. Surreal, Winter thought.

Marie wiped her hands on a tea towel and grabbed the kids before handing them to Stu.

'Upstairs,' she said. 'Now.'

Stu did her bidding, chasing them out of the door. As ever, Lucy began to howl as she tramped up to her bedroom. Winter couldn't be sure but he thought the child had hung onto a couple of the notes. A hundred quid would buy a lot of banana smoothies.

In the kitchen, Marie had emptied the vegetable basket. She began to refill it with banknotes, later after layer. Mackenzie told her it didn't matter, he'd sort the money out later, but she shot him a look.

'Your girlfriend's back any minute,' she said quietly. 'You want her to see all this?'

Mackenzie didn't. Neither did Winter. Stu watched all three of them pack the money into the basket. By the end, there was just enough room for a top dressing of onions, carrots and broccoli. Marie slid the basket back under the work surface. She too wanted to know what her husband was up to.

'It's just in case,' he said.

'Just in case what?'

'Just in case I can talk this guy down. There's a million quid there. He can have it this afternoon, tonight, whenever. Just as long as we get Guy back. Isn't that right, Stu?'

Stu nodded, said nothing. Winter was looking at him hard.

Marie wanted to know how this thing would work.

'Work? We just do it. The guy phones again. I talk to him. I explain that ten million quid's silly money. I tell him ten million quid's going to buy him a lot of trouble because no way do I give that kind of moolah away without having the Filth on board. A million, on the other hand, is different. For a million I can do him a nice discreet private job. We fix a meet, I get the boy, he gets the money.'

'And the police?'

'Are nowhere.'

'How come?'

264

'Because I'll tell them I've had enough. It's our blood, our grandson, our decision. We've decided to play it our way, not theirs.'

'Your way.'

'Whatever.' He looked across at her, his face beginning to colour. 'You've got a problem with any of that? Only now's the time to say.'

Marie stared at him. Then came a ring from the front door bell.

'You think that's Helen?'

Marie nodded. 'You're off your head.' She was still looking at her husband. 'You know that?'

Esme went to the front door. Not Helen Christian at all but Mo Sturrock. He appeared in the kitchen. Winter could hear Esme's footsteps on the stairs, then a squeal from the girls as she stepped into their bedroom. For once, thought Winter, she seemed to be taking an interest in her family.

Sturrock nodded at Mackenzie.

'You just got me in time,' he said. 'I was off home on the hovercraft.'

'Yeah?' Mackenzie got to his feet and headed for the den. 'Come with me, son. There's stuff we need to talk about.'

Helen Christian took the news back to Major Crimes. In Faraday's absence, she knocked on DCI Parsons' door. The DCI, in conference with Willard, asked her to come back later but Willard put a hand on Parsons' arm. He'd seen the expression on the FLO's face, knew it might be important.

'He doesn't want us around any more,' she said.

'Who doesn't?'

'Mackenzie. I got there a bit late this morning. He's saying he'll handle it his way not ours.'

'He can't,' Willard said at once.

'Why not, sir?'

'Because he'll be aiding and abetting. This guy's a criminal. Mackenzie's making it easy for him. That's collusion. Conspiracy. Plus it taints his own money, assuming he plans to pay up. We could have him on any number of charges.'

'Maybe he wants his grandson back.' This from Parsons.

'We all want his grandson back. The question is how. You buy this man off, how many other kids does he lift?'

The question went unanswered. Arguing with the Head of CID in this mood was a lousy career move. At length, Parsons enquired what he wanted *Causeway* to do next.

'We need Faraday,' he said. 'Where the fuck is he?'

Faraday had fixed to meet the engineer from the alarm company at Esme's property. The au pair let him in. Evzenie wanted to find out when she might expect Mr and Mrs Norcliffe to be back in residence. Faraday said he didn't know. The kidnap was at a tricky stage. It was better, for now, that the family were all under one roof in Craneswater.

'It goes well?'

'No.'

'Guy?' She blinked.

'We don't know.'

Evzenie fled to the kitchen. Faraday circled the big lounge at the back of the house. A couple of sensors protected the tall French doors that opened out onto a terrace and there was another on the facing wall. He lingered a moment, inspecting the nest of photos on the mantelpiece. Happier times had taken the Norcliffe family to an exotic-looking beach with the purest white sand. The kids were younger, only Guy on his feet, and the palm trees in the background suggested somewhere Caribbean. Looking at Stu, Faraday could imagine the future that this man had every reason to trust. His face was plastered with sunblock but his arm circled Esme's perfectly tanned shoulders and with two babies in his lap he looked the proudest father in the world. The family had money, freedom and each other. There was nowhere on the planet they couldn't go, no passing whim they couldn't satisfy. If they got fed up with life in the country they could move. If seven acres wasn't enough they could buy more. In a world stuffed with goodies, they had limitless choice. Now this.

Faraday climbed the stairs then checked the bedrooms one by one. Each one was protected by zonal sensors, and there were more on the top landing, but the truth was that no security system in the world could offer 100 per cent protection because the real threat came from within. Not the balaclava-clad intruder somehow ducking all these high-tech sentries but the restlessness in Esme's eyes. You could see it in the pictures on the mantelpiece, a sense of unslaked curiosity that had led, of all people, to Perry Madison.

The au pair was waiting for Faraday at the foot of the stairs. She wanted to know whether he'd prefer tea or coffee. He said no to both but wanted to know more about Guy.

'How trusting was he?'

Evzenie looked confused. Faraday wondered whether she had a problem with the word 'trusting' but it was the tense he'd used that had thrown her.

'*Was?* You think he's ...' her eyes were shiny again '... dead?'

'I meant *is*, I'm sorry. And no, I don't. I think he's still alive.'

'Good.' She nodded vigorously, as if to reinforce the possibility. 'Good. He trusts everyone, that little boy. He trusts me, he trusts people who come, friends who come. He's very easy, very strong, very grown up. He's a lovely boy. Very brave. I love him. Everyone loves him.'

'So you think ... now – given what's happened – he can cope?'

'I think yes, for someone so small, so young, yes. The girls, they are different. Guy? He makes me so proud.'

'A survivor?'

'Always.'

'Good.' Through the open door to the kitchen Faraday could see the boiling kettle. 'Tea please. I've changed my mind.'

The engineer from the security company arrived minutes later. He walked Faraday around the system, explaining a recent update. All the zoned areas were linked by wireless to a central control unit. If any of the motion sensors tripped then a recorded message would automatically be sent to five approved numbers, backed in the case of mobiles by texts. A sixth report would go to an authorised Hantspol number. There was also a 125-decibel alarm that would sound both inside and outside. In theory, at least, the house was intruder-proof.

'Mr Norcliffe says he had a problem last weekend.'

'That's right.'

The engineer had a file. He hadn't attended personally but

he'd spoken this morning to his colleague, who'd driven down from Alton. He'd tested every component in the system and found nothing wrong.

'Is that common?'

'It's not unheard of.'

'But rare?'

'Definitely. This kit is pretty robust. We did the update a couple of months ago. The batteries are first to go but they last a minimum of eighteen months, and there are visual and audio warnings if there's any kind of problem. Like I say, the system was working fine.'

'So there's no way in? Is that what you're saying?' They were outside now, looking up at the house.

'Not without alerting the system. The sensors are state of the art. The science has come on in leaps and bounds. Even the cat would have a problem sneaking in.'

'So how do you get round that?'

'You disable the system with a remote, just the way the owners do. You simply aim and press, just like a car or a telly.'

'And you can buy spare remotes?'

'Of course. But only from us.' The technician gazed at Faraday a moment, then shook his head. 'The answer's no,' he said. 'I took the liberty of checking this morning. There are only two issued remotes on the system, one for Mr Norcliffe and one for his wife.'

Winter managed to corner Esme in the spare bedroom she was using upstairs. Stu had just disappeared into another bedroom across the corridor. The kids were down in the kitchen, helping Marie make brownies.

Esme was sitting on the bed, studying a text message on her mobile. She'd been getting changed and was down to her underwear. A pair of newly bought jeans were on the carpet beside her feet. She looked up, startled.

'Don't you ever knock?'

Winter ignored the question. He wanted to know about the money.

'What the fuck's Baz up to? Anyone care to tell me?'

'He's come up with a plan. You were there, down in the kitchen. You heard him.'

'He's going to pay? You believe that?'

'Yeah, I do.'

'Really?'

Winter's tone of voice sparked a reaction. Esme reached for a T-shirt and then had second thoughts.

'It's called family,' she said. 'If money is what it takes then he'll spend it, I know he will.'

'That's bullshit, love. Bazza never spent a penny he didn't have to. That's why he's living here. That's why you've got more property, more land, more everything than you'll ever need. That came from Baz being clever. A million quid to some bloke he's never met in his life before? How clever is that?'

'He's got no choice. None of us has. And anyway what makes you think it's just Dad with the money? Stu's loaded. It's not down to me to tell you how much he earns but the last Christmas bonus would have covered Guy several times over.'

'So Stu's paying? Is that what you're telling me?'

'I'm not telling you anything. Except it's none of your business.'

'Wrong, love.' Winter was standing over her now, staring down. 'Like it or not, Baz pays me to look after his interests. Just now his interests are in deep deep shit and unless someone gets a grip you lot are fucked. Are you hearing me? Do we understand plain English?'

'You're jealous.' Esme returned his look, unflinching.

'*Jealous?* How does that work?'

'You'd like what we've got. You'd like what it buys – and I'm not just talking property and cars and all that other stuff. I'm talking respect, Paul. Dad isn't joking when he bangs on about doing something in politics. Tide Turn is just the start. You're right, he's a clever, clever guy. I trust him completely. We all do.'

Winter turned away, wondering whether this conversation was worth the effort. Big money shuts you away, he thought. It locks the doors and seals the windows and keeps the real world at arm's length just the way you hoped it would until the going gets really tough. Like now.

Esme had reached for her jeans. She began to tug them on but Winter was back in her face.

'Your dad is this far away from losing it all down the khazi.'

Winter's thumb and forefinger were a millimetre apart. 'You can't see it and neither can he but I spent most of my working life around situations like these, and from where I'm standing you have one big fucking problem.'

'Like what?' Esme was having trouble with the zip.

Winter refused to answer. Instead he asked her about the hotel in Baiona.

'Whose idea was it in the first place?'

'Mine. I just loved it. Dad was with me. Even he had to admit it was gorgeous.'

'When was this? Exactly?'

'Before Christmas. Early December. He'd had a long email from your mate Rikki. That was what put us into the bidding for the apartment block. The hotel wasn't for sale at that point.'

'But after you saw it?'

'I told Dad we had to have it.'

'*You* had to have it.'

'Whatever. It was an investment too. The market's depressed over there, and in any case I think the guy was ready to sell.'

'So what did Bazza say?'

'He agreed. The hotel here works fine for him. He's learned a lot. I know it's Spain and everything but the principles have to be the same. We'd run it as a going concern.'

'Hands on?'

'Yes. That was my idea.'

'You'd run it?'

'Yes.'

'And you'd met Madison by now?'

She didn't answer for a moment. She reached for a T-shirt and put it on. Then she nodded.

'Yes.'

'So he'd be part of this plan? You and Perry out there together? The shag palace of your dreams?'

'Don't be a twat, Paul.'

'But was that it?'

'Yes. Plus the kids of course.'

'And you thought Baz would buy into that fantasy? A couple of million euros to set up some bastard copper who's nicked off with his daughter and his grandkids? Was that it?'

'Yes.' She was defiant now, more sure of herself. 'I could talk him into it. I knew I could.'

'And that's what you told Madison?'

'Yes, sort of.'

'And what did he say?'

'He said he'd go anywhere with me, anywhere in the world. He said he'd had enough of being some bastard copper as you put it. In fact he'd had enough of pretty much everything. He loved me, Paul, believe it or not.'

'Loved?'

'Loves.' She shrugged. 'Present tense.'

They both looked at her phone. Esme covered the text message with her hand then slipped the mobile under the pillow. There was a long silence.

'So what about the hotel?' Winter asked.

Esme gazed up at him. For the first time she was smiling.

'It's still for sale,' she said. 'As far as I know.'

Faraday met Willard in Fordingbridge, an attractive market town on the western edge of the New Forest. They'd made their separate ways to the car park of a pub in the town centre. Faraday had often used the place for a late breakfast after dawn birding expeditions to nearby Martin Down, with its possibilities of turtle dove and lesser whitethroat.

'He lives in Bullingdon Crescent.' Willard had written the address down. 'We'll go in my car.'

They drove to the outskirts of the town. Number 14 Bullingdon Crescent was one of a dispiriting line of post-war bungalows. Madison's had newish-looking dormer windows in the roof.

'I thought he was living in a bedsit in Romsey.' Faraday was looking at the Renault parked outside the house. A man's leather jacket lay across the front passenger seat.

'He was. Until yesterday.'

'He's back home?'

'Yeah, so he says. PSD have also suspended him. My recommendation, if you're asking.'

Faraday nodded. The Professional Standards Department policed the police. Within the space of an hour or so, pending an official hearing, Madison would have become a non-person:

his warrant card surrendered, his email account closed, his work mobe returned to his head of department.

Faraday was still looking at the bungalow. The windows at the front were curtained.

'What's the charge?'

'Officially, it's bringing the organisation into disrepute. Unofficially, the man's been a complete twat. How much of a twat we're about to find out.'

They walked to the front door. Unlike his neighbours, Madison had resisted the temptation to litter the tiny pocket of lawn with garden-centre gnomes.

His wife answered the door. She must have been very attractive once but there were streaks of grey in the blaze of auburn curls and hints of bitterness in the set of her mouth.

'Come in, guys. Help yourselves.' She stood aside. She seemed to be expecting them.

A boisterous Labrador leapt at Willard. She grabbed it. The dog was called Mason.

'Think Perry,' she said. 'It was his idea.'

The joke was lost on Willard but Faraday dimly remembered an American TV defence lawyer of the same name. They walked through to the kitchen. The back garden was longer than Faraday had expected and Madison was visible at the far end attacking a patch of green with a garden fork.

'That's our salad plot. It's the best he can do in the way of therapy.'

They watched Madison for a moment or two. He was wearing nothing but jeans. He kept his head down, thrusting at the soil, bending from time to time to lift a weed and toss it aside. In terms of body language Faraday needed no clues to the coming interview. Every movement spoke of a savage fury.

'Can't be pleasant, any of this.' Willard shot her a look.

'You'd think so, wouldn't you?' She reached for the kettle. 'Gets easier with practice though.'

'He's done it before?'

'Yes.'

'Lots of times?'

'Twice. I suppose the mistake was letting him back in the house but then I'm even crapper with gardening than he is. You want tea?'

Willard and Faraday stepped into the garden. Splashes of sunshine came and went. Faraday knew Madison had seen them but he kept going with the fork until they were barely feet away. There was a light sheen of sweat on his chest. He wiped his face, gave them both a nod.

Willard was looking around. 'Where do you want to do this?'

There was a tiny summer house in a corner of the garden beside the salad plot. Madison organised a couple of chairs out front, leaving Faraday to prop himself against an upright. The summer house badly needed a coat of varnish.

Madison found a sweater and sank into one of the chairs.

'You've been a pillock,' Willard began. 'You don't need me to tell you that.'

Madison said nothing, just looked away. His wife had appeared with a tray of tea. She picked her way through the clutter of garden tools, gave the tray to Faraday and returned to the bungalow without a word.

Willard started again.

'You need to tell us about Mackenzie's daughter, about what's been going on.'

'Why?'

'That's a stupid question, Perry. Because she is who she is. Because she works hand in glove with a Pompey Level Three. Because you've just spent the last God knows how many months leaving yourself wide open.'

'To what? To being in love? To meaning it? To committing myself?'

Faraday, expecting Willard to tear Madison apart, was surprised when he simply nodded.

'Go on,' he said.

'Go on how? You want the details? How we got it on? How often? Where? What she fancies? What really turns her on? Do you have all day or shall I just stick with the headlines?'

'You fancied her,' Willard suggested. 'Why don't we start there?'

The question seemed to deflate Madison. He slumped deeper into the chair, began to pick at his blisters. Then he looked up again and shrugged.

'We used the same gym,' he said. 'She's an attractive lady.

The times we were there the place was pretty empty. We just talked, really.'

'And?'

'She made me laugh. She was witty, bright. She had a mind of her own and she was fit too. A bloke can miss things like that, believe me.'

Faraday resisted the temptation to look up at the bungalow. Was Madison's wife lurking in the shadowed recesses of one of those rooms, watching? Or, more sensibly, was she upstairs, packing her bags? To stay with a man like this you had to have more than patience. Maybe he was a brilliant cook, Faraday thought. Or maybe she had a taste for self-abasement.

Madison was talking about the doors that laughter can open.

'It was so easy,' he said. 'One moment we were having another little chat, the next we were in bed together. And after that it just all made perfect sense. We clicked. We were a couple. We were made for each other. It wasn't me inventing it. It wasn't her taking another scalp. It just *was*. You do it once and it *has* to happen again. And then again. And then again and again. I'd never come across a relationship like that in my life. And neither had she.'

'Did you know who she was at that time? Her name? Her family connections?'

'I knew her name but I never made the link to Mackenzie, no. Not then.'

'And what about her? Did she know you were in the Job?'

'Yes. She asked me what I did for a living and I told her.'

'And then what?'

'She asked me whether I liked it or not, something like that, then we talked about something else.'

'Did she mention Winter at all?'

'No. As far as I knew she was this housewife lady with a law degree she never used who lived with her husband and had three kids and was mad about horses. Her old man obviously had a bit of money because he ran a hedge fund or something. We didn't talk about him much, either.'

'I bet.' Willard was looking at the lettuces. 'So when did you make the connection with Mackenzie?'

Madison frowned, taking his time, thinking back. The earlier resentment had gone. Now, thought Faraday, he seemed glad of the chance to put the whole story together.

'It was way into the New Year. We'd been running together in the forest and she'd left her wallet in my car.'

'And?'

'I did what every copper does. I had a look. There was the usual stuff in there – a bit of money, credit cards – but there were some photos too, a couple with her kids, one of her old man, and one of Mackenzie.'

'You recognised him?'

'Straight off. Back in the early days I used to be a spotter at Pompey away games. Mackenzie was in the 6.57 then. He hasn't changed at all.'

'So now you knew who you were shagging. Am I right?'

'Yeah. In fact I asked her about her dad the next time we met. She said yes, like you would, and when I wondered why she hadn't told me before she just laughed. She didn't want to put me off, she said. As if.'

'But it made no difference?'

'It couldn't. Nothing could. Not by then. Even if she'd told me she had HIV or leprosy something, I'd still have stayed with her.'

'And from her point of view?'

'The same. I asked whether her dad, you know, had cottoned on, but she said no. It was just her and me. Our little secret.'

Willard glanced across at Faraday. Your turn. Faraday wanted to know whether Madison and Esme ever talked about her life outside the home.

'How do you mean?'

'She works for her father. She's legally qualified. She does a lot on the contracting side. If she's told you it's all kids and shopping then she wasn't being entirely ... ah ... truthful.'

Madison nodded. Suddenly he seemed less comfortable.

'I pressed her on that,' he admitted. 'I knew she went away with him sometimes and they couldn't have been just jollies.'

'Away where?'

'Spain a couple of times. Dubai, once. She came back with loads of gold, jewellery and stuff. I remember that.'

'And did she tell you why she went? What they got up to?'

'She always said they had a good time … but no, she never said much else.'

'Did you press her?'

'Yes. She wasn't having it.'

'She said that?'

'Yes. In fact that was the closest we ever had to a row. She said it wasn't my business.'

'Did you want it to be?'

'I didn't want there to be any gaps.'

'You mean secrets?'

'Yes. If this thing was serious, if we were going where I thought we were going, then it had to be for real.'

'Full disclosure?'

'Yeah.' There might have been the hint of a smile on Madison's face. 'Full disclosure.'

Willard stirred. He'd abandoned his cup.

'So where exactly did you think this thing *was* going?' he asked.

'I thought we were going the whole way. Set up together. Live together. Make room for the kids. All that.'

'Where?'

'Abroad. She had some plans.'

'Whereabouts abroad?'

'Spain. She said she'd found a place, a really nice place, a place I'd love.'

'Did she have photos? Anything like that?'

'No. I asked, obviously, but there was always some excuse.'

'And this place was a house?'

'Of course. At least I assume so …' Twenty years of coppering put a frown on his face. 'What are you telling me? It *wasn't* a house?'

Willard dismissed the question. He was more interested in more recent events.

'Mackenzie eventually found out. What happened then?'

'The shit hit the fan. After that, the way I see it now, all bets are off.'

'I'm not with you. What bets?'

'She's a different woman. The spell, the magic, whatever it was, all that's just gone.'

'But you'd just found the place in Romsey, moved out, burned your bridges. Isn't that the case?'

'Yeah ...' Madison's eyes strayed towards the bungalow. 'Tell you the truth, I thought I'd got it all sussed. Bin the job. Take early retirement. Buy the missus off. Scarper. Except that's not going to happen. Not now. Not with Mackenzie on top of her.'

Faraday was trying to work out the timeline. On Saturday last week, Esme had flown to Vigo to sign the contract on the hotel.

'So when was the last time you saw her?' he asked.

'Last week. Friday. I'd just moved into the flat. We had a curry in Romsey. That's when I knew.'

'Knew what?'

'Knew we were in the shit. She said she had to get home to pack. She was going down to Spain for a bit. She didn't say why, and when I asked her about it she was just vague. Stuff she had to do. Early doors next morning. No fucking help at all. Then she just got up and said she was off. At that point I sussed Mackenzie must have found out because I'd had a run-in with Winter.'

'When was that?' Willard this time.

'Earlier in the week. I was coming back across the forest in the middle of the night. Me and Esme had been together that evening and Winter must have plotted us up. He followed me later. We had words.'

'He was warning you off?'

'Yes.'

'And what did you say?'

'I told him to fuck off.'

Faraday leant forward. This was beginning to make sense. 'And what else did you say?'

'That night?' Madison frowned again. 'I think I might have said, might have hinted, that I knew more than I really did.'

'About what?'

'About Mackenzie. Just to put him off in case he was planning anything silly.'

'Stuff you might have picked up from Esme, you mean?'

'Exactly.'

'But that was a lie?'

'A ploy. To keep my arse in one piece.'

Faraday nodded. Winter had obviously reported back, and Mackenzie, like any rational human being, had told Winter to check this threat out. Hence Winter's surprise visit to the Bargemaster's House.

'But in reality you knew nothing?' It was Willard again. 'About Mackenzie's affairs?'

'Nothing.'

'And that's still the case?'

'Yeah.' Madison nodded. 'I'm afraid it is. Life's a learning curve, boss. You can get into bed with one Mackenzie, but the minute the rest find out you're well and truly fucked. You know something? In my line of business I should have seen that coming.'

There was a moment of complete silence. Then even Willard was laughing.

Chapter twenty-five

Marie made an early supper for Mo Sturrock and Winter. Winter, who rarely ate until mid-evening, asked her what was going on.

'Baz has some plans. I take it you know nothing.'

Winter shook his head, looked at Sturrock. Sturrock seemed clueless as well but Winter knew at once he was lying.

'What's going on then? Anyone care to tell me?'

Marie had turned back to the chopping board. A salad of boiled eggs, diced tomatoes, spring onions, olives, tuna fish and slivers of anchovy, Winter's favourite. Winter looked at her a moment longer, still waiting for an answer, then got up and left the kitchen. He found Mackenzie in his den. Baz had recovered the money from the vegetable basket and was packing it into a new-looking holdall. The holdall was black with the Nike motif on the side.

'Baz?'

Mackenzie barely bothered to look round.

'Close the door, mush. It's draughty.'

'What the fuck's this about?' Winter was staring at the holdall.

'I've got a little job for you. I want you to take this lot down to Poole. There's a pub near the ferry port called the Dog Star. There's a guy who'll meet you there. He'll ask you about crowd attendance at the final. You tell him 89,874. Write it down. Go on. I'll tell you something else, mush. That happens to be true.'

'What does?'

'Eighty-nine thousand, eight hundred and seventy-four. And that included me.' He sat back in the chair and nodded at the holdall. 'You OK with all this?'

'With what, Baz? So far I've got to the Dog Star, I'm carrying a million quid in notes, and some bloke's asking me how many turned up at Wembley. Do I give it to him? Do I phone the Bill? Do me and him elope together? Just a clue, Baz, that's all I'm asking.'

'You give it to him, mush. He takes it somewhere safe, somewhere outside, and half an hour later – once he's counted it all – he makes a phone call. Then we hear a knock on the door ... and guess who's home for a late Horlicks?'

'Guy? You're kidding.'

'Never. On my word.'

'What if it's a scam? What if we've just paid a million quid for fuck all?'

'Won't happen, mush.' He patted the breast pocket of his leather jacket, where he kept his mobile. 'I talked to the boy just now. He's been told. He's in the know. He can't wait to get back.'

'I'm not surprised. So where is he?'

Mackenzie smiled. 'Nearer than you think.' He nodded at the money. 'Poole, mush. The Dog Star. I want you down there for half nine.'

Willard ordered yet another council of war. The Crime Scene Co-ordinator was busy with a murder in Southampton but Parsons deemed his presence non-essential. In his place came a D/S from the Totton-based Surveillance Unit. At Faraday's suggestion a lawyer from the Crown Prosecution Service had also been invited to attend.

Much to Dalton's amusement Faraday owned up at once to the blank he'd drawn with the Pole, Cesar Dubroslaw. As predicted, Mackenzie had lured the *Causeway* squad into one of the murkier corners of his business empire. Wasting half an hour of Dubroslaw's time was hardly recompense for Bazza's knock-back on the family-run hotel up the road but Faraday was the first to admit that Mackenzie, once again, had been pulling their strings.

Willard was far from amused. He wanted a full update on developments in Craneswater from Helen Christian. The FLO, expecting exactly this request, spread her hands wide.

'I've got nothing, boss.'

She explained that she'd spoken on the phone to Marie, Mackenzie's wife. She'd confirmed that her husband wanted nothing more to do with Operation *Causeway* and was intending to handle whatever happened next by himself.

'Did you get the impression the kidnapper's been in touch again?'

'I asked her exactly that.'

'And?'

'She said no, not as far as she knew. The last bit is important, boss. Mackenzie's MO never changes. He tells people very little. Even his wife has to fight for every morsel she can get.'

Faraday nodded in agreement. This had been one of the major surprises of the last week or so. Even Winter, who'd practically written the manual on withholding information, had been excluded from the Mackenzie loop.

'So this guy *might* have been in touch?' Willard wanted to be sure.

'It's possible, certainly.'

'And Mackenzie might have negotiated the ransom demand down? Is that what we're saying?'

'Of course. By how much, I've no idea.'

'This morning outside the bank ...' Willard had turned to the D/S from the Surveillance Unit. 'You've got the shots?'

He fumbled in a file and produced a handful of surveillance photos. The sight of Winter toting a bulging pink rucksack across the Commercial Road shopping precinct drew a reaction from the faces around the table. Willard quelled the laughter with a look. Twenty-four-hour surveillance on the ex-D/C, he reminded the meeting, was costing a small fortune.

'So what do we assume?' He'd turned to Faraday.

'We assume, sir, that Mackenzie and Winter have done some kind of deal. The bank disclosure was for a million quid. The money was paid in fifties. There's just about room for the notes in a rucksack like that.'

'And you're telling me this is the ransom?'

'Probably.'

'To be handed over pretty much now?'

'I'd imagine so. Mackenzie likes readies but there's obviously a limit to how much you keep at home.'

Willard took a moment to digest this news. Then he brought

the CPS lawyer into the debate. She was small and very pretty. Her name was Pauline. Suttle couldn't take his eyes off her.

'Pauline, supposing we intercept delivery of the ransom? Recover the money? What are the implications?'

'In legal terms, you mean?'

'Yes.'

She frowned, refusing to be rushed into an answer to what was a shrewd question. Faraday found himself applauding her composure.

'There are two sides here,' she said at last. 'On the one hand I imagine you may end up hazarding the child's life. That's a matter of risk assessment, and as a lawyer I'd suggest you spread the consultation as high as possible. On the other hand, if Mr Mackenzie has refused to accept our help and advice, we might be able to make a case for aiding and abetting or even for obstructing the course of justice. It's tricky, though. Helen's right. There's no way we can force our presence on the Mackenzies.'

'What about the money? The ransom?'

'That would be tainted, definitely. It's being knowingly offered in the commission of a crime. Under the Proceeds of Crime Act, we'd have a case.'

'And that could trigger restraint proceedings?'

'Yes.'

The mobile belonging to the D/S from the Surveillance Unit began to beep. He checked it, muttered an apology and quickly left the room. Faraday caught Willard's eye. He wanted to talk about the Norcliffes' house out in the Meon Valley.

'I can't evidence this yet,' he began, 'but I'm beginning to have my doubts.'

'About what?'

'This whole thing. Number one, the scene was totally protected, state-of-the-art system, sensors everywhere, brand-new installation. The only way in was by someone somehow gaining access to a remote. Only two exist, one held by the father, Norcliffe, and the other by his wife, Mackenzie's daughter. Unless someone's been cloning remotes we have to start asking ourselves questions about both these parties.'

'And number two?'

'Mackenzie's change of mind. I get the impression the

pressure's off.' He was looking at Helen Christian. 'Would that be right?'

'As far as Mackenzie's concerned, yes.' She nodded. 'He was as wound up as everyone else to begin with, but yesterday I definitely noticed a difference. His whole vibe had changed. He was cocky again. He was in *charge*.'

Willard looked at Faraday. 'So what do we conclude, Joe?'

'We ask ourselves whether there isn't more to this kidnap than meets the eye. Quite what, I don't know. Not yet, anyway.'

'You think we might be chasing our tails?'

'It's possible.'

'You think Mackenzie might be taking the piss again?'

'Yes.'

There was a general exchange of looks around the table. Faraday thought for a moment that Willard was going to ask for a show of hands but then the door opened and the Surveillance D/S stepped back into the room. He was still holding his mobile. He paused beside Willard and muttered something Faraday couldn't catch. Willard stiffened, then checked his watch.

'Shit,' he said softly.

Minutes beforehand, Winter had set off for Poole. Now, he eased the big Lexus onto the spur motorway that fed traffic north beside the harbour to the mainland. The Nike bag lay in the footwell on the passenger side of the car. To Winter's amusement, Mackenzie had made a show of padlocking it.

'I sent the guy a key yesterday. If it hasn't arrived he'll have to use a fucking knife.'

Winter settled down for the drive west. At this time of night the traffic was heavy and the streams of homebound cars had been thickened by a line of trucks pouring off a recently arrived ferry. Winter tucked himself behind a French artic and found some decent music on the radio. For the time being, he'd decided, the only sane option was to ride along with Bazza and hope to Christ he'd got it right. It wasn't the fact that he'd been relegated to bagman that rankled. It was the dawning knowledge that this whole kidnap had developed a dimension that Mackenzie simply refused to share.

Something had happened, Winter knew it had. Esme, as self-obsessed as ever, was probably unaware. Marie, who read the tea leaves as astutely as Winter, was looking a wreck. While Stu, after a couple of days on the edge of his own nervous breakdown, seemed to have clammed up completely.

Winter asked himself why. A couple of years back, in the Job, he'd have actioned this. A couple of hours in an interview room, properly handled, could unlock all kinds of secrets, but in this new life of his Winter was left with nothing but his own native guile. Twice over the last couple of days he'd tried to get alongside Stu, tried to build the kind of matey rapport that might lower his guard, but on both occasions sympathy just hadn't been enough. Whatever Stu was hiding from the rest of the world had turned him into a mute.

Did this explain Bazza's abrupt return to form? Had Stu's father-in-law somehow conjured a result from the days and nights of family angst? Winter rather suspected that this had to be true but for the life of him he couldn't figure out how. Neither, for that matter, did he understand the new role that Mo Sturrock seemed to have acquired. It was undeniable that Tide Turn's new executive director had lit a sizeable fire in Marie, and for that blessing Winter was truly grateful, but why had Bazza summoned him back from the hovercraft? And what on earth was he still doing in Craneswater?

The *Causeway* meeting had dispersed. Only Parsons, Willard and Faraday remained in the DCI's office. The Surveillance D/S had received word from the team following Winter that he'd left Mackenzie's Craneswater house. His Lexus had been parked in the road outside and he'd appeared at 18.23, carrying what looked like a black sports bag. His route out of the city had taken him north to the M27, and then west towards Southampton. The assumption had to be that swap arrangements for the release of Guy Norcliffe were under way.

Given the speed with which events were now moving, Willard had abandoned any attempt at a risk assessment. The priority now was to keep tabs on Winter and take out some kind of tactical insurance in case things turned awkward with the boy. The latter, entirely Willard's decision, had involved a call to the TFU. The Tactical Firearms Unit were on standby 24/7. Thankfully, they were based at Netley, five minutes from the M27. With a following wind, they could be hauled in by the surveillance boys and slotted in behind the ever-lengthening queue of unmarked cars accompanying Winter westwards.

'So where do you think he's going, Joe?'

'No idea, sir. If it was Southampton, he'd have peeled off by now.'

'The New Forest? Some link to Madison?'

'It's possible but I doubt it.'

Willard nodded. Both Parsons and Faraday knew that he'd put his head on the block. Deploying the TFU required authorisation from an Assistant Chief Constable. They'd heard Willard, just minutes earlier, assuring the ACC that this plan of his offered the best possible chance of killing three birds with one stone. Within an hour or so they might have recovered the child, the ransom, and gathered enough evidence to start restraint proceedings against Pompey's top face. No wonder the ACC had said yes.

Winter had no difficulty finding the Dog Star. The miracle of satnav took him into the depths of Poole, a westward extension of Bournemouth that sprawled around a huge natural harbour. The continental ferry port was tucked into the northern end of the harbour within walking distance of the pub. Beyond a small marina, through a thicket of yacht masts, Winter could see the white bulk of the cross-Channel ferry. How hard might it be to pop a million quid into the boot of your car, buy a single for Cherbourg and just sail away?

He stored the thought in the back of his mind and retrieved the sports bag from the Lexus. According to a chalked blackboard propped against the Dog Star's front door Thursday was the midweek pub quiz. Half-price drinks until eight and a two-for-one offer if you fancied fish and chips. Winter pushed in through the front door, glad he'd turned down Marie's salad. Once all this nonsense was over, fish and chips would be perfect.

The pub was busier than he'd expected. The quiz was due to start at eight and regular teams had already commandeered most of the tables. He found a spot towards the back with a good view of the door, folded his coat over the seat, and took the bag to the bar. For once in his life, conscious of the importance of what might happen next, he limited himself to a half of Stella. Back in his seat, with the bag tucked between his feet, he settled down to wait.

At Willard's request, the tech adviser from the Comms Intelligence Unit had stayed on at Major Crimes. He'd sorted out a couple of Airwave handsets from his van and tuned them both to the frequency being used by the surveillance team tracking Winter west. The set-up permitted two-way communication, giving Willard overall command of the operation. Parsons had organised a tray of coffees and Faraday had fetched a packet of ginger biscuits he dimly remembered storing in his bottom drawer.

The atmosphere around the conference table was strained. This opportunity had blown in from nowhere, like a sudden summer storm, and Faraday knew how much Willard hated surprises. In a perfect world you'd plan for something like this, carefully deploying your assets, briefing your teams, preparing contingency arrangements, trying to cover every square on the board. That way, as all the training manuals agreed, you'd reduce your exposure to the unexpected and stand a decent chance of emerging with a result. Tonight, though, was very different, and the knowledge that Mackenzie had somehow forced *Causeway* into a corner had darkened Willard's mood.

He was bent to one of the handsets, talking to the D/S in charge of the surveillance team. The D/S, in turn, had been in touch with his oppo on the Tactical Firearms Unit. The TFU were parked up round the corner from the pub.

Willard wanted to know what was happening inside.

'The target's at the back. The place is heaving. Pub quiz night.' Faraday smiled. 'The target' was Winter. Willard must have been dreaming of this moment for the last couple of years.

'You have line of sight?'

'Affirmative. Two of our guys are in there, no problem.'

'TFU?'

'Ready to move. There's a rear exit and a car park at the back. I've got that covered too.'

'Keep me briefed.'

'Affirmative, sir.'

Willard leant back and reached for his coffee. No matter how imperfect his preparations for whatever might happen next, Faraday could sense his excitement at the chance of finally nailing not just Mackenzie but Winter as well. Both men, in their separate ways, had been thorns in Willard's flesh: Mackenzie because of his profile, and his wealth, and his flagrant contempt for law and order, and Winter because he'd crossed to the Dark Side and joined him. In Willard's book there was no sin so grave as betrayal.

Looking up, he caught Faraday's eye. If the wheels came off this one the consequences were unthinkable.

'Are you a betting man, Joe?'

'No, sir.'

'Just as well.' The smile was grim. 'Fingers crossed, eh?'

Winter happily parted with a quid for the quiz entry fee. The girl with the jam jar had a nice smile and Winter liked being told he looked intelligent. Tonight's star prize was a side of lamb, pre-butchered for the deep freeze.

'You want someone to join you? Make a team?'

'No thanks, love.'

'Are you sure? Only I know most people here.'

'Yeah?' He beckoned her closer, lowered his voice. 'How about that guy over there?'

Winter had noticed him a couple of minutes earlier. He had a tiny table by the door. He was young, crop-haired, casually dressed, and had the kind of watchfulness that Winter could recognise at a thousand miles. The face wasn't familiar but after a couple of years out of the Job that meant nothing.

The girl with the jar sneaked a look. Then turned back.

'By the door?'

'Yeah.'

'Never seen him in my life.'

'You're sure?'

'Positive. You want me to ask him over?'

Winter looked up at her a moment. Then he nodded.

'Brilliant idea,' he said.

She took the jar over. It was getting noisier now and she had to bend to make herself heard. Winter caught the shake of the head and the quick precautionary glance in his direction. He grinned back, raised his glass, gestured at the empty chair beside him before the face disappeared behind a swirl of incoming drinkers. When the lounge cleared again Winter realised that the guy had bought a ticket for the quiz. He got to his feet, walked across. Leaving the bag for a minute or two was a risk but he couldn't resist a closer look.

'You're sure, mate?'

'Positive. Thanks for the offer, though. And good luck, eh?'

Winter returned to his seat, trying to convince himself he'd been wrong. Surveillance guys used tiny mikes taped to the inside of their shirts or their wrists. If you knew what you were looking for they weren't hard to spot. This guy appeared to have neither. And what kind of copper ever wished you luck?

'I think he's clocked us, sir, or one of us anyway.'

'Who?'

'The target.'

'You're kidding.'

Willard took the news badly. He should have anticipated this. Winter had decades of experience. He'd been in similar situations a million times before. He knew exactly what to look for, what to expect. With all the sneaky-beaky in the world you couldn't fool the guy who knew exactly how to put the clues together.

'What do you want us to do, sir?'

'Hang in there. See what develops.'

The first round of questions was on the history of *Coronation Street*. Winter settled down, eyeing the sheet in front of him, knowing he was on home territory. His wife, Joannie, had been mad about *Coronation Street*. Winter hadn't shared too many of her evenings in front of the TV but she'd always bring him up to date next morning over breakfast. What Mike Baldwin ought to do with his love-rat pisshead son. Whether Deirdre Rachid would really end up inside after getting it on with her con-man boyfriend. Decades later, those conversations were still fresh in his memory. He could chart the highs and lows of his marriage by what was happening on *Corrie*.

Winter reached for the biro the girl had left behind, waiting for the first question. If, by any chance, he won this thing he'd definitely be dedicating the evening to Joannie. She'd always loved roast lamb.

The quizmaster called for order.

'Question one ...' he announced. 'Who electrocuted herself with a hairdryer in 1971?'

With a little jolt of pleasure Winter realised he knew the answer. Teams at various tables were conferring. Someone said Bet Lynch. Someone else, shaking their head, insisted it was Rita Littlewood. Winter, knowing that only poor Valerie Barlow would have done something like that, glanced across at the lone drinker by the door. The guy was far too young to even have heard of Val Barlow. No wonder he was looking so clueless.

Winter grinned to himself, still watching as the guy turned his body away, shielding it from Winter's sight. Then his head went down and there was a ripple across the denim jacket as his right arm came up. It was the kind of motion you'd make if you were stifling a cough or a sneeze and Winter knew with an alarming certainty that he'd been right first time. The guy had a mike up his sleeve. They'd been following him, doubtless mob-handed. There'd be a couple more in the pub, someone round the back, a car or a scooter outside in case he made a hasty exit. They'd got him plotted up. They'd got him kippered. And the million quid at his feet told him he was in deep shit.

'He's definitely onto us, sir. I think he may be leaving any minute.'

'Options?'

'We can take him now. Favourite would be outside.'

Willard nodded. More control. Fewer punters. Less drama. But what about the handover?

'No sign of anyone else?'

'No, sir.'

'Give it another minute or two.'

'And if he leaves?'

'Nick him.'

Winter was wondering whether to phone Mackenzie but then dismissed the idea. Whatever happened next, it would be Winter himself who'd be carrying the can. Quite how he was going to account for a million quid in fifty-pound notes was beyond him but he still had time to put some kind of story together. Maybe he'd had a big win on the lottery. Maybe he'd found the bag on a bus. Maybe he'd just look them in the eye, have a dig or two about the overtime they must be clocking up, and go No Comment just like every other decent criminal he'd ever potted.

Question three was about a character in *Corrie* he'd barely heard of. Was Joannie up there listening? Might one of her bright ideas get him out of this corner? He shook his head, scribbling something nonsensical, wondering whether it was better to abandon the rendezvous and bail out now or hang around for the kidnapper and give these bastards the satisfaction of two names on the charge sheet. The thought brought him to his feet. He drained his glass, bent for the bag and headed for the door.

Outside, it was still light. The Lexus was parked twenty metres away on the other side of the road. He'd last seen the guy standing next to it a couple of years back. Then he'd been a D/S on Major Crimes.

Winter stopped. A voice in his ear told him to keep walking. He could feel the warmth of the man's breath. He half-turned, recognising the figure at the table by the door.

'Too tough for you, mate?' Winter shot him a grin.

'What?'

'The quiz.'

The man pushed him forward. Winter got to the Lexus. D/S Dave Michaels was pleased to see him.

'Mr Winter ...' He nodded at the bag. 'What have we here?'

'No idea, skipper. You tell me.'

Michaels asked for his car keys. Winter obliged. Michaels unlocked the car doors and told Winter to get into the back. Winter still had the holdall. By now Michaels was in the front passenger seat, his body twisted so he could see Winter in the back. He nodded at the holdall on Winter's lap.

'You've got a key for that little padlock?'

'No.'

'Seriously?'

'Yeah.'

'So what's inside?'

'I haven't a clue.'

'You're having a joke, aren't you? This is no way to treat old mates. I'm going to ask you again. What's inside?'

'No idea.'

Michaels looked at him a moment longer then shrugged. Another of the surveillance officers had a penknife. He offered it through the window but Michaels shook his head.

'Go round there and do it yourself,' he said.

The officer opened the rear door and squatted on his haunches in the road. He took the bag from Winter, checked the padlock, then began to cut into the mock leather. Winter sat back, his head against the soft squab, gazing into nowhere. Then he closed his eyes. He knew what a million quid looked like. He'd had enough of money.

The officer with the knife had finished. He pulled the cut apart. Winter heard the weight of Michaels' body shifting on the seat in front of him. Then a soft curse.

'Take it out. All of it.'

There was a rustle of paper. It didn't sound at all like bank-notes. There was more of it, then more still. Finally, Winter opened his eyes. On the road beside the holdall was a sizeable pile of second-hand books while the footwell in the back of the car was littered with balls of newsprint. Winter reached down for one, smoothing it out on his lap. It was a copy of the Portsmouth *News*, Monday 19 May. Pages 12 and 13. POMPEY WIN BRINGS WORLDWIDE CHEERS. Bazza again. Taking the piss.

Winter gazed at the headline for a long moment.

'Amen to that,' he said.

Chapter twenty-six

'The Marines? Why would you ever get into something like that?' Marie wanted to know more.

'It's kind of hard to remember.' Mo Sturrock was trying to frame a proper answer. 'I was at the old Poly for three years. I was doing a geology degree because that seemed to give me a chance to get out of the country and hunt for oil, but to be honest I was a crap student. In fact I was a crap everything. Crap at the work. Crap with women. Total wuss. Completely hopeless.'

'Really?' Marie glanced across at him. 'I'm amazed.'

'You shouldn't be. I screwed up big time. In the end I tried the Marines, like I just said, but that didn't work either. You need to be brave to hack the stuff they throw at you. I wasn't.'

Marie slowed for traffic lights. A couple of hours in Bazza's Bentley had brought them to the edges of Newhaven. Beyond the town, the last of the daylight was fading over the English Channel.

'So what did you do?'

'I came back home.'

'To Portsmouth?'

'Yeah. It wasn't what I wanted but I had no money so that's what happened. It was a disaster. It was like I'd come full circle, back where I started. I knew within hours I should have stuck with the Marines.'

'Was that an option?'

'Definitely not. I was a gawky little runt of a guy. I had big ideas and nothing to go with it. I lived in fantasy land most of the time. I could talk a good war, no problem, but when it came to the real thing I was clueless.'

'When was this?' Marie was trying to do the sums.

'Middle of the Eighties. It was autumn. The training place is down in the West Country and it never stopped bloody raining. That was bad enough but the Marine instructors were still pumped up after the Falklands and they saw through me in minutes. Horrible. I chucked it in after the second week.'

For a couple of months, he said, he did bar work on the Pier. Then he met an older woman who was acting manageress in a pub on the seafront. She took him in hand.

'She'd spotted that I was good with some of the lippier kids who used to come in, the ones who'd try it on with you. She said I had the knack of getting through to them. It was true too. I did. And I enjoyed it.'

At her suggestion, Mo asked around about jobs in Social Services. If he was serious, he'd have to go back to the Poly for another degree. This time it worked.

'It was totally different. I knew what I wanted to do with this bit of paper they were going to give me, and that changed everything. I was having to work part time too, just to keep my head above water, and that concentrates your mind. When you're on a grant, like before, you piss it all away. This time I was Mr Focus.'

A degree in social work won him a job in a neighbourhood team based in Buckland. The workload was brutal but he loved it.

'Child protection enquiries. Knocking out court reports for kids taken into care. Keeping tabs on short-term placements. Turning up at the Bridewell on a Saturday night to dig the little scrotes out of the mire. All sorts. We were the finger in the dyke and everyone knew that the dyke was bursting. It just went on and on.'

'And has any of that changed, do you think?'

'What?'

'The pressure.'

'Not at all. If anything it's got worse, but I guess we're just used to it now. There are some seriously lost kids in this world and most of them haven't got a clue what to do next. We've taken something away from them. They kick off, they get difficult, they're up in court, and the really sad thing is we end up thinking it's all their fault.'

'It's not?'

'No.' He shook his head. 'If it's anyone's it's ours.'

'You believe that?'

'Yes. And I'll tell you something else. I've got kids of my own, three of them, and you know what? It doesn't have to be that way.'

They were in Newhaven now. Marie spotted a sign for the cross-Channel ferry.

'Where did Baz say?'

'Outside the main railway station.'

'What time?'

'Nine fifteen. We're looking for a black Mercedes. He didn't have a reg number.'

The station was down in the valley. The town was ugly and most of it felt deserted. A trickle of cars headed for the ferry port. Marie pulled onto the station forecourt and stopped. There was only one cab on the rank and the driver appeared to be asleep. Mo suggested she reverse into one of the parking spots. In the gathering darkness, beyond the nearby warehouses, he could see white gashes in the fold of downland that led out to the cliffs.

'How much do you know about this guy?'

'Nothing.'

'So what's in the bag?'

'I've no idea. Money, probably. Remember the key, though. He'll need that.'

Mo grinned. The bag lay between his feet. It was black, badged with the Nike logo. Bazza had got it cheap in a sports outlet in Gunwharf. So cheap he'd bought two.

'Why don't we open it?' Mo's suggestion.

'Bad idea. Working for my husband is one thing, Mo. Being married to him, quite another. I suppose it's a kind of learning curve. He tells you what you need to know. Everything else he takes care of.'

'So why isn't he doing this?'

'I've no idea. There'll be a reason.'

'He hasn't told you?'

'No.'

'So what kind of marriage is that? Do you mind me asking?'

'Not at all.'

'And?'

'I don't know the answer.' She smiled. 'Except it works.'

They sat in silence. It began to rain, big fat splashes on the windscreen, and the cars heading for the ferry became a blur.

'He tells me he's got political ambitions,' Mo said after a while.

'It's true. He has.'

'So how does that work?'

'To be frank, I've no idea. I thought he was joking to begin with, but these last couple of years he's been meeting all kinds of people – councillors, officials, so-called experts – and most of them definitely don't impress him. He thinks he can do better. It's probably as simple as that.'

'But would he want to?'

'Yes.' She nodded. 'I think he does. Take something like Tide Turn. Baz really wants to make it work. We were talking about it the other night. Kids these days see through adults. Unless you've been a bit of a player, a bit of a rogue, or unless you're rich, they've got no time for you.'

'And Bazza?'

'He's a bit of both. They like that. Especially the rich bit.'

The silence returned. The last couple of days had taught Mo Sturrock a great deal about the Mackenzies. In his judgement, Marie was by far the sanest. She checked her watch and then adjusted the seat so she could lie back.

'Been married long, Mo?' she asked. Her eyes were closed.

'Yeah. Though she's my partner, not my wife.'

'Happy?'

'Very. She's a part of me, always has been. The kids were the icing. She's the cake.'

'Wrong.' Marie was smiling. 'You're both the cake, Mo. That's how these things work. I bitch about my husband sometimes but he never fails to make me laugh. We've been in scrapes you wouldn't believe but so far he's never failed us.'

'And if he did?'

'It wouldn't matter in the slightest. He'd still be Mad Baz and I'd still love him for it.'

Mo nodded, looked down at the bag.

'So is this a scrape?'

'Yes.' Marie nodded. 'Definitely.'

The Mercedes arrived minutes later. A small squat figure emerged from the driver's side and crossed the car park towards them. For a moment Mo mistook him for Mackenzie. Then his face appeared at Marie's window. Older, plumper, heavier. Marie lowered the window, readjusted the seat.

'My husband tells me you've got something for him,' she said.

The man nodded, showed her an envelope, biggish, thickish, A4. Marie looked back at Mo then nodded down at the bag. Mo exchanged it for the envelope. The man felt the weight of the bag, examined the zip. Marie watched his every move.

'I gather we have to wait –' she was looking at the bag '– while you count it.'

'No need. We're late.' He nodded towards the ferry port. 'Tell him I trust him. And tell him he's forgiven.'

They looked at each other for a moment. The silence stretched and stretched. Finally the stranger extended a hand, palm uppermost. He had a slight squint.

'Key?' he queried.

Winter chose the baked cod fillet with leek fondue and oregano-scented potatoes. Bazza went for the Dorset rump of lamb dauphinois. The restaurant was pleasantly full. Beyond the carefully gathered brocade curtains, Winter could see the long curve of Studland Bay and the blueness of the hills beyond.

To his delight, Bazza had been parked up beyond the pub in Marie's Peugeot. He'd choreographed the action perfectly and been on hand to capture the final act on his camcorder. The watchers watched. An irony for which Winter had a deep appreciation.

'D'you mind, Baz?'

The camcorder lay between them on a thick fold of linen napkin. For the third time, Winter found the start of the sequence. Bazza was reminding the waiter that they needed the Krug now. Both bottles.

Winter gazed at the tiny screen. The hunched figure in the back of the Lexus was him. He couldn't remember whether he'd been laughing out loud or not but that wasn't the point. Inside, where it matters, he'd been in stitches. All that resource. All those guys on obs. All the suits back in Pompey waiting for word of some kind of result. And all they get is a bagful of books plus a load of balled-up newsprint to bulk it out.

He returned to the screen. The detectives had stepped back, allowing him to get out of the car. Then Bazza had tightened the zoom on the portly figure of D/S Dave Michaels. Winter had always had a soft spot for Michaels. He was a player, he had a sense of humour. He liked to get in amongst the bad guys and mess with their heads, and when the going got tough he wasn't averse to a pint or two to soften the disappointment. Just now, thought Winter, there wouldn't have been enough Stella in the world to make up for the newsprint that littered the back of the Lexus. Instead of money, a second chance to read about Pompey's day in the Wembley sun. Instead of a sure-fire promotion, the near-certain prospect of a major role in the inquest that was bound to follow.

On the camcorder's tiny screen Michaels was talking on a hand-held radio. He walked away from the car, his spare hand chopping at the air, his whole body stiff with irritation, and Winter tried to imagine the conversation. He'd be talking, in all probability, with the SIO. It might be Faraday, it might be the woman Parsons. Given the Level Three target – Bazza – it might even be Willard. By now, wherever these clowns were, the penny would have dropped. Bazza had been pulling their pissers again. And the hunt would be on for someone to take the drop. Michaels, as far as Winter could work out, was blameless. Not his fault the intel was shit. Not his fault he'd just wasted the best part of a Thursday evening outside some gutty pub. Not his fault that Winter, the arch-deviant, had ended up scot-free, extending a hand, wishing one and all good evening and good luck.

He watched himself now, reliving the moment he went round every one of them, a pat on the arm, a wink, a cheery goodnight, before he climbed back into the Lexus and purred smoothly away. Bazza, bless him, had recorded it all, every last frame, phoning him within seconds to announce a nearby rendezvous. A hotel called The Sandbanks, mush. Restaurant with a view to die for. Park the motor and bill the rest of the evening to your grateful boss.

Now, watching the waiter pop the top of the first bottle, Winter felt an anticipatory rush of the purest pleasure. Less than an hour ago he'd been eyeballing a return to Pompey in the back of one of the surveillance cars. After that would come the humiliation of the booking-in procedure at the Bridewell, the call to Mackenzie's brief, the first of two or three interviews, and the indignity of spending the night in a holding cell. Quite how Willard and Co. would frame the charges was frankly guesswork but Winter knew that they'd be burning the midnight oil in a bid to bind him hand and foot. Revenge, to people like Willard, was very definitely a dish served cold.

'Cheers, mush.' Bazza had raised his glass.

Winter answered the toast with one of his own.

'To crime,' he said. 'And capitalism.'

He'd already checked with Bazza about Guy. The kid, Baz had assured him, was alive and well. In a couple of hours he'd be back in Craneswater, reunited with Stu and with Ez. Drama over. Problem sorted.

Winter still didn't get it. The least Bazza owed him was an explanation.

'Easy, mush. There was something dodgy about the kidnap from the start. Stu spent a fortune on that new security system of his. So how come it never worked?'

The same thought had troubled Winter. He'd put it to Stu.

'Stu told me it had been on the blink last weekend.'

'Yeah, he told me that too.'

'And?'

'It's bollocks. I checked with a mate who's got the same system at his garage. He sells top-of-the-range German motors. He says the system's good as gold. Never lets you down.'

'So where does that leave Stu?'

'Away with the fairies, mush. I don't blame him. I don't even hold it against him. If we're talking blame here, we should be looking at my bloody daughter. She's a disgrace, that woman, and one day I'm going to tell her so.'

'Blame him for what, Baz?'

'For Guy. For everything that's happened.'

'*Stu* took him? Lifted his own son?'

'No, mush. Stu cooked the whole scheme up. Turns out he's got a mate in London. This guy's an actor. He's even been in a couple of Bond movies, at least that's what Stu says. For quite a lot of money, Stu had a proposition for him. The geezer said yes.'

The way it worked was simple. On the Monday, around eleven o'clock at night, Stu met his friend in London. They drove in convoy down to Alton, then took a route through the country lanes that Stu had already checked for CCTV. Half a mile from the house, late by now, they pulled in. Stu's mate put on the balaclava and the army top while Stu explained the layout of the house. Guy had a room at the end of the top corridor. You couldn't miss the Pompey transfer on his door.

'Had this bloke ever met Guy?'

'Never. He offered me to give the kid a tour of Shepperton Studios last year but it never worked out. Shame really. Sound stages. Special effects. The lot. Guy would have loved it.'

'Go on.'

'Monday night? Easy, mush. Stu gives him the remote, tells him to cut the phone lines, nick the girl's mobe and get the kid into something warm before sticking a blindfold on him When he gets out of the house all he has to do is follow Stu the way they came, avoiding all the cameras, then fuck off back to London. He's got a pad near Woking, converted place on top of a kebab bar.'

'And the remote?'

'He's given it back to Stu.'

'What about Guy?'

'The kid stays clueless throughout. Stu's mate keeps him in a locked room, never lets him see his face, never talks. He gets lots to eat though, and Stu's bought him a brand-new TV set-up to keep the nipper sweet.'

'And Stu's in constant touch with this bloke? Is that what you're telling me?'

'Yeah. Stu's got umpteen fucking mobes. A couple of them he declared to the Filth. One of the others he used to talk to this mate of his. Apparently the boy had the time of his life. Wall-to-wall DVDs, video games, the lot. Little fella can't wait to get kidnapped again.'

Bazza barked with laughter and drained his glass. The bottle was emptying fast. Winter still didn't get it.

'But why, Baz? Why go to all that trouble? Why hazard the kid? Why expose yourself like that to the Bill?'

'Because he's lost it, mush.' Mackenzie tapped his head. 'Because he's stopped thinking straight. I don't know what Ez does to her men but it certainly works a treat. Stu would do anything to get her back and he thought a million quid of his own money might just do the trick. That's how much he thought the relationship was worth. He wanted to prove it, mush. He wanted to show her.'

'But it wasn't a million quid. It was whatever he was paying his mate for his trouble.'

'You're right. But she wouldn't know that. Not if he pulled it off properly.'

'So what went wrong?'

'I sussed him. I sussed what he was up to, not every last detail but enough to put me on track. The rest was a stroll in the park. The guy was a wreck. He couldn't handle what he'd just done. You pour booze down him, you wait half an hour, you top him up again, then all you need is a locked door and a bit of sympathy. Stu's a fucking infant. He couldn't wait to tell me everything.'

Winter nodded. He took a mouthful of Krug. Then another thought occurred to him.

'So where's the million quid?' he said. 'The money we took out of the bank?'

'Ah ...' Bazza was laughing again '... that's the best bit.'

Faraday checked his watch. Nearly midnight. They were still in Parsons' office, still poking the ashes of Operation *Causeway*, still trying to figure out just how events could have taken such a catastrophic turn.

Willard, as angry as Faraday had ever seen him, had just finished a longish phone conversation with Dave Michaels. The Surveillance D/S had told him that he'd kept a close eye on Winter from the moment he'd walked out of the pub, and in his opinion there was no way that Winter had known the real contents of the bag. He'd worked with the man on dozens of operations, he knew his MO, he could read his body language, and he'd swear an oath that Winter had been convinced that the game was up.

Willard had dismissed this. As far as he was concerned, Winter was a born actor, as devious and bent as anyone he'd ever met. Between them, he and Mackenzie had baited a trap, laid a trail and waited for *Causeway* to tie itself in knots. The only question worth discussing was why it had been so easy. Did Winter have the ear of someone on the squad? Had some of that money already changed hands?

This, Faraday knew, was lunacy. Willard had been taking Mackenzie personally for far too long. Tonight's developments had ripped the dressing from the old sore and by scratching at it like this he'd simply deepen the wound. At every turn in every investigation there were decisions to be made. Some worked, some didn't. Tonight, all too obviously, had been a disaster, but it was their job, round this table, to start afresh.

Willard wasn't in the mood.

'Disaster's a kindness. We're looking at total humiliation.'

'Then the man's won, sir. That's what he wants. That's the kind of language he's after. Why make it easy for him?'

'Because we have to be realistic, Joe. We have to look the truth in the face and admit it. The man's taken us for idiots. And we've let him do exactly that.'

'What about Garfield? What about the Met investigation? This thing still has legs, sir. All we have to do is keep up. He'll make a mistake, I know he will, and then we'll have him.'

'You think so?'

For once Willard seemed beaten, a shell of a man. Whatever he did, however hard he tried to understand this latest twist, wherever he sought to lay the blame, the fingers still pointed at him. He'd trusted appearances, he'd made the wrong inference, he'd scampered all the way to Poole like some trusting puppy, and the consequences still didn't bear contemplation.

He sat back in the chair at the head of the table rubbing his big face. Faraday, he grunted, was right. They'd get a decent night's sleep, they'd reconvene in the morning, and they'd look for a new path to Mackenzie's door.

Faraday nodded in agreement, hearing the trill of his mobe. Midnight was late to be making calls.

It was Helen Christian. She sounded excited. She said that something wonderful had happened.

'Like what?' Faraday was aware of Willard watching him.

'Guy,' she said. 'The little boy. He's back.'

*

At the Bargemaster's House, Faraday finally settled at his PC. He fired up Outlook Express and clicked on Gabrielle's last message. Normally he'd reply in French but he was dog-tired, *tout à fait crevé,* totally knackered, and trusted himself only in English. Gabrielle, a couple of days back, had assured him that she'd been completely sober when she'd written of her yearning to come back to him. Now he half-closed his eyes, wondering how best to give her the answer she deserved.

He toyed with several ideas, all of them too complex or too cheesy. Then, knowing that the simplest things normally worked best, he bent to the keyboard. *Remember the guillemot chicks?* he wrote. *You won't believe this but one just flew back. Still room in the nest. A bientôt. J.*

Chapter twenty-seven

Winter was back in Portsmouth next morning. His first call from the apartment in Gunwharf found Marie doing Guy's laundry.

'So what actually happened?' Winter was still foggy about the details.

'There was a ring at the front door bell last night. According to Stu, it was late, gone eleven. The next thing he knew Guy was standing there on the doorstep. Stu said it was weird because it seemed so normal. It was like he'd never gone. Stu couldn't believe it. He ended up in tears.'

'What did Guy say?'

'He just said this woman had driven him down from London and dropped him off.'

'Did he know her?'

'Not at all. He said she was really nice. Talked to him about crocodiles most of the time.'

'*Crocodiles?*'

'Yeah. She'd spent some time in Australia, up in Queensland, some farm in the outback.'

'And he's OK? Guy?'

'He's fine, just fine. His sisters can't get over it. They can't work out where he's been. Neither can Guy for that matter.'

Winter nodded but said nothing. Last night he'd had his doubts about Bazza's breezy version of events. Now he sensed it was probably true. The kidnap had been a fiction, a heavy broadside in Stu's war for his wife's heart. The last person he'd put at risk was his own son.

Marie was asking about Bazza. Where was he?

'He's gone to London,' Winter told her. 'He's given me a whack of money and told me to take you lot to Thorpe Park.'

'*All* of us?'

'All of you.'

'But the police want to talk to Guy. Before he forgets it all.'

'I bet they do. That's exactly what Baz said. Eleven o'clock, my love. Baz is going to meet us up there. Burger King. Late lunch.'

The news got to DCI Parsons an hour or so later. She looked up from a budget report to find Helen Christian at her office door. The FLO had tried unsuccessfully to arrange a time to interview Guy Norcliffe.

'They're all off out, boss. I gather it's a bit of a bonding session.'

'Tell them it's important. Tell them I have to insist.'

'I can't. They've gone.'

'They have mobiles?'

'They're on divert.'

Parsons stared at her. When she slept badly she had trouble controlling her temper.

'Do you mind trying again? Or is that too much to ask?'

Christian nodded, said nothing, closed the door. Minutes later, Parsons' phone rang. It was Christian again.

'Still on divert, boss. I'm afraid we've lost them for today.'

Thorpe Park was the adrenalin junkie's dream day out, dozens of gut-twisting rides on a huge site off the M25. At Winter's suggestion, they took two cars. Marie drove Esme and the two girls whilst Stu and Guy got into Winter's Lexus. By now, Winter had taken Stu aside. He knew what had happened to Guy because Bazza had told him. What mattered now was to find out how Guy might handle the police interview, which would, in the end, happen.

Guy was delighted to be offered the front passenger seat. Never before in his young life had his dad been relegated to the back. Winter eased through the light mid-morning traffic, then hit the motorway north.

'How's it been then?' He glanced down at his young companion, wondering quite what he must have made of the last few days.

'OK.' He wouldn't look at Winter. 'Scary sometimes.'

'Scary how?'

'Scary because I didn't know what was going on.'

He described the man who'd woken him up in his bedroom at home. The woolly thing he wore on his face. The fact that he hadn't got any shoes. How frightened Evzenie was.

'Did he hurt you at all?'

'No.'

'Did he talk to you? Tell you to do things?'

'No. Only with his hands.'

'And you say he made you wear a blindfold?'

'Yeah. That was really scary. Especially when he carried me downstairs.'

'How long was the blindfold on for?'

'Until we got to the place I stayed at.'

'And where was that?'

'I don't know. It was upstairs, definitely, because he carried me again. I could hear him opening doors. There was a funny smell like in a chip shop. Then he took the blindfold off.'

'And what did you see?'

Guy described the room where he'd spent the next three days. There was no window, he said, just a bed and a thing with drawers in it and a bucket he had to use when he wanted to go to the toilet.

'Just that?'

'No. There was a TV too. It looked brand new. Really cool. And a DVD player. And a Nintendo console.'

'And did the man stay with you? Was he there all the time?'

'Yes. But I never saw his face. He always had the woolly thing. He was terrible at games though. We played Super Mario. I always beat him.'

'Did you ask him what was happening? What you were doing there?'

'Yes.'

'What did he say?'

'Nothing. He never talked. Even when he brought me food he never said anything.'

'What sort of food?'

'All the stuff I really like. Pasta done the way mum does it. Those little sausages. Fish fingers. Really thick chips. It was like he knew exactly … you know … what I like.'

Winter caught Stu's eye in the rear-view mirror. He was smiling. Winter returned to Guy.

'So you never knew when this was going to end. Is that right?'

'No. The man wrote notes to me sometimes. He had a little blackboard and some chalk.'

'What did he say?'

'He said not to worry, I'd be home soon. And he said he was sorry about being so terrible at Super Mario. He wasn't unkind or horrible, nothing like that. Whatever I wanted he tried to get me.'

'Like what?'

'Like this amazing game my friend's got. It's called Commando. I told him what it was like, what it looked like on the outside, and he went out and bought it.'

'Did he lock the door?'

'Always. I didn't like that.'

'Was there anyone else in this place?'

'I don't think so. He had to do everything, even the bucket.'

'You sound as if you almost liked him.'

'I did after a bit. It must have been horrible in that woolly thing.'

Winter laughed. Bazza was right about young Guy. Guts and innocence were a lovely mix.

'So you couldn't recognise this man?'

'No.'

'And you've no idea where he took you? Where you've been?'

'No. Like I say there weren't any windows.'

'Could you hear traffic?'

'Not really. Police sirens sometimes.'

'Did you think you were being rescued?'

'I did the first time.'

'And what about yesterday? Last night? When the woman picked you up?'

Guy explained that he'd had to wear the blindfold again. The man had written a message on the blackboard: *You're going home.*

'Did you believe him?'

'I wanted to, yes.'

'But did you *believe* him?'

'Yes. I don't think he was a liar.'

The man had carried him, blindfolded again, downstairs. He'd been put in the back of a car and then the car drove away.

'And you were still blindfolded?'

'Yes. The woman told me not to take it off. She was nice too. I asked her if I was really going home and she said yes. I liked her.'

'How long was the journey?'

'Quite long.'

'How long?'

'I don't know.'

When the car finally stopped, he said, the woman got out and opened the back passenger door to let him out.

'What did she say?'

'She told me to count to sixty and then take the blindfold off. She said she could see a big house with a wall round it and an upstairs window with a Mr Smiley transfer on it. I knew I was home then because that's Lucy's bedroom.'

'And she drove away?'

'Yes.'

'And you counted to sixty?'

'Fifty. I was cold.'

'But the car had gone?'

'I don't know. I got the blindfold off and I saw the house. Then I just ran in. Lucky the gates weren't locked. So I rang the bell and there was Dad.' He half twisted in the seat and peered round at his father. Winter checked the mirror again. Tears were pouring down Stu's face. He reached blindly forward and squeezed his son's offered hand, then found a tissue from somewhere and blew his nose.

'You did well, son,' he muttered. 'You've been incredible.'

At Thorpe Park Stu and the kids didn't bother with lunch, but disappeared towards Amity Cove for a go on the Flying Fish. It wasn't at all what Guy had in mind, having heard about the legendary Stealth ride, but a promise from his dad that they'd tackle that later kept him quiet.

Winter walked Marie and Esme to the Burger King. Bazza

had already arrived and was busy on his mobile at a table in the corner. Winter paused beside the window. The Stealth ride towered above them. Zero to 80 mph in under two seconds sounded like a short cut to a cardiac arrest but the queues for the loading platform disappeared out of sight.

'Fancy it, mush? Or shall we stick to the Double Whopper?' Mackenzie had joined him.

Winter settled for the Double Whopper. Marie organised an order for all of them. Winter nodded at Esme, sitting alone at a table by the window, her face inscrutable behind her sunglasses.

'Does she know about Stu's little wheeze?'

'No, mush. And neither does Marie. As far as they're concerned, me and Stu ponied up the ransom. Like I said last night, Stu's sending her a message. This is what a proper dad does.'

'Kidnaps his own son?'

'Pays a fortune to get him back. I agree with you, mush. Stu's fucking lost it. But I can just about see what he's driving at, poor sad bastard.'

They joined Esme at the table. Mackenzie reached across and took her glasses off.

'What's that for?' She was furious.

'Because you and me ought to have a conversation.' He folded the glasses into his top pocket. 'Any chance you might start behaving like a human being again? Now that Stu's done the decent thing?'

'What does that mean?'

'You know what it means, love. It means that the music's stopped and we all go back to our own chairs. It means that your shagging days with the Filth are over. And with a bit of fucking luck it might mean that your son hasn't gone through all this for nothing.'

'You're telling me that's my fault too? Some headcase, some pervert kidnapping the child? That's down to me?'

Mackenzie smiled, refused to answer. Marie arrived with a tray of food. Bazza hadn't finished.

'Did I hear a yes?' He cupped his hand behind his ear. 'Can I assume our friend Madison is history?'

'He's gone back to his wife.'

'Poor bloody woman. Was that his decision or yours?'

'His, I imagine. I'm not his keeper.'

'But you'd had enough? Is that what you're saying?'

'I had plenty, thank you. And for the record I enjoyed every minute of it.'

'I bet you did. How come a decent bloke like me fathers an old slapper like you? How come you've got enough between your ears to get to university and not a grain of fucking decency when it comes to people who love you? How come you find it so fucking hard to say sorry?'

'We're talking *apologies*?' Esme got to her feet. 'Maybe you ought to start with Mum and with that nice Chandelle. I'm out of here.'

She turned on her heel and left the burger bar. Winter, looking at Marie's face, felt intensely sorry. When it came to families, he'd concluded, no amount of patience, no amount of glue, could hold the thing together. Having Guy back meant the world to Marie. Now this.

Mackenzie was eyeing his daughter's abandoned salad. He glanced at Winter.

'Half each, mush?'

It fell to Faraday to prepare what Parsons termed an 'interim report' on Operation *Causeway*. Helen Christian had gleaned enough from her phone conversation with Marie to be aware of the circumstances of the boy's return. A car had dropped him around eleven o'clock. He'd lingered a moment on the pavement before removing his blindfold. No, he hadn't seen the driver. And no, he hadn't a clue what kind of car it was.

Parsons had dispatched detectives for house-to-house checks the length of Sandown Road but no one had seen a car arrive at that time of night. Neither would there be any CCTV footage, largely because there were no cameras in the area. Short of tracing every car entering and leaving the city there was no way of building a case prior to interviewing the child. In this sense, *Causeway*'s sole remaining asset was Guy himself. Consciously or otherwise he must have picked up some clues about his captor. Assuming, of course, that the kidnap was authentic.

In his heart, Faraday was far from certain. Bypassing the alarm system without inside help was highly unlikely. Evading every CCTV camera for twenty miles argued equally for specialist knowledge of the area. Esme and Madison had shaken the family to bits. In that wreckage lay the clue to what had really happened to young Guy.

Faraday sat at his desk, brooding about the money. The bank had confirmed the withdrawal of £1 million in cash. Willard, in his eagerness to nail Mackenzie, had taken the bait and assumed – quite wrongly – that the ransom had gone with Winter to Poole. The fact that it hadn't, the fact that the Head of CID had – in his own phrase – been humiliated, still begged a key question: where was the million quid?

Mackenzie, of course, would claim that he'd paid the kidnapper. Guy, in this sense, was his receipt for all that money. It would be *Causeway*'s job to press him for more details – where? when? how? – but Faraday knew that none of these questions would ever be answered. Mackenzie would simply go No Comment, claiming that he had every right to keep the information to himself. He'd secured the child's release. The boy was back home, safe and sound. After the Filth had fucked up – no clues, no leads, no nothing – Grandad had stepped in, spent a bit of money and got the family a result. Framed that way, badged with Mackenzie's trademark grin, *Causeway* was looking at a second humiliation.

Faraday began to scribble himself a note or two prior to drafting the report. When his phone began to ring he was slow to answer it.

'Joe?' It was Willard.

'Sir?'

'Where's DCI Parsons?'

'I've no idea.'

There was a silence on the line. Then Willard was back. He'd just had a conversation with one of the Met guys dealing with Garfield.

'And?'

'He's disappeared. He's supposed to report daily to the local nick. His car's gone. His wife. The lot. Brilliant, eh? That's all we fucking need.'

At Mackenzie's insistence, Winter joined him for a ride on Stealth. Mid-afternoon, the queues had shortened, and as they shuffled forward through a light drizzle Winter tried to avoid the sight of the red train powering down the track towards the dizzying climb ahead. The ride guaranteed blistering acceleration to 80 mph and the track was configured to throw you upside down at the very top of the loop – two good reasons, Winter thought, to part company with his Double Whopper.

'You up for this, mush?' Mackenzie couldn't take his eyes off the girls at the very front of the train.

'Can't wait, Baz.'

'Ever go down Billy Mannings as a kid?'

'Never.'

'I used to think the Wild Mouse was a blast. Just look at this lot. Fuck me ...'

Billy Mannings was the Pompey funfair beside Clarence Pier. The red train rolled off the top of the loop and came thundering down towards them. One of the girls in the front had her eyes shut. The other one was screaming fit to bust. Mackenzie gave them a wave as they flashed by then watched the train pirouette at the other end of the ride.

Winter knew he had to concentrate hard on something else.

'This million quid, Baz ...'

'Sorted, mush.'

'So what have you done with it?'

'Done with it?'

The red train had finally come to a halt beside the concrete jetty that served as a station. Mackenzie was watching the girls help each other out. One of them could barely walk. Winter preferred not to look.

'The money, Baz.'

'I invested it, mush.'

'In what?'

'I'm calling it insurance. Either way it's a sweet deal.'

The queue shuffled forward, and as they mounted the steps to the platform Winter had a sudden feeling of total helplessness. Why was he doing this? How come he'd said yes? What guaranteed that his train wouldn't be the first to rocket straight off the top of the loop and end up in the middle of the nearby M25?

'This one, mush. It's got our name on it.' Mackenzie was nudging him into the twin seats at the very back of the train.

Winter resigned himself to an ugly death. An absurdly young

girl was playing the role of undertaker. She leaned over, told him to make himself comfortable, warned him not to try and stand up. The steel restraints folded down, penning them in.

'Insurance?' Winter muttered.

'Yeah. I did a bit of extra business with Garfield I probably never mentioned.'

'Like what?'

'Like buying a stake in a couple of deals he'd set up.'

'Deals, Baz?' Winter was staring up at a line of signal indicators. Mercifully they were still red.

'Yeah. Instead of money he took a couple of properties off me. Timeshares down near Marbella.'

'You gave him the deeds?'

'I did, Paulie. I did.' Winter felt a squeeze on his arm. This was getting worse. Much worse.

'Not toot though, Baz. Tell me you didn't go shares on some fucking narco-deal.'

'Afraid so, mush.' Mackenzie shot him a look. He was grinning fit to bust. 'A hundred and fifty per cent over less than a year? Who'd say no to a deal like that?'

Winter sat back and closed his eyes. Was it too late to get out? Should he scream, just like everyone else was screaming? Should he wave his arms to attract attention, just like the rest of these monkeys? Or should he find some way to dematerialise? To simply vanish off the face of the earth? Before gravity or the Serious and Organised Crime boys brought his long and distinguished career to an end?

The pressure on his arm had gone. Instead, Mackenzie was patting his thigh, giving him encouragement, telling him to be brave. An experience like this, he was saying, was the ride of a lifetime. Everything thereafter would be just a little bit different.

Winter didn't doubt it. He shut his eyes, trying hard not to contemplate the consequences of Bazza's latest investment. If he survived this, he told himself, then things would indeed be a little bit different.

The screams suddenly got louder. Then he felt a punch in his back, and the rumble of wheels beneath his arse, and a second later he seemed to be lying flat on his back with a hole where his stomach had once been. He couldn't breathe properly. He was too confused, too bewildered, to be frightened. He was going up and up. The screaming hadn't stopped. At speed, the drizzle had become cold needles driving into his face. As the train lurched to the right he opened his eyes. Big mistake. Bits of Surrey yawned beneath him. The speed was falling off. Then the train righted itself and for a single terrifying moment, as they plunged vertically down, he had the jumper's view of the onrushing earth. This is what suicide must feel like, he told himself. This is what happens when you listen too hard to the likes of Bazza Mackenzie. The track began to flatten. The train slowed again. Another couple of twirls, and it was all over. The train juddered to a halt and Winter opened his eyes to find Mackenzie already on the platform, his hand outstretched.

'Fancy another go, mush? Or shall we fuck off home?'

Winter rode south in the Bentley. Stu would be bringing his Lexus back once the kids had had enough of Thorpe Park. Of Esme there was no sign.

'So Garfield's done a runner. Is that what you're telling me?'

'Yeah. New passport. Nice place to go to out in Morocco. No extradition treaty. Marie says he looked happy as Larry. He had a French motor waiting for him in Dieppe and a couple of days would put him in southern Spain. From there he takes the ferry to Tangiers. A million quid off me and fuck knows how much of his own and the last thing he's worrying about is moolah. He buys himself a decent tan and a bit of peace and quiet. Bingo. Sorted.'

'And you?'

'You mean us, mush?'

'Yeah. What do we get?'

'For a million quid? You want the list? Number one, I've got the Spanish deeds back. He never got round to engrossing them so that means him and me never did business. Number two, he's given me an affidavit resigning any interest in the hotel.'

'Whose idea was that?'

'Ez's. She drew it up. She's a pain most of the time but there's still a brain in there somewhere, thank fuck.'

'She talked to Garfield?'

'His solicitor. I wanted to bung him too, just to say sorry, no hard feelings, but she thought it was a bad idea.'

'He's not going to Morocco?'

'No.'

'Then she's right. The guy's a loose cannon.'

'I don't think so, mush.'

'Why not?'

'Turns out he's got a stack of properties in Montenegro. It also turns out he's been knobbing Garfield's missus. So there's another guy who fancies a new life in the sunshine. Esme doesn't think he'll last the course, though. Blokes his age always come back.'

Winter nodded. Surviving three minutes of Stealth had revived his interest in life. Bazza was right. Everything felt just a little bit different.

'So you think you've got it weighed off?'

'*We*, mush. *We*'ve got it weighed off. I know it's late in the day but Marie's right, all the best movies keep you guessing to the very end.'

'And you think this is over?'

'I think we're into something different.'

'Like what?'

'Like Tide Turn for starters. Have you talked to Mo at all? That boy's a fucking revelation. How the fuck did you score someone like him?'

Winter could only smile. 'Boy' was an interesting description. Mo Sturrock had to be mid-forties.

'So what's happened?'

Mackenzie put his foot down, leaving a BMW 5-series for dead. For a second or two Winter was back on the Stealth ride. Then the Bentley slowed to eighty.

'He's come up with this idea, mush, and from where I'm sitting it's a cracker. He's calling it the Offshore Challenge. It's all about rowing, offshore rowing, proper rowing, not the fancy stuff they do on the Thames for the Boat Race. These are real boats. He's showed me pictures, photos. Turns out he does a bit of it himself, over on the island.'

Sturrock, he said, had been a member of the Ryde Rowing Club for more years than he could remember. These were guys who rowed two, three times a week, fit as fuck, trained like bastards, went in for regattas, won every cup ever invented. Mo had got himself a little bit of that, knew what it could do for you.

'We're talking serious fitness, mush. Self-respect is the word he uses. He says it turns your life around, and he should know.'

'How come?'

'He told Marie he had a few problems. When he was much younger.'

'Like what kind of problems?'

'He's not saying or at least she's not telling me. Either way it was a long time ago. Whatever happened, it was the rowing that got him out of it. First in Pompey, then over there on the island. Loads of kids do it in Ryde and it suits them a treat, but these tend to be nice kids, motivated kids, middle-class kids. What Mo wants to do, what he's *always* wanted to do, is set something up for other kinds of kids, scrotey kids, the sort who end up in Tide Trust.'

Winter was trying to imagine the likes of Billy Lenahan in a rowing boat on the Solent. Oddly enough, he could dimly sense the logic. Better to send the boy to sea than have him hot-wiring yet more Escorts.

'So what kind of boats are these?'

'Four blokes rowing, one little guy at the back doing the steering. Mo's got some contacts in the Navy. If we bung some money in for – say – three of these boats he thinks he can talk the Navy guys into giving us some kind of boathouse and maybe a PTI to do the start-off drills, just to get the little tossers fit. Then it's down to regular sessions. He's talking a nine-month programme. We take fifteen of them. That's three crews. He's worked it all out. Talk to him. Like I say, it's brilliant.'

Winter was trying to remember a phrase Sturrock had used when they'd first met in the pub in Albert Road. He'd been going on about just how big a challenge these kids could be. Nine months, he'd said. That was how long it took to win their confidence, to build a little trust, to start to turn their lives around. And nine months on any kind of programme could cost the earth.

'We've got the money, Baz?'

'Of course we've got the money. Three boats? Second hand? How much is that going to cost?'

'I've no idea.'

'He's saying ten grand a boat. The Navy kicks everything else in. We raise a bit of extra sponsorship, blag some more dosh off Social Services, raid the Lord Mayor's fund, talk to the Lottery, probably end up making a profit. But that's not the point, mush.'

'It's not?'

'No way. This is a beautiful idea. Tide Turn Trust, right? The Offshore Challenge, right? Flagship City, right? Turning scrote Pompey nippers into world-beaters, right? Can't go wrong, mush. I've told Mo I want a big summer launch. I want it somewhere special, maybe aboard *Victory*, somewhere like that. I want the press there, celebs, telly, the works. I want us knocking on everyone's door with the Offshore Challenge. And you know who's going to make that happen? You and Mo. Mo sorts the kids out. Mo sources the boats. Mo talks to the Navy. You do the rest. Like I say, mush. Can't go wrong.' He glanced across. 'Deal?'

Winter didn't say a word. A couple of years ago, when he'd first joined up, Mackenzie had thrown him a similar challenge. Then it had been jet skis. Now it was offshore rowing. On both occasions the emphasis was on innovation and scale. Thinking outside the box. Thinking big. Showing what a bunch of scrotey adolescents could really do with their sad little lives. Mackenzie loved taking the world by surprise. As Winter, to his cost, knew only too well.

'Great, Baz.' He tried not to sound glum. 'So when do you want to launch?'

'As soon as, mush. July at the latest.'

Chapter twenty-eight

Faraday officially severed his connection with Operation *Causeway* in a meeting with DCI Parsons. She offered a muted round of applause for the way he'd coped with the ongoing frustrations and hinted that he had her admiration for anticipating the shambles of the stake-out in the Poole pub. However, she said that Willard was less than pleased with the squad's performance on both *Causeway* and *Melody* and without actually saying so she left him in no doubt that the key investigative link between them was Faraday himself. He seemed to have lost his appetite for driving complex investigations forward. There was also, more troublingly, evidence of a crisis of *belief*.

Parsons seldom strayed into territory like this. Her job, and Faraday's, was to gather lawyer-proof evidence as effectively as they possibly could. They measured their success in the number of convictions they secured. Any issues that might lurk on the other side of that mission statement, issues about the real nature or meaning of justice, were of no professional relevance whatsoever. If people did wrong, if they broke the law, they got detected, tried, found guilty and punished. End of story.

Faraday, to his slight surprise, had no quarrel with any of this. Parsons, for once, had tabled her criticisms in a regretful tone of voice that could only anticipate a more permanent farewell, and there was a part of him that welcomed the prospect of a quieter life and an easier conscience. Putting Jeanette Morrissey away had been the hollowest of victories, and getting dicked around by the likes of Mackenzie had soured him still further. If you had the money and the nerve, you'd probably make it. If you'd lost your son to a psychopath and took your chance to get even, you were likely to end up inside.

All the same, he was curious as to where *Causeway* might

be heading next. Would Parsons, as SIO, be pursuing enquiries into who, exactly, the kidnapper might have been? Would the young lad be subjected to a rigorous interview? Would the banks be on alert for the moment the marked fifty-pound notes floated to the surface? Might those sightings flag a path back to Mackenzie's door?

'That's speculation, Joe, as you well know. Of course we don't give up. We never give up. Which is why I want you to focus now on *Sangster*.'

Sangster was the cold case file Faraday had been reading before the phone rang with the news of the kidnap. A stranger rape dating back to 1984 plainly offered him a safe berth. Putting a name to Tessa Fogle's mystery assailant might offer him something more clear-cut in the way of crime and punishment.

Parsons, it seems, was reading his mind.

'Don't be too hasty, Joe. The file tells me this man could have killed her. Even you will admit that's not polite.'

At 13 Sandown Road, in the aftermath of Guy's return, it was Marie who took control of events. When Esme finally turned up, stepping out of a taxi from the station, mother and daughter had a heart-to-heart. Stu and the kids were banished upstairs while Marie and Esme sat at the kitchen table and reviewed the shape of the coming months.

To Marie's relief, Esme appeared to have turned an important corner. The midlife storm that had erupted in the shape of Perry Madison had blown itself out. In her phrase, she'd enjoyed the best of him and moved on. She had no regrets about what she'd done and no plans to ever get in touch again. Marie, who found this dismissal of the last six months rather chilling, wisely declined to comment. The only thing that interested her was the resumption of family life.

Esme agreed. She'd talked to Stu and they'd decided on a new start. They'd be moving back to the Meon Valley that same afternoon. Stu had already told the kids, who to Marie's quiet delight had been less than enthusiastic. They rather liked life in Craneswater with Grandma and Grandad, and Guy in particular was in no hurry to return to memories of the man in the black balaclava.

With this in mind Esme was already hatching plans for the future. In conversation with Stu they'd agreed that Madison had been the symptom rather than the cause of the recent upsets. Their life as a family was out of balance. They needed to see more of each other. Stu spending five nights a week in London might fill the Norcliffe coffers but what use was that if they ended up spending the money as virtual strangers?

Marie, with a sinking heart, anticipated exactly where this conversation was leading. Esme, like her father, never gave up. Her passion for Perry Madison might have cooled but she was still in love with the Baiona hotel.

'It's still for sale, Mum. We could still buy it.'

'How?'

'All kinds of ways. Stu thinks the financial markets are heading for trouble. If we're going to do something radical then now might be the time to sell the business while there's a still a business to sell. He says he can get a bundle for it, serious money.'

'Enough for the hotel?'

'Easily.'

'What about the house?'

'We'd rent it out. Two grand a month, no problem.'

'You're sure about that?'

'I made some enquiries a couple of days ago. We could all live on that money in Spain. Easily.'

Marie said nothing. Esme had clearly worked this whole thing out, done the research, juggled the figures. The conversation with Stu had probably been an afterthought. Now, as ever, she wanted her mother's approval. Clever girl. Well done. Go for it.

'What if it doesn't work?'

'It will, Mum. And think of the kids. They'll learn the language, find new friends. It'll be brilliant.'

'But you've never run a hotel in your life.'

'Neither had Dad. And look what he's made of the Trafalgar.'

'Have you mentioned any of this to him?'

'Not yet. But he'll think it's a great idea, I know he will.'

Esme knew her mother was unconvinced. She'd miss the contact with the kids, the picnics on the beach, the mad rounds of pitch and putt on the course at the bottom of the road. She'd recently found a tennis coach too, for young Guy. Champions always started young.

'There is another option, Mum, something I haven't mentioned.'

'Like what?'

'Like we sell up completely, burn our bridges, take the money and run.' Esme tried to soften the threat with a smile. 'And you wouldn't like that, would you?'

Winter, uncertain about the viability of the Offshore Challenge, knew he was due a conversation with Mo Sturrock. A couple of years working for Bazza Mackenzie had wised him up. The man overdosed on enthusiasm. A gleam in the eye, within seconds, could become a press conference, a media launch, gilt-edged invitations to the city's movers and shakers. Bazza had been a conjuror for most of his life. What rarely bothered him was the small print.

Sturrock had found himself a home in a disused storeroom in the Trafalgar's basement. Until earlier in the week it had been littered with broken chairs, scraps of carpet, miscellaneous shelving, unwanted pictures, cleaning materials and umpteen cartons of glasses that Bazza had lifted from a liquidation sale in Chichester. Marie had helped Sturrock tidy up the mess, bin the rubbish and create a space large enough for a desk and a couple of chairs. The hotel electrician had run in a landline from the exchange in reception and Marie had found a neat little lamp in Habitat that shed a soft light on Sturrock's growing pile of correspondence.

Winter made himself comfortable. Sturrock was deep in a copy of the *Guardian*. The basement still stank of the bleach Marie had used on the 60s lino. She'd already warned Winter that extricating Mo from his previous employer might not be as simple as everyone imagined.

'You've told them about us? About Tide Turn?'

'Who?'

'Your bosses.'

Sturrock nodded. Banned from any direct contact with the office, he'd been obliged to conduct a conversation through a woman in Human Resources. After six months of gardening leave there was still no date for the formal disciplinary hearing. This meant that his bosses were having big problems framing charges against him. His impromptu speech at the conference had undoubtedly been gross misconduct but in an ideal world they'd want to pin lots more on him.

'Like what?'

'Like abuse of my email account. Like making private phone calls. Like poking round for porn on the Internet. Like sexual harassment ... bullying ... racism ... whatever they could find. I ended up managing loads of people. They assume you're bound to make the odd enemy.'

'And you didn't?'

'Apparently not. It must be very frustrating for them. Fingers crossed, I think I may have become a bit of an embarrassment.'

'So how does that work?'

Sturrock had abandoned the paper. These last couple of days, he explained, he'd been trying to negotiate a compromise agreement. He'd write his own reference and agree it with his bosses. He'd sign up to a non-disclosure clause. And in the final settlement he'd acknowledge bringing the organisation into disrepute. In return, he'd get three months' severance money and retain his registration with the General Social Care Council.

'Without that, I'm stuffed. And so is Tide Turn.'

Winter nodded. Twenty years in the Job had taught him how complex these things could be. People didn't just walk out of the door. Not any more.

'You think they'll wear it?'

'Yeah, thanks to you lot. It's a perfect out for them and pretty good for me too. Marie's told you about my little project?'

They discussed the Offshore Challenge for a while. Winter said he loved the idea of making the little bastards sweat but was curious to know how Sturrock had come to rowing in the first place.

'It was way back ... when I was still a student, still pretty clueless, still living over here in Pompey. Stuff had happened, personal stuff, and I wasn't in a good place in my head. I used to run on the seafront a bit, which definitely helped, but then I saw one of these boats, these fours, cruising past. It was the middle of summer, quite late. The guys were rowing out of the harbour, out of the sunset. I remember stopping and just staring at them. They had it nailed, perfect rhythm, perfectly in time. They just made it look so easy and I remember thinking yeah, I'll have some of that.'

The following week he found the clubhouse and made some enquiries. Within a couple of days, after a brief introductory session on a rowing machine, he found himself afloat.

'It was hard, bloody hard, much more difficult than I'd imagined, but the instructor was a good bloke and the rest of the crew were pretty patient, and after a while you start getting the hang of it. One of the crew, the guy I rowed behind, had just come out of the Marines. That's when I had a rush of blood to the head.'

'You enlisted? In the *Marines*?'

'Yeah. The rowing was going really well. It was sorting me out. I'd fucked up my degree and I hadn't a clue what to do. I thought the Marines would be like rowing with a bit of rifle stuff thrown in.'

'And?'

'It wasn't. I was wrong. It was horrible. I couldn't hack it at all.'

'So you went back to the rowing?'

'Yeah. And I've stayed with it ever since.'

'And did it do the trick?' Winter touched his own head. 'Up here?'

'Definitely. And if it worked for me then there's no reason why it shouldn't work with the kids.'

'Headbanger, were you?'

'Worse.' He looked Winter in the eye. 'Much worse.'

Faraday spent the afternoon with the *Sangster* file. As far as he could judge, the paperwork was complete. From the statement of the attending officer, first on the scene, through the medical reports, the raft of house-to-house calls, the interviews with ex-boyfriends and the checks on local sex offenders, the modest squad of D/Cs appeared to have explored every line of enquiry. In a terse final note the SIO had concluded that Tessa Fogle had been the victim of an intruder she probably didn't know. Someone who may have seen her leaving the Student Union, weaving her way home, letting herself in. The back garden was accessible via an alley that lay to the rear of the terrace. The window had been wide open. Chance and alcohol had done the rest.

Faraday looked up, gazing out of the window. The SIO had been a D/I on the old Portsmouth South division, a pleasant enough career copper who raced pigeons in his spare time. He'd died back in the 90s after a brief and painful tussle with pancreatic cancer.

A phone call brought Jimmy Suttle to Faraday's office. Parsons had insisted that the young D/S be available as an intel resource for *Sangster*. The way she'd put it, Faraday felt he was on the receiving end of a retirement present.

Faraday summarised the stranger rape. Blood and semen samples had been preserved but to date they'd raised no names on the PNC database. The next obvious move was to commission a familial DNA search, thus multiplying the chances of a PNC hit. If Tessa's assailant still had no criminal record then perhaps his father, or a brother, or a son might.

'How do we stand for consent, boss?'

'She was last seen in 1999. That's a long time ago. She was living in Chalton then, up near Petersfield. A partner, kids, the whole deal. According to the file she seemed happy enough, but things might have changed.'

'Is the address still current?'

'I've no idea but it might be the place to start.'

'Did she have a job?'

'She was some kind of counsellor. The details aren't clear.'

Suttle scribbled a note and asked for the file. Faraday was looking at the calendar. To the best of his knowledge, submitting a sample for DNA familial testing carried serious cost implications. In return for a four-figure sum you got hundreds of names, all of them to be sorted and prioritised, but that kind of expense would only be sanctioned if a proper squad was ready to action the results. Yet another reason for checking first with Tessa Fogle.

'You'll let me know, Jimmy? When you get her contact details?'

Chapter twenty-nine

Two bits of excellent news on the same day. Marie found Mo Sturrock in the Trafalgar's basement gym. Sturrock had quickly got into the habit of kick-starting each morning with a session on the rowing machine. The 07.45 hovercraft would get him to the Southsea terminal by eight. A ten-minute stroll across the Common would take him straight to the hotel. By half eight he'd be on the machine, sweating towards the end of his first thousand metres.

Marie lingered in the shadows beside the door, understanding at once how years of practice could transform your technique. Mo had set the flywheel on nine, guaranteeing near-maximum resistance, and she watched as he slid forwards down the slide, took up the slack, and then thrust back with his legs, sucking in a lungful of air before finishing the stroke with a powerful tug from his arms and shoulders. The cycle then repeated itself, infinitely smooth, his body in constant motion, and she caught the little gasp of effort at the end of each stroke.

She picked her way towards him, watching his face in the floor-to-ceiling mirrors. Mo had his eyes shut and with each gasp came a tiny facial contortion. With anyone else, she thought, this might have signalled irritation or even boredom but in Mo's case it was undoubtedly genuine effort. Only yesterday, when they'd been discussing exercise, he'd told her that if it wasn't hurting it wasn't working. At the time she'd been in two minds about the phrase. It struck a false note, it sounded glib, but now – watching him – she knew exactly what he'd meant.

'How far do you go?'

Mo's eyes opened. His rate slowed.

'Five K.'

'Five thousand metres?'

'Yeah …' He was still fighting for breath.

'And you set yourself a time?'

'Four minutes per K. Twenty overall.'

'Is that good?'

'At my age? Bloody hard.'

By now he'd come to a complete halt. His singlet was blotched with sweat and his head hung down between his open thighs.

'I've ruined it, haven't I? I'm really sorry.'

'No problem.' Mo reached for a towel and mopped his face. 'You're the perfect excuse. You know what the Marines say? Pain? It's just an opinion.'

She laughed then told him the good news. His employers on the Isle of Wight had been on the phone first thing, wanting to check that the Tide Turn offer was genuine.

'I told them it was and I said we'd like you on board as soon as possible. They didn't seem to think that would be a problem.'

'Really?'

'Yes.' She'd always loved Mo's smile. 'And it gets better. I got an email from the guy you've been talking to on Whale Island. He says the formal go-ahead's beyond his pay grade but the boathouse you're after is definitely available.'

'Free?'

'He didn't say.'

Mo eased himself off the machine. Whale Island housed HMS *Excellent*, a naval shore establishment. From here there was direct access to the harbour, perfect if you wanted to put beginners in an offshore boat.

'Did he say anything else?'

'Yes. I gather you'd asked him about getting hold of a PTI. He says he's got just the right bloke in mind. Real animal. Can't wait to get stuck in.'

Mo grinned again.

'Perfect.' He was watching her face in the mirror. 'You know something? This just might work.'

Faraday was still at home when Suttle rang. These days, Faraday told himself, there was no pressing need to crawl to Kingston Crescent in the rush-hour traffic. Better to hang on for a late breakfast and a stroll round the nearby saltwater ponds. The dabchicks were still in residence amongst the reed beds at the water's edge and he had high hopes for an invisible but very male Cetti's warbler, singing its heart out from the cover of the scrub.

'Jimmy?'

'Me, boss. I've got details on Tessa Fogle. She's moved to the Isle of Wight.'

'Have you spoken to her?'

'Not yet. I thought I'd leave that to you. If you want me to go over today there might be a problem. I'm in court until twelve and in Basingstoke after that.'

Faraday wrote down the address details and hung up. *Dimpsy. Newchurch. IoW.* There was a number too. He studied it for a moment, wondered about the dabchicks, then reached for his mobile again. The number answered on the third ring. A woman's voice. She sounded, for some reason, amused.

'Yes?'

'Ms Fogle?'

'That's me.' The voice changed. More formal, more cautious. She must have been waiting for another call, Faraday thought. He introduced himself, asked whether she had time to talk on the phone, then briefly sketched in the circumstances. There was nothing but silence on the other end.

'Are you still there?'

'I am. Would it be possible to meet? This is all a bit sudden.'

'Of course. When can you manage?'

'Today?'

She gave him directions. When he got to the village he was to look for a pub called the Pointer Inn. A hundred yards beyond it, on the left, he'd find an old converted chapel.

'That's you?'

'That's us. Would lunchtime be OK for you? I have to be away by half two to pick up the kids.'

'Of course.' Faraday checked his watch. 'I'll be with you by one o'clock.'

Upstairs, he found a map of the island. To his delight, Newchurch was only a couple of miles from the RSPB site at Brading Marsh. The Isle of Wight could be disappointing from the species point of view but short-eared owls wintered in the marshes and with luck one or two might still be around. Late spring also attracted pairs of breeding lapwings, and the reed beds beside the River Yar were another favourite haunt of the reclusive Cetti's warbler. He packed a rucksack with his walking boots, a light anorak and his precious Leica red spots. Back downstairs, he phoned Wightlink for a ferry booking while the kettle boiled. The flask of sugared coffee should last him all afternoon.

By now, the traffic was thinner. By five to eleven, with the Mondeo stowed on the car deck below, Faraday was leaning on the rail in the sunshine, watching a swirl of gulls fighting for scraps from the fishing boats in the Camber Docks. Peace, he thought.

Newchurch was a tiny village south of Ryde. The fact that the Pointer Inn had survived was a tribute to the locals and the passing trade. An elderly couple were sitting at a table outside, enjoying an early lunch. Faraday pulled into the car park and fumbled for his mobile. The woman was tearing off tiny shreds of bread roll and tossing them to a waiting blackbird.

'Ms Fogle? I'm afraid I'm earlier than expected.'

'No problem. Early's good. Where are you?'

'Virtually outside. The Pointer Inn?'

'Oh!' She sounded startled. 'I'll put the kettle on. The place is a tip, I'm afraid.'

Faraday was on her doorstep within minutes, eyeing the battered Land Rover parked on the verge outside the garden gate. He could hear footsteps inside, then came a grunt as someone tugged the door open. Tessa Fogle was in her mid-forties. She had a weathered, lived-in face lightly dusted with freckles. She wore a loose cotton top over a pair of worn jeans and her feet were bare on the flagstones inside the door. Two toe rings, both silver.

'Come in. Like I said, it's a mess.'

She was right. Faraday picked his way past a litter of toys and abandoned clothing. He remembered the file. Three kids, he thought, at the very least.

She took him through to the kitchen. More chaos. Faraday found a stool and propped himself beside the breakfast bar. The calendar on the corkboard was covered with crayoned crosses, most of them blue.

'My daughter, I'm afraid. They're kisses. She's very affectionate.'

'She has special days for kissing?'

'I'm afraid so. Saturdays and Sundays mainly ... as you can see.'

Tessa was right. There wasn't a single weekend that hadn't escaped a big waxy blue cross.

'How many kids have you got?'

'Three. And three's enough, believe me. We love them to death but forget real life.'

'They *are* real life.'

'You're right. Tea? Coffee?'

Faraday asked for tea. Wherever he looked, the bones of the old chapel poked through. The lower half of a stained-glass window, bisected by the floor above. An old timber pew, high-backed, deeply uncomfortable, piled high with newspapers and half-finished kids' drawings. The flagstones underfoot, polished by age and tiny dancing feet. The conversion was piecemeal, haphazard, a sketch at best, but somehow it worked. The place, even to a total stranger, felt like home.

'Why Dimpsy?' Faraday had noticed the name etched on a slate beside the front door.

'We used to go to the West Country a lot, years back. We had a camper van. Dimpsy's an old Devon word for twilight. We couldn't resist it.'

'Twilight?'

'Sunset. You get beautiful sunsets here. The back of the house faces west. Great for dimpsy. Even the kids say so.'

Faraday grinned. He liked the idea of living in a house called Twilight. Twilight, on a rising tide, was when the birds on the harbour flocked home to the roost. Twilight, in a couple of months' time, would see Gabrielle back at the Bargemaster's House. Smells of garlic and fresh ginger. An open bottle of something delicious on the kitchen table. *Dimpsy*. Nice.

Tessa was decanting hot water into a teapot. The only tea bags she could find were chamomile.

'Fine.' Faraday shrugged. 'Whatever.'

She left the pot to brew and turned back to him. She wanted to know why now was the time to reopen an inquiry on something that had happened so long ago. Faraday, sensing she'd had a bit of a think since he'd phoned her earlier from the Bargemaster's House, said at once that nothing had been decided.

'So I can say no?'

'Absolutely. That's why I'm here. Without your consent, your go-ahead, nothing happens.'

'But you'd like it to? You want to get to the bottom of this thing?'

'Of course.'

'Why?'

'Because it might happen again. To be frank we've no idea who did it but there are new DNA techniques that might give us a lead. This man, whoever he is, might be on the other side of the world. He might never touch another woman in his life. He might even be dead. But we know what he did to you all those years ago and that's something for which he should be caught and punished.'

She nodded. She agreed. Over the years she'd thought long and hard about it.

'And?'

'Exactly what you said. He's done it before. He might do it again. That gives me a bit of a responsibility, doesn't it? As well as … I don't know … offering some kind of closure.'

The word 'closure' took Faraday back to the file. He asked whether she was still working as a counsellor.

'Yes.' She poured the tea. 'The kids keep me busy most of the time but I've got clients who go way back and if I can still help them at all then of course I do my best.'

'And has that –' Faraday frowned, hunting for the right phrase '– made it any easier to come to terms with what happened?'

'Yes, definitely. In fact I'd never have gone into counselling otherwise. Counselling was incredibly therapeutic, believe it or not. So I guess I owe him my career, such as it is. Weird, don't you think?'

Faraday didn't answer. The tea was foul. He looked up.

'Are you married?'

'No. Partnered.'

'And does your partner know what happened?'

'No.' She shook her head. 'Oddly enough we got together quite soon after it happened but I took a decision never to tell him. The only people who knew were my mum and dad, and my dad's dead now so that just leaves my mum.'

'And she's the only one who knows?'

'Yes. Apart from the other people in the house where it happened, of course, but I lost touch with them pretty quickly. I think that's the way it affects you. You just want to get away, burn your bridges, try and forget it all.'

Faraday toyed with his rainbow mug. Every investigation came with a health warning. Especially this one.

'This new technique is powerful,' he said. 'There's a reasonable chance we'd get a result. If that were to happen then you'd be in court as a witness. People would know. Your partner would know. Your kids. Everyone. You'd have to be prepared for that. Quite aside from the trauma of having to go through it all again.'

'I can cope with that.'

'With what?'

'Going through it all again. To be honest it now feels like something that happened to someone else. It's like a script or something. I'm word-perfect about what happened but my life's moved on. Does that make any sense?'

'Of course, but you're still left with having to cope with other people. Take your partner. You think the relationship's strong enough to survive something like this?'

'Absolutely. We've been together more than twenty years. We're mates. We have a really solid relationship. He's going to want to know why I haven't told him all this time, but he's a sane guy, I know he is.'

'So you think he can cope?'

'I know he can. I can read that man like a book. I know him inside out.' She caught the ghost of a smile on Faraday's lips. 'Is that arrogant, do you think? Presumptuous? Thinking – *assuming* – he loves me enough to forgive me?'

'Not at all. I think you're very lucky.'

'Because he loves me?'

'Yes. And because you've made a life for yourselves in spite of what happened.'

'Sure.' She nodded. 'But he doesn't *know*, does he? And that's the point you're trying to make.'

She'd hacked a path of her own through this thicket of what-ifs and come full circle. Faraday asked her whether she needed time to reflect a little longer.

'I've had twenty-four years,' she said at once. 'Don't you think that's time enough?'

'So it *has* mattered.' Faraday's voice was soft.

'Of course it's mattered. There've been nights and nights and nights when I've thought about that man, what he did, the liberties he took, the way he *defiled* me. I know I was pissed but you can't feel dirtier than that, believe me. You feel worthless, useless. And you're right, it doesn't go away.'

'Even now?'

'Now's different. It's been different for years. Now I've got kids, a family that works. We laugh a lot, we enjoy each other. The odd night? A bad dream? Sure, it all comes back. And maybe that's why I know it's right for you guys to go off and do what you do. I've got no doubts about that. Absolutely none. I'd only ask one favour.'

'What's that?'

'You'll warn me if you find him.'

'Of course.'

'I'm serious.'

'I know. But he'll be in custody so there's no need for you to worry.'

'It's not that.' She shook her head. 'It's my partner. I'll only tell him if I have to. And that will only happen if you get lucky.'

'Lucky?'

'By finding him.' She nodded at the rainbow mug. 'More tea?'

Bazza drove Winter and Mo Sturrock to the dockyard. The Victory Gate lay at the end of the Hard, a busy stretch of waterfront beside the harbour station. He parked the Bentley, had a brisk word with a woman on the security gate, and shepherded Winter and Sturrock through. This was the Historic Dockyard, the jewel in Pompey's crown, acres of museums, boat sheds, and – her masts already visible – Nelson's flagship HMS *Victory*.

Winter had a shrewd idea what was coming next. Already, as far as Mackenzie was concerned, the dramas of the past week were history. Guy was back where he belonged, the Garfield problem had been sorted, and thanks to Esme's sudden passion for married life there might even be a possibility of resurrecting the hotel deal in Baiona. No one else's money this time, just family cash.

Most of this was lost on Sturrock. He wanted to know where they were heading.

'The Victory Gallery, son. A mate of mine hired it last year. The people here do you proud.'

The Victory Gallery turned out to be part of the Naval Museum. It was available for private or corporate functions and Mackenzie regarded the £500 fee as entirely reasonable. Two hundred guests could get cheerfully pissed while Tide Turn explained the magic of the Offshore Challenge. The Lord Mayor would be there, together with the councillors who mattered. The top honchos from Social Services, educational welfare and the magistrates' court would all be getting an invite together with a whole bunch of high-profile people from the voluntary sector. The Navy would obviously be turning out in force and Bazza planned to lure every head teacher in the city with the promise of a Tide Turn goody pack for their school library. He was even considering a special invite for the police.

'I need a name, mush. You'll know.'

Winter was studying a scale model of the Battle of Trafalgar. Nelson's flagship was in the windward column of vessels heading for the French line.

'Willard, Baz. He's in charge of CID.'

'You think he'll come?'

'Bound to. He loves a nice day out.'

The implications of this recce were beginning to dawn on Sturrock.

'This is the launch party, right? For the Offshore Challenge?'

'Spot on, mush.'

'Do you have a date in mind?'

'Yeah. They've got a free slot in a couple of weeks. Wednesday 18th. You think you can handle that?'

Sturrock blinked. Local authorities never worked at this

speed. He began to tally the boxes he'd have to tick: the preparation of detailed training programmes, finding suitable boats, firming up the partnership with the Navy, getting some kind of AV presentation together. The list went on and on and he was about to mention his own status – still suspended from Social Services – when Bazza cut in.

'This is a launch, son. This tells the world we've arrived, we're in business. Think of it as a selling opportunity. It's your baby, your idea. Get out there and flog it.' He shot Sturrock a grin. 'I've said yes to the 18th. You happy with that?'

Faraday spent the rest of the day on Brading Marsh. The wetlands extended south from the wide sweep of Bembridge Harbour and he ducked off the main road that skirted the waterfront, following the path that led deep into the reserve.

Before leaving Tessa Fogle he'd borrowed her PC for a quick check on the RSPB website. Birders had recently reported nine breeding pairs of grey herons. Grey herons had always been a favourite with J-J, and Faraday remembered the evening after he'd first laid eyes on the bird. J-J had been a child then, barely nine years old, and Faraday could still picture him strutting up and down the kitchen in his *Star Trek* pyjamas, his arms glued to his sides, his skinny neck stretched forward, trying to master the elements of being a heron while his dad ladled out another helping of spaghetti hoops.

The memory warmed him, drew him back to this morning's encounter with Tessa Fogle. He hadn't given much thought to what he'd find at the converted chapel. Day after working day he stepped into other people's lives. Often he was there to deal with the consequences of family breakdown. A single mother on the game battered by a drunken client. A vengeful husband taking it out on his luckless wife. A son kicked to death for drug debts.

Case by case, incident by incident, the evidence mounted, and Faraday knew it was hard to avoid the dark conclusion that he and others like him were watching a society tearing itself apart. For some unfathomable reason, all the post-war miracles hadn't worked. Better health care, shorter working hours, greater affluence, even the guarantee of a longer lifespan had failed to make people happier. We whined more. We worried more. And we started wondering when the shiny must-have bubble that was modern life would burst.

Then, all of a sudden, you walked into the seeming chaos of the Fogle household and you realised that there was still plenty of room for warmth and laughter in the world. Faraday didn't doubt for a moment that times would have been tough for them, maybe still were. Kids weren't cheap to run and three of them would cost a fortune. Tessa hadn't volunteered anything about her partner and trying to imagine what he did for a living was pure guesswork, but jobs were scarce on the island and the pay was lousy.

A glance through the kitchen window told Faraday that much of their veg was home-grown and she'd mentioned a local fox that had designs on the chicken coop beyond the onion sets. Her oldest, she said, had recently acquired a .22 rifle and sat up late some nights. The boy had turned out to be a natural with the gun and was on the promise of a trip across to Fratton Park for a decent home game if he ended up nailing Mr Hungry.

The story had made Faraday laugh. It was funny, and real, and smacked of a proper family. One way or another, he'd concluded, Tessa Fogle and her brood were making it work. Before leaving, Faraday had given her a card. Any problem, he'd told her, just get on the phone.

At the far end of the marsh Faraday stopped to watch a circling buzzard. According to the RSPB website, there were two breeding pairs. Later, enjoying the last of the coffee from the Thermos, he spent a contented hour hunkered down beside a stand of reeds. Through the red spots he had perfect line of sight on a family of lapwings, busying around beside a lined scrape amongst the scrub and heather. There were three chicks with Mum and Dad, tiny little speckled pompoms, battling to keep up with their parents as they foraged for food. Another take on domestic life, Faraday thought, wondering about the possibility of a pint before he returned to the ferry.

By the time he finally left the marsh, it was sunset. The shadows were lengthening over the harbour and he paused beside the long crescent of beach, hearing the soft lap of the tide. The beach was littered with debris and there was a faint tarry smell he always associated with waterside evenings like these at the Bargemaster's House. He paused for a moment, enjoying the silence, then came a distant flap of wings and a distinctive harsh croaking sound and he looked up to see a pair of grey herons flying overhead, heading home to their roost. He half-turned to follow their progress, catching the wide spread of their wings against the failing light, knowing it was a moment to treasure. Dimpsy, he thought, fumbling for his car keys.

Chapter thirty

Mo Sturrock had never worked so hard in his life. Ten days, flat out. A week and a half of hurried phone calls, snatched conversations, carefully noted promises. Ignoring the stipulation that he was meant to stay at home, awaiting the call to his final disciplinary hearing, he'd come across daily on the hovercraft, begging time with senior city officials, cornering key social workers, making his case with a magistrate or two, spreading the word about Tide Turn's bold new initiative. He'd even sacrificed his morning session on the rowing machine to squeeze an extra half-hour from his working day.

The reactions, though, had been worth it. Everywhere he went there'd been agreement that issues around youth offending were in dire need of a good shake. The Every Child Matters agenda had provided a launch pad for all kinds of enterprising schemes, some effective, others not, but the brutal truth was that lots of kids were still getting lost, still getting into bad company, still getting into trouble.

Many of their problems were rooted in their early years, the product of a chaotic home life, and sorting out that kind of damage once the child had got to early adolescence was a real challenge. Social workers, in theory, could do it. And mentoring schemes, properly funded, had met with a degree of success. But the real need was for what one ex-policewoman called 'credible messengers'. Kids these days listened to no one. Except that rare individual who stepped into their lives, shot them a smile, tossed them a challenge and – in the process – left them seriously impressed.

This, to Mo Sturrock, was the essence of his Offshore initiative. It had to be ongoing, building session on session. It had to be physically daunting, confronting the kind of kids who already deemed themselves tough. And it had to be led by hard bastards who'd clearly seen a bit of real life. Kids would listen to people like this. The Navy PTI, with his shorn scalp and eagle tats, was perfect. You could see it in his eyes, in his body language, in the way he knew how to use silence. That guy had been somewhere horrible. And that, to many of Pompey's problem kids, made him very credible indeed.

Bazza agreed. Sturrock was sitting in his office at the Trafalgar, going through the PowerPoint presentation for next week's launch. The PTI would be present to field questions in the Victory Gallery, and Sturrock had been canny enough to acquire some video footage from the days when he'd been part of the Pompey field gun crew. He'd built the archive pictures into a longer sequence and now he cued the video and sat back, half-watching Bazza's face.

'Fabulous, son.' The PTI was riding the gun barrel along a cable strung between two trestles. 'Just look at that fucker.'

The next sequence showed the crew reassembling the gun. Everything was a blur, the drills perfectly rehearsed, each man aware that the smallest mistake could lose a finger or break a leg. Seconds later, the PTI slammed a shell into the breech and gave the order to fire. Smoke from the charge curled round the gun crew before the picture dissolved into a slow pan across Portsmouth Harbour, accompanied by the PTI's growl. That same discipline, he said, would lie at the heart of the Offshore Challenge. And here on the harbour is where the adventure would begin.

Bazza was spellbound. For a moment Sturrock thought he was going to demand a rerun. Then he turned to Sturrock and gave him a playful punch on the upper arm.

'Brilliant, mush. Fucking mustard. Works a treat. What else have you got?'

Sturrock had taken his own video camera on his travels over the past ten days and every time he sensed agreement or enthusiasm he'd been bold enough to ask for an on-screen endorsement. These he'd later edited into a sequence intercut with shots of kids hanging out on Pompey street corners: Lacoste trainers, Henri Lloyd tops, baseball caps and lashings of attitude. The Lord Mayor came first. An ex-matelot himself, he wished the Offshore Challenge every success. Other faces followed: men and women Sturrock had plucked from every corner of the city's establishment. Bazza knew them all, surprised that a County Court judge had spared Tide Turn five minutes of his precious time, delighted that both the Pompey MPs had given him the thumbs up, and intrigued by the surprise appearance of a leading newscaster from BBC South. Clearly smitten by Sturrock's pitch, she wished Tide Turn bon voyage and a safe landfall. The Offshore would offer kids a fighting chance, she said. And the rest was down to them.

'How did you get to her, son?'

'I phoned in. Told her what we're about. Told her the way it would work. Turned out her little brother's in trouble with the Bill. Nice lady.'

'You *met* her?'

'Yeah.'

'And?'

'Nice lady.'

Bazza turned back to the screen. He couldn't get enough of this stuff. During the months that Winter had been in charge he'd had the faintest glimpse of what might be possible but this was beyond his wildest dreams. Paulie had been right. Sturrock was a genius.

Sturrock wanted to know how the invites were going.

'That's Marie's baby. I'm surprised you haven't been in touch.'

'No time, Baz. I've been flat out.'

'Then you'd better bell her, son.' Bazza gave him a wink. 'I think she's missing you.'

To Faraday's surprise, it had taken more than a week to prepare for *Sangster*'s next step. An hour with the deputy head of Scientific Services at the Netley Training HQ had established the ground rules. A familial DNA search would cost over five K. To justify that kind of money, *Sangster* had to pass certain tests. Number one, the original paperwork on the Fogle rape had to get the nod from the CPS. If it turned out not to be lawyer-proof then there'd never be any prospect of taking *Sangster* to court. Number two, Faraday had to guarantee enough detectives to action the findings of the familial search. *Sangster* was liable to be looking at hundreds of names. There were ways of prioritising this list but every action had to be individually authorised at ACC level and there'd still be dozens of doors to knock on.

Faraday was in conference with DCI Gail Parsons. She'd summoned him to a small, bare office at force HQ in Winchester where she appeared to be working. Faraday wondered whether she and Willard were still trying to extract some shred of self-respect from the shambles of Operation *Causeway*. If so, Mackenzie still seemed to be in the driving seat.

'I haven't got much time, Joe. Just give me the bones of the thing.'

Faraday summarised the steps he'd taken to revive *Sangster*. The CPS had okayed the paperwork. He'd reviewed every investigative step taken by the squad at the time and saw no prospect of reopening any of their lines of enquiry. The only way forward lay in a familial DNA search, for which, of course, there'd be a cost.

'But that's down to Scientific Services, Joe. It's their budget, not mine.' Her attention had been caught by an email that had just appeared on her PC. Whatever she was reading brought her no joy. 'You've got a squad?'

'Two D/Cs.'

'Will that be enough?'

'That's all there is. Netley seem happy enough.'

'Intel?'

'D/S Suttle.'

'Good.' She began to tap a reply to the email. 'You've seen the survivor? Got her consent?'

'I went over last week. She lives on the Isle of Wight.'

'And she's happy?'

'More or less.'

Faraday summarised Tessa's thoughts on the matter. Like most raped women, she nursed an understandable resentment against the perpetrator. If there was a decent chance of finding the man, then so be it. Her only worry was her partner.

'He knows?'

'No.'

'Is this someone new? Someone recent?'

'They've been together more than twenty years.'

'Really?' She stopped typing. 'And she's never told him?'

'No. In fact she never told anyone apart from her parents.'

'And that's worked for her?'

'Yeah.' Faraday nodded. 'I think it has. They've got three kids. She says they're very happy. How common is that?'

'Good question, Joe. What happens when we take the guy to court?'

'Then she'll have to tell him, obviously. She's asked for a heads-up if we make an arrest. Seemed reasonable enough to me.'

'Of course.' Her head turned to the screen and her fingers settled on the keyboard again. 'Let's go for it then, eh?'

Mo Sturrock found Marie at home in Craneswater. He hadn't been to Sandown Road since Guy's return and he sensed at once that something was missing.

'They've gone home, Mo. The place feels like a tomb.'

'You miss them?'

'The kids? Definitely. The rest of it was horrible.'

'No repercussions, though?'

'Only the police. That nice Helen Christian fixed up for Guy to be interviewed. It happened at the end of last week. They've got a special place up in Havant where they take kids his age.'

'How did he get on?'

'I only talked to him on the phone. He said it was OK but that means nothing. I think they fall over backwards to be nice to the kids but Guy doesn't give much away when it comes to things like this. Between you and me I think he was pretty traumatised by the whole thing.'

'Anyone would be.'

'That's right. He asked after you, by the way. You made a bit of a hit there.'

'I barely saw him.'

'That's not the point, Mo. You were the Man as far as his sisters were concerned and some of that's rubbed off. You should take him out one day, go swimming or something. Shame you didn't come to Thorpe Park. That was another nightmare.' She forced a smile. 'How's the Big One?'

The Big One had become private code for the Offshore Challenge. Mo told her what he'd organised. Bazza had seen the PowerPoint.

'I know. He couldn't stop talking about it. No offence, Mo, but he's easily pleased by that kind of stuff.'

Sturrock wanted to know about take-up on the invites. The launch was scheduled for Wednesday. By now, she might have a rough idea about numbers.

'Very good. In fact excellent.'

'You sound surprised.'

'I'm not, Mo, I'm pleased. Pleased for Tide Turn and pleased for you. You've worked your socks off. I haven't seen my husband so impressed for years.'

'Good. Have you got a list?'

Marie nodded and left the kitchen. Her files were next door. She returned with a Waitrose bag and emptied it on the table. Adding email acceptances to phone messages and replies sent in by post, Tide Turn was already expecting over a hundred guests.

'That's amazing.' Mo was studying the list. 'Some of these are quality names.'

'Shouldn't we be adding your ex-bosses? Just to make a point? There's still time.'

'I'd love to, I really would.'

'So why not?'

'Because they wouldn't come, and even if they did I wouldn't want to talk to them. There are bits of your life it's better just to forget. Stuff never happened. You were never there. Don't you ever find that?' He looked up, catching her eye, then realised he'd touched a nerve. 'I'm sorry.'

'Don't be.' She ducked her head a moment, one hand feeling blindly for his.

Mo did his best to comfort her. 'What's the matter? What did I say?'

'Nothing. Of course it's better to forget, Mo, but that isn't always possible. Do you know what's happened now?'

'No. Tell me.'

'Esme and Stu are selling up. They're leaving, taking the kids, going to bloody Spain.' She looked up at him, her eyes streaming. 'Can you believe that?'

Faraday was at Kingston Crescent shortly after lunch. Before he returned to his office, he checked in with Jimmy Suttle. His carefully laid plans for *Sangster* were at the mercy of events. If something had kicked off this morning, taking Jimmy with it, then he'd have to cancel the trawl for familial DNA.

'Nothing, boss. Quiet as the grave.'

'Nice one. We'll do it then, yeah?'

Suttle nodded. It was so quiet he'd had time to leaf through a holiday brochure he'd nicked from the office next door. Lizzie fancied somewhere with a bit of culture. He was all for lying on the beach. Odds on they'd end up in Florence with overpriced cappuccinos and a week touring the art galleries.

'How about you, boss? Montreal again?'

'No point. I told you – she's coming home.'

Faraday returned to his office. A precautionary call to Netley put him through to the Senior Staff Manager.

'Terry? It's Joe. Just to confirm we're ready for the off. You're still happy we meet the threshold?'

'No question. Come Monday, you'll be looking at a trillion names.'

'Thanks. I'll bell Birmingham then.'

Faraday hung up. The Serious Crime Unit occupied premises in Birmingham. Familial DNA searches were their responsibility. Faraday's contact was a woman called Lee. She answered on the second ring.

'Lee? It's Joe Faraday.' He paused. 'Operation *Sangster*?'

'Yep.'

'Do it.'

Chapter thirty-one

Faraday was at his desk early. A relaxed weekend had taken him to Dorset. At Radipole Lake in Weymouth he'd spent a happy hour with bearded reedlings before driving down to Portland Bill for pied flycatchers and ring ouzels resting after their long cross-Channel passage. There'd also been a gaggle of puffins paddling around in the shallows, their beaks full of sand eels, and higher up the cliffs he'd spotted nesting kittiwakes and fulmars. As the sun began to drop towards Lyme Bay he'd returned via a favourite birding site in the New Forest. The sight of a nightjar at dusk, noisily patrolling his territory, had reminded him of Willard at full throttle. The same manic defence of turf, the same eagerness to take on all comers. Faraday had made his way back to the car park by torchlight, sublimely content.

He settled behind his desk and fired up his PC. Anticipating the DNA results from Birmingham reminded him of long-ago days of waiting for O-level results at school. Then, as now, he wondered whether the minimal work he'd put in might somehow conjure a grade or two above his expectations.

He spotted the email at once, number three in a pile of dross. It was flagged 'High Priority', addressed to Operation *Sangster* and accompanied by a 37KB attachment. The message was from Lee. It directed his attention to the attachment and wished him luck. Opening the attachment, he scrolled through the list of names. At a rough guess there must have been a couple of hundred. He'd made a point of asking for a non-Y-chromosome search. A few of these names would therefore be female, not because they could possibly have been the rapist but because the DNA familial finger might point at a brother or a dad.

He powered up the printer and ran off two copies of the list. Between them, he and Suttle would now apply various matrices to boil down the numbers into manageable packets. One matrix would look for persons living in Hampshire. Another would target individuals within a certain age group. A third might explore names on the PNC database with a family history of sexual offences.

Footsteps along the corridor paused outside his office. Faraday glanced over his shoulder to find Jimmy Suttle standing in the open doorway.

'You're early, boss. What's this?'

Faraday passed him a copy of the list.

'Take a look through, Jimmy. See if there's anything obvious.'

Faraday's phone rang. He picked it up. It was Willard. An email from Mackenzie's bankers had gone astray. He wanted to know whether it had ended up with Faraday.

Faraday checked his emails and drew a blank.

'Nothing, I'm afraid.'

'You're sure?'

'Positive. What's the matter?' He was thinking about the marked notes. 'Have they got their million quid back?'

Faraday waited for an answer but Willard had rung off. He turned to find Suttle still at the door. He was staring at the list.

'Have you seen this, boss? Halfway down. Page two. Under M.'

Faraday reached for his own copy. Suttle saved him the bother. He was standing beside him at the desk, the list still in his hand.

'There. Look.'

Faraday followed his pointing finger. Jeanette Morrissey, 33 Harleston Road, Paulsgrove, Portsmouth.

'That's our Jeanette Morrissey, right?'

'Must be. It's the same address.'

'From *Melody*, yeah?'

'Yes.'

'So what are we looking for here, boss?' Suttle seemed thrown by the name. He'd never done a familial DNA trace before.

'It means she's on the PNC, which we know already, and it means she may have some family tie to the rape.'

'Jeanette *Morrissey*? She's Madame Respectable.'

'Sure. Of course she is. But say she has a brother ...' Faraday was already doing the sums. 'We're talking 1984 for the Fogle rape. Morrissey's in her late forties. If the brother is broadly the same age that would put him around twenty, twenty-one at the time of the rape. There's a geographic link too. Pompey.'

'You think she'd have known about it? Had suspicions?'

'I've no idea. She's on remand, isn't she?'

'Yeah.' Suttle nodded. 'Winchester nick. There's no point in interviewing her though. She has phoning rights. She could be onto anyone the minute we left her.'

Faraday pushed his chair back and told Suttle to shut the door. They were getting way ahead of themselves. First they needed to find out more about Jeanette Morrissey's relatives. And Suttle was right: there was no way they should involve Morrissey herself.

'Open sources, Jimmy. Voters' register. Births and deaths. Facebook. You know the drill.'

Suttle was backing towards the door. He had a better idea.

'You remember *Melody*, boss? The lad Tim Morrissey, the victim, kept an address book. He was very organised that way. We seized it in case there were names that might be of interest. Some of them were starred to remind him about birthdays.'

'You mean mates and so forth? Relatives? Cousins?'

'Yeah.' He nodded. 'And maybe uncles.'

Suttle backed out of the office with his list. Faraday studied his own copy for a moment longer then put it to one side, knowing there was no point applying any kind of matrix until they'd eliminated Jeanette Morrissey. Hunches were often a detective's worst enemy but in this case Faraday sensed that the path to Tessa Fogle's attacker might well lie through some relative of Morrissey's. The coincidences of age and probably location were simply too strong. He stared at the name a moment longer then realised the logical next step. Morrissey would probably be her married name, the name of Tim's father. What *Sangster* really wanted was her maiden name.

He got up and went to the window. The index of births, marriages and deaths was an open source. A phone call or a visit to the library would yield Morrissey's maiden name. He was still deciding what to do when the phone trilled. It was Suttle. He'd retrieved Tim Morrissey's address book from the

Exhibits cupboard and was in the process of going through it. There hadn't been as many names as he'd remembered. Already he'd got to S.

'Either I'm going mad, boss, or this thing's getting out of hand.'

'What's the matter?' Faraday could sense the quickening excitement in Suttle's voice.

'Mackenzie's place, a couple of weeks back. You remember a tall guy who had something to do with that Trust of theirs, the one Winter was in charge of?'

Faraday was thinking back. The tensions inside 13 Sandown Road seemed to belong to a different age. *Tall guy. The Trust. Winter.* The name came to him. The tumble of greying hair. The twist of scarlet ribbon.

'Sturrock,' he said.

'That's what I thought. Stay where you are, boss. Don't move.'

Faraday returned to his chair wondering if the DNA list was already surplus to requirements. Then his door burst open. Suttle seldom ran anywhere.

'Here, boss.'

The address book was open at a page near the back. Faraday read the entry, read it again, then closed his eyes. It simply wasn't possible. It couldn't be. Not that man. Not that family.

Suttle was still beside him, staring down at the open page.

'Dimpsy?' he said. 'What kind of address is that?'

Marie had invited Mo Sturrock for lunch. She took him to Sur-la-Mer, where a month earlier she'd had a somewhat fraught meal with Paul Winter. She'd booked the same table beside the window. Second time lucky, she thought.

Mo settled in. He couldn't remember when he'd last had time for a sit-down lunch.

'You deserve it. Baz says the same. This is his idea, not mine. He's terrible at saying thank you.'

'It hasn't happened yet. This is really tempting fate, you know that?'

'It'll be fine. Baz knows a winner when he sees one.'

'The Big One?'

'You, Mo. You're the big one.'

He shot her a smile. There was a part of him that had been trying to figure out this marriage of theirs and he still hadn't quite got it. Was she there to put a coat or two of social gloss on Mackenzie? To raise the tone at 13 Sandown Road? Or was she the kind of woman who needed a bit of rough? Either way it didn't matter, especially now.

A pretty waitress arrived with a couple of menus. Marie had already recommended the prawns in garlic. Mo pulled a face. He loved garlic but his kids loathed the smell.

'And your partner?'

'She's like me. We used to live on the stuff before the kids came along. The closest we get now is growing it.'

Marie wanted to know more. How had they met in the first place?

'I was in a pub in Petersfield. Tess was there with a girlfriend. The girlfriend was on the course I was doing at the Poly, second time round. She did the introductions and bingo!' He smiled.

'Just like that?'

'Yeah. Just like that. For me, at any rate.'

'And Tess?'

'It took a while. I courted her. It was very old-fashioned.'

'But you won?'

'Big time. It turned out she'd been at the Poly the same time as me but that was first time round.'

'Before you took it seriously?'

'Before I became a human being.'

'Do you mean that?' She frowned at the phrase.

'Absolutely. Some people take a while to grow up. Maybe that's why I get on OK with kids. You can't necessarily have what you think you need. You have to work for it, you have to earn it. It's a kind of apprenticeship. Life can be tricky that way. Sometimes it takes a while to suss it out.'

'Apprenticeship? Isn't that where the Big One comes from?'

'Yeah. The Big One is a crash course in growing up. At the end of it you're fit for only two things. Rowing round the Isle of Wight is one of them. Real life is the other. Should I write that down? Give it to Bazza for his speech?'

The news that Mackenzie planned to address the guests at the Victory Gallery had come as a bit of a surprise, especially

347

to Marie. To her knowledge, he'd never made a formal speech in his life.

Mo was intrigued. 'You think that's part of the political thing? Staking out his ground? Grabbing a bit of profile?'

'I hate to say it, but yes.'

'You don't want him in politics?'

'It's not that. To Baz, politics is like anything else. If he fancies it, he'll have it. I just don't see him in the role. Be honest, have you ever met an interesting politician in your life?'

'No, but then I haven't looked very hard.'

'Me neither, but the guys I see on TV are on a different planet to my husband. He's got a mouth on him. You might have noticed. And he's got absolutely no time for democracy. To be honest I'd give him a week, and that's tops.'

'Have you told him? Broken the news?'

'Of course I have, but that's the other thing. He never bloody listens.'

The waitress returned for the order. Marie went for the prawns in garlic; Mo settled for lamb shank and another pint of Kronenburg.

'Thirsty?'

'Knackered. Tess says I need to slow down. I'm not used to this kind of pace.'

'Is she happy about us? About Tide Turn?'

'Relieved. She'd never admit it, but I think she was starting to worry about what was going to happen next. Not just the money but how I was going to fill my time. Digging veg and mucking out chickens is OK for a month or two, and it's great being around the kids, but she thinks I need more than that.'

'And is she right?'

'She is. She knows me inside out.' He gazed at the remains of his first pint. 'At least that's what she tells me.'

Gail Parsons was back in her office at Kingston Crescent by mid-afternoon. Faraday had given her a brief update on *Sangster* over the phone and she'd heard enough to realise that they needed a full discussion. Mo Sturrock may well have raped the young Tessa Fogle. Suttle had been onto the university authorities and confirmed that he'd been at the Poly at the same time as she had. Soon afterwards they'd started a proper relationship. Two decades later they'd had kids, put down roots, become – in Faraday's phrase – a proper family. Only a DNA sample from Sturrock himself would prove his guilt, but if he turned out to be the rapist then surely *Sangster* was looking at a number of delicate issues.

Parsons didn't see it at all. Neither did Suttle. Faraday sat with them both at the conference table.

'It's simple,' Suttle said. 'We knock on his door. We make up some fairy tale about an incident in the area. We say we're taking lots of gob swabs and would he mind? We fast-track the sample and – bosh – he either did it or he didn't.' He was staring at Faraday. 'You're telling me I'm wrong, boss?'

'I'm telling you I gave the woman my word that we'd be in touch if there were developments.'

'Why?'

'Because she'd need to tell her partner.'

'But it *is* her partner, boss. Or it might well be. What on earth is she supposed to do with information like that?'

Parsons agreed. There was an edge of impatience in her voice, even exasperation.

'You're a detective, Joe, not a marriage counsellor. Why on earth do you think there's a problem?'

Faraday took his time trying to frame an answer. In the end it was simple.

'Because they've made it work for themselves,' he said. 'Because they're a family. We're going to wreck all that. We're going to tear it apart.'

'So we do nothing? Is that what you're suggesting? This is a guy that may well have raped a woman he probably didn't know at the time. Not just that but he may have tried to kill her as well. The fact that they later formed a relationship is irrelevant. Rape is a crime. So is attempted murder. Why am I having to spell this out?'

'Because it's wrong.'

'What's wrong?'

'Smashing up a family. We have to think of the consequences of what we do. We're going to rob those kids of their dad. And we're probably going to put them into poverty.'

'Really?' She was staring at him now, the way you might

stare at somebody who'd suddenly become a total stranger. 'And that's worse than rape?'

'Of course it is. Twenty-three years together tells me they're good with each other. Kids need a dad. The thing works. Why wreck it all?'

Parsons pushed her chair back and gazed up at the ceiling. Suttle tried to play the peacemaker.

'DCI Parsons is right, boss. The kids thing works both ways. Those kids are vulnerable. And so are the ones he'll be trying to sort out professionally.'

'Vulnerable to whom?'

'To him.'

'But he's their father, Jimmy. He's their *dad* for fuck's sake. Don't you see that? OK, let's assume he did it. Let's say that twenty-four years ago he had a moment of madness. He was pissed. He lost it. He did what he did. Since then he hasn't put a foot wrong. Are you really saying we punish him for that one moment? Punish all of them?'

Neither Parsons nor Suttle answered. The implication behind Faraday's outburst was all too clear. You don't have kids. You don't know what it's like to be a dad. Finally Parsons produced her mobile and put it carefully beside her notepad.

'How do you know that's true, Joe?' she said.

'What's true?'

'That he hasn't put a foot wrong?'

'I don't. Of course I don't. But he certainly hasn't raped anyone else otherwise the same DNA would have come up again.'

'Maybe other rapes went unreported. Have you thought of that?'

'Unlikely.'

'But how do you *know*?'

'I don't. You're right. I can't *prove* it.'

'Good word.'

'What?'

'Proof. We're one swab away from proving this man raped Tessa Fogle. If that's the case, and we have the evidence, then our job is done. Everything else is irrelevant. Consequences, as you put it, are not our concern. Can you imagine what would happen if we did nothing? If we *didn't* take a swab? If we ignored the match with this woman Morrissey? You tell me this guy will be working around kids. He has kids of his own. Jimmy's right. Something kicks off, he has another moment of madness, and there's an inquiry. What does that inquiry discover? It discovers that we, the *police* for Christ's sake, knew all along that this guy was probably a rapist. But we did nothing. We put hurt feelings before the law. We pussyfooted around the problem and decided to look the other way. This is crazy, Joe. We're here to gather evidence not deliver judgement. Since when has forgiveness been part of our brief?'

Faraday had held her gaze throughout this speech. It was, he knew, a statement of the blindingly obvious. For the second time in a month events had conspired to corner and punish individuals for whom Faraday felt some sympathy. First Jeanette Morrissey. Now her brother. The law drew a very narrow bead on the consequences of particular actions. Morrissey had killed someone. Mo Sturrock may once have raped the woman who was later to bear his children. The wider ripples of these small tragedies should be of no concern. And yet Faraday was still left with a deep foreboding. Families in good working order were becoming a rarity. And this one was probably doomed.

Parsons clearly regarded the meeting as over. She'd reached for her mobile. Looking up, she caught Faraday's eye.

'I'm referring this decision to Mr Willard,' she said. 'In deference to the strength of your feelings, Joe.'

Mo Sturrock's whirlwind blitz around Pompey had won him an interview with a journalist from the *News*. At Winter's suggestion, he'd phoned Lizzie Hodson. Winter had known Hodson for years and knew she specialised in major features. The fact that she was now living with Jimmy Suttle sweetened the bid still further.

On the phone, Hodson had been impressed by Sturrock's pitch for the Offshore Challenge. She'd arranged to meet him at La Tasca, a café-bar in Gunwharf. Sturrock, arriving from his lunch with Marie, had held her attention for more than an hour. By the time Winter strolled over from Blake House to join them, Lizzie had filled seven pages of her notepad and knew she had enough for a decent feature. Wayward kids were always good copy for the Pompey readership. The fact that someone might have dreamed up a scheme to turn them into human beings was definitely worth a feature slot.

'We'll need a photo,' she said. 'We like to take our own.'

'When would this be in the paper?'

'Thursday. That way we can cover the launch as well. I fancy a photo with you and your own kids. When could we do that?'

Sturrock was watching Winter ordering refills at the bar. He'd lost count of how much he'd drunk since meeting Marie.

'Tomorrow would be good,' he said. 'Though you'd have to come over to the island.'

'No problem. What kind of time?'

'Late afternoon would be best. After the kids get back from school. I should be back by five.'

'Half five, then. You'll give me directions for the snapper?'

Sturrock nodded. He'd never learned shorthand and looking at Hodson's pad he wondered which bits of the Offshore story had caught her eye.

'You've got enough?' He nodded at the pad.

'Loads, thanks. You're sure you don't want to talk about that conference speech?'

'I can't. I've signed a non-disclosure agreement. They'd sue the arse off me.'

Hodson grinned, making room for Winter at the table. She'd googled Sturrock before the interview and had shared his unscripted remarks with half the newsroom. How often did public servants break ranks like this?

'Gentle, was she?' Winter nodded at Lizzie and put the drinks on the table. Another pint for Sturrock. San Miguel this time.

'She was fine,' Sturrock said. 'We'll all be famous by Thursday night.'

'Yeah. Here's hoping.'

Winter swallowed a mouthful of Stella, spotting Jimmy Suttle as he stepped in from the waterfront boardwalk. The moment he saw Sturrock he paused, but Winter was already on his feet, organising another chair.

'Party time,' he said. 'How are you, son?'

'Fine.' Suttle was still looking at Sturrock. 'I just came to pick up Lizzie. We're off to Southampton.'

'Are we?' Hodson looked up in surprise.

'Yeah. That movie you wanted to see. It's on at the Harbour Lights. You remember?'

The question had the force of an order. Winter was still on his feet. He nodded at the glasses on the table.

'My shout, son. What are you having?'

Suttle checked his watch then shook his head. The movie started at half six. The traffic on the M27 was a nightmare. They'd have to leave now.

Hodson shrugged. Then she gathered up her notes and pushed her glass of Chardonnay towards Sturrock.

'It's been a pleasure,' she said. 'I'll give you a ring about tomorrow afternoon.'

Moments later, they'd gone. Sturrock gazed after them, bewildered. Then he turned back to Winter.

'What was that about? Something I said?'

Faraday was home by six o'clock. He prowled around the house gathering up bits of laundry, checking his food stocks, running the hot water in the kitchen to do last night's washing-up, trying to throw a blanket over the day's developments. *Sangster* had become a nightmare. He felt trapped by events. As a serving detective, as Parsons had pointed out, he had a duty to gather evidence. That evidence was about to take a wrecking ball to a bunch of people who seemed to have weathered most of life's storms. Was that why he'd joined up in the first place? To be complicit in the destruction of yet another family? Was this a new definition of Major Crime?

He sensed that madness lay in questions like these and he wondered how to silence the voices in his head. He'd known other cops who'd shared similar qualms, similar misgivings. Most of them had had the good sense to keep their mouths shut and the rest had quickly become the butt of endless canteen jibes. To survive in a job like this you had to kill a part of you. You had to become hard, or unforgiving, or simply indifferent to the consequences of a particular action. The law was nothing more than a set of rules. That's the way society functioned. Break the rules and people like Faraday would be on your case. If you were lucky, you got away with it. If you weren't, and the Faradays of this world did their jobs properly, you suffered. That was the deal. That's what he'd signed up for.

But it wasn't enough. He stepped out into the garden, scanning the harbour. Torn shreds of cloud were scudding in from the west and he could taste rain in the air. He lingered a moment, watching a pair of cormorants revving up for take-off, and he tried to imagine the conversation that Parsons must have had with Willard. If there'd been a suspicion that Faraday had lost his appetite for the Job then here, surely, was the proof. The guy was one swab away from nailing a rapist. A DNA match would turn *Sangster* into a stone-bonker, the sweetest of victories. Yet here was the Senior Investigating Officer, the captain on *Sangster*'s bridge, turning the ship around and heading for the open sea.

Faraday slipped through his garden gate and onto the towpath. He found the image of the trackless ocean oddly comforting. Better to have no clues at all, he thought, than this morning's grim tidings from Birmingham.

It was nearly dark by the time Winter and Sturrock struggled back through the rain to Blake House. Drinks at La Tasca had developed into a bit of a session. Afterwards Winter had insisted on a curry. Now he had no choice but to offer Sturrock a bed for the night. No way was he in any condition to make it home.

Sturrock phoned his partner from the lounge in Winter's apartment. Listening from the kitchen, Winter heard him mumbling something about garlic. He'd be home tomorrow. He loved her passionately. He loved the kids. He'd had a few to drink. Night night. God bless.

He appeared at the open kitchen door asking whether there was any brandy. Winter found a bottle of Armagnac. He poured a couple of glasses and they went through to the lounge, where Sturrock collapsed full length on the sofa. He appeared to have no idea where he was.

Winter eyed him from the comfort of his recliner. Jimmy Suttle was troubling him. The line about the movie at the Harbour Lights had been bullshit. Why had he been so keen on a hasty exit?

Sturrock's eyes were closed. Winter asked him about the interview with Lizzie Hodson. Had he mentioned the possibility of an endorsement by Harry Redknapp? Even a personal appearance at the Wednesday launch?

Sturrock appeared not to have heard the question.

'The conference,' he muttered. 'She wanted to know about the conference, man. That fucking speech of mine. Know what I mean?' He dragged himself upright, feeling blindly for the glass of brandy Winter had left beside the sofa. 'Conference?' he said again. 'That fucking speech I made?'

Winter nodded. Conversation was pointless. He was tired of being addressed as 'man'. He'd quite like to go to bed.

'Brave boy, weren't you? Telling it the way it is?'

'Brave, bollocks. Not brave.' Sturrock shook his head. 'I just fancied it, man. It just happened. Bang. You go for it. That ever happen to you? You just go for it? Just do it? Fuck the consequences? Bang? In? Do it? Just like that?'

He'd found the glass but missed his mouth. Most of the brandy was dribbling down his chin.

'That was it then, yeah?' Winter yawned. 'You just fancied winding them up?'

'Big time.' Sturrock nodded. 'Big fucking time. That ever happen to you, man? Something happens? Bang? You're in there? No fucking about? Just in there? Doing it?' He smiled then wiped his chin. 'Good bloke.'

'Who?'

'You, man. You. Good bloke.' He nodded. 'Yeah, just do it, man. Just get fucking in there. Know what I mean?'

Winter studied him for a long moment, watched his eyes slowly closing, his body slumping sideways on the sofa, watched the way he drew his knees up towards his belly, the way his hands found the warmth between his thighs. He'd seen this same pose a million times. On heavier nights he adopted it himself in bed. Umbilical, he thought, retrieving the glass and padding off in search of a blanket.

Chapter thirty-two

Faraday was at the Wightlink terminal early, in time to make the 7.30 crossing to the island. The tide was high, and debris from the overnight storm washed against the stout timber pilings. Out in the Solent the ferry wallowed in the swell, setting off a couple of car alarms, and Faraday was glad to feel the nudge of the berthing ramp in Fishbourne Creek.

A maze of country lanes took him to Newchurch. He drove past the converted chapel, found a place to turn, and eased back until 'Dimpsy' was in sight again. Of the Land Rover he'd seen on his previous visit there was no sign. She must be taking the kids to school, he thought. He settled down to wait.

Tessa Fogle was back within minutes, taking him by surprise as the Land Rover clattered past. A child was sitting alongside her on the front seat and a single glimpse of the puckered face was enough to tell Faraday that the kid was Down's syndrome. She parked on the grass verge outside the house and carried the child inside. Moments later she was out again, in the back garden this time, pegging out her washing. The clouds had parted in the backwash of the storm and a boisterous wind snatched at the line of tiny garments. The Downs child lingered in the open doorway, watching her mother, and Tessa scooped her up with her spare hand as she returned with the empty basket.

Faraday lowered his binoculars, still uncertain. He'd come over to keep his promise. As a human being he owed her some kind of warning. That the miracles of genetic science had, in all probability, put a name against the man who had raped her. That she'd been living with him all this time. That she'd carried his babies, made a life together, weathered the bad times, enjoyed each other. And that this idyll, if that's what it had been, was over. Was that really his responsibility? To break the

356

news a day or so earlier than strictly necessary? Or should he cut his losses, go back to being a cop, and leave Tessa Fogle to find her own way through the looming catastrophe?

Spotting a movement in an upstairs window, he reached for the binos again. She was standing beside the milky billow of net curtain, the child in her arms. She must have been singing to it because the pair of them were moving very slowly, almost imperceptibly, the child's tiny moon face tucked against her mother's cheek. If there was a single moment, a single image, to get Faraday out of the car and down the road to the front door then this was surely it. He watched them a moment longer, closed his eyes, muttered a prayer, then turned the key in the ignition. It wasn't until he was back at Fishbourne, waiting beside the car for the next ferry, that he took the call from Parsons.

'Mr Willard wants a meet with us first thing this afternoon.' She paused. 'Can I hear seagulls?'

Mo Sturrock didn't wake up until gone ten. To Winter's surprise, he showed no traces of a hangover. Neither did he address Winter as 'man'. His memories of last night were admittedly vague but Winter's suggestion of a mug of tea and a thick bacon butty won an immediate nod of approval.

'Brilliant.' He yawned. 'And brown sauce if you're offering.'

They were at the Trafalgar within the hour. Sturrock disappeared to the basement gym while Winter chased Bazza for a list of last-minute decisions for tomorrow. The Victory Gallery people were still waiting for a steer on Mr Mackenzie's preferred choice of red wine. A teacher from Buckland wanted to bring her entire PSE team. And Fratton Park had sent their regrets. As far as the launch was concerned, Mr Redknapp, sadly, was otherwise engaged.

'Fucking shame.' Bazza had been looking forward to shaking the great man's hand. 'How's Mo?'

'Bloke must have two livers. The amount he got through yesterday would have slaughtered most of us.'

'He's suffering?'

'Not at all. In fact he's on that bloody rowing machine again. Dunno how he does it.'

'And the *News*?'

'Sorted. Big feature piece on Thursday. They're coming to the launch as well. Be nice to them, Baz. Those bastards eat politicians.'

'You think that's what all this is about? Me and politics?'

'I know it is, Baz. That nice Marie never lies.'

Faraday met Helen Christian in the car park at Kingston Crescent. The FLO was already working on another murder in the west of the county and was about to leave for a squad brief in Southampton.

'This won't take long, love. Ten minutes tops.'

She accompanied him back to Major Crimes. When they got to his office he shut the door. On the assumption that this was about Guy Norcliffe, Helen started telling Faraday about last week's interview. The kid had given them a full account of the days he'd spent with his kidnapper. Nothing in that account had offered *Causeway* anything useful in the way of new lines of enquiry and the investigation, for the time being, appeared to have stalled. She began to talk about Esme and Stu, how they'd decamped back to their house in the Meon Valley, when Faraday interrupted.

'I'm interested in Mo Sturrock,' he said. 'You remember him?'

'Of course.' Helen looked blank. 'What do you want to know?'

'He's working for Mackenzie now. Am I right?'

'Yes.'

'In the youth offending field?'

'Yes.' She nodded. 'He's brilliant with kids, I watched him. Stu's aren't delinquents, far from it, but Sturrock's got the knack, you can tell. That's rare in blokes, believe me.'

Faraday didn't doubt it. He wanted to know whether Sturrock had ever stayed over at the Mackenzies' place.

'Yes. A couple of times at least.'

'And what did he do about a toothbrush?'

'I think Marie's got spares. She's like that. She'd have sorted one out for him.'

'And you think it might still be there? For the next time he stays?'

'I've no idea. You could try Winter if you don't want to talk to Marie.' She paused, staring at him. 'Why? What's this thing about?'

Winter was at the Victory Gallery with Bazza and Sturrock when he took Faraday's call. Mackenzie had settled on a fruity Australian red and they were in the process of putting a bottle to the test. Winter stepped through to the outdoor viewing platform. From here he had a perfect view of HMS *Victory*. The last person he expected to be talking to was Faraday.

'Boss?'

Faraday asked him about Sturrock. Did he keep a toothbrush at 13 Sandown Road?

'Haven't a clue, boss. You want me to check?'

'Please. And phone me back.'

'What's the urgency?'

'Asap.'

'For a *toothbrush*?'

Faraday had gone. Winter returned the mobe to his pocket and lingered by the rail for a moment, staring at the huge triple-decker. Faraday was looking for DNA, he knew it. He returned to the museum, made his excuses, and walked back through the dockyard. A cab from the rank outside the harbour station took him to Craneswater. Marie was in the kitchen, doing the ironing.

Winter asked her whether she kept toothbrushes for the kids.

'Yes, of course I do. Esme's hopeless that way. Always forgets to bring them.'

'You've got one for Guy?'

'Absolutely. It's green if you're interested.'

'What size is it?'

'Small. Obviously.'

'Do you mind if I take it?'

'Take Guy's toothbrush? Why would you want to do that?'

'Doesn't matter.'

'Is this important?'

'Very.'

'And you're really not going to tell me why?'

'No.'

She shrugged, then abandoned the ironing. At the door, she paused.

'I've got an adult-size one if you want it. Mo's been using it.' She looked at him a moment longer. 'No?'

Parsons and Faraday drove to Winchester for the meet with Willard. The Head of CID's office was on the third floor. Parsons bustled up the six flights of stairs, trailing Faraday in her wake. Faraday liked to set key moments in his life to music. For this afternoon he'd already chosen a passage from Berlioz's *Symphonie Fantastique*: 'The March to the Scaffold'.

Willard's office was big enough for a long conference table but he had no intention of leaving his desk. The windowsill behind him was piled high with old copies of *Yachting Monthly*.

'Gail?' There was a briskness to Willard's manner that Faraday recognised only too well. This wouldn't last long.

Parsons summarised what she called 'the Mo Sturrock situation'. She was scrupulously fair. On the one hand he was obviously prime suspect for the *Sangster* rape. On the other, he and the victim had been living together for half a lifetime and seemed to have survived the experience. In one sense, the relationship clearly worked. But that would make Mo Sturrock no less guilty.

'You agree, Joe?'

'I do, sir.'

'And you also agree we have to secure a swab?'

'Yes.'

'I understand Suttle's suggesting some kind of subterfuge. A house call. A cover story. Yes?' Faraday nodded. 'Gail?'

'I'd advise against it, sir. If Sturrock's guilty it gives him a week to get away. In my view we need to keep him in custody until we get a result. There's a real chance of flight.'

'I agree.' He sorted through the correspondence on his desk until he found a long white envelope. Faraday found himself looking at an invitation to the launch of something called the Offshore Challenge. It came from Tide Turn Trust and Mackenzie had scrawled a personal line across the bottom. *All welcome*, he'd written, *Even you*.

'I also got this last week.' Willard opened a drawer and showed Faraday a DVD. 'It contains footage from our little expedition to Poole. Mackenzie has been kind enough to share it with us.' He glanced at Parsons again. 'Gail?'

'The launch party starts at ten, sir. It's scheduled to go on until lunchtime. They're serving canapés and wine.'

'And Sturrock?'

'He's doing the main presentation along with a PTI from the Navy.'

'Guest list?'

'The usual suspects, sir. The great and the good.'

'Media?'

'The *News*. BBC South. A couple of radio stations. And there's a rumour about someone from the *Guardian* turning up.'

'Excellent.' Willard turned back to Faraday. 'You're still SIO on *Sangster*, Joe. I want you to arrest Sturrock at ten o'clock tomorrow morning. I want you to do it on the premises, that's to say within the venue. When the gentlemen of the press ask you why, you tell them what you've just told Sturrock. We've arrested the man for sus rape and attempted murder. If they want more put them onto me.'

Faraday nodded. He should have seen this coming. After years of dogging Mackenzie's footsteps, after years of watching the man get richer, the Head of CID finally had a chance to post a small but very public victory. The would-be politician, the self-styled King of the City, had just hired a suspected rapist to head his precious Tide Turn Trust. The perfect chance for Willard to rain on Mackenzie's parade.

Willard was beaming. 'Any comments, Joe? Any thoughts of your own? Any other way we might deal with this?'

Faraday had the toothbrush in his pocket. One glance had already told him that it couldn't possibly have been Sturrock's. Wrong size. Wrong state. Some child had been using it for years. Pointless, therefore, to test it for Sturrock's DNA. Winter again. As devious as ever.

'Well?' Willard wanted an answer. 'You're up for this?'

Faraday nodded. He felt strangely light-headed.

'My pleasure, sir. As always.'

Chapter thirty-three

Tessa Fogle woke early. The window was half open and the curtains stirred in the wind. It was barely dawn and the room was still shadowed in the thin grey light. She rolled over, reaching for Mo, but he wasn't there. She frowned, then rubbed her eyes. Recently, since his banishment on gardening leave, he'd made the occasional early-morning expedition, following the bridle paths across the neighbouring fields. He said it helped him clear his mind, get things in perspective. He also liked the silence.

She drifted into sleep again, wondering about the photos from last night. The photographer from the *News* had been later than expected, turning up with the reporter who was writing the story. They'd taken lots of shots with all five of them, various informal family groups, and then they'd gone with Mo down to the woods at the edge of the village for a couple of more personal photos. He'd returned alone. When she asked him whether or not he'd seen the results, he'd shaken his head. He was nervous about tomorrow's launch. There were still so many things that could go wrong. He'd retired early, pleading a headache. By the time she'd come up to bed, he'd been asleep.

She woke again to the sound of the phone. Mo had still to return. She thought he might be downstairs, might answer the phone, but it rang and rang. She pulled on his dressing gown and made her way down to the living area. Whoever was ringing wasn't going to hang up. Finally, she lifted the receiver. To her horror, it was nearly half past eight. She had barely half an hour to get the kids to school.

'Hello?'

A voice she didn't know asked whether she knew a Mr Sturrock. She said she did. She gave her name.

'This is the police in Ryde, Ms Fogle. I'm afraid I have some bad news.'

Guests started to gather for the Tide Turn launch around half past nine. Winter had left an attendance list with the security guards at the Victory Gate and slowly the first-floor gallery began to fill. Marie had insisted on a choice of coffee or fruit juice on arrival, resisting Mackenzie's preference for a glass or two of wine, and now she moved from group to group, making introductions, welcoming familiar faces, warmed by the comfortable buzz of conversation.

Most of these people already knew each other. They met at function after function. Together, as she was beginning to understand, they formed that critical mass of movers and shakers that made any city work. Mo had likened it to what happened in a nuclear reactor. These were the people responsible for the smooth flow of power. Without their support, their approval, very little would get done. Hence the importance of today's launch.

Of Mo himself there was no sign. According to Winter, he'd been due off the hovercraft at ten past eight. He had stuff for the PowerPoint to pick up from the Trafalgar and he wanted a final run-through before setting off for the dockyard. Winter had waited for him until nearly nine and then taken the equipment himself. Maybe Mo was running late. Maybe he'd gone straight to the venue.

Now, for the umpteenth time, he was trying to get through to Mo's mobile, but calls were being diverted to the messaging service. Never had he bothered with Sturrock's landline, an oversight he was beginning to regret. The gallery was filling fast. In a couple of minutes, if Mo still hadn't shown, they'd have to think about starting without him.

Mackenzie was locked in conversation with the Lord Mayor. Winter chose his moment and took him to one side.

'Mo hasn't turned up.'

'What?'

'He's not here, Baz. And I can't raise him on the mobe.'

'So where the fuck is he?'

'I've no idea.'

Mackenzie was eyeing the pile of equipment that went with

the PowerPoint. Mo ran it through his laptop. Neither he nor Winter had a clue how it worked.

The PTI was body-checking his way towards them through the mill of guests. At Mackenzie's insistence he was clad in a tracksuit rather than anything more formal. One or two people were beginning to check their watches.

'You got a problem, guys?' The PTI had to be away by eleven.

'No, mush.' Mackenzie was staring at the top of the stairs that led up from the entrance below. 'What the fuck are they doing here?'

Winter turned to find Faraday and Suttle eyeing the assembled guests. They seemed to be looking for someone. Then Suttle spotted Winter. He came across, took Winter by the arm, found a space behind a model of the French flagship at Trafalgar.

'You've heard?'

'Heard what?' Winter's heart sank.

'About Sturrock?'

'Tell me.'

'Someone called in a body first thing this morning. Over on the island. It turns out to be him.'

'So what happened?'

'He put a bullet through his head.' He nodded towards Mackenzie. 'You'd better break the news.'

As a mark of respect, the launch was cancelled. At Mackenzie's invitation, the PTI muttered a few words about the Offshore Challenge. It was, he said, a bloody fine idea. Kids needed something special in their lives. They also needed someone special to make all that stuff happen. He hadn't known Mo Sturrock very long but everything he'd seen and heard had convinced him that this guy would make a difference. The fact that he'd gone was a real shame, a real loss, and whatever the circumstances he deserved a moment of silence. Heads bowed around the room. Mackenzie hugged his wife tight. She was sobbing.

Afterwards, as the guests drifted away, the journalists wanted to know more. Mackenzie did his best, distributing Mo's fact packs about what the Offshore Challenge involved, but that was no longer what they were after. There was a rumour that Tide Turn's new boss had committed suicide. Was Mr Mackenzie in a position to confirm that? Mackenzie shook his head, aware that Faraday and Suttle were still on the premises. Lizzie Hodson was nowhere to be seen but a pushy young reporter from Meridian TV had sussed the presence of the police. He cornered Faraday on the viewing platform outside.

'*Maurice* Sturrock? Is that correct?' He spelled out the Christian name.

'Yes.'

'And can you confirm he's killed himself?'

'I can confirm he's dead.'

'Would there be any reason why he *might* have committed suicide?'

'I've no idea.'

'Is there someone else we can talk to? Someone who might know?'

'Not at this point. I expect there'll be a press statement later.' Faraday stepped back inside, thankful that the reporter hadn't enquired exactly what CID were doing at a function like this.

Willard and Parsons were waiting for Faraday at Kingston Crescent. At their insistence, Suttle joined them in Parsons' office. Willard, once again, was incandescent. He'd just conferenced with the duty D/I at Newport police station. Sturrock had taken a single .22 bullet through the temple. There was no indication of foul play. The rifle evidently belonged to his seventeen-year-old son.

'He knew, Joe. Some fucker told him. Am I getting warm?'

'I've no idea, sir. I imagine you must be.'

'So where were you yesterday?'

'When?'

'Yesterday morning.'

'I went to the island.'

'Good. That's a good start. You know why? Because that's exactly what we thought you might do. And you know something else? I asked DCI Parsons to run a check on the ferries. 07.30 to Fishbourne. Am I right?'

'Yes.'

'So then what?'

'Are we talking PACE here? Should I have a lawyer?'

'Just answer the question, Joe. Tell me why you went to the island.'

'I went to see Tessa Fogle.'

'Why?'

'To tell her where we'd got to with *Sangster*. To warn her, I suppose, about what was about to happen. I'd given her my word. It was the least I owed her.'

'And what did she say?'

'She didn't. I got as far as her house and there it stopped.'

'She wasn't in?'

'I didn't knock on the door.'

'She *was* in?'

'Yes.'

'So you got up early, you took the ferry, you drove over to her place, you confirmed she was there, and you didn't take it any further? Is that what you're telling me?'

'Yes.'

'Then I don't believe you.'

'You think I'm lying?'

'Frankly, yes. Either that or you've totally lost it.'

Faraday held his gaze. Then he stood up. His warrant card was in the top pocket of his suit. He slipped it out and laid it carefully on the desk. He'd had enough. His tussle with his conscience was one thing. This was quite another.

Then came another voice. Suttle's.

'It was me, sir.'

'What?' A tiny frown clouded Willard's massive face.

'Me. My fault.'

'How does that work?'

'I live with a journalist. She interviewed Sturrock on Tuesday, ahead of the launch. She was preparing a big piece on him. She was really impressed, really *really* impressed. After the interview we had a bit of a run-in. In the end I marked her card.'

'Told her what he'd been up to? All those years ago?'

'Told her what he *might* have been up to.'

'Same thing, son. I'll put money on it.' He glanced at Parsons, then went back to Suttle. 'So what did she do, this girlfriend of yours?'

'She went to the island yesterday with a photographer. She

must have had a word with Sturrock. That's the only way it could have happened.'

'Are you sure about that?'

'Positive.'

'Why couldn't it have been Joe here?'

'Because D/I Faraday's straight, sir. He doesn't lie. He doesn't hide from the truth. And if you don't mind me saying so, we ought to be able to cope with that.'

Afterwards

A DNA swab from the post-mortem on Mo Sturrock provided a perfect match with the scene sample preserved for Operation *Sangster*. Faraday got the news personally from Willard. His call found Faraday in the Bargemaster's House. Pending a decision on whether he really wanted to resign or not, he'd been granted what Willard had been careful to describe as 'compassionate leave'.

'He did it, Joe. He raped that woman. Even you can't deny it.'

'It's not denial, sir. That was never my point.'

'I know, but it's black and white, isn't it? The guy was a rapist.'

'You're right.' Faraday had wearied of this conversation already. He no longer knew or even cared where it led.

'So what next? Have you made a decision yet?' Willard was trying to sound upbeat. It didn't work.

'No, sir. DCI Parsons said two weeks. I'll let you know by Monday.'

'You feel OK?'

'I feel fine.'

'Have you seen anyone?'

Faraday smiled. He meant a psychiatrist.

'No, sir.'

'Still away with the birds, then?'

It was a poor joke. Faraday didn't laugh. There was a long silence.

'Monday then. We'll talk again.'

He rang off.

Two days later, Faraday took another call. It was a woman's voice this time and it was several seconds before he placed it. Tessa Fogle.

'I'm in Portsmouth,' she said at once. 'If it's possible I'd like to talk to you.'

'How did you get this number?'

'You gave it to me. You left a card.'

'I'm sorry. Of course I did.'

He gave her directions for the Bargemaster's House and wondered whether to put the kettle on. Within minutes she was stepping out of a cab and walking up the path to the front door. She looked terrible.

'Come in.'

Faraday led her through to the big lounge that looked onto the harbour. Mercifully, it was a beautiful day.

'Are you happy to stay in here or would you prefer to go outside?'

'Here's fine.'

She sank onto the sofa, refusing Faraday's offer of tea. She said she'd been talking to the girl from the *News* again, Lizzie Hodson. After the trauma of Mo's funeral and ongoing problems trying to settle the kids, Lizzie had come back to her. At first Tessa had thought she was after a story, some kind of exclusive interview, but it hadn't turned out that way at all.

'What did she want?'

'She wanted to tell me about you.'

'Me?'

'Yes. I never realised at the time, but it seems you came over the day before Mo ... you know ... did it. She said you wanted to tell me what was going on, what I should expect. And she said there'd been all kinds of trouble about it, between you and your bosses.'

Faraday nodded, saying nothing. This was Jimmy Suttle's doing, he thought. He's leant on his partner, asked her to pass a message. If so, it was a kind thought.

Tessa wanted to know if it was true. Faraday said yes. He'd made her a promise. That promise flew in the face of all kinds of other stuff but he'd still felt compelled to keep his word.

'Why?'

'*Why?*' He shook his head. To be honest, he said, he no longer knew. Lizzie was right. There'd been big trouble, huge trouble, but nothing that would hold a candle to what she must be going through.

'Do you think some kind of warning would have made it easier for me?'

'I don't know. I suppose it might.' Faraday frowned. 'Did you ever suspect it was him?'

'Mo, you mean?'

'Yes.'

'Who did it? Raped me?'

'Yes.'

'Never.'

'So if I'd have warned you, would you have told him? Would you have confronted him?'

'Of course I would.'

'And then?'

'I would have forgiven him. It wouldn't have mattered. Back then we were different people. That's what I'd have told him.'

'So he'd still be alive? Is that what you're saying?'

There was a long moment of silence. Outside, two gulls were squabbling over something on the foreshore. Then she shook her head.

'He'd still have gone. He'd still have done it, still have killed himself. Nothing I could have said would have changed that.' She studied him for a moment then ducked her head. 'I've brought you this. It's a copy, I'm afraid, but I know you'll understand.'

She searched in her bag and produced a folded square of A4. It was typed, single space. At the bottom, a row of inked kisses.

Tessa was on her feet. She'd asked the taxi to hang on for her at the end of the road. She'd come to tell Faraday that he wasn't to blame for what had happened. Faraday stared up at her.

'So you don't think it made a difference? Me not telling you?'

'No.' She offered him a wan smile. 'But thanks for trying.'

She left the room, refusing Faraday's offer to walk her up the road. He heard the front door open and close. Then silence again.

He turned to the letter, aware of a sudden chill in the room. A dead man's voice, sepulchral, beyond reach.

My lover, it began.

By the time you read this I'll have gone. I know it's the

coward's way out but I've always hoped and prayed that what we have, and what we've had, would last forever. I've loved you since I first laid eyes on you. You won't remember because I never had the guts to do anything about it but I was the geek who trailed around all those years ago trying to summon the courage to chat you up or ask you out or any of that stuff.

You were beautiful and I loved you from a safe distance and then one night I got as pissed as a rat and decided to do something about it. That was the night it happened. You were out of it too. I followed you home. I found the little alley at the back. There were two rooms that looked onto the garden but yours was the window that was open. I could see you inside. I couldn't help myself. I knew you'd be off the next week, just like all the other third years. When would I ever see you again?

So that's the way it happened. I remember getting in through the window but the rest of it I've pretty much blanked. The police got nowhere and after a while I started asking around after you. You were mates with a girl on my course. That's how we both ended up at that pub in Petersfield. The rest you know about.

I love you, Tess. I've always loved you and I always will. Kiss the kids from me and never forget the family we've been. What happens next I could never cope with. To tell you the truth I thought we'd cracked it but it turns out I was wrong. Maybe I was greedy. Maybe I wanted too much. Maybe our kind of heaven is beyond reach.

XXXXX

Faraday folded the letter and then looked up. *Beyond reach.* Too right. He blinked, wiped an eye with the back of his hand, stared out through the big glass doors. The harbour was a blur. He didn't know what to do, who to phone, who to talk to. He didn't know anything. He'd never read anything so sad in his entire life.

The following afternoon he phoned Winter.

'Have you got a moment?'

Winter didn't want to talk on the phone. He said he'd drive over from Craneswater. Sandown Road was a tomb. He was back in charge of Tide Turn. Life, he thought, couldn't possibly get worse.

Faraday opened a bottle of wine. Already, he felt like a convalescent. Tessa's visit seemed to have blown away some of the fog in his head. He was beginning to think straight again. He was beginning to sense the need for decisions.

Winter had shed his jacket. It was another perfect day. They sat in the garden, two men deep into middle age, sharing a bottle of decent Rioja.

Faraday told Winter about Operation *Sangster*, about the doors that familial DNA could open, about the dawning realisation that he'd walked into a horror show. The guy was a loyal partner, a great father and the kind of social worker that gave the profession a good name. A thimbleful of semen, shed in a long-ago moment of drunken madness, had destroyed all that. Where was the logic? Where was the justice?

'There isn't any.' Winter was monitoring the approach of a young blonde jogger along the towpath beside the harbour. 'So how come you got the familial hit?'

Faraday told him about Jeanette Morrissey, Sturrock's sister, and what had happened to Kyle Munday. Winter abandoned the jogger.

'She *killed* this bloke?'

'Ran him down.'

'Deliberately?'

'No question about it. She spelled it out for us. She saw him in the road and put her foot down. She'd been wanting to do it for ages, just never had the chance.'

'And this is a *nurse*?'

'Pillar of the community. Straight as a die. Saw the opportunity. Took it.'

Saw the opportunity. Took it.

Winter nodded and then turned his head away, remembering Sturrock sprawled on his sofa, pissed as a rat. *I just fancied it*, he'd said. *It just happened. Bang. You go for it.* At the time, Winter had assumed he was talking about the speech he'd made at the conference. Only now did he realise what he'd really been getting off his chest.

'Something the matter?' It was Faraday.

'No, boss.' Winter shook his head. 'Nothing you shouldn't expect.'

'Share it with me?'

'One day maybe.' He reached for the bottle then raised his brimming glass. 'Jimmy Suttle tells me you might be looking for something new. It happens I know just the man to talk to.'

On Monday the weather broke. Faraday, who'd spent most of the weekend on the phone talking to Gabrielle, drove to Kingston Crescent in pouring rain. Faintly surprised to find his name still on his office door, he shed his coat, sat down at the desk and lifted the phone. Willard's secretary was about to put him on hold when Willard himself came on the line.

'Joe?'

'Me, sir.'

'Had a think?'

'Yes, sir.'

'And?'

Faraday suddenly saw the message scrawled across his whiteboard. *Sangster* was having a modest celebration upstairs in the bar at six o'clock. Be there. Faraday started laughing. Suttle must have been in.

Willard was getting impatient. He was demanding an answer. Did they still have the pleasure of Faraday's company or not? Faraday bent to the phone, trying to compose himself. He needn't have bothered. Willard made the decision for him.

'I'll take that as a yes then, Joe.'

The phone went dead.

If you enjoyed

Beyond Reach

Don't miss

BORROWED LIGHT

Graham Hurley's thrilling new novel

out now in Orion hardback

Price £12.99

ISBN: 978-1-4091-0123-9

Prelude

Faraday was asleep when he went through the windscreen. He heard neither the warning klaxon from the oncoming truck, nor the shriek of the tyres as Hanif stamped on the brakes, nor the Arabic oath so abruptly smothered by the final collision with a roadside tree.

As the Peugeot settled in the dust, Gabrielle tried to reach forward from the back. Hanif, like Faraday, hadn't bothered with a seat belt. His chest crushed by the steering wheel, he was limp within seconds, expiring with a barely audible sigh which Gabrielle later chose to interpret as surprise. The blaze of the truck's headlights. The split-second swerve that avoided a head-on collision. The gnarled stump of the acacia briefly caught in the headlights. And then darkness again.

Fighting to make sense of what had just happened, Gabrielle was aware of the receding thunder of the truck. She could taste blood in her mouth. She felt herself beginning to shake. She called Faraday's name. Then she too lost consciousness.

The lost hours that followed took them to a hospital beside the Mediterranean at El Arish. Faraday's first clue, his eyes still closed, his breathing laboured, was the shouts of men running in the corridor outside the ward. For a moment he was back in the Bargemaster's House, unable to account for people yelling in Arabic on their way to his bathroom, then he drifted away again, awaking some time later to see a bearded face above a white jacket bending over him. English this time, lightly accented.

'Mr Faraday? You can hear me?'

Faraday nodded. More or less everything hurt. His head was bursting. For some reason he could barely swallow. He tried to

3

speak, tried to struggle upright. Failed on both counts.

'You're in hospital, Mr Faraday. You understand me? Hospital?'

Faraday closed his eyes. Opened them again. Hanif. The driver. He'd borrowed Hanif's cap. It had been night, dark. He was tired. He'd tried to sleep, the cap pulled down over his face. It was a baseball cap. He remembered the taxi bumping along and the murmur of Gabrielle's voice as she chatted to Hanif and the smell of the cap, sweet with hair lotion, not unpleasant. So where was Hanif? And where, in God's name, was Gabrielle?

'You've been in an accident, Mr Faraday. Your lady too.'

The alarm in Faraday's face sparked a reassuring smile. He felt a hand cover his.

'Your lady is OK. Not so bad. Soon you will see her.'

Faraday withdrew his hand. He wanted to touch his own face, reacquaint himself with its familiar features, find out what had happened. He too wore a beard. So where had it gone?

'You're in a special unit, Mr Faraday. You understand?' The doctor tapped his own skull, pulled a face. 'We must do some tests, get you better. Rest now. Be still. Your lady is OK.'

Faraday's fingers were still exploring the heavy swathe of bandage around his head. Blood had dried and crusted on his temples. When he tried to answer, when he tried to do anything, he felt a stabbing pain in his chest.

The doctor told him once again to relax. Two of his ribs had been broken. There was a little damage to his shoulder. But on the whole he'd been very, very lucky.

Faraday was thinking of the baseball cap again. He shut his eyes, trying to visualise what it had looked like, trying to bridge the gap between the moment he must have drifted off to sleep and this bright place of pain with the splashes of sunshine on the wall.

'Should ...?' He tried to shape a sentence, failed completely, but when he opened his eyes again the presence beside the bed had gone.

Then, from somewhere close by, came the cry of a child, plaintive, lost. He listened to it for a long moment, totally bewildered, then darkness swamped the sunshine and he drifted away.

Over the next couple of days he began to recover. Gabrielle, as promised, came to his bedside. Already walking, her arm in a sling, one eye blackened, a swelling around her mouth, she brought him fresh orange juice and crumbled biscuits on a paper plate. He was in a high-dependency unit on the hospital's top floor. They'd taken away the tube that helped him breathe and a second set of X-rays had confirmed that the skull fracture was less severe than they'd feared. His broken ribs were already on the mend and his shoulder, badly dislocated, had been reset. With luck, she said, he would soon be back on his feet again.

Faraday wanted to know more. Where exactly were they? And what had brought them here?

Gabrielle explained about the car crash, about Hanif losing concentration, about the truck that had so nearly wiped them out. Hanif was dead, she said. His chest crushed against the steering wheel.

Faraday stared at her. They'd been with Hanif for two days. He'd driven them to birding sites high in the mountains. With his quick intelligence, his grin and his wealth of local knowledge, he'd become a kind of friend.

'Dead?' he said blankly.

Gabrielle nodded. There'd be a session with the local police soon. They wanted a witness statement about travelling with Hanif. But in the meantime there was something else he needed to know.

'We're in a place called El Arish. It's very close to Gaza. You remember Gaza?'

Faraday nodded. They'd come to the Middle East on a midwinter break. The day after they'd landed in Amman the Israelis had begun to bombard the Gaza Strip. Jordan was full of exiled Palestinians. Wherever they went, it was impossible to avoid Al Jazeera TV in the cafés, newspapers in the hotels, huge demonstrations on the streets.

'And?' Gabrielle had his full attention.

'A lot of the people wounded come here. Terrible. Just terrible.'

The wards below, she said, were full of casualties from Gaza. Worst of all were the children. Kids. *En petits morceaux*. In bits.

'There's a child here ...' she nodded towards the door '... in the next room. A girl. Maybe five, maybe six, nobody knows. They call her Leila. She has burns, chemical burns, here and here.' Her hands touched her chest, her wrist, her fingers. 'The poison makes her very sick. *Phosphore, n'est-ce pas?* The doctors think she may die. Maybe that would be for the best.'

Faraday was doing his best to follow these developments. He hadn't a clue about *phosphore*. He wanted to change the subject.

'How about you?' he said.

Gabrielle shrugged, said she was fine, a little bruised, a little shaken up. Then she checked her watch and glanced again at the door.

'They try and wake the little girl every morning.' She got to her feet. 'Maybe there's some way I can help.'

Faraday was nearly two weeks in the hospital at El Arish. Mobile again, waiting for the doctors to tell him he was fit to travel, he took to wandering the corridors, passing ward after ward, tableau after tableau. Gabrielle was right. The hospital was slowly filling with seriously wounded from the killing zone that had once been Gaza. Men with no legs, lying inert, their eyes dead, staring at the ceiling. A woman who'd lost part of her face to a mortar blast, her head turned away towards the wall. Sitting outside in the winter sunshine, Faraday could hear the roar from the city's airport as flights lifted more broken bodies to specialist facilities in Cairo and Saudi Arabia. Back inside the hospital they were burning incense to mask the stench of rotting flesh.

This, to Faraday, was disturbing enough. Seeing the sheer physical damage inflicted on these people, it was difficult not to share Gabrielle's growing sense of outrage. They were defenceless civilians with no greater sin to their names than the urgent desire for peace and some kind of security. Instead, through no fault of their own, they'd lost everything.

Worse, though, were the moments Faraday paused outside the glassed-in rest room where the orderlies gathered between shifts to drink mint tea and gaze up at the big wall-mounted screen. The TV was permanently tuned to Al Jazeera and its non-stop torrent of live pictures from Gaza: wrecked schools, hysterical women, maimed kids sprawled in the dust, men filling ambulances with yet more bodies. From time to time among this grim carnage a camera would tilt skywards to reveal hanging white tendrils from an airburst artillery shell. This, according to Gabrielle, was white phosphorus, the evil wafers of burning gunk that had done the child Leila so much damage. She was still alive, just, and one of the reasons Faraday so rarely saw Gabrielle was the position she'd taken up on a chair beside the child's bed. This little girl has no one left in the world, she said. So it has to be me.

Faraday, in his heart, agreed. He'd glimpsed the tiny pile of bandages that was Leila and he was only too aware of the faces of the orderlies in the TV room when they noticed him out in the corridor. It was the tiny reproachful shake of the head that made him feel helpless and somehow complicit. It had been the same in cafés in Jordan and Egypt before the accident. The unvoiced accusation: you in the West did this, *you* with your American friends, *you* with your stake in Israel, *you* made all this possible.

At moments like these Faraday would beat a slow retreat to his room. His possessions had been returned from the wreckage of the taxi and he'd sit through the long afternoons sorting through his birding logs. There'd been a ring-necked parakeet glimpsed near the Old Fort on the seafront at Aqaba and a Barbary falcon a little further south along the coast. Earlier in the trip Gabrielle had been the first to spot a pair of Sinai rosefinches drinking at a spring near the Royal Tombs in Petra, and later that same day they'd spent nearly an hour watching a Bonelli's eagle riding the thermals above the deepest of the wadis. These were the kind of exotic sightings that he'd dreamed about in the depths of an English winter at the Bargemaster's House, but the excitement had gone now, swamped by the human wreckage that surrounded him.

On his last evening at the hospital he packed his rucksack and waited for Gabrielle to appear. She'd been in town, confirming the flights home, negotiating a decent price for a taxi to Cairo airport. Finally, when she turned up, she appeared to have no luggage. The flight left late the next day. Still exhausted, Faraday had little taste for sightseeing but wondered whether they might have time for a detour into downtown Cairo.

Gabrielle seemed surprised. There was something she clearly hadn't told him.

'I'm staying over, *chéri*,' she said. 'The taxi man will look after you.'

'Staying over?'

'*Oui*. The child will need lots of care. I can help there. I know I can.'

Leila, it seemed, was at last out of danger. Gabrielle had been talking to the consultant looking after the little girl, who spoke French as well as English. He was a nice man, *sympa*. He knew London well, had friends there. He'd done a lot of his training in the UK and had good contacts at the Burns Unit in Salisbury. At Gabrielle's prompting he'd been on the phone, looking into the possibility of a surgical bed there for Leila, even taken a provisional booking on a medical evacuation by air. Around 30 per cent of her body had been burned. She'd need a series of skin grafts and lots of specialist nursing, but the care in the UK, according to the consultant, was world class. With luck, *inshallah*, Gabrielle's *pauvre petite* might have a half-decent future.

Gazing at her, Faraday realised just how cut off, how isolated, he'd become. The accident and its aftermath had locked him away in a bubble of his own making. How come all this was news to him? How come Gabrielle had never mentioned it before?

'But who pays for all this? How does it work?'

'*J'sais pas, chéri.*' Gabrielle offered him a tired smile. 'That's why I have to stay.'

Several hours later, more than a thousand miles to the south-east, Paul Winter was making a difficult phone call. Dubai time, it was three in the morning.

'It's over, Baz. Kaput. Finished. We have to take the hit, move on. It's the only sane thing to do.'

'Take the hit? Bollocks. The market'll turn. It'll come good. In this game you need patience, my friend. Thank Christ one of us hasn't bottled it.'

Winter tried to picture the scene in Craneswater. It would be late evening in the UK. Post-Christmas, Bazza was doubtless tucked up in his den, scrolling through the spreadsheets on his

PC, patrolling the battlements of his commercial empire, doing his best to ignore the obvious. A glass or two of Black Label often helped.

Winter went through the numbers again, standing by the window, staring out at the long curve of the Corniche. Hotel after hotel after hotel, most of them unfinished, pools of darkness under the forest of cranes.

'The market's collapsed, Baz. The guys in the know out here are talking about a 40 per cent fall in property – and that's just the first quarter. Year end, we could be looking at 60 per cent off.'

Mackenzie grunted something that Winter didn't catch but he knew he was tuning in at last. You didn't get to a £20 million fortune without the ability to count.

'The hotels are dead, Baz. Most of the white guys I've met are on their way to the airport.'

He described conversations he'd had with bankers, lawyers, architects, consultant engineers. All of them had spent the last couple of years with their noses in the Dubai trough, feasting on near-vertical rates of growth. But those days were suddenly over.

'Half the construction projects are either on hold or cancelled. Take a stroll round the airport and you'll find parking lots full of dumped four-by-fours. These guys are totally maxed out. They leave the keys in the ignition and their credit cards in the glove box and leg it.'

'Why would they do that?'

'Because they've got brains in their heads. If you default here, everything stops. Bank accounts frozen. Assets frozen. Passport confiscated. House arrest. You end up in court and they're all speaking Arabic, and before you know it you're sharing a jail cell with some drugged-up zombie from fuck knows where. Probably for ever. You wouldn't know it to look at, but this place is medieval, Baz. I just hope they're not listening.'

Mackenzie wasn't giving up. He'd invested £750,000 in 10 per cent deposits, buying thirty apartments off-plan in a promising waterside development. Last year's spreadsheet told him he could sell on for a 20 per cent mark-up after just six months – £1.5 million for doing fuck all.

'Listen, mush. You're tired. You've been talking to the wrong guys. Take a break. Treat yourself to a couple of those nice Russian toms I keep hearing about. Then go and find Ahmed and get the thing properly sorted.'

Ahmed was Mackenzie's local agent, a smooth trilingual twenty-something with tailored white robes, wire-framed glasses and an Australian air hostess girlfriend.

'I can't, Baz.'

'Why not?'

'He's gone too.'

'Legged it?'

'Probably.'

'How come?'

'He went into liquidation last week. Like I said, it's not something you want to hang about for.'

'Shit.'

'Exactly.'

There was a long pause. In the background Winter could hear the opening music to *Match of the Day*. Saturday night, he thought grimly. And me stranded in fucking Do-Buy.

Mackenzie came back on the line, suddenly businesslike.

'You're right, mush, we have to liquidate. Find yourself an attorney, a real-estate agent, any fucking monkey. Get those apartments sold on. Whatever it takes, mush. Whatever you can screw out of these people. You got that?'

'Yeah. One problem. Did I mention the building itself?'

'No.'

'It doesn't exist, Baz. They never even started it.'